Marry YOUR Billionaire

The Reluctant Bride
Book 1

Marry YOUR Billionaire

CYNTHIA SAVAGE

Cover design and layout by C.J. Anaya

Publisher: C.J. Anaya Publishing LLC

ISBN 10: 1-7373366-3-1

ISBN 13: 978-1-7373366-3-1

CHAPTER 1

Midge

*U*nbelievable!

Madelyn Knightly—Midge to her friends—took one look at the handsome stranger who'd had the audacity, the outrageous nerve, to steal her usual seat at Café Canapé and felt an irrational pang of anger surge to the surface.

He looked vaguely familiar, but she knew she'd never met him before. He was clearly a man of importance, but she failed to place him as she glared at him from the corner of her eye. He was probably a player in Hollywood. Maybe an associate of her father's, though she wouldn't know who her father was hobnobbing with since she hadn't had much to do with Corbin Knightly for awhile now.

Annoyed beyond what most might consider reasonable, she stood in the cafe's entrance and surveyed her other options while the man sat at *her* table engrossed in some heated discussion. She tromped past him and huffily planted herself at the table furthest away from the arrogant seat stealer and the man's associate, a self-important looking gentleman with a large tablet held at the ready, possibly dictating the man's schedule to him as if anyone out of high school wasn't capable of something as idiotic as that.

Midge couldn't muster a single ounce of goodwill as she opened her laptop, flipped to her Scrivener program, and then chanced an open glare at the two miscreants.

She sighed at her illogical anger, an obvious sign that after six years of working through her personal issues she wasn't any closer to actually *working* through her personal issues.

The loss of the table bugged her. She loved sitting in that particular spot since it gave her such a spectacular view of a small portion of Huntington

Beach. But what disturbed her even more was this nagging familiarity the handsome stranger's presence produced; this blatant reminder of a life she'd purposely turned her back on, a life she'd avoided like she would a cracked out actress or the paparazzi.

Thinking about the paparazzi, her troubled musings turned to the scheduled visit with her father, which filled her stomach with stone-cold dread. She had no idea why he had summoned her or what he could possibly have to say after several years of sporadic phone calls and little else.

She was just a semester away from graduating with a Masters in English. Nothing in the world was going to mess up her well-laid plans, not even the abrupt loss of her scholarship due to budget cuts, information her counselor had bombed her with just moments before her father's secretary called to schedule an appointment for that very afternoon.

The scholarship had been a godsend, something that came to her a few days after her falling out with her father. To have it dry up now was a serious problem she didn't, as yet, have a solution for. Student loans were an obvious option, but the idea of debt didn't sit well with her even though it was generally considered acceptable debt. She didn't like owing anyone anything.

A few quiet moments at her favorite café writing her romance novel, one which was sure to get her foot in the publishing world, should be giving her the opportunity to step away from her current problems. Instead, fate threw in a ridiculously good-looking guy and favored him with the most amazing beach front view, which was completely lost on him.

She glanced out a nearby window and had to admit her view wasn't all that bad either. Café Canapé was located in the downtown district area where fun shops and restaurants catered to tourists. Midge loved the freedom she felt whenever she walked along the streets, enjoying the surf and turf atmosphere and inhaling that salty sea air.

She dropped her eyes from the tempting view and adjusted her non-prescription glasses on her nose. She always felt more confident when hiding behind them, something she'd never vocally admit to anyone. She reached into her bag, pulled out her laptop, and dove into her story. Midge managed only one paragraph before a sense of someone critically studying her flooded her concentration. Instinct made her peek above her laptop, straight into the eyes of the very man who had stolen her table, her concentration, and her peace of mind.

His manly perfection was definitely at its peak. His dark hair was styled in a way that screamed straight-laced and altogether too perfect to be true, while the hint of natural wave looked ready to rebel against its gelled structure. She imagined the image he presented and the real man lurking behind the facade worked much the same way: bad boy with all-American charm. Dark lashes, a square jawline, and defined cheekbones just added to his allure.

Totally yummy.

And totally familiar. Why couldn't she remember where she'd seen this guy before?

Midge lowered her eyes to her work, but her mind strayed to the gorgeous stranger. Without consciously trying, she began to pick apart the low murmur coming from their general direction. Soon it morphed into distinctive phrases. The subject matter, unfortunately, was right up her alley.

"Brody, you can't back out of this now. It's too late. The network is offering you an opportunity here, one that shouldn't be sniffed at simply because you feel appearing on television is beneath you."

Aha. She *knew* he looked familiar. The handsome billionaire seated at *that* table was none other than Brody Prescott, founder and CEO of Shackled And Loving It, an online dating service which boasted outstanding reviews and thousands of successful pairings ending in marital bliss. There'd been a scandal attached to his name several months ago; allegations of breaches in privacy policies. The tabloids had painted the confirmed bachelor as a playboy who used member information to score himself one-night stands. The ensuing debacle had wreaked havoc on his personal credibility and threatened to sink the whole company.

Not that Midge paid attention to the tabloids...much.

She didn't believe the accusations for one second, at least the allegations he'd broken his company's privacy policies. A wealthy and powerful man like Brody Prescott didn't get to where he was by making stupid, career-ending blunders of that magnitude. Most likely, the lie had been weaved by a spurned lover...or lovers.

She *did* absolutely believe he was a playboy.

The handsome stranger shook his head, clearly frustrated.

"I don't understand how this reality TV show is going to improve my image, Gregg. I'll only look desperate and stupid."

Reality TV? Midge groaned as she thought of her father and his profession. Corbin Knightly was a filmmaker, director, and producer. The last several years of his career had been spent dedicated to developing gritty reality TV series. Before Midge had walked away from the family business, she'd had to work on some of those projects with him. She had not been a fan of the process.

Mr. Prescott's assistant let out a long-suffering sigh, giving her the impression that this argument had been visited and then revisited with essentially the same outcome. She could almost visualize his body deflating into a small puddle on the vinyl covered chair. She'd have to disinfect the whole thing if she ever wanted to sit at that table again.

"Brody, you've already signed the contracts. All the marketing for this show centers solely on you. They're announcing you as the star of this new series next week. Do you have any idea the kind of legal ramifications we're looking at if you back out now?"

"Look, when this whole scandal blew up, I was ready to jump on board for some serious damage control. I did the interviews, signed the contracts, and even hit the gym so my abs would be film ready once shooting started. At the time, this looked like our only chance at fixing the damage Felicia's lies caused, but now I'm having some major doubts about how this is going to work in our favor. I never watch this crap myself and have zero respect for people who do."

Midge's opinion of him rose by exactly point-five percent. After all, he was still a rich, spoiled womanizer.

"Brody, we have to fix this. You already have a certain...reputation with women. No one is interested in joining the most successful online dating community if its creator isn't successfully matched or at least attempting to stick with one woman for an appropriate length of time, and you can't use your own company to find yourself a match. That'd be feeding fuel to the fire of these spreading allegations, no matter how on the up-and-up you go about it. This is the only other avenue available to us. By publicly demonstrating your desire to find a wife, and then going through that very process on television, you're giving people a reason to trust and believe in you again."

"Do you have any idea how many women I've dated without ever having been tempted, even once, to make the situation permanent? All they're after is my money."

Tough gig. Never knowing a person's true intentions.

She hated that she could relate to him.

"That's why this show is so important. It will paint you in a different light. The women you meet will be vetted to ensure there isn't a single gold-digger in the bunch. You will have the opportunity to go from playboy to steady suitor within just a few months, and hopefully your image will be saved in the process."

"Ha," Midge said, and then quickly bit her lip. She hoped they hadn't heard her staccato burst of derision.

"Excuse me, did we say something funny?"

Well, she'd certainly stuck her foot in it. No possible way to duck behind her laptop now. She prepared herself for Brody Prescott's compelling gaze before looking up from her work. Even then, his perusal of her left her a bit disconcerted. Having dealt with a few arrogant playboys in her day, she knew better than to exhibit the slightest hint of fear or intimidation. Nothing less or more than total indifference was the way to go in this situation. She squared her shoulders, met his assessment of her with a critical one of her own, and brazenly answered the question.

"I find it amusing that either of you think reality TV is going to paint you in a favorable light. These networks are interested in ratings, and they'll get them any way they can." She pulled her glasses from her nose and pinched the bridge of it, frustrated to have inserted herself into the conversation.

"And you think you know the inner workings of what makes reality TV an actual reality?" the assistant asked.

"Far better than you, I'm afraid." Midge turned her gaze to Mr. Prescott and watched as his expression changed from skepticism to a strange kind of interest.

Wonderful. He finds me about as fascinating as one might find a few juggling chimpanzees: bizarre and inexplicably entertaining.

She used the pointed end of her glasses to gesture toward Brody while directing her comments to the assistant. It was a way to avoid the billionaire's stare while simultaneously letting him know she felt comfortable talking about him as if he wasn't present, a tactic her father had taught her as a result of dealing with one too many self-important players in Hollywood.

"These dating shows resemble the type of interactions you might find in a cult community where plural marriage is condoned because some zealot broke away from mainstream Mormons and dubbed himself king of the county."

He turned a slightly amused look on Midge. "I'm sorry, but what does polygamy have to do with this conversation?"

"Multiple women all vying for your affections, and you can't find one similarity to that of a man marrying an obscene number of females?" Midge shot back, giving him a look that implied he was brain-dead for even considering it.

Gregg held up a scrawny arm to get her attention.

"The pictures taken of Brody with different women, and the accusations involved, have painted a rather unpleasant persona. We need to revamp his image."

"And your solution is to put his playboy personality on the screen, allow him to date multiple women at one time, and hope he doesn't offend anyone in the process?" Midge wondered who Mr. Prescott's image consultant was because the middle-aged assistant resembling a withered tree branch couldn't possibly be the one calling the shots here. "You're absolutely right. I would never label Brody Prescott as a heartless womanizer after watching a full season of him kissing twenty plus girls and breaking all of their hearts once he finally decides which one he'll marry, only to call the wedding off when the season is over."

Brody pointed a finger at Gregg as if to say, *I told you so.* "Finally, someone on my side, though I'm offended by your attack on what I've always considered to be a sparkling, affable personality." He gave Midge a cheeky grin. "You should spend time getting to know me before making snap judgments like that. Would you like to start by grabbing some dinner with me tonight?"

She narrowed her eyes at this and quickly redirected her attention to Gregg.

"In the short time I've listened to you two speak, I can already tell your boy here doesn't have the patience for preening prima-donas or high maintenance, self-absorbed drama queens. These types of women run rampant on any reality TV series no matter the subject. Not everything is going to go according to plan."

She doubted that either of them would take her seriously. She was only twenty-four, after all, and her tight, frizzy bun paired with her frayed jeans and white T-shirt hardly screamed, "Hey, my father produces reality TV for a living. You should totally listen to me!"

"You don't think I'm capable of diplomatically handling an emotional female?" Brody asked.

Midge thought he looked slightly amused but couldn't fathom what might have sent him there.

"You probably handle emotional women about as diplomatically as I handle the rise in price of chocolate croissants here at Café Canapé." Midge turned to the owner of the shop, a balding Italian with whom she'd developed a love-hate relationship over the last six years. She yelled a playful greeting to him in Italian, and then in English said, "It's still totally unacceptable, Giacomo. No one in their right mind would ever willingly pay ten dollars for a croissant the size of my palm. I don't care how sinful that Italian chocolate is."

He threw a few Italian expletives at her, shook his fist, and then walked into the back of the store. When she turned back to Brody it was to see that his shoulders were shaking ever so slightly as he fisted a hand to his mouth.

Midge trudged forward, figuring she may as well disillusion both of them before they continued on with this ridiculous scheme.

"You are dealing with an attack on your image, and since your image of happily wedded bliss is crucial to your company's means of survival, it makes more sense to actively pursue one woman rather than throw the inner workings of your dating life on a screen for everyone to see and possibly make yourself look like more of a horses rear end than you already have."

The assistant choked on his espresso—a poor choice considering his abundant nervous energy—and continued gasping for air as the billionaire stared at her with a transfixed expression. She had expected him to become indignant at her unbecoming description of him, but he stared her down as if he were inspecting a curious organism under a microscope and couldn't quite identify its subgenus.

"One woman, you say? And how will I find one woman to pursue when pursuing several dozen hasn't produced any winners for me?"

"Were you really in earnest with any of them? Let's be honest with ourselves, Mr. Prescott. Your choice in women is typical: fake blond hair, fake double-D boobs, fake booty, fake personality. Are we noticing any themes here?" By the smirk on his face she gathered he'd grasped the theme all too well. "You essentially date the same woman. She may look good on your arm, but you need someone who will challenge you, listen to you, and actually respond to what you have to say rather than someone who looks at you vapidly and giggles when she has no idea what you're talking about." Midge leaned back in her chair, getting ready to return to her laptop to resume her now useless efforts in world-altering story telling. "In short, Mr. Prescott, you should try dating someone with half a brain. You might be surprised how much that one factor lengthens your relationships."

She put her glasses back on and began typing, feeling satisfied that she had given the undeserving seat-stealer sufficient cause to nip this madness in the bud.

A dark shadow hovered above her and then lowered itself atop the chair directly across from her.

Midge raised her eyes above the black rims of her glasses.

"Was there something else, Mr. Prescott?"

He appeared delighted by the question, a reaction that surprised her.

"There certainly is. I find your advice much more applicable than Gregg's over there." He threw a dismissive wave over his shoulder, and she watched as Gregg sank a little in his seat and then bounced upward as if the caffeine in his system wouldn't allow for bad posture.

"If I'm going to be taking advice from you, I'd like to know your name."

The idea that Brody Prescott might be taking her warnings to heart loosened her lips when she normally would have told him to take a hike.

"Midge," she said.

Brody waited, looking as if he expected more.

"I don't get a last name, here?"

She contemplated the idea of giving him her full name, the one name tied to Hollywood, her father, and the inadvertent fame she'd done a bang-up job of turning her back on. She didn't want him to know her true identity. She didn't want him to begin calculating what her ties to Hollywood might do for him. She simply wanted him to go away.

"You're a desperate person, and I really don't have time to solve all your problems. I don't want you hunting me down for more advice. Midge is all you get."

He smirked. That delightful smile of his widened even further.

"That's too bad, since I want you to take the job."

Midge couldn't have felt more perplexed if Giacomo had come swinging out of the back kitchen, arms flailing, offering his chocolate croissants for free.

"The job? What job?"

"I want you to pose as my girlfriend."

"Not a possibility," Gregg said in a warning tone.

Brody waved away his protest as he continued to study her.

"Pose? You *do* want to actually find someone to marry, correct?"

He shook his head and laughed.

"I'm a confirmed bachelor, Midge, but my image is more transient. If I do the show, I'll probably end up with someone I can't stand. We'll break up once the show is finished, which will only confirm my playboy status to the public."

"Not if you actually fall in love and get married....or...at least get married," Gregg interjected in exasperation.

Midge watched as Brody rolled his eyes but essentially ignored his assistant.

"You've suggested I date a woman of intelligence who covers herself as a nun would and is about as blond as the day is dark."

She slammed her laptop closed and pointed a warning finger in his face.

"Just because my cleavage isn't reaching my ears and my hind end isn't exposed for all the world to see doesn't mean I dress like a nun! It means I understand the difference between what's classy and what's...ah...pushing the envelope." He playfully reached for her finger, but she pulled it back before his skin could make contact. She was not interested in finding out what his touch might do to her central nervous system. "There's no doubt I'm more intelligent than the lumps of flesh you sport on your arm, but any woman within a ten-mile radius could claim that accolade, and my hair color isn't really up for discussion."

"I like the flaming red curls. They suit your personality."

She narrowed her brows into a tight V, feeling certain he hadn't intended that as a compliment.

He held his hands up in surrender. "You're the one who thinks I should chase after a girl who is the exact opposite of everyone else I've ever dated."

"Yes." Midge punctuated her response with a slap of her hand on the table. "A relationship that you enter into willingly with an equally willing partner instead of hiring someone for a job and then walking away once you feel the damage to your image has sufficiently recovered." Midge shook her head at the amused gleam in his eyes. She couldn't tell if he was seriously being this obtuse or if he simply enjoyed bating her. "At the very least, be in a relationship where both parties are attracted to one another."

"I don't mind your mousy librarian look. Throw on a pencil skirt and some high heels and you can take me to the library any day."

Midge didn't miss a beat. "I was talking about finding someone who is attracted to *you*, genius.

Surprise flickered across his features before that look of amusement returned. "Are you saying you don't think I'm hot?" He leaned forward in his seat, practically crawling across the table to hear her response.

This man was the essence of too-hot-to-handle and whoop-der-it-is, and Midge would have died a torturous death at the hands of her materialistic, Hollywood producer father before she ever admitted to Mr. Prescott or herself just how attractive she found him.

She raked him over with her eyes, giving a cool assessment of his appearance before allowing her gaze to meet his again. She shrugged her shoulders.

"I'm sure *someone* in this world finds you attractive. It just isn't me."

Instead of sending him away with his tail between his legs, all Midge got for her disinterested response was a low chuckle that sent a rush of heat swiftly curling around her heart, securely lodging itself there in the process.

"Bull," he said.

"Excuse me?"

He quickly reached over and plucked her glasses from their perch across her nose, eliciting a startled gasp from Midge. "If we're going to be an item, I want to see all of you. Those freckles are too cute to cover up."

She might have lunged across the table to grab them if he hadn't placed her spectacles in his jacket pocket. Retrieving them now would require more physical contact than she was interested in. She had no intention of wrestling Brody Prescott for cheap Wal-Mart glasses.

"So now we'll add thief to the list of your promising characteristics," she muttered.

He considered her for a moment, allowing his eyes to study her face with little reserve. It was unnerving to say the least.

"Like what you see?" she snapped. That goal of complete and total indifference had just gone sailing out the café window.

"Oh, you definitely hold some appeal, young lady."

She opened her mouth to let him know exactly where he could stick his own appeal when Gregg butted in.

"You know, she might be the perfect candidate. She looks like a woman of intelligence, and with an adjustment to hair and make-up she'd clean up quite nicely," Gregg said in an all too pleasant tone. Then an angry scowl crossed his face. "That is, if you're seriously interested in getting sued for breach of contract!"

"So you two assume I'm just going to go along with this?" She folded her arms across her chest and leaned back in her seat.

"Of course," Brody said with assurance. "You'd be in the spotlight. You'd be plastered on the cover of magazines on the arm of a handsome, wealthy, powerful man. Isn't that what every girl wants?"

Midge's experiences with that kind of attention had led to nothing but pain, embarrassment, and rejection. The spotlight had become dull. The glitz and glamour of a life among the rich and famous had become as dark and dangerous as a pit full of tigers.

Brody seemed to think her lack of response signified a consideration of his offer.

"At the very least, I'll show you a good time, and in the end, you'll have a fun story to tell your friends and family."

She allowed her face to morph into a fake, exuberant smile before giving him her answer.

"I'm afraid I'll have to decline the offer, Mr. Prescott. If the outcome of this entire exchange is for you to end up a bachelor once again, then having me as your fake girlfriend is going to be problematic for you."

"Why is that?"

Midge leaned forward, reached for his hand resting on the table, and turned it palm up. She then drew lazy circles around his palm and up his wrist. His eyes darkened a bit with a heated look that communicated her affect on him.

She continued that soft contact as she said, "Spend enough time with me, and you're liable to fall desperately in love. How will you be able to let me go after that?"

Without hesitating, he captured her fingers in his grasp. Raising them to his lips, he softly kissed the tips of them, never breaking eye contact with her. She hadn't been prepared for him to rally like that, and she found herself just as mesmerized by his actions as he had been with hers.

"Maybe I'm okay with the idea of never letting you go."

Sweet maple syrup!

Unable to handle the smoldering heat of his gaze, she abruptly pulled her hand back and shot to her feet, grabbing her laptop and shoving it in her bag.

"Now," she said, attempting to gain back that clinically indifferent tone she'd perfected over the years, "you can take my advice and find a girl with some substance who will be interested in you for your mind instead of your billions, or you can go on a reality TV show and run into the same mind-numbing scenario you're doing your best to distance yourself from."

Midge moved to leave, but Brody placed a restraining hand upon hers, causing her heart to nearly stop with the adrenaline that shot through it. He rubbed his thumb in a slow circle around the inside of her wrist and gazed at her suggestively.

"Are you sure you don't find me just the slightest bit attractive?"

He was using her move now, was he? He wanted to play games? Well, Midge could handle battleship like any old seasoned pro. She slowly bent over a little so that her lips hovered just centimeters from his. She heard his sharp intake of breath, as if he was a little surprised by her boldness, or possibly affected by her proximity, and it emboldened her further. She hovered for just a moment longer, one centimeter closer to give him the right illusion, and then she paused again.

"Not even the slightest bit attractive, Mr. Prescott." She straightened her posture, reached inside her purse, and pulled out a pair of humongous sunglasses, which, when worn, covered nearly the entirety of her face. She quickly put her glasses on and took a moment to peruse his gob-smacked expression.

Priceless.

"Enjoy your jaunt with reality TV and all the craziness that's sure to follow." Midge saluted the assistant with mock seriousness as she strolled past the billionaire.

Walking out of Café Canapé with her pride intact made her feel as if she had just managed to lasso the moon.

CHAPTER 2
Brody

rody Prescott allowed the tempting librarian to walk out the café's entrance, listening to the cheery bell that chimed as the door swung open and then closed, as if to announce the departure of a woman of significance.

Brody suspected her abrupt entrance into his life held a plethora of possibilities conveniently carried upon a sweet, serendipitous breeze. His eyes followed her figure through the café windows, watching her lithe form as her narrow hips swayed hypnotically from side to side in a clipped, no-nonsense manner. Her fiery curls bounced out of her tight chignon, desperate for a bit of freedom as they fought their suffocating prison.

Her movements were precise as she lifted those irritating sunglasses from her face and cleaned them with the bottom of her white tee. If he'd have known she had more glasses hiding away in that purse of hers, he would have broken them in half on the spot. They hid her exotic green eyes, pert nose, and an adorable array of freckles generously sprinkled across said pert nose's bridge. Thank the Good Lord above for that last bit of detailing in the creation of this new and intriguing female.

He dug the freckles.

She placed the offensive sunglasses back on her lovely face and climbed into a light blue truck that had seen better days.

As she drove off, he felt certain he would see her again. Knew he would. He planned on making it happen one way or another.

"Gregg," he barked.

Without having to look behind him, he knew his assistant startled in his seat. He had to fight the urge to chuckle. Gregg had been with him since the start-up of the company, understanding the ins and outs of marketing and branding. He was a nervous, edgy man with gray hair, a bulbous nose, and a constant five o'clock shadow. Brody considered him family but never missed an opportunity to mess with him.

Gregg joined him at the table the mysterious girl had vacated. Brody felt a strange prickle of longing.

"What do you think of her?" He never minced words with Gregg.

The man folded a freakishly long leg atop its twin and gave Brody an exasperated look.

"Absolutely not, Brody. Don't even think about pursuing that...that... young lady. Backing out of a TV deal is not a decision you make lightly. We're talking hundreds of thousands of dollars in legal expenses if Corbin Knightly decides to sue you. Plus, that Midge woman didn't exactly jump at your offer. If she's not amenable to the agreement, we can't waste our time on a doomed venture."

Brody gave him a grin. Gregg couldn't adequately describe the enchanting little minx either. Perfection came to mind, but then he risked sounding like some cheesy guy in a chick flick.

"It isn't likely that Corbin will go for the jugular since they haven't released the news of my involvement yet."

"They've already spent their budget on marketing. Marketing that revolves around you!" Gregg said. "A guy like Corbin Knightly is going to recoup his losses one way or another, and what if he decides to publicize your backing out? We're trying to save your image as a respectable businessman."

"I'll reimburse them for their time and money, Gregg. I'm not worried about the financial hit this will take, and maligning my image will only give his show bad press."

Gregg rested his forehead in his hands and moaned.

"I can't believe you're actually considering this!"

Brody leaned forward and caught Gregg's eye with his intensity as he pointed his finger toward the door where his mousy librarian had just exited.

"She is the solution to our problem. She's the polar opposite of those debutantes and celebrities you've thrown at me, and she has an actual personality and brains to go with it. Dating her will debunk these rumors about my professional and personal life." Brody leaned back and nodded. "Yep. Any man could bring her home to his mama." He smiled thinking about his mom's likely reaction to Midge. His mother was a sassy lady who didn't suffer fools well. They'd get along great.

Gregg pinched the bridge of his nose before replying. "Brody, the lies leaked to the tabloids and press are career-ending unless we can prove them wrong."

"You and I both know I would never break company privacy policies. I would never be desperate or stupid enough to contact women within the program unless they contacted me first."

"Give me some credit here. I've known you for ten years, and your character and integrity are what convinced me to join you when you started your company. I did *warn* you right from the beginning that the founder of an online dating service who insisted on remaining a confirmed bachelor would eventually run into trouble. Your last mistress has played the part of a woman scorned to the very best of her abilities."

Brody pointed a warning finger at him.

"I've never had, nor will I ever have, a mistress. You know how I feel about sleeping around. I don't do casual, and I won't get involved with women who do. Felicia was your idea, by the way, along with the others." Brody shook his head. "You have to admire her cutthroat initiative, though. She brilliantly retaliated when I refused her loaded proposition for drinks at her place."

"Hell hath no fury..." Gregg mumbled.

Brody sat back with a weary sigh. He should have seen it coming with Felicia. The minute Gregg introduced them, he had noted her cat-like eyes devouring him, ready to pounce the moment he gave her the signal. When he replaced that signal with a firm yet civil rejection, the she-cat went for blood. The lies Felicia had fed to several tabloids and magazines had called into question Brody's ethics and his own ability to find a match for himself.

According to Gregg, Brody's single status was a constant thorn in the company's side, but if he were to be seen out and about with gorgeous females —some of whom were the daughters of rich senators, directors, CEO's of other corporations, the elite crèm de la crèm of society—then at the very least his dating life would look like one long string of successes.

Brody knew that a confirmed bachelor heading an online dating service was a bit of an oxymoron. Despite his bachelor persona, he really was interested in finding someone he could settle down with, but he was in an impossible position. He couldn't ethically use his own dating company to find that perfect match, and meeting someone with zero ulterior motives where his money was concerned was just plain impossible. He should have had it made. His wealthy bachelor status meant that women were lining up, practically throwing themselves at him.

But that was the problem.

They were all too eager, all too available, and all too happy to be whatever they thought he wanted them to be. He wanted someone with substance, someone who challenged him, tested him, and encouraged him to be a far better individual than he was at the moment. He also desperately wanted to love someone without any fears or reservations. He wanted to share his wealth and success with an equal partner for the rest of his life—so long as that partner loved the man and not the money.

Midge hadn't cared about who he was or how much money he had, which meant any interest she showed in him would be genuine. So how was he going to attract her interest? He didn't even know where she lived?

"I know Felicia is most definitely my responsibility, but repairing the damage she's inflicted also falls under my jurisdiction. This TV series is going to be good for you. With any luck, you'll actually meet the right girl and use that sparkling personality of yours to charm America in the process. This is a win-win."

"Gregg, I really don't want to do the show. I was in panic mode when I agreed to this idea. Finding love on TV where women are most likely there to further their acting careers sounds pathetic and desperate. As far as my personality goes, its more snarky than sparkly. Midge was right when she said I'd look like an idiot."

"I seem to remember her wording it a bit differently than you." Gregg's look was sly. "That's why editing is going to come in handy. The director can chop and cut as he pleases to maneuver you in the best light. I'm telling you, Brody, you need a fiancé and you need one soon. We have to nip this in the bud before America permanently sees you the way Felicia has painted you."

Brody would have rather been drowned in a sea of blind dates than be the star of *Marry Your Billionaire*. This dating series where numerous females spent weeks vying for some coveted engagement ring as he slowly got to know them and then callously eliminated them one-by-one was like some game show gone wrong.

It wasn't like he was narrowing it down to his favorite flavor of ice cream. At the end of the series, they fully expected him to find "the one" and propose. He'd look like the playboy the media had pegged him for if he didn't marry one of them, and he wasn't about to marry for his image's sake.

He looked up to find Gregg studying him.

"What?" Brody barked.

"What did *you* think of her?"

Brody swallowed hard. "I think it took me everything I had to allow her to walk away from me. Around her it felt like I was breathing fresh air for the first time."

Gregg nodded. "Well, that was poetic. Sickeningly so. I can't say I'm not thrilled about it. I've been waiting for someone to turn that jaded head of yours, but it couldn't have come at a worse time or with a worse female. Did you really have to bait her like that? You came across just as shallow as the tabloids have stated."

"I couldn't resist. The way her green eyes flashed and her cheeks flushed every time she got rattled was intoxicating. Her face is so expressive. Don't you think?"

"I think, not only is she not impressed with you, she's not the least bit interested in you. She wasn't exactly subtle about that."

"Then I can only improve upon further inspection. Correct?"

"Theoretically. There is that snarky personality of yours to contend with. You plan on wooing the lady? You're actually going to make an effort when it comes to dating?"

"I plan on sweeping her off her feet, turning her world upside down, and laying bare my heart while winning hers in the process."

Gregg smirked. "You're a hopeless romantic, you know that? How a sappy guy like you has managed to stay single for the past ten years is absolutely beyond me." He leaned forward, and his intense energy caused the table to lurch a bit with his movement. "You have a meeting with the producer of the series in a little over an hour. What exactly do you plan on telling him?"

Brody furiously scrubbed his fist into the side of his head, a nervous habit he was convinced helped him think better. "I'm out. I'm done." Gregg let out another agonized moan. "Even if I *did* decide to continue on with this ridiculous rat race, I'd never be able to focus with Midge on my radar."

Brody watched as Gregg took a moment to accept this drastic game-changer. He finally nodded his acknowledgment.

"And then?"

"We're going to track down that mousy librarian."

Gregg let out a rueful chuckle. "How many hours of sleep is that going to cost me?"

"Cost me, you mean? You're an insomniac anyway. Neither one of us is sleeping until Midge has agreed to a first date with me."

"So let it be written..." Gregg intoned dramatically while fisting a hand to his chest.

Brody's grin broadened and he made a similar gesture, wondering if the longing he had previously felt was what made his chest ache as he gently touched it with his fist.

"So let it be done."

CHAPTER 3

Midge

Midge seethed and mumbled under her breath as she headed further into LA, doing her utmost to avoid her propensity for reckless driving whenever her flaring temper got the better of her.

She failed miserably.

Brody Prescott had managed to ruffle her usually unflappable composure. Their conversation had her fuming one minute and then wondering how his hair might feel if she ran her fingers through it the next.

The last thing she needed to be was another notch on that man's exceptionally long belt.

She prided herself on her cool head and her ability to respond logically no matter the situation she found herself in. One too many scenes and manic meltdowns from her actress mother, and Midge had learned if she wanted her father or anyone else to take her seriously she needed to be the exact opposite of the woman who'd given birth to her.

As far as childhoods went, Midge couldn't say hers was either good or bad, simply unusual. Her mother played the put-upon socialite whenever situations demanded her parental insights—for which she had zero—and then she managed to completely transform into the doting mommy whenever fashion, hairstyles, or boys came into the picture.

Once her mother realized Midge preferred casual, sensible clothing like jeans, t-shirts, and Converse shoes, considered boys to be an epic waste of time, and had no desire to smear chemicals all over her sensitive skin, her mother gave up all hope of turning her daughter into a big-named actress and slithered away to her bedroom where she'd spent the majority of her time drinking and reminiscing about her glory days. That is, until her final meltdown occurred.

Her father generally had bigger fish to fry but insisted Midge learn the art of film production to become his partner in the company when she reached an appropriate age. She reveled in the attention afforded her whenever her father was available. She found that the best way to share in his life was to insert herself into every aspect of his career.

From the time she was six, Midge and her father had been inseparable. The more she questioned him about his work, the more attention she received. It was the only way to relate to the overachieving workaholic, and she hadn't minded it one bit until adolescence kicked in and other worlds opened up to her. Eventually, she decided to pursue a career in writing.

To say that Mr. Knightly was shocked by this abrupt change in plans was the understatement of the century. He played the wounded victim while Angelica, their housemaid and Midge's surrogate mother, scrubbed the house with a vengeance, asking the patron saint of broken families to hurry and do something about this particular family—all in Spanish, of course.

Her father threatened to take away her trust fund and any and all support if she refused to join the family business.

Hurt and betrayed beyond anything she had ever before experienced, Midge gladly relinquished all claim to her trust fund, packed a few bags, and stormed out of the house, having absolutely no idea how she was going to fund her dream without her father's help. Receiving news of a scholarship a few days later had been nothing short of a miracle, helping her with tuition and housing. Six years later, she had reached every goal she'd ever set and would soon graduate with the degrees and accolades she wanted. Her life was perfect.

Perfect.

Her father's request for a meeting left her feeling queasy. Their relationship had remained unstable after she set out on her own, but he made an effort to speak with her on the phone during Christmas and her birthday—all scheduled through his secretary, as if the man couldn't pick up his own cell phone and call her like any normal, half-way decent parent.

It hurt.

For six years this break from her father had pained her more than anything she'd ever experienced, and she missed him. She missed the dinners they'd shared, the adventures they'd gone on together while filming in strange and exotic locations all over the world, the late nights discussing his latest project, current visions, or the politics and gossip of the industry.

She'd never considered herself a brave individual, but with her father by her side she'd felt virtually invincible, attempting new things and moving out of her comfort zone whenever he suggested she try something in the industry such as singing, dancing, film, and writing classes.

She'd done it for him. To share in his life the only way she knew how, but her father had never understood how difficult it was for her to make friends or even keep them, and dating had been an absolute nightmare. No one was ever really interested in Madelyn Knightly. They were interested in how their connection to Madelyn Knightly gave them an advantage with her father.

Those writing classes had been the one thing that managed to give her a voice. To set her apart as Madelyn Knightly and not Corbin Knightly's daughter. She'd found who she was while creating compelling characters and developing complex plots and story lines with themes that forced her to form her own opinions and solve her own problems. The possibility that she might have her own projects, ideas, and individual choices kept her grounded in an environment she felt certain she could rely on.

In her stories, the good guys won and the bad guys were vanquished. Maybe real life couldn't play out like a fairy tale, but creating words on a page gave her the freedom to rewrite the outcome of tangible wrongs. It wasn't all sunflowers and rainbows, but her stories played out exactly how she wanted and needed them to.

That kind of control appealed to her.

Not necessarily something Corbin Knightly had been grooming her for.

And then that reprobate of a billionaire had to ruin her mojo and the serenity of Café Canapé by reintroducing her former life to her and reminding her of everything she'd given up so very long ago.

She felt violated, tainted—and Heaven help her slightly curious. What kind of reality TV show did Brody Prescott feel desperate enough to debase himself on? Why? He could easily date a sensible woman until the media found something else to gnaw at.

Of course, it seemed clearer than glass that the type of woman he desperately needed in his life was not the type he actually wanted.

Like she cared!

Midge furiously pushed all thoughts of Brody Prescott and his devilish good looks to a far recess of her mind, promising herself upon pain of death she wouldn't give one more consequential moment of her precious time to that conceited, idiotic, egotistical, charming, intriguing...gah!

About thirty minutes later, Midge pulled into the spacious parking lot of her father's film production building of which he owned several. It was safe to say that Corbin Knightly had made quite a name for himself in the filming industry. His accomplishments varied in their size, scope, and subject matter, but every single project always ended in one outrageous success after another.

After several years of a career in blockbuster movies, he had decided reality TV was the new wave of entertainment and wasted no time in sticking his green thumb into the competitive scene, quickly making a name for himself in that industry as well.

Midge jumped out of her car, squared her shoulders, and tilted her chin to an appropriate battle-ready level. She would not be intimidated by a face-to-face discussion with a father who couldn't be bothered to visit her at her own apartment even though it was located less than an hour away. She looked at her watch and swallowed hard.

Late. If she hadn't been so distracted by that seat-stealing billionaire she would have made it back to her apartment to grab a few necessary items for her classes later that evening before the bad traffic hit.

Upon entering the building, the frosty air from the silent central cooling system tickled the back of her neck, drying a line of sweat that had made its way down her back. After all this time she might have tried to give herself a pep talk when it came to her father, but in the end all she really desired was his approval. The fact that she didn't have it anymore made this meeting all the more nerve wracking.

Midge approached the receptionist—a young girl with a cheesy smile plastered across her face—and gave her a syrupy sweet smile of her own.

"Do you have an appointment?" she asked.

Midge prevented herself from grinding her teeth. "Unfortunately, I do. Would you please inform Mr. Knightly that his daughter is here?"

The young girl's face drained of color. "Oh, I am so sorry, Ms. Knightly. I've never met you so I didn't know..."

Midge held her hand up, trying to calm the frazzled girl down while wondering what had caused her to become so undone in the first place.

"Not a big deal. I never come here if I don't have to, so how would you know who I am?"

The relieved expression on the intern's face made Midge want to slap her father. Was he incapable of being decent to any of the people who worked under him? The poor girl looked terrified.

"I'll...I'll show you right in," she stammered.

"Thank you."

BRODY

"I'll sue," Corbin Knightly threatened again as Brody let out a tired sigh.

"Corbin, I've already told you I will reimburse you for this little setback."

"Little setback?" Knightly looked like he might spontaneously combust. "We'll have to change everything about the show. The marketing, the girls, the locations, the dates, the entire theme. I can't just whip all of this together and still plan on having a show ready to shoot two months from now!"

"You mean to tell me there's no plan B? Weren't you considering other billionaires for this show?"

"The only other billionaire who is dealing with as much scandal as you at the moment is Alexander Montgomery, and there's no way I can shift the focus of the show to him before the first of June."

Brody felt a little sick at the thought of any of the contestants having to deal with the advances of Alexander Montgomery. The guy was a scumbag disguised in tailored Armani suits. He didn't have a problem sharing every sordid detail of his many conquests with anyone interested in listening.

"Look, if you have to push production back until the fall, I will happily pay for every financial loss you incur."

"You may be a billionaire, but you're crazy if you think this won't set you back financially, and I'll drag your name through the mud while my lawyers have a field day with you in court."

Brody let out a few curses under his breath. All of Gregg's predictions were coming true. He really hated it when his assistant was right.

"Do you plan on telling me why you've decided my show isn't good enough for you when the benefits of this exposure for you and your business are positively exponential? Don't be an idiot, Prescott. Pull your head out of your arse and have a little pow-wow with that weird assistant of yours. There's no way Gregg is backing you up on this."

For a few moments, Brody doubted the wisdom of his decision when faced with the consequences of being sued by Knightly. He hadn't expected the man to be so ticked off. He thought if he flashed the offer of a few hundred thousand dollars in his face, the guy would give in and take the pay-out.

Apparently, Knightly was the type to take things personally. The lawsuit could get very ugly. Brutal. How would he have time to chase after Midge if he was embroiled in a messy lawsuit? How would he even have time to find her? But what else could he do? He absolutely could not get that girl out of his head.

"Mr. Knightly, your daughter is here to see you," came the harried voice from the intercom atop the expansive desk.

Brody thought the little receptionist a bit jumpy, though he wondered if the intimidating figure of Corbin Knightly had anything to do with it.

"Late," Mr. Knightly muttered. "She's doing it on purpose. As if I didn't have enough to deal with thanks to you." Knightly stood up in an angry huff. "I need to get a few things squared away with my daughter, though my conversation with her may not matter if you're intent on screwing everything up. I'll give you ten minutes to think very carefully about your next course of action." Knightly strode around his desk and headed toward the door. He paused before turning to look at Brody. "Just remember, Brody, Felicia Davenport may have put a slight dent in your armor, but I'll completely pulverize it for the simple satisfaction it will afford if you don't get your head in the game ASAP."

Knightly's threats and the sinking sensation in the pit of Brody's stomach laid waste to his former plans.

Knightly gave him one last menacing look before turning back to the adjacent door that must have led into another office. The moment the door opened, Brody heard the most beautiful sound in the world.

"Hello, Dad," came a cheerful greeting from within.

Brody thought his ears were playing tricks on him. It sounded like...no way. No chance he was that lucky.

Knightly walked through the door, and it began to close behind him. Brody, never one to dismiss Serendipity when she blatantly threw herself in his face, stealthily rushed to the door and placed the toe of his shoe right in front, leaving it open a tiny sliver, just enough for him to sneak a quick glance at the young lady before her father's bulk got in the way.

Midge.

He smiled at the sight of her.

After that one glorious confirmation, Brody felt content to shamelessly eavesdrop.

CHAPTER 4

Midge

Upon entering the small office space, Midge's panic descended like an old, persistent nemesis. She gritted her teeth and told herself that she had pushed beyond her loathsome insecurities. This place, though it held her father's sole interest, attention, and affection was no longer something she felt inclined to compete against.

Her father's first love had been, and always would be, his production company. Films, directing, the interchange between celebrities, Hollywood gossip, and the endless network of parties all amounted to one thing and one thing only: his theatrical works of art. A child had been an afterthought, and in her parents' case, one mighty screw-up in regards to her mother's inability to remember to take her birth control pills on a consistent basis.

She wondered if her father had any idea of the psychological effect his offices had on her. Probably. His ability to read people and nail down their weaknesses had aided him in a business as cutthroat as entertainment.

Midge took a few steadying breaths and reminded herself that these walls and her father's consistently indifferent attitude toward her in the last few years were no longer sources of anguish or misery. She had lived on her own merits for some time and made something of herself without her father's connections, money, or interference.

Big girls like her didn't need to feel intimidated by unresolved daddy issues.

Her internal pep talk managed to stiffen her backbone and sharpen her courage. Just in time too. Within a few seconds her father's solid frame stood before her.

"Hello, Dad," she said with as much happiness as she could muster. She even managed a tepid smile, giving herself a mental pat on the back.

Corbin Knightly entered the room and shifted to the side, tilting his head and critically studying the whole of her. He hadn't really seen her in six years. She hoped for some kind of loving response, but knew better than to expect it.

After a few more punishing moments of silence, Midge spoke up.

"Have I passed inspection or is there some suggestion you're aching to make in regards to my appearance?"

Her father's eyebrows drew up in surprise and a slight smile teased the corners of his mouth, though she noticed some strain around his thin lips and the corners of his eyes. He wasn't a big man in the sense that he was burly. His six-foot-two frame was what gave him the ability to look down upon others if he felt so inclined. His sandy blond hair always managed to look perfectly windblown, creating the impression that he'd just been surfing and didn't give a hoot about how he appeared to others. He was striking. No doubt about that, and many women had tried to snare him into one illicit affair after another. Yet despite her mother's mental health issues, Corbin had remained surprisingly faithful to Celeste Knightly.

She remembered a conversation they'd had when she was fourteen years old.

"Daddy, I think these women are totally into you, and I don't like it."

Her father gathered her in for a massive bear hug. "Don't you know you're the only woman I can handle taking care of? These ladies are too high-maintenance for me."

"What about Mom?" she asked.

She almost wished she hadn't. The quick stab of pain that flickered across her father's face may have gone unnoticed by anyone else, but Midge was highly attuned to her father's cantankerous moods. He swallowed hard and then moved to pick up a spreadsheet on top of his desk.

"I'll always love your mother, Midge girl."

"Then why don't you ever spend time with her?" The answer to her question was important. She wanted to know exactly where her parents stood. How did she, as Madelyn Knightly, fit into this familial picture if she couldn't pinpoint some kind of stability in the chaotic dealings between her parents.

"Your mother is searching for her own brand of happiness, and most of the time I can't travel along the same paths with her. She'll get there someday. We just need to be patient."

Midge wanted to point out that someone as ill as her mother wasn't capable of finding her own happiness. Nothing short of an intervention would do, but she knew her father didn't necessarily know how to handle intense situations like that. Confrontations in his industry were never a problem for him, but saying no to his wife and meting out a little tough love in the process seemed to be beyond him. He tended to shy away from emotionally charged conversations. So everyone in the household tiptoed around her mother, pretending that this phase would eventually play itself out, and she would go back to being ambitious, successful, and happy.

Midge snapped out of her sad reverie as her father moved in front of her and took her shoulders in his large hands.

"I've missed your spunk, Midge girl. Too many people around here tend to kow-tow and agree with everything I say."

"How boring."

Her father threw his head back and laughed for a moment. Midge let the surprising tone and texture of it slide across her skin like a loving embrace. The one thing she had always been capable of doing well was coaxing a laugh from her father.

"Have you gone to visit Mom lately?" She hated to bring it up, but she felt like someone needed to remind him of her existence.

Her father's eyes darkened in pain before he cleared his throat and spoke.

"I sent her some flowers on her birthday. The nurse knows that it's best to tell her it's from a secret admirer."

Midge nodded. Over the past year, her mother's condition had begun to deteriorate much more rapidly than before. She became agitated when Midge introduced herself as her daughter. Yes. It was probably for the best.

He let go of her shoulders and motioned for her to take a seat as he slid behind the desk.

No hug then. Midge didn't know why she had hoped for it.

"You're too skinny, young lady. Doesn't that scholarship provide enough money for groceries?"

She rolled her eyes at this, getting ready for the next critical volley to follow.

"My scholarship covers tuition and housing. My freelance work as an editor and writer is what feeds me."

She waited for him to comment on business being slow or how much more lucrative an internship and subsequent partnership with him might have been. Subjects they had argued in circles over. Instead, he demonstrated great restraint by changing the subject.

"How is your writing going?" He appeared a bit uncomfortable asking, but she answered despite her certainty that he didn't care.

"At the moment, I am in the middle of a contemporary romance, a rags to riches story."

"Will the love interests live happily ever after?"

"This isn't a tragedy, Dad. You know I hate a gloomy ending."

Her father steeped his hands together and rested his chin atop his fingers.

"When do you graduate with your degree?"

Midge narrowed her eyes. They'd been over this last time they spoke.

"I have two more months left in this semester and then one more semester starting in the fall."

"But you have nothing going on this summer?"

His question seemed overly casual. She sensed a trap and smelled a rat.

"I wouldn't say I have nothing. I have my freelance work and my own writing, not to mention marketing for my website and my book once it is finished."

"Yes, of course." Her father's hand whisked in the air as if swatting down something annoying and inconsequential. "What I mean is you have no set schedule or routine for the summer. No classes you are locked into?"

Midge eyed him suspiciously and decided to avoid his question altogether.

"Dad, let's cut the chit-chat and get to the heart of what exactly it is you want from me."

Her father feigned shock at her accusation.

"What could I possibly want from you other than spending some quality time together inquiring after the details of your life?"

"You haven't been interested in my life for a while now."

"That's completely untrue. I've followed you on Facebook and Twitter, haven't I?"

Midge shook her head, wondering if there were parenting classes specifically catered to those individuals with narcissistic tendencies.

"Not the same as actually having a conversation."

"We speak on the phone."

"Twice a year, Dad, and only because your secretary schedules it for you."

She noted that, for once, he actually had the decency to look guilty, though that lasted for one—maybe two—seconds.

Midge blew out an exasperated sigh and sank a little lower in her chair, hoping it would release some of the tension accumulating in her shoulders.

"Why am I here? You've never once asked me to come to your office and speak with you. Not once in six years. So instead of pretending you're actually interested in my life, how about you tell me what you want so we can end this forced family fun and you can get back to creating mind-numbing drama."

Her father's smile looked more like a grimace, but his shoulders seemed to relax a little. "Here's the deal, Midge girl, you know how I've been working on about three different reality TV series following the lives of celebrities and their budding romances?"

Reality TV again. She'd heard enough about it for one day.

"I don't want the details, but yes, I've seen advertisements for them."

"Well, we're starting a new dating series, hoping to create a safe environment for wealthy men to find women who are more interested in them as individuals rather than their money or assets."

"Novel idea," she muttered.

"Isn't it? I certainly could have used something like this when I was dating your mother."

"In all fairness to her, you were using her career as an in for directing your first major motion picture."

Her father snapped his fingers and nodded in agreement. "You see? There are unscrupulous people with ulterior motives running rampant around the dating scene. What is a wealthy bachelor to do if he wants to find true love in a sea of gold-diggers and fame seekers?"

"A truly compelling dilemma. I'm assuming your question was rhetorical?" She yawned in order to emphasize her boredom, but her father had just stepped upon his soap box and wouldn't be descending so soon.

"This new reality TV series will follow the dating life of a wealthy bachelor as he gets to know several different women, all hand-picked and vetted to be the perfect wife for any wealthy man. Each week he will decide which relationships are not progressing until he narrows it down to the girl he wishes to propose to."

"Propose to? Hand-picked and vetted? Tell me the truth, here. How many of these women are actually aspiring actresses? How many will be prepped and coached for creating wildly emotional scenes where the man in question is either getting his face slapped one minute or being desperately kissed the next?"

Her father grinned at her. "Oh, that's good, Midge girl. I'll have to add something like that to a few of the episodes. This is why you should have come to work for me instead of pursuing something as ridiculous as a Masters in English."

Well, she'd been waiting for it and there it was. At least he'd gotten it off his chest and they could move on.

"You do realize that creating stories for your episodes involves creative writing, yes?"

"I'm just saying, you could have done an internship with me and learned everything you needed to know. What's so great about being an author when you could work with your own father? I thought you loved this company," he said in an aggravated tone.

Midge stared at him in shock. Oh sure, he had said this the very night she'd left her home and never looked back, but he was notorious for evading these kinds of conversations.

In a softer voice he said, "I wish you had stuck to the plan we mapped out for you."

"Why are you telling me this? We've been through it before, and we differ with one another's take on where my future is headed. So let's just agree to disagree while you tell me why I'm here."

Her father remained silent for a few moments and then nodded, quickly bouncing back to his previously jaunty behavior.

"I'll get to that in a minute, but first, I want to know what you think about it."

"You...you want my opinion?" Her disbelief couldn't have been more obvious.

"Of course. What do you think about a guy dating several, specially picked women to find the perfect wife?"

"Coming from a woman's point of view, I can't imagine anything more humiliating than throwing myself at a man who is dating several other females at the same time. Seriously, do these women have no self-respect? Do they really want their pathetic attempts at snaring a man—and then subsequently being rejected by him—splashed across national television?"

"Wonderful, isn't it? The things people will do to get themselves on TV. I can't imagine this show tanking when the subject matter is so controversial."

"You're sick, you know that?"

Her father's mischievous grin gave her the willies. "So I've been told. Now then, twenty women have already received vigorous background checks, screen tests, and other necessary vetting to come up with the best possible fit for the bachelor who will be starring in the first season."

"The sorry sucker." A worrisome thought struck Midge. "You haven't signed on Brody Prescott for this series, have you?"

Her father looked at her in surprise.

"Not that I would be able to leak that kind of information to anyone who isn't working on the project..." He eyed her askance. "No. Brody Prescott has not agreed to work on this series. Now how about you tell me why his name popped into your head. Do you know the guy?"

Her father's question was delivered with far too much interest. She had to tread carefully here.

"The scandal surrounding him, and your tendency to cast controversial people in your shows, made his involvement a natural conclusion to come to."

He considered this for a moment while she held her breath. Then he smiled and nodded in agreement.

"You know me well, Midge girl."

"Far too well," she muttered.

"Anyway, back to why you're here. We start shooting two months from now, but I've hit a snag and need your assistance."

"I'm not helping you shoot this series. I don't want to have anything to do with this."

"I'm not asking you to shoot it with me. I'm asking you to be one of the contestants. A cast member."

Midge's jaw dropped well below the level of her father's desk. The suggestion was absolutely ludicrous. She finally broke the silence with a quiet chuckle which quickly turned into one of the best laughs she'd had in a very long time.

Her father didn't appear the slightest bit perturbed by her hysterical laughter, merely waiting patiently as if he had more to spring on her.

"I can't...I can't imagine what in the world might possess you to believe that...that I would ever willingly end up on one of your shows...it's just...it's so..." Her laughter returned again, rendering her speechless once more. She gave her father a condescending pat on the hand and leaned back in her chair.

"Thanks for that. You have no idea how badly I needed a good laugh. Tell me the *real* reason you brought me here."

Her father's intense look remained linked with hers as he explained his situation. "We've had a cancellation. One of the contestants on the show had to drop out due to a botched nose job and several reconstructive surgeries scheduled for the summer. She won't be face-time ready, and we have to have twenty contestants. It's the number this production has been planned around. I need you to fill in for this girl for the first night. I promise you, at the end of the night the bachelor will be instructed to include you as one of three girls eliminated during the diamond ceremony."

Midge's horror increased with every word uttered by her father.

"Absolutely not," she said in a hoarse whisper. "Absolutely not." Midge gave it a little more backbone the second time around.

"Consider it for just a few minutes."

"I won't consider it for few *moments*. You are not dragging me back into this lifestyle, this fake, unfeeling world that you reside in where everyone is competing for the best hair, the biggest boob jobs, the most expensive mansions, or the most impressive vehicles. I walked away from it for several good reasons, Dad, and I will not get sucked back into this endless black hole of immoral decay. Plus, what does it matter if you have twenty contestants exactly if you're planning on doing the first round of eliminations that very evening."

"I already explained the necessity of having twenty contestants."

"Get someone else."

"I know you, and I trust you to conduct yourself appropriately on camera. I don't have the time or the patience to do more auditions and screen testing to find someone new."

Midge gave him a perplexed look.

"You may not have the patience for it, but you certainly have the time. Two months is plenty of time to—"

"I hear your scholarship won't be renewed next semester."

The change in subject caught Midge completely off-guard.

"How on earth could you possibly know that?"

"Despite your beliefs to the contrary, I *do* take an interest in your welfare and your personal life. You walked away from your trust fund when you refused to go into business with me. What if I offer you that trust fund back in exchange for one night of being a contestant on the show?"

Midge swallowed hard at this. Why would he offer her that? Why would he even consider going to her in the first place? What was really going on here?

"You can't be serious."

"I am. I absolutely am. You could pay for your last semester of college and do whatever you want after that. Invest it, spend it, I honestly don't care. I'm willing to let bygones be bygones and allow our past differences to disappear if you help me out."

She shook her head, feeling dazed by the generous offer and the hidden strings that were most likely attached. She'd be digressing if she agreed to take the money she'd turned her back on in an indignant, self-righteous huff six years ago, but she couldn't graduate without that last semester, and despite her hard work, her freelance jobs wouldn't cover expenses.

"I want it in writing." Her voice sounded hollow to her ears.

"What?"

"I want it in writing. I know you. I know how you are. If I do this show for you, what's to stop you from demanding other favors and eventually roping me back into the business simply because you gave me back my trust fund? I want it written down that once I'm eliminated from the show, I get my trust fund and that's the end of it."

Her father's study of her held a hint of respect, possibly admiration. She didn't care at this point. She felt sick inside. After everything she'd accomplished in order to assert herself and her independence, he'd managed to find a way to pinpoint her weakness and go in for the kill.

"I'll have the contract written up and the money ready for transfer." He stood, giving his usual signal of dismissal now that their business had concluded. "I think you'll see this has all worked out for the best. In the end, you'll finally get your trust fund, and I'll get my TV show."

"I also want my cell phone and laptop available to me."

Her father sighed in exasperation. "You can't go a single evening without it?"

"Dad, I'm fully aware of the way you immerse people into the reality you stage for them. No outside contact with anyone. Complete and total brainwashing when it comes to how isolated everyone is once they step onto a reality TV series. My world cannot shrink to a few rooms in a mansion even for one day."

"Fine. I'll allow it."

"One more thing."

Her father groaned and sat back down.

"I can turn my mic off whenever I want to."

His head shot up. "Absolutely not."

She stood up and pointed a warning finger at him.

"I will go completely insane if the only time I get a break for myself is when I'm in the bathroom. You will allow me to turn my mic off and send your cameras packing whenever I want. I am not signing up for such an enormous breach of privacy. Your methods rival that of any surveillance techniques the government has employed, illegal or otherwise, and I will not be your puppet or play to the cameras when it isn't completely necessary. If I'm only going to be there for an evening this shouldn't be a problem. Should it?"

Her father grimaced as he thought through her stipulations. She could see the wheels working in his mind as he fought for a way to insert a loophole into the contract.

"Okay, Midge girl. I accept your terms."

He held out his hand as if to seal the business deal, but Midge turned on her heels and walked to the door. She rested her hand on the silver door knob for a moment, hesitating to leave before saying to her father what she'd been wanting to say for the last six years.

Making up her mind, she turned around, but leaned against the door for support. She didn't know why the tears began to fall, but they did, and at that moment she couldn't have cared less whether her father used that weakness to his advantage or not.

"You know it was never about the trust fund, right?"

"What?" he asked in surprise.

"Your money was never important to me. Your fame and your name were never the things I wanted you to share with me. I simply wanted you to know that—unlike most people in your life—I really cared about you. I am the one who loved you whether there was a trust fund in the mix or not. Despite who you were to others, you have always been Daddy to me." She took a steadying breath and let it out slowly. "I wanted to be a part of your life, not cast aside like Mom."

Midge cleared her throat and opened the door, leaving a depressing silence in her wake.

CHAPTER 5

Brody

The minute Midge exited her father's office, Brody spun around and quietly went to his seat.

Midge was Corbin Knightly's daughter. No wonder she'd refused to give him her full name. Madelyn Knightly had been known throughout Hollywood as the next Corbin Knightly. She was considered a savant in the industry due to some of her own projects produced through Knightly's company. She'd virtually disappeared from the public eye six years ago, but Brody remembered the woman's picture plastered all over the news when she broke with her father.

She'd certainly blossomed since then. He hadn't even recognized her. Her hair had always been straight and blond in all of her photos, and she'd definitely had more of a baby face at that point in her life. She must have reverted back to what was most obviously her natural hair color to trip people up. It had certainly tripped him up.

And now, the woman he'd nearly risked court for was going to be on *Marry Your Billionaire*. There was no way he planned to step down and let someone like Alexander Montgomery take his place. He didn't want that creep to have even five minutes of alone time with Madelyn Knightly. Not that there was any reason to step down when the most interesting woman he'd ever met was going to be a contestant on the show.

His show.

He'd learned a great deal about Midge during that brief conversation she'd shared with her father. She was a trust fund baby, yet shunned the life of a pampered, spoiled rich girl, opting for a more down-to-earth lifestyle, walking away from a trust fund that most likely held several million dollars. The fact that she had accepted it now didn't even faze him. Her father had basically blackmailed her into it, and her own desire to use it for something as worthwhile as a college education instead of buying a half-million dollar wardrobe—or something else as equally frivolous and insane—was admirable.

There were three things he knew with certainty.

One: Midge was no gold-digger.

Two: Midge was going to be on the show.

Three: He absolutely wanted and needed her in his life.

His thoughts were interrupted by the inward swing of the door as Knightly came barging into the room looking a bit out of sorts.

"Is everything okay?"

"What?" He sat down across the desk from Brody with a distracted air. "Never better. Now, where were we? Oh yes, I was threatening you with financial ruin if you didn't wizen up and see things my way."

"To be perfectly frank, your threats did their job. I'm all in."

Knightly's eyes widened in surprise and then a pleased grin took over. "Marvelous. I love it when threats pan out. We'll just pretend our previous conversation never happened and continue on like the good friends we are."

Anyone who considered themselves good friends with Corbin Knightly was probably the type who felt comfortable swimming in a tank filled with hungry sharks.

"Gregg explained to you the necessity of my phone and laptop being with me while I'm there?"

Knightly grunted. "I'm getting tired of everyone throwing conditions at me, but yes, I understand that you need to run your business. Just remember you're not allowed to post things or comment on social media during the filming of this series."

"Wouldn't dream of it."

"Good. Now, I want your whole heart and soul invested in this. You better show up on the first of June anxious and raring to find true love. Are you ready to be the first star of *Marry Your Billionaire*? Ready to find a woman you can spend the rest of your life with?"

Brody smiled back, thinking it hilarious that this man had no idea who he intended that woman to be.

"Knightly, I've never been more ready for anything in my entire life."

MIDGE

Midge shared an apartment with Lisa Rassmusen, a girl with whom she'd originally had very little in common. She'd met Lisa on campus after placing an advertisement for a roommate on one of the many community boards spread throughout the vast university's grounds. Their shared pitiful level of poverty and mutual need for an able body to split the rent had thrown them together, and since they never seemed to get in each other's way the arrangement had become permanent.

As Midge entered the tiny apartment she took note of Lisa's shoes on the floor. One shoe was stuffed with a pair of used socks—something to do with recycling footwear to save money on laundry detergent. Midge shook her head and gave the shoes a rueful grin, finding Lisa's quirky penchant for pinching pennies rather endearing. It was usually Midge's job to make certain her roommate actually washed her socks after three uses.

Lisa had pushed for ten, but after thoroughly grossing out a guy she'd been dating for a few days she finally saw the wisdom in Midge's kind suggestion and changed her OCD behavior...at least in that respect.

Their first year together, Lisa hacked into a professor's laptop to change a grade on a test that Midge had quite vocally complained about. Apparently, her roommate was a talented hacker with activities firmly located under the delinquent category.

After that one incident, she made certain to never complain about her grades around Lisa again, though she warned her roommate about the evils of her online criminal activities. After Lisa claimed to be hacking into the airport's database to secure herself a seat on a flight to her hometown in Washington, Midge begged her to never again give her the details of her online criminal adventures. Best to remain ignorant on that score.

Midge stepped over Lisa's shoes as the need to pummel something began to dissipate. A few more deep breaths and she could almost forget about her agreement with her father and the way she'd finally sold out to the trust fund baby stigma.

One glance in the kitchen confirmed that Lisa was home. The remains of left over peanut butter and jelly sandwiches littered the table along with a couple of string cheese wrappers and a jug of orange juice.

How her roommate could be such a stickler about money while simultaneously being the ultimate slob never ceased to amaze her. She just figured penny pinching ought to go hand-in-hand with germaphobic tendencies. Unfortunately, that phobia belonged in Midge's corner.

Not that it was a phobia, really. She just liked to keep things tidy and organized. Nothing wrong with disinfecting the apartment three times a week...or more. With a roommate like Lisa it tended to be mandatory.

"Lisa, are you home?" Midge entered the small, square kitchen, opened up the freezer, and pulled out a Marie Calender's microwaveable dinner. She didn't have much of an appetite after her conversation with her father, but she needed to eat something. A loud clank carried down the hall and then a pain-filled moan soon followed. Heavy footsteps approached, and Lisa sprang into view with half of her blond hair in curlers, a toothbrush in her mouth, and a bottle of mascara in her right hand.

"Hot date tonight?" Midge smirked.

Lisa rolled her eyes heavenward, making her look even more ridiculous than she already did, and pulled the toothbrush from her mouth.

"You completely forgot the double date I set up for us tonight, didn't you?"

"The what?" She did *not* like the sound of that.

"Dang it, Midge, I told you last week that Danny wanted you to meet one of his super cute, super single friends this weekend. Don't you remember?"

"Vaguely, but what I also don't remember is you ever giving me an actual date and time."

"You told me to set it up, so I set it up." Lisa paused for a moment, screwing her face into a serious frown, her thinking face as Midge liked to call it. "Okay, so maybe I forgot to mention exactly when I set it up, but we have hot dates within the next two hours so get a move on baby. We're getting fed tonight."

Midge groaned. "Do you think Danny has any idea that he's the reason you haven't starved to death over the past few months?"

"If he does he isn't complaining." Lisa slid her hands over her ample hips and gave them a little shake. "Not when I'm keeping him nice and warm at night."

"Please spare me the details of your love life, Lisa. You know there are other ways to show him you appreciate him rather than jumping into his bed."

"So I'm a kept woman. So what?"

"If only," Midge grimaced. "If you really want to play the role of a kept woman, you need to be demanding more from this guy. Next time the plumbing breaks, have him pay to fix it. Or better yet, how about he finds us a new apartment and pays our rent."

Lisa shrugged. "You don't mean that, Midge. You and all your talk about being independent and never relying on your father's money to get you through college. Even if I *was* a kept woman, I doubt you'd ever accept a single penny from me. Speaking of, how did the meeting with your dad go?"

Midge's shoulders slumped. "I'm getting my trust fund back."

Lisa's jaw couldn't have become further unhinged if Mohammad Ali had sucker punched it. "Why am I settling for a goof like Danny when my roommate has a trust fund?"

"Oh, so now *I'm* responsible for your kept woman status?"

Lisa smirked, but her face became serious once again. "What happened, Midge? I thought you walked away from that years ago?"

"My father is heading a new reality TV series, *Marry Your Billionaire*—"

"Oh, yeah. I read a little bit about the new series on the internet. They'll be unveiling the identity of the billionaire in question next Monday."

Midge shot a hand up to prevent Lisa from going any further. "Don't tell me. I don't want to know the details. Anyway, they start shooting in two months, but Dad had a cancellation and needs me to step in as one of the contestants for the first round of eliminations. He said if I did it, I would get my trust fund back with no strings attached."

Lisa's squeal vibrated from the back of her throat like the revving of a race car engine before take-off. When her squeal finally made its way out of her mouth the results were ear-shattering.

"I can't believe this. I can't believe it." She jumped up and down in a circle, losing half her curlers in the process. "My roommate is going to be famous. My roomie is a reality TV superstar." She said the last part in a dramatic whisper while jumping to one knee and throwing her hands in the air, flinging the mascara and her toothbrush in opposite directions and wiggling her fingers in true jazz hand style.

"Lisa, its one day and one night, okay? I have to be on TV for less than a twenty-four hour period, and then the guy will be instructed to eliminate me with however many other girls he decides to let go. I'll hardly be a superstar."

"You'll get to be on a billionaire's radar for a whole day. I'm so freaking jealous of you right now."

"You shouldn't be. The guy will probably be arrogant, self-centered, and about as personable as a dead fish."

Lisa jumped up from her position and went in search of the items she'd torpedoed through the air. "Can you, for once, get excited about the male species? Be thrilled to go on television like any normal twenty-four-year-old woman? You get your trust fund back, you're doing your dad a favor so it isn't like he can hold anything over your head. You'll be on TV for one full day, *and* you'll get to hob nob with all sorts of famous people. This can only help push your writing career further. Don't you see that? Win-win, my dear."

Midge attempted to look at it from Lisa's perspective, but could only view this latest development as a major setback in her life. She loathed the fact that she had to depend on her trust fund at all, but her desire to graduate held more sway than her pitiful pride.

She'd made a deal with the very devil and she knew it. Only time would tell when that devil might pull out his own set of tricks, and then the whole thing would blow up in her face, trust fund and all.

"So I assume you'll be staying at some immaculate mansion to film this thing?"

"My father's secretary will send me the details soon. Who knows where we'll be?"

"You're going to be sharing a mansion with nineteen other women. I can already picture the cat fights *that* little scenario will produce." Lisa clasped her hands together and let out a wicked cackle.

Midge shook her head. "It's a good thing I'll only be there one day. Can you imagine how miserable it would be to live in the same mansion with so many other women all competing for the same man?"

"Freaking drama, girlfriend. I can't wait for all of the gory details. Just make sure you have someone taste-test your food and drinks before you eat anything. Oh, and lock your bedroom door at night. I wouldn't put it past any of those girls to slip a black widow in your bed or cut off your gorgeous red curls while you're sleeping. That's what I'd do, anyway."

Midge snorted. "I'm not entering a war zone, Lisa. It'll be the most uneventful, painfully boring experience I've ever been unfortunate enough to suffer through."

Lisa grinned and shrugged. "You *would* describe your big Hollywood debut as boring."

"It's unbelievable that I agreed to this."

"Unbelievable, is correct. That's reality TV, for ya."

Midge studied her roomie for a moment and then let out a snicker. "You plan on curling the other half of your hair before we go out tonight?"

Lisa reached into her pocket, grabbed her phone, and checked the screen. She groaned and bolted down the hallway. "We're gonna be late if you don't get a move on."

"Where are we going?"

"Some fancy restaurant where Danny claims all of the most fashionable celebrities frequent."

"Danny can afford that?"

"Of course he can. Did I not mention he's a trust fund baby like you?"

Say what?

Midge stomped down the hall and entered the bathroom. "Please tell me the guy he's setting me up with isn't some scumbag playboy who has never worked a day in his life."

"Okay, I won't." Lisa's grin became more pronounced.

"Dang it, Lisa. Playboys like Danny have expectations after they fork out money for elaborate dinners."

"Oh believe me, I know."

"I'm not giving up my virgin status for a thousand-dollar dinner, do you understand me?"

"Of course, I do. I know you can handle these guys. You've had a lifetime of dealing with their come-ons. We'll have a great dinner and benefit from the joys of leftovers for a week. Please back me up on this. Please?"

Midge grunted and then headed to her bedroom.

"Throw that black sequined number on, Midge. I swear if you walk out of your bedroom in a t-shirt and jeans I will have no choice but to delete your current manuscript and any backup files you've created."

"You wouldn't dare. Besides, my computer is password protected," Midge hollered back.

"Have you forgotten who you're talking to?"

"That's illegal!"

"Again, have you forgotten who you're talking to?"

"Fine, fine. Curse you and your vicious life of crime."

Midge entered her bedroom and began getting ready for what was sure to be one excruciating dinner date.

Club 23 was the type of restaurant you found Hugh Jackman or Reese Witherspoon frequenting. Everything about the establishment, from the vaulted ceilings with dangling, crystal chandeliers, to the red velvet cushioned chairs and circular tables with gold plaited florets weaved along their outer rims, reminded Midge of that fancy restaurant, Harmonia Gardens, from the movie *Hello Dolly*. The seating had been arranged in the exact same manner with the same floor plan. Open tables were located on the ground floor and positioned directly beside an expansive dance floor where a live orchestra played anything from classical music to big band standards, depending on the night in question.

Midge begrudged the sweet sense of homecoming as she entered Club 23 on the arm of her blind date, Alexander Montgomery, the son of some oil tycoon recently transplanted from Texas. She hadn't really paid much attention to the details of Danny's introduction, too distracted by the evident leer disrupting the perfect symmetry of Montgomery's face. She'd made a mental note to never find herself alone in the lecher's presence.

As a teenager, her father had brought her to this very place for quality time. Even though the discussion tended to center around his latest project, he'd always asked for her opinions and involved her in the process. He'd also encouraged her to move past her stage fright by forcing her to get up with the orchestra and sing jazz standards whenever Mac, the band's director, asked her to. To say she was a crowd favorite during her teen years was an understatement, and it had been a great confidence booster for a girl who only received attention from the male population due to her last name.

A short waiter appeared out of nowhere—no small feat considering his rotund figure—and approached the group with an expectant air.

"You have a reservation?"

Alexander Montgomery gave him a condescending nod. "A private dining area under the name Montgomery."

The waiter's eyes widened.

"Yes, of course. Forgive me, Mr. Montgomery. I'll show you to your table immediately."

The man spun on his heels with impressive grace and speed, defying all laws of physics with his portly frame. She thought she heard Lisa let out a tiny snort and gave her a warning look. She hated it when the patrons of this place treated the staff as if they were less than human, and she wasn't about to let her roommate behave that way. Danny was quickly becoming a bad influence on her.

The private dining areas were situated on the balcony above, encircling the floor below like boxed seats in an opera house. A red velvet curtain hung around each dining booth to offer more privacy should one wish to use it.

Midge most certainly did not.

Once they ascended the curling staircase, their host directed them to two separate booths. Like a lightning bolt to the brain, it dawned on Midge that she and Alexander would be separating themselves from Danny and Lisa. The sick feeling in her stomach took wings after that, fluttering a nauseating rhythm as she seated herself across from her date.

"Something to drink?" the waiter asked.

"We'll start with some champagne."

"Actually, if you could bring me some water, that would be wonderful," Midge cut in.

Alexander quirked an eyebrow at this and then nodded to the man. She watched with some amusement as his tiny legs whipped back and forth, carrying the rest of his body gracefully across the balcony floor.

"You're only drinking water?"

"I suppose I could have ordered some juice." She squeezed out a smile which didn't even come close to reaching her eyes.

"No, I meant to ask if you would prefer some wine."

"I don't drink."

His eyes widened at this. "You...don't drink. How on earth do you get through the monotony of your week?"

Really?

Midge held back the urge to pinch the bridge of her nose and possibly punch him in his. She felt a massive headache coming on. Her original fears about this night had transformed from boring to miserable. The guy's personality was about as engaging as that of a disgruntled college professor delivering his millionth chemistry exam.

The fact that he had maneuvered them alone together didn't signify any promising developments.

"I've always found that a little alcohol tends to loosen people up a bit. Nothing like lowered inhibitions to make for a pleasurable evening, and I certainly don't mind finding out just how pleasurable our evening could be. Maybe you could give me a little preview."

His eyes dove directly toward her chest. She was grateful her dress had a modest neckline.

Midge whistled at him to get his attention.

"Up here, Alexander."

He raised his eyes to her questioningly. Once she was sure she had his undivided attention she continued, "My body really isn't on the menu for this evening. Got it?"

He smirked and leaned forward.

"I love it when chicks play hard-to-get."

She gritted her teeth and took in some air, attempting to rein in her temper before her scathing tongue got the best of her. Abandoning him right then and there was all too tempting, but she couldn't afford the cab fare, and she didn't relish the fifteen-mile walk home. Instead of throwing her cutlery at him, she took another cleansing breath and opted to change the subject.

"So tell me a little about yourself, Alexander."

He gave her a pleased smile and ran a hand through his light blond hair. He might have been handsome if his weak chin and condescending sneer hadn't ruined his face.

"As much as I enjoy discussing anything centered around me, I am much more interested in learning about you."

Midge puzzled through this unexpectedly selfless response.

He reached to his right and pulled on a small tassel which brought the red velvet curtain down around the opening of the booth. The small light directly above them let off a seductive glow, attempting to sell the romantic atmosphere and failing to succeed due to the company seated across from her.

Midge felt the space within the room diminish by several square feet.

Alexander reached across the table and enveloped her hand within his cold, clammy paw. "What's it like being the daughter of a famous Hollywood producer and director? I was actually one of the billionaires considered for this season of *Marry Your Billionaire,* but I wasn't chosen. Any chance you could put in a good word for me with your father for next season?"

Midge gritted her teeth.

Lisa and her big mouth!

CHAPTER 6

Brody

"Mom, I know this reality TV show is ridiculous, but I swear it has absolutely nothing to do with fixing my image," Brody said as he brought a virgin piña colada to his lips and downed it like it might be the last one he'd ever have.

As much as he loved his mother, the last fifteen minutes of their dinner had consisted of persistent questioning into every feeling, thought, and motive behind his decision to film *Marry Your Billionaire*. Like a bloodhound in hot pursuit, his mother had caught wind of an ulterior motive and intended to sniff it out until Brody surrendered any and all pertinent information.

"I'm aware of that, dear child. Why on earth do you think I'm playing twenty questions with you?" His mother shrugged her wide shoulders as if to say, *Honestly, what did you expect? I'm your mother*, before picking up her fork and delicately spearing a succulent piece of shrimp. "If you'd consider giving me a straight answer, we might be able to move on from this interrogation." She popped the shrimp into her mouth and chewed, but her eyes never left her son's face.

Brody, ever aware that is mother saw much more than he felt comfortable with, squirmed in his cushioned seat like a chastised five-year-old. He enjoyed taking his mother out to dinner once a week to catch up on the latest news, relishing in the easy camaraderie of her company. As a single mother, Blanche Prescott had done her best to raise Brody with every advantage a working mom could manage, and well he knew it. His gratitude for her sacrifices was what had motivated him to build his company. Giving her the life his father had wanted for them before he passed away was more gratifying than Brody could possibly describe.

She was just so darned insightful sometimes!

He had to look at his nearly empty plate when he finally disclosed his secret. "I...met someone this morning, Mother."

A fork clattered upon a glass plate and his head shot up to witness his mother's completely dumbfounded expression. He took a moment to enjoy her surprised and speechless condition. Then her face broke into an excited grin, making her high cheekbones and slender nose look almost elfish in nature.

"My dear boy, you've finally met someone? A girl you actually plan on dating for longer than a day?"

Brody scowled at this. "I have had relationships last longer than a day."

"Try naming one, please. It'll be entertaining."

Brody's scowl released into a reluctant grin. He wasn't excited to reveal the existence of a previous relationship gone bad when he'd never introduced the money-grubbing woman to his mother. He'd wanted to. He'd been planning on it, but then his ex-girlfriend had made it painfully clear that his desirability directly correlated with the amount of money he had in his bank account.

It'd been a huge blow to his ego. Yep. His self-esteem had taken one mighty hit. He'd never wanted to go through that again. Worse than that, he'd been afraid to trust in his own judgment. He'd dated Rita for some time and never suspected she was seeing someone else or that she was merely dating him for his money. Weren't there supposed to be gradual signs, little nuances in behavior, an occasional slip-up with texts and phone messages instead of the eventual explosion that took place?

He'd been clueless for ages, and after that he'd convinced himself that others would have seen it coming, which made him a terrible judge of character when it came to his own personal life. He simply didn't trust himself anymore. Not in that department.

"All right. I suppose I haven't been too willing to pursue anything with anyone for a while."

"A while? Brody, the last time you brought a girl home to meet me was in high school, and she was your prom date. As I recall, she asked you. You hadn't planned on going since you thought it was a waste of time when you could have been making money."

"Well, you were working three jobs, and I wasn't gonna waste money we didn't have on something as lame as prom when one night of work would have given us an extra hundred bucks."

His mother reached a consoling hand out to her son and placed it upon his. "I am not criticizing you. I'm merely pointing out how much you've sacrificed over the years."

"I hated seeing you so tired. I had to...do something about it. Fix it."

"Iit was my job to provide for you, and we did just fine back then. We learned plenty over those hard years, wouldn't you say?" She held a loving twinkle in her eye. "I never wanted billions, you know. But I couldn't be more proud with how hard you've worked and how far you've come."

Brody swallowed a foreign lump in his throat. Only his mother had the power to reduce him to tears. His main motivation from the moment he'd nabbed his first job was to obliterate that tired look from her eyes and provide a future for her where she would never have to suffer like that again. He'd never imagined that too much money might become a double edged sword, always wondering whether a woman was interested in him for him alone or for the billions attached to his name.

"Now then, who is this darling girl that's captured your eye, and when do I get to meet her?"

"Her name is Madelyn Knightly. She's the producer's daughter and quite a firecracker."

"Hold on a second. You're dating Mr. Knightly's daughter? Sounds like a conflict of interest. It could get very messy."

"We're not actually dating. In fact, when I ran into her this morning I had no idea who she was." Brody related the exchange he'd shared with Midge and the conversation she'd had with her father, admitting his shameless eavesdropping in the process. He watched his mother as her eyes danced with amusement.

"You say she showed absolutely no interest in you even though she knew exactly who you were?"

"She claimed to show no interest, but that girl blushed one crazy shade of red every time her eyes caught mine."

"Maybe she was simply showing signs of distress because she was afraid you might molest her." His mother gave him a wicked grin.

"In a public place with Gregg there to witness the entire encounter? Believe me, she was not even remotely afraid of either one of us."

"Gregg, was there? Well, that will certainly put a damper on any romantic entanglements."

"Mother—"

"I love Gregg as much as you do, but that man hasn't a clue what romance is as evidenced by the many floozies he's set you up with." His mother gave a disdainful sniff.

"Yeah. Midge definitely touched on that subject. She told me I should date someone with half a brain. Honestly, it's been a long time since I've had such a stimulating conversation with a woman around my age."

Understatement of the century. Brody couldn't remember the last time he'd actually picked out his own dates. Gregg had been in charge of his social life for so long, he wasn't even sure he knew how to ask a girl out anymore. Worse, Gregg's ideal woman tended to be aggressive. They were all too eager to jump into bed with him without really knowing him as a person. He suspected his money had everything to do with that.

"And her father is now blackmailing her into filling in for a last minute cancellation? Do you think she has any idea you're the billionaire starring in this first season?"

Brody shook his head. "Nope, but she'll find out next week."

"Oh, this is marvelous," his mother sighed. "I suppose I'll have to wait to meet her then."

"We'll be shooting the first week in Hawaii, and I won't be bringing any potential future wives home to meet you until the last week or so of the show."

Brody paused for a moment to again consider what a meeting between his mother and Midge might be like.

Entertaining.

They were essentially the same person when it came to cutting through the bull crap of any situation. His mother couldn't stand insipid, flighty girls, and Midge didn't fall under either category. No. His Midge was strong and determined. There was substance there. An inner light he desperately wanted to bask in.

Blanche pointed her fork at him in warning.

"You're going to have to figure out a way to keep her on. She fully expects to be eliminated after the first day."

He'd spent the last few hours contemplating that very problem.

"Oh, I have a plan. Don't you worry about that."

"My darling Brody, when it comes to you and plans, I'm never worried, but you have a variable you can't control in this one, and it sounds to me like she's a spirited girl with a mind of her own. So a bit of advice for you."

"What's that?"

"Don't screw this up."

"Thanks, Mom."

"Of course. Now if you'll excuse me, I need to go to the little ladies room."

"Am I ordering you dessert?"

His mother placed a hand on her ample waist as she stood. "Does it look like I'm counting calories?"

"I'm going to dodge the trap embedded in that loaded question and just order the usual."

"Smart boy."

MIDGE

Midge continued to linger in the restaurant's elaborate ladies room, dreading to return to her shallow date and the monotony of their inane conversation which centered solely around him. His hints at future dinner dates with her and her father had been about as subtle as an elephant wearing a clown suit while holding a sign that read SUBTLE in bold red ink. His roving hand under the table proved difficult to dodge in such a tiny space.

A trip to the ladies' room had been her only solution.

She leaned her elbows against the marble counter near the porcelain sink with its tiny soaps and lotions. Her face sank into the curve of her hands and a quiet moan escaped her lips.

"That bad, is it?"

Midge's head popped up at the slight intrusion. She glanced in the mirror and saw an older, elegant looking woman with naturally wavy hair the color of snow. Midge had never encountered a woman brave enough to leave her hair untouched by dyes and highlights, but the pure white of her hair made her striking blue eyes more pronounced. There were fine lines that rested within the creases of her brow and the corners of her eyes. She looked rather timeless, and Midge had a wild thought that her fairy godmother had come to spirit her away to a more promising prince where she would find true love at last.

"Wh...what's that bad?" Midge asked.

Her fairy godmother's sympathetic smile reflected back at her through the mirror. The kind woman rested a weathered hand upon her shoulder.

"Is it a first date or are you suffering through the, 'It's not you, it's me' speech?"

Midge couldn't help but grin at the perceptive question.

"First date. Not necessarily the most hellish date I've been on, but there's nothing worse than getting to know someone you would normally avoid like the plague."

"Ah, then it was a set-up?"

"More like an ambush."

Her fairy godmother chuckled. "Oh dear! Those are the worst kind. Are you dealing with someone who can't keep his hands to himself or is he simply centering the conversation around his many virtues minus the vices?"

Midge snorted. "Both. I honestly don't think I'll be able to get through the rest of dinner without throwing my water in his face."

Her fairy godmother's eyes lit with amusement. "Please tell me you're seated somewhere on the first floor where I can watch the action unfold and possibly throw a few pieces of shrimp over the balcony's edge."

"We're on the balcony, unfortunately, and as much as I would love to have someone armed and dangerous in my corner, I think it would be better to keep you out of the crossfire."

"Pity. I have such wonderful aim."

Midge grinned widely. "Of that, I have no doubt. Are you here with someone special?"

"My son. He likes to treat his old mother to dinner, and I'm a huge fan of eating food I don't have to cook."

"Ah, a restaurant junkie after my own heart."

Her fairy godmother washed her hands under the sink, nodding in approval before saying, "It surprises me that a girl like you is on a first date instead of out with a serious boyfriend."

Midge thought carefully before responding. "I think I'm a little too blunt for the men I've been introduced to. I've been told I'm an acquired taste."

The older woman dried her hands. "Like a fine wine, then? Sounds like you're someone worth savoring. My name is Blanche Prescott."

Prescott? Probably a coincidence. There were plenty of Prescott's in the area.

"I'm Madelyn Knightly. It's very nice to meet you." At the sound of her name, recognition set into her fairy godmother's features. She sometimes wished her name didn't bring to mind her producer father. Once her name was mentioned, an uncomfortable air of expectation usually descended like a smothering blanket. She then felt it her duty to share all sorts of anecdotes concerning the life of a Hollywood producer's daughter.

Instead of the interrogation she dreaded, her fairy godmother merely smiled and said, "What a beautiful name, Madelyn. Is it a family name?"

"Honestly, I have no idea. My mother doesn't discuss her background, and my father's parents passed away when he was in college. I've never thought to ask."

"Well, either way, it suits you."

"Thank you."

Midge wanted to splash some water on her face before returning to her date, but her make-up prevented her from that reviving course of action. She thought it might fortify her nerve to see the evening through, a sort of protective cleansing.

She noticed her fairy godmother giving her a searching stare in the mirror. She smiled and received a self-deprecating smile in return.

"Do you think I could trouble you to help me back up that menace of a staircase? I assured my son that I would manage just fine, but I'm beginning to feel a slight twinge in my knees."

"Oh, of course."

The poor woman must have been embarrassed to ask for help.

Midge looped an arm through Blanche's and opened the bathroom door, ushering her through.

Blanche hardly seemed to struggle as they ascended the staircase, and Midge noticed that she didn't seem out of breath. Strange to think of this vibrant woman needing anyone's help with anything.

As they neared her private dining table, Midge saw a man's sleek black dress shoe peeking out the side and noted that the son was seated with his back to them. She refrained from looking at him, too preoccupied with making certain her fairy godmother was seated comfortably.

Blanche turned her attention to her son. "My dear, I ran into an angel in the ladies room, and she was kind enough to help me up that treacherous staircase."

"I'd recognize that fiery red hair anywhere."

Sweet maple syrup!

Midge stood stock still at the sound of a voice she feared was far too familiar. She spun her head around only to have those fears confirmed, and then turned her head back to her traitorous fairy godmother. Instead of delivering her into the arms of a prince, she'd been thrown into yet another ambush.

"Brody Prescott is your son?"

"Why, yes. Do you two know each other?" Her question held nothing but innocence.

Midge's attention quickly swiveled back to Brody. She felt irked at the delighted smile spreading across his lips and the way it tugged at her heart just a little.

"This lovely young lady is Midge."

"Oh, you're the girl from the café? How delightful!" The surprise Blanche exhibited seemed a bit forced, almost rehearsed. The knowing grin on her face certainly told its own story.

Midge couldn't believe he'd been discussing her with his mother. A fierce blush rose to her cheeks. She worried about the unfavorable way in which he might have described her.

"I'd...better return to my table." Midge attempted to back away, but she was detained by a firm hand encasing her own. She glanced toward Brody in surprise.

"I'm not going to allow you to leave without first learning your full name."

Midge hoped her fairy godmother would remain quiet on that score, but she didn't like the knowing grin Brody wore. Did he already know who she was?

"And I'm not going to keep my date waiting just so you can learn something you'll never have need of."

She thought she heard a choked chortling sound coming from Mrs. Prescott and cringed at the thought of offending the sweet woman by giving her son the cold shoulder. She liked the lady immensely, but Brody's unexpected presence had undermined her steady composure.

"You're here on a date? Who is he?" Confused by his irritated tone, she watched in amazement as he stood up and gripped her just above the elbow, turning her body to face him. She heard a breathy, "Oh, my!" from his mother, causing an angry blush to slink its way across her cheeks.

The nerve of this man! Does he really believe my dating life is any of his business?

"That's really none of your concern. Now if you'll excuse me—" She felt a firm tug on her arm.

Brody's eyes sparkled in amusement, interest, and an angry possessive fire whose origins left Midge completely baffled.

"I'm afraid I don't excuse you. I must admit to being intrigued by the notion that any man on this planet might possibly meet up to your stringent expectations when it comes to character and personality."

"Stringent?" Midge placed her free hand on her hip and began tapping her foot. Its soft thudding wasn't quite as satisfactory as it would have been on a hardwood floor. "I merely gave you some suggestions, a few guidelines if you will, since you're so woefully inept at chasing after anything that hasn't been filled with silicone." Another chortle from the mother sounded to her right. "As far as my dating life is concerned, well, I'm not the one attempting to save it with reality TV now, am I?"

"A low blow, young lady. I'm beginning to think you've grossly misjudged me."

"You mean in the same way you misjudged me by scoffing at my mousy librarian appearance while simultaneously calling me a nun?"

"He *didn't*," Mrs. Prescott said.

"He *did*." Midge turned to Brody's mother and the two ladies shared a look of commiseration, as only females can.

"I didn't exactly put it that way, but you definitely don't look like a nun tonight. That black sequined dress sheds you in a new light."

Midge raised her eyebrows in outrage as he made a great show of looking her up and down...in front of his mother.

"I'd tell you to eat your heart out if I thought it would have any impact, but since I'm nowhere near your type, I'm afraid it would be a waste of time."

"It is quite a daring little number, dear girl. Your curves and legs look so feminine. Wherever did you get it?" Mrs. Prescott asked.

"Macy's clearance sale. Two weeks ago."

"No!"

"Yes!"

"Such a steal. What else do they have over there?"

In that moment, Midge went from liking Brody's mother to absolutely adoring her.

Dang it.

"Mom, you and Midge can discuss shopping some other time. I'm trying to figure out if I should steal her away and drive her home tonight." His teasing smile nearly coaxed a returning smile of her own. "Your date is an idiot for leaving you alone like this. Any red-blooded male around here is bound to pounce."

Horrified, Midge took a step back, but Brody still had a firm hand around her arm.

Cretin.

"Mr. Prescott, you're making a scene. We're embarrassing your mother."

"Oh, don't worry about me. This dinner has just gone from dull to delightful. No offense, Brody."

"None taken," he said with a grin.

Midge narrowed her eyes at Brody and attempted to pull away with no success.

"You are *not* driving me home."

"Well, I'm not letting you leave until I know for certain that your date isn't hammered."

Midge hesitated for a moment, remembering the several glasses of champagne Alexander had already worked his way through.

"Aha." Brody's smile smacked of satisfaction. "I'm not the only one worried. Now, how about you introduce me to the man lucky enough to earn a date with you, and we'll inform him of the abrupt change in plans."

Midge shook her head, letting out a disbelieving snort. "There is absolutely no way I am leaving my date only to enter a vehicle with you."

Blanche lifted a hand to grab her attention. "You'll be quite safe, my dear. I'll be there to chaperon should my son have any ideas of seduction or conquest. Though who could blame him, really. That dress looks positively sinful on you."

Midge's shocked expression did little to quell the innocent smile upon Blanche's face.

"Madelyn, what's keeping you? Hello, Brody."

Dismayed, Midge turned to see her date sidling up to her with a drunken leer upon his face. It didn't surprise her that he knew Brody. Same social circles, after all.

She noted Brody's face lighting with surprise then quickly turning to irritation.

"Alexander Montgomery. I had no idea you knew this lovely lady, Madelyn, is it?" He turned his irritated look on her. "That guy gets to know your real name, and I don't?"

Midge squeezed her eyes tight, hoping her date wouldn't reveal her last name.

Brody's eyes glittered with repressed rage as he pulled her closer to him.

"You have the nerve to nail me for my dating choices while you're schmoozing with the biggest womanizer of them all?"

Midge wasn't about to defend herself to Brody Prescott of all people.

Alexander's drunkenness must have impaired his hearing since he didn't even register the insult.

"Have you two never met before? Allow me to make those introductions," Alexander said as he wavered upon his feet.

"Not necessary. I believe Mr. Prescott and I are as acquainted as we'll ever need to be. Let's get you back to our table."

She discreetly pulled her arm from Brody's grasp and gave her date her other arm for support.

"Absolutely lovely meeting you, Mrs. Prescott," she said.

"Don't be a stranger, dear. Brody may bite, but I certainly don't."

Midge's lip curled in amusement, and then she was off with her inebriated date in tow, and not a moment too soon. Brody Prescott had almost convinced her to allow him to drive her home.

CHAPTER 7

Brody

rody's gut clenched at the sight of Alexander Montgomery draping an arm around Madelyn Knightly. He couldn't fathom what had induced the levelheaded girl to go out with him. Had her father introduced them? *Why* would he do something like that?

He took his seat almost mechanically, not allowing Midge out of his sight until she seated Alexander and herself in a private dining area three booths down.

Not too far away, then. He could keep an eye on her and make certain that reprobate didn't try anything. His thoughts were interrupted by a swift jab to his shin.

"Brody, for Heaven's sake, have you heard a word I've said?"

He blinked twice and gave his mother a chagrined grimace. "I'm sorry. I seem to be a bit preoccupied with Madelyn's sudden arrival."

"Obviously." His mother put all the force of her sarcasm behind that one word. "You called her a mousy librarian? No wonder the girl behaved so hostilely toward you, and you didn't improve upon further inspection, what with ordering her about and attempting to terminate her date without her consent. Women don't like to be manhandled, Brody." His mother smiled, bringing a glass to her lips before saying, "At least, not right away."

Brody didn't want his mother to elaborate on that last remark.

"Oh, but I do like her. She's got spirit and refuses to let you get away with anything. I heartily approve."

He let his eyes wander toward Midge's booth, hoping for a brief glimpse of her creamy shoulder, made creamier by the stark contrast of her black gown with it's swooped neck-line and daring V in the back.

"She's quite miserable, you know?"

Brody broke from his trance to take in the sly expression on his mother's face. "What?"

"In the ladies room she appeared upset. From what I gathered, she was forced into this blind date and couldn't be more unhappy about it."

His relief at his mother's explanation nearly bowled him over.

"I knew she had more sense than—you knew exactly who she was when you brought her up here, didn't you?"

His mother's satisfied grin was contagious.

"I fell in love with her the moment I met her and couldn't wait to see what fireworks a little run-in between the two of you might produce. Neither one of you disappointed on that score."

"She doesn't like me much, does she?"

"Oh, I'd say you've gotten under her skin. She just needs a little time to adjust."

He couldn't help but worry that he had managed to make a mess of everything. Madelyn Knightly was not the type of girl to be easily impressed by flowers, chocolates, or expensive jewelry. No, she was an enigma. The most beautiful enigma he'd ever encountered.

"Brody, this idea of dating her on a reality TV series is absolutely insane. Pursuing her in that setting holds too many variables you can't control."

"I can't convince her to *not* do the show, Mother. She needs her trust fund to pay for college, and I'd rather avoid Corbin Knightly's wrath if at all possible. I'd happily pay the tuition for her, but I can't see a way of suggesting it without her taking offense or assuming there would be sexual strings attached."

"Good point."

"If she's going on the show, then so am I. She can hardly avoid me then, can she?"

Her mother gave him a warning look.

"Call me when this plan comes falling down around your head, will you dear?"

"I appreciate your vote of confidence."

"It's a mother's job to tell it like she sees it." She gave his hand a squeeze and then continued, "In any case, I honestly do think that young girl could use your help tonight. Otherwise, I never would have supported your suggestion to tear her away from her date." She reached for her purse. "I'll hail a cab to take me home while you wait to see just how inebriated that Alexander gets."

Brody took his mother's work-calloused hand in his own and kissed it gently. "Thank you. Even now, you still take care of me."

"A mother's work is never done. Her children will always need taking care of." She stood and moved around the table, planting a kiss on his forehead. "I must ask you one thing before you continue with your pursuit of that adorable young lady."

"Yes?"

"Are you interested in her because she presents a refreshing challenge or do you genuinely like her? Most women are all too eager to be readily available to you. The glamour and glitz of your billionaire status has done little to impress Ms. Madelyn Knightly."

Brody carefully considered his words for a moment, knowing full well that his mother would accept nothing but the candid truth from him.

"I can honestly say that her initial disdain was more than a little intriguing, but there's substance there, and definite chemistry between us. If there's any chance that she could be interested in me and not my billions, I'll move Heaven and Earth just to be close to her." He let out a tired sigh and leaned back against his chair. "This is no game of cat and mouse for me, though I suspect with her reticence it might turn into one."

"Well, I hope the cat catches the mouse in the end."

"I intend to, mother."

"I didn't mean you, dear boy. I was talking about Madelyn."

MIDGE

Midge's heart sank to the bottom of her black high heels after reading a text message from Lisa. Apparently, she and Danny had decided to leave without them. Since the group had arrived in separate vehicles she could hardly fault her friend's logic, but Alexander was in no condition to drive, and Midge was in no mood to drive him home. She'd be stranded at his place after that.

Not an ideal situation.

Why couldn't Alexander have behaved like any normal billionaire and used his own chauffeur?

For one brief, desperate moment she considered taking Brody Prescott up on his offer, but discarded the thought almost immediately. She could honestly admit to herself that asking anything of him at this point was the kind of hardship her pride couldn't handle. Not after such a disastrous date, with Brody Prescott witness to Alexander's drunken behavior.

She wondered what his motivation behind the extended invitation had been. She suspected he simply enjoyed pushing her buttons, giving her a hard time in return for her rude yet honest assessment of his taste in women.

Still, his offer, whether given in earnest or not, was terribly tempting, all things considered. She rubbed her arm along the spot where Brody's hand had held her. Her traitorous body tingled at the thought of his warm touch and easy smile.

She looked at her drunken companion as he continued his monologuing about summers in Italy and how the women there tended to be much more affectionate than women in the United States, a factoid she barely believed.

With the amount of money this man possessed, she doubted the type of women he generally associated with—no matter their nationality—would withhold their affections from him.

She felt one of his hands dodge past her defenses and land with a possessive smack upon her knee.

"Shall we call it an evening and head over to my place for some quiet conversation?"

Midge abruptly stood, shoving his hand aside and squaring her shoulders. There was simply no help for it. Whether she could afford the cab fare or not, there was no way she was allowing this man to drive her home.

"I think I've had quite a night, Alexander, and you seem a bit indisposed at the moment. I'll have the waiter call you a cab and grab one for myself. Good night."

Midge dashed out of the booth and headed to her left in order to avoid Brody's table. She wound around the balcony, arriving at the stairs in record time and flew down them, hoping to dissuade Alexander from chasing after her in case, for some inexplicable reason, he'd managed to pull himself out of his inebriated fog.

On the last step, her shoe slipped from her foot and remained on the staircase, impeding her progress. She let out a frustrated sigh and turned around only to discover Brody Prescott just three steps above her, looking for all the world like some fairy tale fantasy come to life. Electricity jump-started her heart, creating an awareness within her, a certain longing and possible wish she hadn't known she possessed.

What were the words to that song from Cinderella?

A dream is a wish your heart makes...

She felt as if her heart had managed to communicate its wishes to a mind finally conscious and capable of recognizing their depth.

It hardly prepared her to accept it.

Brody pointedly glanced to her shoe and then to her bare foot resting lightly against the hardwood floor.

He took the last few steps with all the grace and dignity of a man who felt comfortable in his own skin, gallantly retrieving her shoe in the process. Soon he stood before her on the dance floor, and his manner as he bent low on one knee could only be described as princely. He held her shoe out before him like he was gifting her the most magnificent engagement ring and humbly begging her acceptance.

"May I?"

Too dumbfounded by her epiphany and the sudden emotions he'd managed to draw from her soul, she barely achieved a swallow and a stiff nod, giving him permission to proceed. He gently placed a warm hand upon the back of her ankle, lifting and then guiding her foot into her shoe.

And there she remained, gazing at his exquisite face with one foot grounded and the other resting upon his knee while he gave her a smoldering look.

The start of a sweet waltz from the orchestra merely enhanced the bewitching spell fate had expertly woven around the couple. Brody lifted a hand to her and she took it, replacing her high-heeled foot upon the floor with the other. She watched as if in some kind of foggy dream while Brody rose to his full height with her hand in his, never once breaking eye contact with her.

"We should dance, you and I."

The rich baritone of his voice floated over her senses. She could hardly resist when he placed a hand at her waist and drew her into position, leading her across the dance floor to the hypnotic lift and swell of the one-two-three rhythm created to unify and ignite a certain kind of beautiful recognition and remembrance for those hearts truly meant for one another.

She followed him easily, and for the first time in her life she felt she had finally encountered someone who operated within the same sphere of existence she did. Her own world within a world where no one, up until now, had ever been granted access. Her heart and soul had never been willing to open that door for anyone.

His arm around her waist tightened, bringing her flush against his chest and mere centimeters from his lips. They whispered something soft and sweet, taking her a few moments to register.

"Why did you tell me your name was Midge? Is that a nickname or something?"

"Or something," she responded, feeling a little lightheaded with his nearness.

She noted his dissatisfaction with her response and felt a weird compulsion to tell him the truth.

"Madelyn, what's your full name?" his eager eyes entreated her with sincerity. The warmth radiating from his touch shared a promise of comfort, safety, and peace.

"My...name...I..." Midge fought the passionate current keeping her mind from logical thought and reason. She did her best to focus on his question and the answer she must give as she continued to gaze into his gentle eyes. He wanted to know her name. She needed to tell him who she was.

Madelyn Knightly. Madelyn...Knightly!

"No...no, I can't." Sharp fear sliced through her. It was an uncommon emotion that jarred violently with her previously serene demeanor, causing her to wrench herself from Brody's arms.

Sudden thoughts of how he might look at her if he knew who she truly was pierced the sweetness she experienced within his arms. Flashes of a different kind of interest from other men with far different goals and agendas pummeled her in a relentless onslaught of one failed dating attempt after another. Men interested in her father, her connections and her trust fund. Men interested in fame and what her father might do for them if they managed to get in good with his daughter.

She may have possessed a tiny fraction of hope that Brody's billions would negate possible interest in her father and her Hollywood connections, but her recent experience with Alexander Montgomery strangled that hope and squashed it out of existence. Alexander was also an established billionaire. He'd looked at her with nothing but lust and calculating greed. What kind of look would radiate from Brody's eyes the minute he found out who she was? She could more than guess the outcome of such a revelation. Her predictions never failed her where most men had.

He reached for her then, the determined glint in his movements giving her the impetus needed for physical flight. She turned on her heel and immediately jostled her way through other couples on the dance floor. She didn't pause once she reached the front doors, hardly believing he might pursue her after her stunning behavior. She made it out the exit, rushed to the curb in a panic, and hailed a cab while ignoring the questioning look of the valet attendant.

She never wanted to see him again. Never wanted to feel the heat of his eyes lingering upon her or the warmth of his hand guiding and supporting her as if she belonged there when so many other women had most assuredly felt or thought along the same vein. Brody Prescott was dangerous, not because of what little he was capable of feeling for her, but because of her capacity to care for *him*. Nothing placed Midge in a more vulnerable position than recognition of affection most certainly unrequited. Having never been so emotionally exposed in all her life, the only response she could now muster was one of instinctive flight.

Nothing but escape mattered.

She barely registered the pummeling rain as she jerked the cab door open and made to enter. She was roughly pulled backward and then spun to face the very threat she'd been running from. Brody's eyes hungrily raked her face as he pulled her against him and wrapped his arms around her struggling frame.

"Don't run from me, Madelyn. You can no more outrun me than you can outrun fate."

She opened her mouth to form some sort of protest, but Brody seemed to take that as an invitation. He crushed his lips to hers in the most wonderful melding she had ever experienced. Her first instinct was to fight the currents of passion and bolts of electricity that surged between them, but her muscles and tendons refused to acquiesce to her desperate wishes.

Brody's kiss completely unraveled her, shooting a direct hit to her heart where she knew it would never recover. She was never going to get over this man, and he didn't even belong to her. With just one kiss, Brody Prescott had managed to claim her heart as his, and she would now have to deal with the aching hunger of his absence for the rest of her existence. Ignorance would have been preferable to this crushing awareness. It angered her enough to give her the fortitude to push away from him, pull her arm back, and deliver a resounding smack across his cheek.

Her breath came in heavy gulps as Brody stood with glittering eyes full of passion and hunger as if he'd hardly registered the punishment she'd firmly dealt. She had nothing to say; no witty retort or snappy reparté to throw back at him. The only thing she felt capable of doing after sharing such an earth-shattering exchange with a man she felt certain she could never possess was to turn around, step into her cab, and pull the door shut with a finality that nearly tore her heart in two.

She sucked in deep breaths, fearing she might never be capable of taking in enough oxygen. Her desperate gasps of air turned into quiet sobbing which shook her entire frame as her cab carried her far away from the restaurant and the man who remained standing in the rain.

BRODY

The rain pummeled Brody's broad figure, a definite punishment for manhandling the only girl he'd ever taken a true interest in. He hardly felt the wet shards as they sliced at his skin and clothing, too distracted by his tumultuous emotions and the way Madelyn's kiss, though stolen from her soft lips, had shaken him to his core.

What in the world had possessed him to chase after her and force himself upon her like that? Panic? A foreboding sense of loss? He'd managed to make progress with her upon the dance floor, catching her by surprise in a weak and vulnerable moment where she actually allowed him to look at her, speak to her...touch her.

He wasn't one to believe in magic, supernatural occurrences, or fairy tales, but he could have sworn he'd stepped right into one the minute Madelyn had turned around and spied him on the staircase. And then he'd bungled the entire thing by pushing her for a name he knew all too well. He never should have ruined the moment by asking her to reveal a part of herself she was so obviously trying to hide. She was skittish and resistant to his advances, and not just because of his rocky first impression, but because of some nameless fear rooted within her.

Tracking her down offered no problems. He had the connections and the resources to find Madelyn no matter where she might live, and he thought, with a grimace, where she might flee to. No, that wasn't the way he wished to go about this. There were things he had to prove, obvious dragons he needed to slay, and having her father throw them together made it easy for him to escape blame while doing everything within his power to bring back the Madelyn he'd discovered on the dance floor.

He'd do the show, but he'd be darned if she only stayed on it for one day. Brody had a plan, and it did not include eliminating Madelyn Knightly.

CHAPTER 8

Midge

Bent over her father's desk with a pen in hand, Midge let her flowery penmanship flow across the contract her father's lawyers had written up. She noted her hand shaking the minute she finished. Mentally cursing the traitorous appendage, she placed the pen upon the desk before her shaking caused it to involuntarily jump from her hand.

Her father's grin was filled with genuine happiness. Though she hated the circumstances she found herself in, she suddenly felt enormously happy to have his approval. She was never going to stop wanting or needing it.

I am so pathetic.

"We start shooting two months from now," he said with some excitement. "Did my intern email you your itinerary for the first day's schedule?"

"She did."

Apparently, the first week of shooting had been planned in Hawaii on some island owned by a celebrity so rich he hadn't even bothered to name it. An enormous mansion on the property had been rented for the occasion. Twenty girls in a mansion. Fortunately for Midge, they would each receive their own suite. She had no idea where the billionaire in question was residing and she didn't care so long as it was far away from her room.

"How exactly are we getting to the island from Honolulu?" she wondered.

Her father's features took on an air of mystery. "That, my dear girl, is a surprise. I have no intention of spoiling it for you."

"I hate surprises."

"I know." His gleeful expression irked her.

"All right, now that I've signed a day's worth of my life into your hands, I guess there's nothing left to do but go home, finish up the rest of this semester, and possibly make out a will in case the plane crashes on the way over there and all twenty contestants perish in one grand explosion."

Her father chuckled at that.

"You've always been so dramatic. I certainly hope you'll employ that while you're on camera."

"If you're looking for someone to start a cat fight, create harmful gossip, or fake a panic attack and begin hyperventilating, you've coerced the wrong girl. I don't even plan on getting drunk while I'm there."

"Ah yes, you and your strange aversion to alcohol. Too bad, really. I've always thought you were more fit for appearing on the screen than typing in front of one."

"One day my novels will be New York Times bestsellers, and when you come with an apology, begging to turn my books into movies, I plan on laughing in your face and giving the movie rights to Steven Spielberg."

His wry look was annoyingly absent of outrage. "I doubt anything you write will fit what he produces."

"I stand by my threat." She grabbed her small purse and pulled the strap across her shoulder. "See you in two months."

"Aren't you interested in finding out who the bachelor for this season will be? Now that we're working with one another again, I can give you the inside scoop before his identity is revealed tonight on live TV."

"I couldn't care less, and I have *The Mindy Project* to catch up on tonight. I guess I'll just have to wait for my roommate to spill the beans."

It was a total lie. She was going to be glued to the television, waiting to find out just who she'd have to cozy up to and pretend to play nice with for an entire evening, but she wasn't about to acknowledge her interest—or her trepidation—in front of her father.

He chuckled and shook his head. "See you in two months, young lady. Unless..."

"Unless what?"

Her father cleared his throat, looking slightly uncomfortable. The shock of Corbin Knightly appearing less than completely confident almost prevented her from catching her father's invitation.

"Well, I was thinking, maybe we could skip TV altogether tonight and grab a bite to eat at one of our old dives."

Midge's mouth went dry. "You'd have time for that?"

He was about to respond when his cell phone rang. The sweet stab of hope Midge had harbored dissipated as her father became engrossed in a heated argument with one of his colleagues.

She waited for a few minutes, but when it became clear this latest issue was going to need his immediate attention, she turned around and walked out of his office without even bothering to say goodbye.

Old wounds resurfaced as she drove to Huntington Beach and paid for parking, leaving her tiny parking permit on the console of her car and walking toward the soft sand and calming sounds of the ocean in the distance. The wind whipped her hair in her face. She brushed it back and let out a rueful laugh at the brilliant red hue, the color she'd finally embraced when she'd left home.

The blond, straight hair of her teen years had been an attempt at relating to her mother in some way. When Midge had matched her hair to Celeste's as a teenager, it was the first time in a long time that her mother had actually become excited about anything.

It was stupid for something like that to be so important, but it had been to Celeste. Seemed like a moot point once her mother lost her mind and failed to recognize her anymore.

The shrill ring of her cell phone brought her out of self-pity mode. She reached into her pocket and grabbed her phone.

"What's up, Lisa?"

"Midge," she squealed. "Where the heck are you? The big reveal for *Marry Your Billionaire* is airing in like thirty minutes. Get your hot booty home."

Midge checked the time on her phone for confirmation and was soon sprinting back to her little truck. She sped all the way home with a severe knot in her stomach.

As she pulled in front of her apartment, she couldn't help but wonder at the strange niggling sense that the Universe was about to throw her another curve ball. Lisa met her at the door with an offering of popcorn and a bag of Hershey's kisses.

"Time management, Midge. Your priorities are seriously screwed when it comes to television."

"I'm here, aren't I?" Midge followed Lisa into the living room where a small flatscreen sat atop a bare desk.

Lisa pulled her down onto the couch as the opening for the Evening Show with Mark O'Brien began playing. The girls suffered through the first fifteen minutes of the program before Mark finally began discussing the up and coming reality TV show.

"As you all know, the identity of this first season's bachelor will be revealed tonight. Right here. Right now."

"Mark, honey, I love ya, but you need to get on with it," Lisa groused. As if in answer to Lisa's impatient demands, Mark finally got to the point.

"I'm excited to introduce to you the star of the new reality TV series *Marry Your Billionaire*...Mr. Brody Prescott."

Midge choked on her popcorn, and Lisa began screaming like a banshee as Brody Prescott walked on screen flashing that million gigawatt smile.

Her father was an unmitigated liar!

She fought to clear the popcorn from her throat and then tried to blink Brody out of existence, but no matter how many times she opened and closed her eyes, his beautiful face stared back at her from her own television set.

Lisa took a few quick victory laps around the couch as she continued to voice her enthusiastic approval with shouts of, "Brody Prescott is smokin' hot," and "Marry him, Midge. You'll have beautiful babies."

As for Midge, she felt like a complete and total idiot. Why hadn't she seen this coming? She was a smart girl, right? Hadn't Brody planned on starring in a reality TV show with his assistant? She should have pressed her father when he denied Brody's involvement.

She couldn't do the show. There was no way she would be capable of total indifference with Brody after the way he'd kissed her, and how in the world was she going to be able to stand seeing him with those gorgeous women, even if it was just for one evening?

She'd have to convince her father to rip up her contract. There had to be a way for him to let her off the hook.

Midge quickly disregarded this. She needed that money. Had to have it. Her graduation and future depended on her trust fund, and she couldn't give that up. Was Brody irresistible? Of course. Was her heart invested in him a little more than was prudent? Possibly. Was avoiding his presence far safer than confronting him on the show? Indubitably!

Fine. He was a dream, wrapped in a fairy tale, dipped in chocolate, and laden with dollops of whip cream. But she had far too much invested in her future to let that delicious concoction distract her.

She'd do the show and schmooze with Brody on live television, dang it.

But she wouldn't like it. Nope. Not one bit.

Lisa took a detour from her over-the-top celebrating to plant herself on the couch again.

"OMGoodness! I cannot believe how lucky you are. Your life is charmed, I tell you. Every time I see his yummy face on commercials and billboards for his company I just wanna stop whatever it is I'm doing and have a crazy make-out session with any male present."

"That's...really disturbing, Lisa. Your hormone levels rival that of the most virile of males. You should get your thyroid checked."

"You need to figure out a way to stay on the show, girlfriend. If I were you, I'd charm the pants off him the very first evening."

Midge decided to keep her own personal experiences with Brody to herself. Any sharing at this point would only fuel Lisa's zealot-like fire, and there would be no end to her maniacal matchmaking after that.

She stared at the TV screen again, taking in Brody's chiseled perfection and the way his smile lines drew attention to his yummy lips. The guy she'd been trying to forget about, the man who'd turned her whole world upside down with one crazy kiss was going to be on the show with her. Her and nineteen other eligible females.

BRODY

"I think you've made the right decision," Gregg said as he brought a few more papers for Brody to sign.

"Of course you do, Gregg. You're the idiot who got me into this in the first place."

Brody studied Gregg's features, bothered to find a hint of self-satisfaction lurking behind his stoic façade.

"Your mother, for once, is on my side. Are you going to label her an idiot as well?"

"My mother knows I'm going after Madelyn. That's the only reason she isn't in this office giving you your weekly dose of a reality check."

"Thank Heavens for small miracles."

Brody leaned back in his chair, anxious to be done with the last of his work before heading home to pack for this new and reckless adventure he'd landed himself in. Two months had passed since his last encounter with Madelyn Knightly, and he found himself more than a little anxious to finally start shooting the series just so he could have the opportunity to see her again and possibly repeat their last encounter...minus the smack to his face.

He glanced at the cluttered walls of his office, studying the various wedding announcements and family pictures of clients who had found their perfect match and dived into wedded bliss with the kind of fearless determination he'd always admired.

They represented a decade's worth of hard work and success. Those wedding invitations, pictures, and baby announcements proved to him, day in and day out, that finding someone who wanted to love and work with you to build something special was possible. Happy families really did exist amidst the sea of vicious divorces and heartbreaking family dysfunction.

As he studied them now; however, they also represented something he still hadn't managed to attain for himself. It was a venture he hadn't considered himself ready for until he'd met Madelyn. Though these decorations on his wall still gave him hope, they also brought home the truth of just how isolated he'd allowed himself to become.

Lonely.

Some may have felt pathetic admitting that openly or even to themselves, but he was man enough to recognize that he'd been lonely for quite some time, and after meeting Madelyn, he didn't feel quite so lonely anymore. The past two months had been a bit difficult for him without Madelyn around. He'd consoled himself with watching some of the movies she'd helped her father produce and reading old interviews she'd done for magazines. He'd even dropped by Café Canapé occasionally to see if he could orchestrate a chance encounter.

Nothing. He supposed he could have hired someone to get him a copy of her schedule and then showed up outside the door of one of her classes, but that move screamed of desperation and made him feel like a stalker.

"I wonder if you should set your sights on Madelyn Knightly, Brody. I know she caught your attention, but it might be easier to simply chase after someone willing to be caught."

Brody glowered at his assistant.

"Gregg, throughout my years as a businessman I have found that anything worth achieving or attaining in this life is always going to be hard won."

"Madelyn isn't a business acquisition. You're dealing with a very strong personality when it comes to that girl. For Heaven's sake, Brody, you grabbed her and kissed her like some wild hillbilly. She slapped you in the face. Generally, a kiss involves two consenting parties."

"She did consent." Gregg's skeptic grimace prompted him to explain further. "Okay, so I caught her off-guard, but she could have pushed me away at any time—which she did, now that I think about it—but the fact that she momentarily returned my kisses with just as much enthusiasm must be a sign that she felt something. Right?"

Gregg shook his head. "Don't mistake her momentary shock at your forwardness as acceptance. I don't think your savvy business skills are going to help you out when handling this female. She seems to activate your Neanderthal button. Not the image we're working for."

"Everything I've ever accomplished has been done with the single-minded goal of providing for my mother and making others happy. This time, I'm going after what makes me happy, and I have no intention of failing."

"Well, I hope for your sake you succeed," Gregg said as he grabbed the papers and placed them in a tan folder. "Something tells me the next time Madelyn sees you, she'll be prepared for your more aggressive overtures."

Brody chuckled low and deep. "Let's hope not. I'm worried the element of surprise is all I've got going for me."

CHAPTER 9

Midge

Midge's flight to Honolulu was blessedly uneventful. She had no idea if any of the other women on the show had been booked on her flight, but she didn't attempt to make small talk with anyone. No point in trying to make friends with women she never planned on seeing again. The last two months had passed in a whirl of classes, studying, testing, and her freelance jobs on the side. She'd kept herself so busy, she hadn't even had time to finish the rest of her manuscript.

She'd done it on purpose in hopes of pushing Brody Prescott and his passionate kiss out of her mind. It hadn't worked one iota, but she gave herself props for trying. Now she was one sleepless night away from seeing him face-to-face after slapping him and making an idiot of herself at Club 23. She was not looking forward to it.

She arrived at the airport in the evening and went straight to baggage claim, aware that one of her father's employees would be picking her up and driving her to a nearby hotel where she could rest for the night and prep herself for the next day of filming.

She was both surprised and delighted to see her father's receptionist shaking with excitement as she held up a card that read "Midge" in her trembling hands.

"How nice to see you again. I didn't realize you would be here," Midge said in greeting.

"Oh yes, I know. I mean, I am the receptionist, but I'm also interning with your father's company so I have the amazing opportunity to be a part of this season's filming."

Midge gave the girl a smile, taking note of how nice she looked with her light blond hair in a loose ponytail. The severe bun she'd arranged before at her father's office hadn't suited her. She was definitely pretty. Not necessarily someone you would label as exotic or gorgeous, but kind of adorably cute.

"Am I the only one you'll be picking up?"

The young receptionist grimaced. "You're the last one. Several other contestants came in on different flights, and a few weren't very friendly."

She clamped a hand over her mouth as if she might have said something unconscionable.

Midge laughed, deciding this girl would be someone worth liking. "I can't imagine any of these ladies were all that considerate. Several of them are most likely here for their own devious purposes and will perceive every pretty female as a threat, even females like you who aren't competing."

The receptionist laughed and stuck her hand out in greeting. "I'm Stacey Bedford," she said.

"My friends call me Midge." She took Stacey's hand in her own and gave it a firm shake. "So Stacey, what does our day look like for tomorrow?"

Stacey gave her a sympathetic look. "Honestly, it looks like chaos. I'm not sure whose crazy idea this was, but apparently the contestants are going to be landing on the island via skydiving."

Midge's eyes popped wide at that. "We're skydiving onto the island to make our grand entrance?"

"Yep." Stacey shook her head. "Bringing girls in by limousine one at a time is overdone and too cliché. Your father was looking for a more exciting approach, and when he asked for suggestions I guess someone on his committee thought it best to have the show located in a place where a limousine would never be capable of driving. Thus a private island and skydiving were born."

"But surely each girl could arrive on the beach with their very own motorboat. Why the extreme sports?"

Stacey shook her head. "I guess the whole thing is more dramatic. He's hoping some of the girls will be afraid of heights and cause a scene before they jump. He also thinks it will be hilarious for these girls to have their hair messed up and their dresses crumpled."

Midge couldn't believe what she was hearing. "Are you saying my father expects us to wear cocktail dresses under our skydiving equipment?"

"Yes. You'll parachute onto the island and meet Mr. Prescott within twenty yards from where you've landed. Mr. Prescott will be helping you get out of your gear. Stripping off the equipment and revealing what's on underneath is supposed to add some excitement to the show as well. Like unwrapping a beautiful present."

Midge shook her head, wondering why on earth she was even surprised by this insane development. Her father never filmed anything like anybody else. Then she considered the possible hilarity that would arise if any of these girls were averse to the idea of skydiving.

Dear old Dad was a bloody genius.

"Well, I suppose that'll start the season off with a bang."

"It gets better. Any girl who decides she can't skydive onto the island will immediately give up her place in the season and be disqualified."

"He's raised the stakes before the show even gets started." She gave a rueful laugh at the sheer ingenuity of his plan. "Well, I suppose that ought to level the playing field for most of the other girls intent on vying for the attentions of some billionaire who is eager to date twenty women at the same time."

Stacey quirked an eyebrow. "Does it surprise you that a man might want to date twenty different women at the same time?"

"No, what surprises me is that we as a society have condoned it—on national television, no less. How many girls have already backed out?"

"None. No one has been told about the way they'll be arriving. They won't find out until they get to the small airstrip that's supplying the staff and airplanes."

"Then why did you confide in me?"

"Oh, because you're only going to be here a day. Your dad let me know why you're really here. I figured it wouldn't matter whether you knew or not."

"Well, I'm excited to go skydiving. I haven't been for quite some time. At least there's *that* to look forward to."

"I'm looking forward to the total horror on the contestants faces when they see what they're up against. It's going to be so much fun."

Midge chuckled as she pictured wilting make-up, disheveled hair, and crumpled cocktail dresses shoved under skydiving gear.

"You know, Stacey, I think we're both looking forward to that."

The resort housing the contestants for the night was grand, glorious, and ostentatious. Midge might have considered a quick swim in the pool, but her muscles were sore from traveling. All she truly desired was a nice soak in a large tub filled with bubbles and perfumed soaps. Just because she'd turned down her father's opulent lifestyle didn't mean she couldn't appreciate it.

As she dragged her heavy suitcases into the elevator, the visage of a dark-haired Adonis popped into her mind and all thoughts of the show, skydiving, or the misery she had agreed to fled. All she pictured at that very moment was the way Brody Prescott had taken her in his arms and embraced her lips with his.

It bothered her, this power his memory held over her, the way her senses filled with him when he lived so far away. She'd battled her traitorous thoughts and feelings, smashing down the desire to investigate the billionaire further or possibly cyber stalk him on search engines and social media.

When she'd caught herself making plans to scout out the location of his residence, she'd decided that maybe shooting the reality TV series wouldn't be such a tragic setback if it succeeded in getting Brody out of her system while watching him romance nineteen other girls.

Right. She really was full of it.

Before the elevator doors closed completely, a finely manicured hand shot between the silver walls, holding them open. The doors parted with the same alacrity the Red Sea had for Moses. A blond beauty wearing a tight mini-skirt paired with a hot pink halter top strode into the elevator. To Midge's eye, it looked as if the woman's make-up had been applied more than a dozen times without any washes in between, and her teased hair stood at least five inches from the top of her forehead.

The hairstyle looked like a large yellow dome had transplanted itself on top of her head. Midge wondered what would happen if she took a sledge hammer to it. She feared the hammer wouldn't survive the confrontation.

The lady in question looked vaguely familiar. Probably an aspiring actress who had already been on a reality TV series or a few beer commercials. Though conversation with this particular brand of woman held little appeal for Midge, she refused to judge a person on appearance alone.

"Hi there. Are you one of the contestants for the reality TV series they're shooting here in Hawaii?" Midge asked.

The girl gave her a baffled look, as if she wasn't sure why Midge had addressed her, and then looked her over with a calculating air, sizing her up and dismissing her with one offensive perusal of her person.

"Of course, I am. Haven't you paid attention to any of the tabloids or magazines? My picture has been broadcast all over the news." The girl waited expectantly for a response.

Midge had no idea what kind of response she was required to make.

"I guess I haven't. I wasn't aware the contestants had been unveiled."

"No, no, dear. I'm a tabloid favorite for far different reasons." She ran a dagger-like fingernail through the ends of her hair and gave Midge a long-suffering look.

"Why is that?"

The elevator dinged and the doors opened on the third floor.

"Because I used to date the billionaire in question. Should make for some scintillating controversy, don't you think? None of those other contestants are going to stand a chance, really. Bye now." She wriggled her fingers in the air and stepped out of the elevator without a backward glance.

Midge's first assessment had been spot on. That girl was not someone she planned on spending any of her precious time with.

She pondered the familiarity of the woman's face as she exited onto the fourth floor and awkwardly pulled her suitcases into her suite.

The snotty woman's face continued to eat at her as she drew herself a bubble bath and settled in for a long soak. Just as the blessed heat from the water began to loosen the knots in her muscles, her brain worked out the puzzle.

Felicia Davenport. The woman in the elevator was none other than the conniving slanderer who had accused Brody of breaking privacy policies within his own company. The soothing heat of the bubbling water now felt uncomfortably warm, smoldering even, as Midge's temper burned bright in the knowledge that her father had given that shameless hussy air time on *Marry Your Billionaire*. As if she hadn't received enough publicity with her ridiculous, slanderous claims. She'd already managed to ruin Brody's career, and now she was out to make a name for herself in television.

She'd wager a billion dollars Brody had no idea her father had put Felicia on the show.

Midge shook herself, attempting to cool the anger burning in her belly as she realized how outraged she felt on Brody's behalf.

Now the urge to protect Brody, his company, and his image in the face of that obvious gold-digger churned up a tempestuous storm within her tiny frame. This did not bode well for her firm resolution to avoid any and all emotions linked with Brody Prescott. What did this overprotective, knee-jerk reaction say about her emotional state? Certainly something she didn't care to analyze.

Still, that little vixen deserved a few rugs pulled out from underneath her spiky stiletto heels, and Midge was bound and determined to be the one giving those rugs a good, hard yank. Giving up all pretense of relaxing, she jumped out of the tub, threw a towel around herself, and sped into her suite, searching the area for her laptop.

It was time to do some research on one, Ms. Felicia Davenport.

BRODY

Brody fiddled with the mic pack attached to the back of his waist, annoyed at the undignified bulge it caused which interrupted the fine lines of his dress shirt. He nearly laughed at himself for such vain musings, though he had to concede it masked the nervous energy he felt whenever he considered Madelyn Knightly's reaction to his presence on the show. He'd be heartbroken if she showed nothing but disdain in his presence after waiting all this time to see her again.

Unless the memory of that kiss he'd stolen from her had somehow managed to get under her skin. Maybe she actually wanted to see him again. The happiness he felt at that outrageous thought dimmed when he considered her volatile response to his barbaric advances that night.

Brody was used to getting what he wanted, barreling through obstacles like a bull in a rodeo. Never in his life had he ever considered any goal out of reach, and he pursued his goals with single-minded determination. Granted, he'd never had to convince a girl to give him a chance. Most women fell into line with little persuasion, but he didn't want most women. He wanted Madelyn. And as with any other goal he set out to accomplish, he believed perseverance and determination would win the heart of his mousy librarian.

"Now remember, Brody," Knightly called from the director's chair, "When each girl arrives, you're to help them out of their gear. I want an honest reaction from them."

Brody nodded and fiddled with the mic again. It was starting to itch his skin where it rested on the small of his back. A cool breeze caressed his cheeks, momentarily whisking away the damp heat of mid-afternoon, though it hardly cut through the humidity. A buzzing sound from above caught his attention, and he lifted his hand, shading his eyes from the brightness of the blistering sun. Was Madelyn on that particular plane? He had no way of knowing if she would be first, last, or somewhere in between, but until the moment he unveiled her from her skydiving gear his heart seemed intent on lodging itself within his throat.

MIDGE

Free falling.

In Midge's humble opinion, there really was nothing quite like it, and though she didn't claim to be an adrenaline junkie, she wasn't averse to the crazy butterflies she'd experienced the few times she'd gone skydiving with her father. Now, as she flew thirteen thousand feet above an obscure island, the butterflies tumbling around her belly were present for an entirely different reason.

Reality TV.

She felt like such a sellout. Only one day of possible screen time, but a sellout none-the-less. She sighed as the goggled professional strapped to her back asked if she was ready to jump.

"Yeah, let's do this," she said, preparing herself for the plastic smile and fake greeting she'd have to give Brody. She couldn't wait to see his face when he helped remove her gear and got a glimpse of the girl he'd toyed with two months ago. She hoped he'd be worried once he recognized her, wondering if she'd make a scene and attempt to discredit him for his behavior with her earlier. Midge would never do that, of course, but wouldn't it be fun to see him squirm a little? Then again, what if he didn't care—or worse, what if he didn't remember her?

Suddenly, her bright and pithy greetings were swiped from her mind in the face of her insecurities. Hopefully a, *Hey there, fancy meeting you on a deserted island dressed for prom with nothing but cameras in our faces,* might do the trick.

"Okay, then," the guy said. "One, two, three."

As their bodies picked up speed, she allowed the freedom of the moment to blow away the tight tension in her shoulders and neck. The beauty of the ocean and the tiny island below beckoned, tugging her forward just as forcefully as gravity did. Moments before the chute opened, errant thoughts of Brody disrupted the quiet peace of her jump. Then the chute deployed and she was temporarily sucked upward, straining against gravity before descending back down to her new and demanding reality.

Her landing was smooth and efficient, she wasn't a total novice after all. Once detached from her jumping partner with her feet firmly planted on the unstable sand, she removed her head gear and goggles and began unfastening the straps of her jumpsuit.

"Here, allow me," said an unforgettable voice.

Midge's fingers froze along the collar of her suit as her eyes snapped to the person standing before her.

She sucked in a mouthful of air and failed to give him the greeting she'd practiced a million times on the plane ride over. Had his eyes been that blue the last time she'd seen him? She didn't remember him being this handsome. She certainly didn't remember finding it difficult to speak in his presence. She doubted he'd forgotten her snide remarks either, which made her cringe a little at the thought.

"You're on camera, Madelyn." His urgent reminder gave her a second to pull her frantic thoughts in order before she said something too telling on national television.

To say she felt like the biggest imbecile on the face of the planet would have been a gross understatement.

Fake smile. Fake smile. Are we having fun yet?

Midge was like a block of solid wood, incapable of movement or sound as Brody continued to help her out of the ugly gray jumpsuit. She finally managed to pull her wits about her as her cocktail dress caught the breeze and whipped daintily around her legs. It was a red sequined number with capped sleeves and a slit up the right knee.

Once unveiled, Brody's eyes followed the tight curves of her dress, making her feel exposed and vulnerable in front of several cameras, not to mention all of America.

"I'm Brody Prescott, but then, I believe you and I have met before," he said, extending his hand. She accepted it as if on autopilot, while he pulled her forward and into a tight embrace. He placed a feather-light kiss on her cheek and then stepped back, giving her a knowing smile.

He definitely remembered her, but he didn't seem the least bit ruffled by her unexpected appearance. The contestants hadn't been unveiled, and yet his face didn't register even a hint of surprise.

What was up with *that*?

Midge cleared her throat, gave herself a millisecond of a pep talk and leaned heavily on all the acting classes her mother had insisted upon during her adolescence. She performed for the cameras.

"Madelyn Knightly." *Why was that so hard to spit out?* "So nice to run into the founder of Shackled and Loving It again. I hear you're looking for your own version of happily ever after."

Brody let out a soft chuckle that sent yummy tingles down the length of her spine.

Dang it all.

"That's definitely why I'm here. After meeting a brave and enchanting woman such as yourself, I can't imagine going home with anything less."

His tone and look held a specific meaning, one that Midge felt certain she'd misunderstood. No. He was merely playing a part, the consummate host welcoming his first prospect. Well, why not join in the game? Might as well embrace the awkwardness at this point and move on. One day. That's all.

Yes, but Brody will be here for the entire show with nineteen other beautiful women.

The melancholy descending upon her took her by surprise. Was she really falling for this guy?

Fake smile. Fake smile. Play to the cameras.

She quirked a flirtatious eyebrow and gave him her best smile. "Well, I did fall out of the sky for you." She felt awkward. Flirtatious banter didn't necessarily come easily to her. She attempted to pull her hand back, but met with resistance.

He rubbed his thumb along her wrist, eyes smoldering, he took a single step forward as she fought to hold her ground rather than retreat. Everything she wanted to do—like flee the scene and hop the nearest canoe back to Honolulu—couldn't be filmed on camera.

"You most certainly did, Madelyn, much like a shooting star."

"Midge," she said without thinking.

"What was that?" he stepped closer until her chest was flush against his.

She licked her lips, unintentionally drawing his attention to them. "My friends call me Midge."

Brody's own lips slid into a satisfied, victorious smile as if he'd managed to achieve something significant.

"Midge. I like that name very much."

Unfortunately, she did too. The way he said her name made her naked toes curl in the warm sand.

"Okay, Midge," her father yelled from his position about fifty feet away, "Let's have you enter the mansion so we can film the next arrival."

She felt her body relax a little as several cameras shifted into different positions and people off-set began milling about the beach, completely ignoring their interactions now.

She glanced at Brody again, disconcerted at the intense way in which he studied her. Casting a wary look at her father and his crew, she reached behind her neck and yanked on the chord attached to the mic pack underneath her dress. Pulling it up and out felt much more comfortable than having it pressed against the small of her back. She quickly turned it off and then motioned for Brody to do the same with his.

He raised his eyebrows at her behavior, but seemed to be willing to play along with what was most definitely a cardinal sin in the world of reality TV. He quickly removed his own mic and turned it off. Midge didn't waste any time. Her father was bound to notice this egregious affront to his program.

"I thought I warned you about reality TV," she hissed. She'd been waiting for two months to lecture him.

"Funny, considering I'm not the only one standing on this beach dressed to the nines for all the world to see."

"My reasons for being here have nothing to do with finding a husband."

Brody's lips turned up at the corners. The dimples this slight movement created made Midge want to lean forward and reenact that kiss he'd stolen from her a few months ago.

"We'll see," he said.

"We'll see? What in the world is that supposed to mean?"

"Midge, honey, I really need you to get inside the mansion. We're on a tight schedule here." Her father tapped his wrist even though he never wore a watch. He then turned to one of his crew and shouted, "Jane, there's something wrong with their mics. I thought you checked everything out before we started."

Midge hurried to warn Brody before her father discovered the truth.

"Are you aware that Felicia Davenport is on the show?"

Brody visibly flinched. "What?"

"My father plays dirty. He knows your history. He knows her presence is going to stir up trouble. The woman who slandered you to the press is now fighting to become your future wife?" Midge shook her head. "I don't like it. Watch yourself, Mr. Prescott, and prepare yourself for her arrival. At least now you won't be caught unaware."

Midge made to leave, but Brody placed a hand on her arm. "Thank you for the warning. You didn't have to tell me that."

"Well, I just hate watching dumb animals suffer." She hoped her sweet smile drove the sarcasm home.

His lips twitched. Not the reaction she was shooting for as he drew just a little closer, invading her personal space.

"Is that all? Because I thought maybe you'd forgiven me for hijacking that delicious kiss from you—and you're ready for round two."

Her mouth gaped open, and he gave her a wink. Unbelievable. Was everything just a game to this guy?

"Midge, honey, are you really gonna stand there while the contestants come flying down around you?" her father shouted.

Annoyed beyond measure, she wrenched her arm from Brody's tight hold and turned from him, hastily speeding toward the mansion. "Okay, Dad. I'm going." She flipped her mic back on and raised it so he could see. "All fixed."

Now Brody knew who her father was. It wasn't like he could use that knowledge against her anymore. He already had his own TV show, but more importantly if he knew she was the producer's daughter then her presence there made more sense. Heaven forbid Brody Prescott get the idea that she'd joined the show just for him.

Still, his presence here hurt her pride. Some small part of her, some infinitesimal sliver of the romantic in her yearned to believe the kiss Brody Prescott had so brazenly stolen had shaken him as much as it had her. Like a relentlessly determined Prince Charming, he intended to search the countryside of Southern California, diligently seeking the lovely young lady powerful enough to leave such an indelible impression upon his heart, not to mention his lips.

Ha!

She could certainly write a fairy tale, but experiencing one in this sex-crazed, commitment-phobic era was about as likely as convincing her roommate to deep clean their freezer.

Nope. If his presence here was indicative of anything it was that she'd left little to no impression at all. He might be here to save is image, but he was still a playboy.

So how exactly was this womanizer going to paint a monogamous picture when the temptation of playing the field amongst the various contestants became too much for him? Midge's stomach rolled at this. A recipe for disaster.

No doubt her father was well aware of this possibility. Probably counted on it. He didn't give a hoot about Brody's image, or how reality TV might expose the billionaire.

Thoughts of Blanche and how she would react to the bad press her son might receive brought her up short. She stood on the threshold of the mansion, wondering what she could possibly do to protect Brody from whatever her father had in store for him. Felicia Davenport's presence was just one weapon in her manipulative father's arsenal.

Again, dang it.

She saw no alternative but to coach Brody as much as possible before he eliminated her from the show. Which meant more time spent in his yummy presence.

Did she really want to do that to herself? Poised with one hand on the gold-plaited handle of the mansion's front door, she considered the alternatives if she stayed silent and allowed her father to play his mind games. Felicia Davenport being his biggest ace in the hole.

Nope. There was no avoiding it. She'd have to help him navigate the treacherous waters of reality TV before she left him to fend for himself. That decided, she turned the door handle and crossed the threshold.

Game on.

CHAPTER 10

Brody

S he looked like a fiery seductress in that red ensemble. A tempting piece of literature he wanted to study and learn more about. Watching Midge walk to the mansion just out of his reach brought a hollow feeling to the pit of his stomach, especially since he had waited so impatiently for this moment to arrive.

He'd fought the impulse to seek her out and spirit her away to some romantic destination. Unlike at Club 23, she had nowhere to run to, no way to avoid his presence. He could pursue the smoking hot librarian for the duration of the show so long as everything went according to plan.

Felicia's presence put a damper on things, but he wouldn't allow this tiny setback to interfere with his plans for wooing, Madelyn Knightly.

Midge.

Her friends called her Midge.

He couldn't help the boyish grin stealing over his face as he contemplated the significance of her statement. One wall down, several hundred more to go, no doubt, but he'd witnessed a definite chink in her armor just now, and he planned on chiseling away at the tiny crack until all of Madelyn's reservations came tumbling down.

As the director called action and the next contestant descended to the sandy beach, he couldn't help but feel that everything was going exactly according to plan.

"Hello stranger," said a sugary sweet voice that left him feeling nothing but dread. The contestant took her goggles and headgear off, and Felicia Davenport was not only unveiled, but in Brody's opinion, unleashed, the she-cat herself in the flesh.

Okay, so maybe not everything was going according to plan.

MIDGE

After a brief visit to the bathroom, Midge entered the main hallway and was directed to a large room where the contestants were supposed to gather once they arrived. It housed several couches made of plush, satin looking fabrics. Midge felt certain her inelegant behind would feel severely out of place housed within the folds of a couch assembled for nothing less than royalty.

She'd just tentatively seated herself upon a less intimidating love seat when Stacey came into the room bearing a cup of steaming hot tea and a large, fluffy croissant.

"You can turn your mic off for the moment, Midge. Your father explained to me the terms in your contract. There are no cameras here right now, but once the girls start coming in you'll have to turn it back on and behave...or not behave." She gave her a furtive smile. "Any drama is good drama, you know what I mean?"

"Got it. Thanks for the brief reprieve." She flipped it off and settled back in her seat.

Stacey nodded, handing over her offering and taking a seat next to her with a tired sigh.

"It's chamomile," she said. "You looked a little unnerved after your encounter with Brody."

Well, she was perceptive. Midge blew on her tea while considering what the safest response might be.

"I wasn't unnerved—"

"It's all right." She placed a comforting hand on Midge's shoulder. "You don't have to explain anything to me. You didn't expect to have that physical reaction to him, did you? After all, you're not really here to pursue the bachelor. It was probably a bit of a shock."

"Stacey, what are you getting at?"

"Why, the chemistry between you two. Seriously, the moment you and Brody locked eyes for the first time—to say that sparks were flying would be an understatement. That man wants you, and if I'm not mistaken, you're probably not opposed to the idea."

Midge studied Stacey's owl-like glasses. There was keen intelligence in those hazel eyes and a bit of the whimsical romantic within her sweet expression.

"I'm willing to admit he is attractive, but I'm contractually obligated to leave tonight, and I plan on doing so."

"Well, that's a terrible idea. You should stay and see how this plays out."

"How this plays out? Stacey, this is reality TV, which by definition means that everything happening on this show will be completely staged. You can't develop a relationship with a guy who is dating nineteen other women. It's hard enough to get to know someone exclusively let alone in a harem-like setting. It may make for entertaining television, but trust and commitment can't exist when the boyfriend in question is pursuing other women. That's the very epitome of a playboy, something I told Mr. Prescott he needed to avoid, but did he listen? Oh no. Heaven forbid anyone listen to the daughter of a film producer."

Stacey's eyes glowed with interest. "You knew Mr. Prescott before the show?"

Midge hesitated. "Well, I...we met briefly. I tried to talk him out of reality TV. Told him to save his image by dating one woman who was capable of wearing an entire dress."

That got a laugh from Stacey.

"My advice fell on deaf ears."

"Interesting. I do wonder, though." She pushed her spectacles up the bridge of her nose and settled into the love seat.

"Wonder what?"

"Hmm? Oh, nothing. I'll keep my musings to myself for now. How about we go over what to expect for the evening?"

"I think we can save that for later," Felicia Davenport said as she charged into the room. "Right now, I need coffee with lots of alcohol in it. Stat!"

Stacey's entire demeanor changed from relaxed and confident to nervous and submissive. She shot from the love seat and made a beeline for the door, mumbling a, "Yes, Ms. Davenport."

All too quickly, Midge found herself alone with the despicable woman. She flipped her mic back on and then took a sip of her tea to refrain from commenting on Felicia's curt treatment of Stacey.

"I didn't realize you were a contestant as well," Felicia sniffed. "You might have mentioned it in the elevator."

"You seemed to be in a hurry. I didn't want to take up any of your precious time." Midge flashed her a winning smile, but Felicia gave her an unhappy scowl.

"What did you say your name was?"

"I'm Madelyn Knightly. The director's daughter."

Now Felicia appeared even more upset.

"So just like that you land a role in a critically acclaimed reality TV series because your daddy is the director? Must be nice to have such high connections even though you possess zero talent where acting is concerned."

Critically acclaimed? Was there such a thing when it came to reality TV? This was the first taping. No one had even had time to critically acclaim anything.

"Acting? I thought this was reality TV," Midge said. "Do you mean to tell me you're not here to make amends with Brody Prescott and win his heart?"

Midge saw the door to the room open up a crack while something peeked through, though she couldn't catch much of a glimpse since Felicia moved in front and stood, looming over her.

"Of course, I am. I'm not the one who'll be acting. Some women are here for less than genuine purposes." Her pointed look underscored her subtle accusation.

Eyes are everywhere, her father used to say whenever they were on location. Someone was definitely filming this encounter.

"Well, *I'm* certainly here to give it a try," Midge lied. Right, like she was going to divulge the truth behind her presence to the she-devil standing before her.

Felicia gave her another condescending perusal. It was a talent really, the ability to stick your nose up while looking down on everyone around you. Probably one of the few she actually possessed.

"Well, good luck with that, sweetheart. From everything I've observed, Brody Prescott isn't interested in gingers. His preferences tend to lean toward curvy blonds." She smoothed her hands over her hips and then gave her butt a firm smack.

"Then it's a wonder, considering your ample figure, that Brody failed to take full advantage of your curves when he had the chance. You went out how many times? Once?" Midge tsked as outraged anger emanated from Felicia's quivering frame. She knew she needed to bite her tongue, be the better woman, and show a little restraint, but her disgust with Felicia had pushed her over the edge. "Perhaps he's outgrown the flighty Marilyn Monroe types and is looking for a classic beauty."

Midge might have resembled a mousy librarian to those unwilling to give her a second glance, but she was definitely no pushover, and beautiful glitzy women like Felicia didn't scare her one bit. She had her mother to thank for that. As she set down her tea and stood, ready to leave Felicia's distasteful company, the woman grasped her wrist and applied a painful amount of pressure.

"You're out of your league here, sweetie. You're not ready to play with the big girls."

Midge showed no reaction to the painful increase of pressure on her wrist. Instead, she met Felicia's hateful gaze and leveled her with an icy look of her own.

"Don't be so hard on your own body type, Felicia. You're not *that* big."

The debutante's indignant gasp made her lips quiver with pent up laughter. Felicia had grossly underestimated her. Though she'd turned her back on this kind of Hollywood lifestyle she'd been groomed for it since day one. She knew how to deal with the likes of Felicia Davenport.

"Now, if you'll excuse me, I need to go freshen up before the rest of the contestants join us. You might consider it as well. You have a smudge, just here." Midge moved her finger across her cheek, indicating the area where a non-existent blemish was located. Felicia turned around in a panic and grabbed for her purse, probably looking for a compact mirror.

Before she could reach the door, a few crew members wielding cameras came in. Bill Thompson, her father's right-hand man motioned her to stay.

"That was great ladies, but we were hoping for something even more hostile. Midge, I think you should splash your drink in Felicia's face and then Felicia can move to hit you. We could throw in a stunt double to get that initial face slap. We've got your conversation recorded and we can just edit, dub, and adjust where we need to."

Midge raised one eyebrow in disgust and then shook her head, feeling ashamed at how she'd already taken Felicia's bait and behaved like a shrew. "Not happening, Bill." She moved around the crew, marched through the door, and headed toward the staircase.

She noticed Stacey in the hallway with a small video camera in her hands. She gave Midge a thumbs up and a conspiratorial wink before turning around and heading in the opposite direction.

Eyes everywhere.

BRODY

"Why is Felicia Davenport here?" Brody demanded.

He felt tired, annoyed, and emotionally drained. Not a single female—besides Madelyn—held an ounce of intelligence unless you counted the calculating looks he'd received from a few of them, no doubt wondering about his assets and stock holdings and how they might get their hands on every single penny he possessed.

What an unendurable nightmare. The only thing that made the endless line of introductions bearable was the idea that Madelyn was in the mansion waiting for him. Well, maybe not waiting for him, per se, but at least present, and for all intents and purposes available for some slotted alone time with him.

As he stood in a makeshift office where Knightly and his crew followed up with edits and post production—apparently each episode would be shot and edited during the week and then unveiled the following Monday night—he waited impatiently for Knightly to get on with his explanation.

"This is exactly what the show needs. The public is aware of Felicia's accusations. Are they true, are they false? Perhaps she is here to patch things up and make amends for her vicious attack on your image."

"Is *that* why she's here?"

"Or," Knightly said, pointing a finger at him, "she's come to forgive you for your abhorrent behavior due to her undying love for you. We're trying to save your image here, and the best way to do that is to kiss and make-up with the woman who caused this whole hullabaloo to begin with."

"Knightly, if you think I want to have anything to do with that psychotic female, you're crazy. I turned her down for a nightcap. Her ego was hurt and she attacked me the best way she knew how. Her claims are completely fraudulent."

"Of course, of course, but whether real or fake I believe the public will be ready and willing to forgive any and all scandals if they are privy to the details of your fairytale romance unfolding on screen. An engaged founder of an online dating community is much more trustworthy than a playboy CEO."

Brody's anger at this kink in his flawless planning caused him to plant a fist on Knightly's desk, upending a triangular paperweight and a cup filled with ballpoint pens.

"I have no intention of falling in love with that nightmare."

"Love? Who said anything about love? I'm not asking you to follow your heart. I'm telling you to give the American viewers exactly what they want."

"And what is that?"

"An entertaining love story filled with jealousy, betrayal, emotional turmoil, and eventually the happy ending we're all programmed to expect."

"It's nothing but a lie," Brody said in amazement.

"Exactly. Welcome to reality television. Now Prescott, I have a few last-minute things to go over before the cocktail party tonight."

"And that is?" Brody asked impatiently.

"First, as you know, it will be important for you to make some kind of grand opening speech, something nonsensical about finding the woman of your dreams in the room, true love yadda yadda yadda, you know the drill. I've heard you speak publicly so I know you won't need any coaching in that area. Do you feel confident that you'll be able to say something meaningful and heartwarming?"

"I think I can manage."

"Good. Great. After all, we're trying to repair that damaged image of yours."

"Are we? Why do I get the feeling I've just been submarined?"

"On to other important details. Tonight, you will be eliminating three individuals from the group. I don't care who the first two are, that's completely up to you."

"How thoughtful, thank you."

Knightly smiled at the heavy laden sarcasm. "Obviously, Felicia stays so don't even think about eliminating her." Brody growled at this, but Knightly ignored him. "There is one contestant who must be eliminated from the show tonight."

Brody anxiously waited for the response he knew was coming.

"My daughter, Madelyn Knightly. You see, she's merely here as a stand-in due to a last minute cancellation. She promised to step in just for tonight, but she's not an actual contestant for the show."

Brody had already rehearsed his response.

"She didn't sign a contract like the rest of the contestants?"

"She did sign one, but it slightly differs from the others in scope and compensation."

"Ah, then she signed a contract stating she would remain for only one night?"

"Essentially. The wording for that contract is basically the same as the others. She stays until she is eliminated."

"No specific time frame, then?"

Knightly narrowed his eyes at Brody. "Why do you ask?"

The phone rang before Brody had to face more of Knightly's suspicious questions. He decided to hightail it out of there before the producer got off the phone. He'd found out everything he needed to know. Her contract wasn't specific in the length of time she'd agreed to stay. She fulfilled her end of the contract and was allowed to leave once she was eliminated.

And Brody Prescott had no intention of ever eliminating the tempting little minx.

Once he reached the mansion, he had one of the crew escort him to his own suite where he could quickly shower and change into a less wrinkled, less sweaty, tux for the evening.

"You have about an hour before we start shooting," the crew member said, a sweet looking girl with owl-shaped glasses.

"Thank you, ah…"

"Stacey," she said. A knowing smile perched itself upon her lips. "Let me know if you need anything."

Puzzled by her demeanor, he automatically responded, "Of course. Thank you, Stacey."

He closed the door and turned to study the grandeur of his stately room with an immaculate king sized bed and a large chest of drawers situated in the corner. The decor was decidedly male in nature with dark blues and greens interspersed in the carpeting, furniture, and bedding. Well, at least he'd be comfortable. In here, anyway. He held no hope of ever feeling comfortable in front of all those cameras.

He turned to his left and opened the door to what he assumed was his private bathroom. Nothing could have surprised nor delighted him more than to find Madelyn Knightly pacing back and forth along the pristine floors.

She'd come to him, to his room, without the slightest bit of convincing or even coercion. His planning had included slowly seducing the woman, gaining eventual ground until she willingly fell into his outstretched arms. And yet here she was, waiting for him as if she couldn't bear to waste another moment without the warmth of his lips on hers.

His abrupt arrival caused her to gasp in surprise, her mouth taking on the most alluring O-shape imaginable. He didn't think, he didn't plan, his response to this young lady was anything but calm and controlled. In two large strides he crossed the distance between them, pulled her into his arms, and crushed his hungry lips to hers.

She let out a slight moan of surprise which was quickly muffled as he deepened their kiss. She fisted her hands against his chest, applying slight pressure, but not enough for him to believe for one moment that she intended to actually push him away. If she did, he would stop. If she pulled back, he would let her go no matter how much it pained him to do so. In the back of his mind he had to acknowledge that he was once again behaving like an incorrigible beast, but he hoped to high Heaven she wouldn't make him stop. He'd waited two months for this.

Neanderthal button, indeed.

His heart warmed as the pressure against his chest lessened, her body relaxing against his. Just when he thought she was ready to surrender herself to the inevitability of the chemistry between them, he felt a sharp pain in his left shin and immediately released her.

He stared at her wild, disheveled hair—courtesy of his roving hands—and her deliciously red, swollen lips—courtesy of his administrations—and realized the look in her eyes wasn't that of a woman in the thralls of passion. It was a woman ready to kick some serious fanny, and she'd done so by lashing out at his shins!

He was so taken aback by her fierce stance and fiery spirit he couldn't help but laugh out loud at her irresistible pout. She was simply incredible. He adored her more for pushing him away, and rightly so. His impulse control around this woman was non-existent. His mother would be mortified.

Before he could apologize for his caveman-style behavior, she pointed a finger in his face.

"Am I the first contestant you've made-out with, or is there a pecking order I need to be made aware of?"

Absolutely adorable.

What a firecracker!

CHAPTER 11

Midge

Midge moved to the edge of the bathtub to catch her breath, keeping an eye on the irresistible billionaire just in case he pulled another fast one on her and caught her completely by surprise again.

Cheese and crackers, this meeting had not gone according to plan. When she realized how much time the contestants had before the evening's cocktail party, she wanted to meet with Brody as soon as possible and impart as much reality TV knowledge as she could before she left the show that night. She didn't like the thought of him completely unprepared for Felicia's endgame, whatever that might be. She was still researching that crazed woman's background at the moment—and coming up with nothing.

Stacey had agreed to sneak Midge into Brody's room so she could have a private word with him without any cameras lurking in the shadows. One look at the king sized bed— hinting at all sorts of things she didn't plan on doing until her wedding night—encouraged her to move the location of their conversation to the bathroom, assuming it would make their meeting feel less like some clandestine, romantic rendezvous.

The billionaire had managed to blow that assumption right out of the water.

Did the man have to be such an accomplished kisser?

"Pecking order?" he asked, referring to her previous question. "Madelyn, you're under the distasteful belief that I'm some kind of lip whore."

"A playboy generally falls under the lip whore category. And to think I came here to help you."

She lifted a hand to her heart, trying to prevent it from beating right out of her chest. He'd gotten to her. No doubt about it. What an unfortunate turn of events. How was she supposed to keep it together after that emotionally charged kiss?

"Help me? I want to hear about that later, but first I'm going to defend myself against your offensive accusation. I'm not a playboy." He folded his arms across his chest and leaned against the bathroom door. Unfortunately, it made him look even more appealing.

Midge quirked a disbelieving brow at this. "Aren't you? Shall we review your dating history?"

"I've never dated a woman for longer than one night," he exclaimed.

"Not helping your case, here. Playboys can't stick to one woman. Do you see how this looks from a woman's perspective?"

He appeared amused yet slightly frustrated. "You're only a player if you get some actual play time in with various women. I never slept with any of those girls. Scouts honor. All of those dates were set up by Gregg to help me appear as if I knew my way around the dating scene."

Midge, truly baffled by this revelation, took a step forward. "Do you mean to tell me that for the last ten years you've never slept with any of those set-ups?"

He hesitated before speaking, seeming to wince at some memory or thought her question had elicited. "If Gregg hadn't set those dates up for me, they never would have happened to begin with. I'm not chasing after meaningless one-night stands. I don't do casual."

"Then why did you casually kiss me? Twice?" she shot back.

"Who says kissing you is casual?"

Midge swallowed hard. "What are you saying?"

"I don't waste time with people who hold no interest for me." He approached her with slow, measured steps. She wondered if he was afraid she might bolt for the door. More likely she'd dive out the window since his impressive frame blocked the most logical exit. "But you've held my attention from day one, and there is nothing casual about the pull I feel when I'm around you."

He couldn't be serious. Weren't playboys notorious for their smooth talk?

"Right. You're so captivated by my presence you decided to join a dating show rather than pursue something serious with me. Not buying it, Casanova."

Brody had the nerve to give her an engaging smile.

"I can explain my presence here."

"I'm sure you can. With flowery words and empty compliments." She waved her hand in the air as if she couldn't be bothered and then motioned for him to take a seat on the closed porcelain throne. She hoped seeing him seated upon a toilet might diminish the magnetic pull he had on her. He sat down and gave her a smoldering, come hither stare. How in the world did someone sitting on a toilet manage a look like that?

She sighed heavily and continued.

"I don't want to hear your reasons for being here, but I will share with you why you found me in your bathroom."

"Yes, I believe that explanation ought to be extremely entertaining."

Midge gave him a glare, but refrained from throwing out any counter attacks.

"Look, I'm sure by now my father has informed you that I'm to be eliminated after tonight."

"Yes, he did mention the reasons for your short stay on the show."

"All right. Obviously, the plan for salvaging your image hit a snag the minute Felicia Davenport parachuted from the sky. My father isn't interested in what is best for you, and he is going to make this series entertaining no matter whose persona gets dragged through the mud. So I'm here to coach you on what exactly you're going to say during your initial speech to the group."

"Really?"

"Yes. This first impression you give to the viewers is crucial. It doesn't matter if any of the contestants are actually paying attention to what you are saying so long as the American viewers are hearing every single word."

"What do you think I should say?"

"You're going to be honest, realistic, and in the process lay out some definitive ground rules that will set the tone for this season's madness."

"Set the tone?"

"Absolutely," Midge said as she sat back down on the edge of the bathtub. "Your character needs to be beyond reproach. Now, most viewers aren't going to be surprised if you kiss every girl on the show. You're getting to know them, right? American's ideals and values have changed enough that everyone seems to assume the only way to vet a potential spouse is to rate them on their kissing ability and sexual prowess. That's how a relationship stands the test of time. Great sex, amazing chemistry. I can get to know you after I've slept with you."

"You believe that kind of thinking is wrong?" It sounded as if he really wanted her honest opinion.

"Of course it is. How many marriages have ended in divorce simply because one of the spouses decided the sex wasn't that great anymore? Instead of building a foundation of mutual respect, love, and trust, the marriage is solely carnal in nature. There's nothing but sex holding the couple together, and you can get good sex anywhere, so there's nothing in that relationship noteworthy enough to stick around and fight for."

"Nothing," he replied.

Midge failed to note his understanding as she continued on with her coaching.

"Billionaire Brody is different, though. Brody Prescott is not the playboy the media has pegged him as. He's interested in personality, true friendship, mutual respect. Chemistry is important. There has to be an attraction there to begin with, but it's what draws him in rather than what convinces him to stay. When you start your speech, you need to make it clear that you have no intention of kissing anyone on the show until you are serious about someone and know them well enough for that to matter."

"I can say that."

"Yes, but can you do it? Can you keep your paws off the girls until you've developed a real relationship with one of them?"

Midge balked at the twinge of pain she felt when discussing his entering into other relationships. She had to ignore this useless attraction she felt for him. She knew next to nothing about his personal life. Her feelings for him were based on pure physical attraction. Nothing more. Did she have a desire to explore something more than this physical attraction?

She found that she did and was terrified with the very idea. It took two to tango, and she didn't want to step onto the dance floor if Brody held no interest in joining her, and she didn't believe his claims of interest where she was concerned.

"It's like I told you before, Madelyn, I never had an intimate moment with any of those women. Why start now with women I don't even know? I can keep my hands off."

"You don't show any restraint where I'm concerned, so forgive me if I'm slightly skeptical, and quit calling me Madelyn. I told you my friends call me Midge."

"You're saying we're friends, then?"

"Acquaintances would be a better term."

"I think I'll stick with Madelyn?"

"Why?"

He fixed her with another one of those smoldering stares.

"Because I'd like to be much more than your friend."

Midge nearly choked on her response. "Then why are you on the show?"

"Are you saying you would leave this island with me if I asked you to?"

"Leave with you? Of course not."

"Then you've given me very little choice in the matter, Madelyn. I'm determined to get what I want."

Confusion washed over her in discombobulating waves. *What on earth is he talking about? Getting what he wants? What exactly is that?*

She waited for him to explain further, waited for those deep blue eyes to hold a hint of mirth, to tell her it was all simply a game to him and apologize for leading her on. When his expression began to reflect that determination he'd just mentioned, she rushed to the door. Once she opened it, she turned around half expecting him to be mere inches behind her. He remained sitting on the toilet seat, hungry eyes following her every gesture.

"Just remember, we're reshaping your image. If you're not a playboy then prove it tonight. Set an appropriate and respectful tone for your fairy tale, Brody. Choose one woman to slowly develop a relationship with and pursue her until the very end of the show."

"I plan on pursuing her for much longer than that," he said in a deep, rumbling voice.

Confused with the double meaning behind his words and her own tempestuous emotions, she spun around and sailed out of his bedroom, taking care to not be noticed by the crew and contestants within the mansion.

BRODY

Brody stood just outside the main room where all twenty contestants were gathered. He wasn't nervous for the things he planned to say. Nothing about this night truly set him on edge, unless he considered the fifteen minutes he'd been allotted to spend with every single female present. Essentially five hours spent in aimless chit chat with women who were most definitely not as intriguing as his mousy librarian.

He didn't relish the idea, but Madelyn refused to acknowledge his open invitation to leave the island with him. He had to see this through.

"Ready when you are, Brody," came a voice from behind him.

He entered the room and immediately sought out the gorgeous redhead—who happened to be in the back behind the other excited contestants. Their eyes met. She gave him a pointed look and then an encouraging smile. It was enough for now.

Directly on his heels followed TV icon and host for the season's show, Les Lassiter. His regal bearing and camera-ready smile reminded Brody of a tacky game show host.

"Ladies," Les began, "I want to congratulate you on being part of this season of *Marry Your Billionaire*." He paused with a patient smile as the girls applauded his words and appearance. "As you know, this season's bachelor is a man well-versed in the art of bringing couples together, and now he has the opportunity to find that special someone of his own. The question we must all ask ourselves is this: which one of you lovely ladies will it be?"

There were titters and murmurs from the girls as Brody forced himself to make eye contact with every woman present rather than fix his gaze on Madelyn and leave it there for the remainder of the evening. Out of the corner of his eye he noticed Felicia Davenport mincing her way towards the middle of the room. He assumed she was simply trying to maintain the focus of everyone's attention, but the way her angry glare landed on Madelyn made him warily clock her movements. She sidled up right next to her and looked to be reaching toward Madelyn. His focus was interrupted by a rough slap on the back from Les Lassiter.

"This evening you'll have the honor and opportunity to get to know one of America's most eligible bachelors. Are you ladies ready to get started?"

A hearty "yes" resonated within the room, signaling Brody's cue to deliver that first speech with as much charisma as possible.

"I wanted to let you know how truly honored I am to be here. It has come to my attention that many of you came here for me specifically, and I am thrilled to spend time with every single one of you."

Various ahhs and ohhhs floated across the large room as most of the women did their best to slowly inch toward him.

"I would like to say something that I feel is incredibly important before we get started." The room quieted with an expectant air. "This situation we're in, one man dating several women at one time, is unusual to say the least. Feelings will develop and attachments will be made. I don't want to hurt anyone, but in the end I'm looking for one woman to spend the rest of my life with, and damaged feelings are inevitable. I would like to minimize this as much as I can. I really feel that intimacy is something shared between two people who are serious about one another. I'm hoping that you'll understand me when I say that I would rather not kiss any of you as we get to know one another."

He thought he heard a few surprised noises from the crowd, but the commotion quieted as he continued. "I can't think of anything more confusing than having someone you care about kiss you one moment and then turn around and kiss someone else the next. Did those kisses mean anything? Was he just using you? That kind of cavalier use of your time and affection will only cause unnecessary pain and confusion. I'd like to think I'm a better man than that."

This time his gaze zeroed in on Madelyn. He hoped she sensed the sincerity of his words. This wasn't just a speech being made due to her encouragement alone. He'd had something like this in mind all along, but it had warmed his heart to think she'd cared enough about him to help him salvage his image, enough to continue on with this crazy plan of his.

"So please, if there is any show of affection to be made, let me be the one to initiate it. That way, if and when I do, you'll know I'm seriously pursuing a relationship with you. You'll feel no confusion on that score if that moment presents itself. Does that work for you ladies?"

A collective sigh of agreement washed throughout the room. All the women, even the ones he suspected were present to further their own career, seemed to take note of him as not just a lucrative bank account, but as a truly worthwhile individual. Everyone, that is, except the she-cat making her way over to his side.

"I believe I called first dibs on alone time with this handsome guy."

Felicia was all smiles and laughter, but her tight grip on his bicep let him know her level of displeasure. This woman had cornered the market on holding a grudge.

He followed her into an adjoining room where they were able to sit down and supposedly "get to know" one another, cameras at the ready, of course. He figured the best way to deal with this situation was just as Madelyn had suggested: with honesty.

"I must admit, Felicia, I was terribly surprised to see you here. Especially after the hurtful things you said about my ethics where my business was concerned." He helped her sit down and then seated himself across from her.

"Darling, I came here specifically to apologize to you for the awful things I said. When I received that anonymous tip claiming that you were calling and stalking women on your dating service, why, I simply did what I thought was best. After all, my dear friend happened to be one of your victims."

"Felicia, you know I would never do something as unethical as breach the trust of my clients."

"I know that now, of course. Some people will tell just about any lie they can to get into the spotlight."

"And yet, that friend of yours never once came forward with her own statement as to her claim about my abhorrent behavior. You would think someone interested in the spotlight would have taken the tabloids by storm—much like you did."

Felicia couldn't have failed to catch his subtle dig, but she responded with a chagrined smile, pouting her lips in a placating way.

"Can you ever forgive me for impulsively hurling such false accusations against you without verifying whether or not they were true?" Her eyes brimmed with unshed tears. Her acting skills were quite believable. He wondered how many men had been swindled by her little damsel in distress display.

He saw exactly what she aimed to accomplish here. If he refused to forgive her it would make him look like an unfeeling monster on national television, but forgiving Felicia gave him no valid reason for avoiding her presence or eliminating her from the show, at least not right away. He would have to come up with something more substantial later. If he was going to play this farce, he might as well do it convincingly.

"Of course, I forgive you, Felicia. You were merely looking out for your dear friend, and with such pure motives, who could ever fault you for that?"

She delicately wiped the moisture from the corners of her eyes and gave him a grateful smile.

"How kind. Thank you for being so understanding. I'm happy to put this all behind us and start over again."

"That's a wonderful notion. We'll begin from the beginning. Where were you born?"

Felicia gave him a light-hearted chuckle and he joined in. The entire charade caused nausea to wash over him, but he continued to play his part to perfection. He'd never again allow Felicia Davenport to get the best of him.

CHAPTER 12

Midge

Midge sat in a corner of one of the mansion's libraries, curled up on a love seat with a book propped on her lap. She'd done her fair share of mingling with the girls and felt justified in sneaking off even though a camera still ended up following her to the library, which hadn't been easy to find. Once it became obvious that she'd be doing nothing more than some light reading, the camera and its wielder quickly left her to her own devices. That never would have flown with any other contestant, but Midge's status as the director's daughter gave her some massive leeway.

"Why am I not surprised to find you hiding out here?"

Her head shot up at her father's abrupt appearance. He leaned against the door frame with his arms folded and a deep frown etched on his face.

"You said I was allowed some freedom, and I don't see any point in spending time with nineteen other women who are sizing me up and analyzing all of my facial flaws when I could be enjoying some classic literature."

"We need some shots of you mingling with the other girls." He strode into the room and settled himself across from her on a white settee with ornate carvings along the legs.

"Nice try, Dad. I've paid my dues in that department. Just ask Bill."

"We also need to film your fifteen minutes with Brody. From your earlier comments on the beach, it sounded like you two already knew each other."

He flicked some lint from his pants, behaving as if he wasn't eager to find out the details. His suspicion made her shoulders tense. If he discovered how explosive her first two run-ins with Brody had been, that would be it for her. He'd do everything he could to keep her on the show and have this "romance" play out. She'd never get away.

She raised her eyes to his and gave him a nonchalant shrug.

"I ran into him once a few months ago at Club 23." Staying close to the truth was the best possible solution.

"You were at Club 23? Without me?" His wounded expression surprised her.

"I was on a blind date. My roommate set me up with some scumbag who introduced me to Brody while we were there."

Anger flashed across his features.

"Who?" he growled.

"Alexander Montgomery."

Her father let out a few expletives, surprising her with his vehemence.

"That guy is a jerk, Midge. How could you be stupid enough to get stuck with someone like that?"

Midge's anger spiked.

"I'm pretty sure I mentioned that I was on a blind date. Had I known what I'd be dealing with, the date never would have happened. Give me some credit, here."

Her father took a deep breath, puffed his cheeks out, and exhaled.

"I'm sorry, Midge girl. I just worry about you sometimes."

"Um...thank you."

Her anger deflated with his unexpected concern.

"Now then, I want you to work on getting to know Brody. Really delve into his family and his past. We want to know about rough break-ups, traumatizing childhood experiences, and any other possible sob stories that will garner more sympathy from the audience."

Midge nodded her head. "Right. I'm on it."

"If you sniff a scandal, push for information on that as well. I'm all about revealing skeletons from the past, and nobody is better at sniffing out smut than you, Midge girl."

"Not really a compliment, Dad."

"Fancy meeting you here," Midge said as she seated herself next to Brody. She couldn't help but notice the way his eyes lit up at her approach and hoped for a moment that the reaction was genuine and not some play to the cameras. She'd noticed Brody escaping to a wide balcony overlooking the ocean. A set of wicker chairs were strategically placed facing one another. A bottle of champagne was seated on a small holder on the side. Getting this fifteen minutes over with had been the sole motivation behind aborting Brody's attempted escape. She simply couldn't stand the inane small talk from the other contestants, her hovering father reading over her shoulder, or the anticipation building at the idea of spending more time with Brody.

"Hello, Madelyn," he said.

"How are you holding up, Mr. Prescott?"

"Brody. I'd very much like it if you called me Brody."

What she wanted to do was get up and run like mad to the nearest sailboat, but she'd promised to follow through with this night while helping Brody avoid the many pitfalls her father had planned for him. She'd rather be pretending that the interest he showed her held a glimmer of sincerity.

Sigh.

It was so much easier to relate to people when they were characters in books. Then again, maybe this scenario could be exactly like a good book. Fictitious situations created by an artistic mind. Why not converse with Brody in the way she wished to without worrying about her growing feelings for him or the lack thereof on his part? It was all a fairy tale anyway. She might as well let her guard down and simply be herself.

"I like the name Brody. Does it hold any special significance for you or your family?"

Her question appeared to catch him off-guard. He took a moment to clear his throat before responding.

"It's my father's name. Well, my full name is Broderick, but my parents shortened it to Brody just after I was born. My dad wanted to name me something else, but mother felt that there could be no higher honor than naming her son after a man as strong, caring, and kind as the man she married."

"That's a wonderful legacy. Are you close to your parents?"

Brody swallowed hard at her question. Midge felt slightly perplexed at the reticence with which he approached the subject.

"My father passed away when I was a teenager. Pancreatic cancer. We barely found out he was ill and then suddenly he was gone."

"I'm so sorry." Midge felt her heart slam into her throat. She instinctively reached for his hand as raw emotion engulfed his features, furious with herself for opening up that can of worms. No wonder he'd approached her questions as if he were approaching a land mine.

"It's okay," he coughed, clearing his throat. "I'm not the only person who has ever lost a parent. I certainly won't be the last. But to further answer your question, my mom and I grew very close as a result of my father's passing. We really had to rely on each other for support and simple survival. She's an incredible woman."

She'd only met Blanche once, but once was all it took to leave an unforgettable impression.

"How so?" Midge prodded.

"When my father passed away, my mom took on extra work to provide for us. At one point, she was working three jobs, waitressing at nights, cashiering during the days, and walking dogs on the weekends. Seeing her struggle like that just for me, all for me, I knew I had to get my act together and eventually become the kind of man who could take care of her. I didn't want that life for her. I needed to make something of myself."

"So you became an entrepreneur," Midge stated.

He nodded and gifted her a small smile. He squeezed the hand she'd offered him and pulled it closer to his chest. Without realizing it, she rested her other hand on his knee completely enthralled in the story he told and this more vulnerable side to the powerful CEO.

"I worked every job imaginable through my teen years and then went to college and studied business. Lots of late nights, sleep deprivation, and peanut butter and jelly sandwiches, but I think I managed to make out just fine in the end."

Midge smiled at his humble description of himself.

"Now enough about me. What's your legacy, Madelyn?"

"Your guess is as good as mine. I've never actually asked my parents why they named me Madelyn, but since they're both involved in show biz in one form or another, I'm assuming their name choice involved some serious wishful thinking on their parts. No doubt, I was expected to become some Hollywood starlet."

"Is that something you would have enjoyed?" he asked. He seemed genuinely curious. It looked like they were both playing their parts to perfection, and she couldn't help but enjoy the whole charade.

"A professional acting career? Hardly. No, I enjoy being creative in my own way, but that usually involves creating my own stories rather than playing out stories created by others."

How ironic that that was exactly what she was currently participating in.

Brody's eyes alighted at this. "You're an author?"

"An aspiring author," she corrected. "Currently working on my first manuscript."

"Sounds fascinating. I would love to read your book when it's finished."

"I'll be sure to keep you on speed dial."

"I'm counting on it."

His thumb grazed that sensitive spot along her wrist, and she glanced down, taking note of how close their bodies were positioned. In her periphery she noticed two cameramen, and for one brief moment felt saddened by the inevitable conclusion of this evening. Though it was glamour, glitz, and make-believe, she'd enjoyed the small glimpse of Brody, vulnerable and hardworking, getting to see a personality under all that male bravado.

"That was great, you two. A really nice ending to this section of the evening's events," her father said as he came to tower over the two of them. Though he appeared relaxed, his taught smile said otherwise. Confused at the hint of annoyance she picked up on, Midge released Brody's hand and stood, giving her dad a crisp smile.

"I'm impressed, Midge girl, for someone who hates the limelight you sure know how to command all the attention in the room."

"Red hair is a natural eye-catcher," she said, downplaying her father's praise —or was it an accusation? "Anyone with this much frizz is bound to stand out in a crowd."

Her father chuckled, finally letting go of whatever had been bothering him.

"I was going to attribute it to your intellect and the fact that you're a natural beauty," Brody said. He stood as well and pinned her with a dimpled smile.

"You can cut the charm, Brody," her father stated in annoyance. "Cameras aren't rolling at the moment."

"Who said they were?" he asked all innocence.

Midge felt a slow tension coiling within her father, making the sudden silence more than a little uncomfortable.

She shifted her feet.

"I suppose I'll go wait in the other room with the girls while you and Brody discuss the next scene." Midge hurried out the door before she gave in to the urge to offer Brody a goodbye hug. He was here to save his image and enter into a committed relationship in the process. No matter her own interest where Brody was concerned, it was time for her to go home.

Next stop: elimination.

BRODY

"What was that all about?" Knightly demanded.

Brody studied the producer, marveling at the sudden change from director to overprotective father. About time, really.

"I'm not sure what you mean?"

"Don't you? You were holding my daughter's hand. You looked at her as if she was the only woman who would ever matter to you."

Brody gave a nonplussed shrug. "Your daughter is extraordinary. Are you really upset with me for noticing?"

Corbin Knightly let out a frustrated hiss and then rubbed his temples in a slow circular motion.

"Of course not. Any man who doesn't notice Midge is either dead or gay, but I'm not accustomed to seeing her...like that."

"Like what?" Brody asked.

Knightly appeared truly upset over something as simple as a fifteen-minute conversation.

He speared Brody with a piercing look.

"Like she's finally found her place in this world."

The producer's quiet revelation made Brody feel as if he'd just been given a sign, a significant nod from the Universe that this path he'd chosen, this woman he pursued was the only thing that mattered. He simply had to continue to work for it, work for her.

Brody felt the urge to help Knightly understand his interest in his daughter, but at that moment Stacey came rushing in.

"The crew is all ready to go, Mr. Knightly."

The producer turned to her and gave her a slight nod then turned back to Brody.

"Do you know who you're going to eliminate?"

"Yes."

Knightly tapped his finger against his bottom lip.

"Then let's get to it, shall we?"

MIDGE

When a man tells a woman he simply isn't interested in her, the woman is humiliated and the man makes himself out to be a first rate jerk. Fortunately, television has found a way for a man to reject several women at one time without offending America's social sensibilities.

Thus the diamond ceremony, an innovative, ritualistic method of offering up a consolation prize—a red rose whose blossoms are encrusted with tiny genuine diamonds—while simultaneously implying that the woman isn't suitable enough for marriage without having to tell her why. The fact that the woman is found wanting, whether she is, in all actuality, the most incredible individual or not is swept to the side.

The entire farce made Midge feel as if her soul was dying just a little.

The first diamond ceremony had the women fluttering about, fixing hair, smoothing down invisible wrinkles, and nervously chatting about their fifteen-minute conversations with the enigmatic billionaire.

"Oh, you wouldn't believe the amazing talk we had," said a gorgeous brunette seated to Midge's right. She was the type of person who talked with her hands, flinging them here and there at the end of each sentence as if they were visual exclamation points. She grabbed Midge's arm and gave it a friendly squeeze. "I mean, he is a perfect gentleman. So considerate and thoughtful, asking me questions about myself instead of just talking over me like most men do."

It seemed as if hundreds of bodies pressed in around Midge, cutting off her air supply. The temperature in the room had increased by at least ten degrees. Had someone turned the AC off?

"Oh, I know what you mean," said another brunette to Midge's left. "We just talked and talked about my family, my schooling, and everything I was interested in." She let out a heart-wrenching sigh. "I felt such a strong connection with him. I really think he's my future husband. I can't imagine being sent home tonight."

Midge felt bile rise up the back of her throat as she listened to other women talk about Brody as if they held some kind of ownership over him. Why hadn't the ceremony started yet? What was taking so long?

After a few more excruciating minutes filled with shallow professions of love at first sight, Les and Brody mercifully came striding into the room. Everyone, including Midge, moved to their respective positions to wait out the results of this first humiliating round of eliminations.

Midge didn't feel at all sorry for herself since being eliminated was exactly what she had asked for—exactly what she wanted, but two other girls would be sent home tonight, and what if they really *had* developed feelings for Brody? Being slapped in the face with an actual rejection from a man as desirable as this particular billionaire probably wouldn't go over well with several of the women present.

Her eyes traveled to the back of Felicia's blond beehived head. She'd positioned herself in the front row, smack dab in the middle.

Seriously? With her hairdo rivaling the height of Mount Everest, the cameras weren't likely to miss the attention hungry wannabe. She hoped Felicia might get the ax tonight right along with her, but if her father's wishes and desires for ratings took precedence she figured Felicia had earned a place on the show due to her own vicious personality.

Poor Brody. Hopefully, her brief instructions continued to help him throughout the rest of the season until he found the woman he wanted to claim as his fiancé.

The thought soured her stomach.

"As much as we all wish that no one had to be eliminated tonight, the time has come for Brody to decide who he has connected with and who must, sadly, be sent home." Les turned to Brody and gave him a nod. "Good luck, Brody."

The bachelor of the season took center stage and gifted them with one of his dazzling Crest-white smiles. Midge's stomach did an Olympian somersault before taking a nosedive.

"Ladies," Brody began, "I enjoyed speaking with every single one of you. To the women I am letting go, I hope you will understand that this is not a personal reflection on whether or not you are lacking in some way. With only a brief amount of time to get to know each of you, I have to make my decision based on how I felt in your presence and whether or not we shared anything in common with one another. So please, do not leave this house feeling as if you are unattractive or unwanted because that is simply not the case."

Oh, he was good. Emphasizing that his choice hadn't been based on looks was a stroke of genius. No one could dub the man shallow or insensitive. Brody briefly made eye contact with Midge, as if searching for her approval. She gave him an imperceptible nod, just a slight gesture of support that couldn't have possibly been picked up by the cameras. The small twinge of his lips hinted at a hidden smile. Then he reached toward the table at his left and picked up the first diamond rose of the season.

"Charlene," he said.

The brunette to Midge's left let out a soft squeal of delight and moved forward to accept her rose. Midge swallowed the bitter taste of jealousy and mentally chastised herself in the process. She wasn't here for him. She didn't have feelings for him. She didn't have any desire to get to know him, and she continued to tell herself that with every name that left his yummy lips. Every name that wasn't hers, and every rose entrusted to some other woman's care, made taking in more oxygen difficult.

Get a grip! He's a playboy, a womanizer, and one humongous heartache just waiting to happen. You're not here for him.

After several minutes of this excruciatingly painful procedure—Midge felt certain that open-heart surgery with no anesthetic would have been less agonizing—they were down to five women, Felicia Davenport being one of them. Midge had surreptitiously studied the growing outrage on the woman's face as one contestant after another graciously accepted a diamond rose from Brody's steady hand.

If she hadn't been writhing in her own emotional turmoil she might have laughed outright at the subtle setback he'd administered. Midge didn't believe Brody intended to send Felicia home, not if her father had any say in the matter, but at least Brody had found a way to rebel a little against her father's directives and put Felicia in her place—*nearly* last place it would seem.

Once Felicia was finally called forward, she tilted her head and adjusted her expression to that of feigned delight, accepting the rose and giving Brody a loving peck on the cheek, though her eyes shot daggers as she walked back to her position. That left three other desirable contestants and Midge, with only one more rose to give away.

Brody picked up the rose and then gazed at the crowd of girls assembled. "This last rose is perhaps the most important one of all. In truth, I wanted to call this young lady forward first, but then I realized that sometimes the best, most beautiful things in this life must be saved for last. It makes the journey that much more meaningful. So the woman who stood out to me this evening and stole my heart with her kind words and sincere concern is...Madelyn Knightly."

Madelyn's mouth hung open, her heart rate elevating to a resounding roar. This could not be happening. Why was this happening? He'd been instructed to eliminate her. He knew she wasn't here to pursue a relationship with him, and yet he'd called her forward anyway, kept her here to continue this silly, stupid charade, and for what purpose? To what end?

Though her mind instructed her body to remain still, Brody's eyes pulled Midge forward with the force of a tractor beam. She stood mere inches from him, heart racing, limbs tingling, filled with outrage and frustration one second and then sheer relief the next. She didn't want to stay, but she also didn't want to leave.

"Madelyn," Brody murmured, "will you accept my invitation to stay?"

"Yes," she croaked, and then more firmly, "Yes, I accept your invitation to stay."

For now.

Brody rewarded her with a broad smile and gave her a soft kiss on the cheek. The significance of that gesture wasn't lost on her. Though every single woman present had gifted him with a kiss on the cheek when they had accepted their rose, she was the only one who had received such a gesture from him, and she was the only one who refrained from giving one herself.

As she turned around and walked back to her position, she couldn't help but notice the hatred and jealousy lurking in several of the contestant's glances. So now she had a large bull's-eye on her back.

Wonderful.

Hopefully, once the cameras weren't rolling, she could go have a very long chat with Brody and her father about the terms presented in her contract. For now, she had to stand there and simmer in silence.

CHAPTER 13

Brody

B rody was in big trouble and couldn't have been happier about it.

After the shoot and everyone's dismissal for the evening, Knightly had herded he and Madelyn into a luxurious looking office, the kind one might encounter on the movie set of *Sense and Sensibility* or *Emma*. So far, the intimidating director had simply listened to Midge's angry comments, seeming to assess and weigh her reaction against Brody's. He had no idea how Knightly would react to his decision to keep Midge on the show, and it unnerved him.

"What in the world were you thinking?" Midge hissed, finally pausing her angry tirade long enough to take a deep breath.

Brody noted her livid expression and decided it might be best to appear apologetic rather than one hundred percent elated.

"Madelyn, I know I was supposed to send you home, but I couldn't do it. I want you here."

"Why?"

"I think you know why."

He took her hands in his, but she pulled away and folded her arms across her chest. He didn't dare make another move toward her for fear she might bolt at the slightest provocation.

"Just because I gave you some sound advice for your opening remarks doesn't mean I'll do it again. You can't force me to stay on the show in order to play the role of your image consultant."

"No, that's not—"

"Well, I'm feeling slightly clueless at this point," Knightly interrupted. He leaned back in his office chair wearing a bewildered expression. "Why didn't either of you tell me you already knew one another?"

"I already told you we met briefly at Club 23."

Brody shook his head in silent disagreement. That lie wasn't going to work on someone as perceptive as Corbin Knightly.

Knightly shot her a skeptical look and proceeded to turn his laptop around so that the screen was visible. A YouTube video of Brody and Madelyn kissing in front of Club 23 played back at them. He couldn't believe it. Some miscreant with a camera had recognized him and posted their passionate exchange on social media.

"Sweet maple syrup," Madelyn exclaimed, pressing both of her hands to her flushed cheeks.

Brody's mouth twitched at the adorable expression.

"How many people have seen this?" she asked.

Knightly turned the laptop to face him and studied the screen. "It was posted a few days ago and has over a million hits." He continued to study the screen, a small smile tugging at the corners of his lips, waging war against the grimace attempting to pull them down. "You know, from a director's standpoint, this is one of the most fabulous kissing scenes I think I've ever witnessed. There's passion, there's tension, and that slap you gave Brody…" He chuckled softly. "Hells bells, Midge girl, who knew you were such a fire cracker?"

Brody cringed a little at Knightly's cavalier attitude. He was the worst wingman ever—not that he'd volunteered for the position.

"Are you freaking kidding me right now? My personal life has just been plastered all over social media, and all you can do is comment with your director's hat on?"

"You two need to explain yourselves," was all her father said.

"We met briefly before the show," Midge explained. "I encouraged Mr. Prescott to repair his image by dating one woman rather than throwing himself at the mercy of reality TV."

Brody looked from father to daughter and noted two strong, stubborn personalities. This was about to get even more interesting.

"That doesn't explain why you were kissing Mr. Prescott." Brody noted the edge to Knightly's tone.

"I didn't kiss him. He kissed me."

Knightly took another measured look at his screen. "I'd say you definitely kissed him back. You clearly have feelings for this playboy. Midge, I thought you had more sense than that."

He talked as if Brody wasn't standing right in front of him. Brody's anger at being relegated to playboy status yet again began to fester.

He worried as he watched the color drain from Madelyn's face and edged closer to steady her trembling form, but she jerked away from his touch.

"I do not have feelings for Brody Prescott. Nor do I intend to stay on the show. My contract states that I can leave after the first night."

"Actually, your contract states that you have to stay on the show until you are eliminated, and Midge girl, Brody did *not* eliminate you. I'm not happy about the way this played out, and I know you aren't exactly thrilled about being on the show, but you're contractually obligated to stay until Brody says otherwise."

Brody noted her clenched fists as she ground her teeth together.

"You promised me no strings attached. I could go home after this first night. You promised me."

"I know what I promised," Knightly said. He rubbed his eyes. "But that was before I knew about this kiss. There's no way I can let you go home now. Fans of this short little YouTube video will follow the series just to find out if this fairy tale between you and Brody has a happy ending. It's amazing publicity for the show."

On the one hand, Brody wanted to strangle the man for putting the success of his TV series before the needs of his daughter. On the other hand, he had no intention of continuing with the show if Madelyn wasn't the prize at the end of it.

"Publicity," Madelyn stated.

The crestfallen look on her face almost convinced Brody to give in and allow her to walk away.

Almost.

"I suppose I shouldn't expect anything more from a man who has spent the last six years pretending I'm not his daughter."

Without sparing either of them one last glance, Madelyn turned around and walked out of Knightly's makeshift office.

Brody wanted to chase after her, explain himself and convince her of his interest and budding feelings for her, but he suspected that nothing he said at the moment would be well received, and he had a few things he needed to clear up with Corbin Knightly.

MIDGE

After storming out of her father's office, Midge stood just outside the door, attempting to reign in her chaotic emotions. She wanted to cry, rant, and throw a few breakable items in the process, and she wasn't about to allow any of those things to happen in front of the crew, cameras, or contestants. She just needed a moment to cool her anger and steel her emotions. Her father's voice floated to her through the crack in the door.

"What is going on here, Brody? Are you feigning interest in my daughter? Has this all been some calculated attempt at getting in good with me? Because I don't trust your intentions one bit."

She heard Brody let out a frustrated sigh.

"Isn't that exactly what a playboy would do, Knightly? Get in good with the producer's daughter to further his own ambitions and get more favorable publicity for himself and the company he represents? I can just use her as a valuable resource for coaching me through this series. Or perhaps I can use her as a shield to avoid the advances of Felicia Davenport while simultaneously improving the viewers' opinion of me."

Midge swallowed down the bile rising to the back of her throat. It was just as she had feared. He wasn't interested in her, merely using her as every other man in her life had. She alone would never be enough to hold a man's interest, and Brody Prescott was solely interested in her usefulness, her ability to guide him through this mess he had landed himself in.

She clutched her chest and bit her lip to keep herself from letting out the gut-wrenching sob ready to explode from within. The two men she cared for most were concerned with their own publicity and success. She was a pawn in their Hollywood politics.

She silently sped off to the privacy of her bedroom, unwilling to listen to anymore of their poisonous, hurtful words.

Well, two could play at this game. If her father wasn't willing to cut her loose then her only option lay in convincing Brody to eliminate her, and she had a few ideas as to how to make that happen.

Look out, Brody Prescott. You're about to get torpedoed.

BRODY

Brody continued on with his sarcastic tirade.

"Or perhaps I find that your daughter is the most captivating creature to ever walk the face of this earth. Has it ever occurred to you that a man like myself might find your daughter to be someone worth loving?"

"Are you in love with her?" Knightly asked. The question was casually delivered, but Brody sensed the wrong response would bring out a side of Corbin Knightly he was less than eager to experience.

Brody took in a steadying breath and lowered his voice, aware he'd nearly been shouting at Knightly. "I've never fallen in love before, and in all honesty, I can't say that I've had enough time with Madelyn to get to that point, but what little time I *have* shared with her has shown me that caring for her and liking her are as easy and natural as breathing. Falling in love with her is a given. I want her in my life. The reason I tried to back out of the show was because I'd met Madelyn the very day I came to your office."

Knightly's eyes widened in surprised.

"You didn't agree to stay on due to my threats, did you?"

"I overheard you blackmailing her into standing in for that other contestant. I'm here for her. She's the only reason I agreed to continue on with this show. I have no intention of eliminating her. Ever."

The producer nodded, sizing him up as if seeing him for the first time.

"I'm allowing this to continue because of what I see in her eyes when she looks at you," Knightly said. "Midge does not trust easily. Most of her friends, boyfriends, and colleagues were interested in her because of her connection to me. Your feelings for her may be genuine, but she's been a means to an end far too many times, and this little feud we've had over the years hasn't helped either. Do you understand what you're up against?"

Brody nodded. "I think so."

"I can't guarantee you a happy ending, Brody. And I promise you, if you hurt my daughter I will do far more damage to your reputation than Felicia Davenport ever did."

"Understood."

"Okay, then. Good luck to you, man. You're certainly going to need it, and now I need to rethink the entire angle for this season's show."

"I'm hoping that means I can let Felicia go."

Knightly's concerned, fatherly demeanor changed, and in its place the director fully emerged.

"Are you crazy? Absolutely not. She's going to go insane with jealousy when she realizes you're pursuing Madelyn. I can't wait for the temper tantrums that are sure to follow." Knightly's face took on a gleeful cast. He'd just proved he cared for his daughter, but the director in him just couldn't seem to stay in the background for long.

Brody rubbed a tired hand over his face.

"You're kind of scary, Knightly."

Knightly gave him a wicked smile. "Glad you think so."

FELICIA

Felicia Davenport paced the white carpeted floor of her luxurious suite, glancing intermittently at her phone—it was a good thing she'd had the presence of mind to sneak her phone onto the shoot—where a YouTube video of Brody Prescott and Madelyn Knightly was prominently displayed for all the world to see.

One million views and counting.

Things were *sooooo* not going according to plan.

"How could you not know about this?" she asked the trembling contestant seated at the edge of her bed.

"I don't know...I...he never once brought her back to his apartment, never went on a single date with her. Their relationship must have developed right before the show started."

"A detail I've paid good money for you and your company to uncover and report. This no-name woman totally blindsided me tonight. It's obvious her father placed her on the show so she could continue to win Brody over, but he's supposed to fall in love with me. Not this dumpy redheaded nobody."

Felicia's methodical planning over the past several months had not included unexpected competition. Another rival for her rightful place at Brody's side. Her initial plan several months ago had involved bedding Brody and then faking a pregnancy where he'd have no other choice but to marry her. Once the divorce came, half of his fortune would be hers. The plan had been brilliant, perfect, until Brody had refused her invitation to join her in her apartment for drinks.

Refused *her*, of all people!

It ate at her, the idea that any man might not want her. It simply wasn't possible. Soon her obsession with snaring Brody began to outweigh her desire to swindle him for his billions. She had to convince him that his life was better with her rather than without her.

At first, she determined to ruin him for his callous rejection, hoping he would crawl back to her and beg her to be with him. Then when her private investigators discovered he was in talks with Corbin Knightly about shooting a reality TV series she knew she had to be on the show. It was perfect, really. Brody would see her in a different light, all would be forgiven as their love story played out on national television. Their engagement and subsequent marriage would be the talk of every existing social media platform. She'd make this man, this stupid, stupid man fall in love with her, and just maybe she would consider sticking around and loving him back.

And now this...this little girl thought she could win his heart.

She has no idea what I'm capable of, but she'll find out soon enough.

"I want to know everything about Madelyn Knightly. Her interests, her secrets, anything I can use to blackmail her into going away. Do you think you and your pathetic group of investigators can handle that?" She speared Liz with a dangerous look.

The contestant quickly agreed, pulling out her cell phone and rattling off instructions.

Felicia had thought it a stroke of genius to have a spy on the show using a completely different name, giving her useful details about the progress between Brody and any possible rivals. The young lady was good at her job, for the most part, and a little sabotage on her end would help maintain Felicia's standing in the competition.

The stakes for this game were high, and Felicia Davenport intended to win.

CHAPTER 14

Midge

Midge punched her pillow several times, picturing her father's face and then Brody's in quick succession. Each pummel with her fist filled her with a sense of sick satisfaction.

She'd been duped once again by her father's manipulative tactics, and now Brody had joined forces and was in on it.

She was stuck on the show at the mercy of the egotistical billionaire until he decided when to let her go. Confusion blossomed within her as she considered the conversation she'd overheard. It contradicted the soft side Brody had presented to her during their quick conversation before the diamond ceremony.

A man intent upon taking care of his own mother the way Brody had couldn't be capable of such cruel behavior. Could he? The consultant angle made more sense. Maybe he simply needed her there to coach him through this entire ordeal. He was in desperate need of a publicist, crafting a specific image for fans and viewers to latch onto, taking advantage of her many years in the film industry—like so many other men in her life had.

On the one hand, it made practical sense for Brody to use her like this. She might have agreed to the advantageous idea if he'd been upfront with her about his true motives. That nonsense about his interest in her being sincere instead of casual irked her. Why lie to her face when all he had to do was ask for her help? Her normally implacable feelings were now involved, and she was stuck on the show with a man who wanted nothing more than someone to groom him for live TV.

A devilish smile took hold of her features. Oh, the mischief she could make knew no bounds.

Jumping from her bed, she walked to her bedroom door and opened it, pausing for possible sounds of movement. Satisfied that most everyone was sleeping, she tiptoed across the hall, down the long, ornate staircase, and then made a sharp right toward the enormous kitchen. She needed food coloring. Purple, green, and blue to be exact. She nearly giggled at what she was about to pull. She hadn't pranked anyone like this since her freshman year of college.

She couldn't believe the level of immaturity she'd sunk to—just to get kicked off the show, but desperate times called for desperate acts of sabotage. It felt good to take back a little control. Nobody used Midge Knightly as a pawn in their own games.

Nobody.

Speaking of games, she wondered again what Felicia Davenport's endgame might be. As much as she hated the corner Brody had backed her into, she despised the snotty debutante even more. The little message she'd managed to slip into Midge's purse that evening had been so predictable.

"I'm warning you one last time. Leave Brody to the big girls, and I'm not referring to my size, which is a size four by the way."

Typical.

Before she left the show, she planned on revealing Felicia's secrets and exposing her real purpose for being here. Not to help Brody, of course. No. That woman simply deserved to be thwarted.

But first, round one of *Escape from Billionaire Island*.

Midge awoke from her troubled sleep with the sound of a surprised yell followed by a few angry expletives. She smiled and threw off the covers, rushing to her door and wrenching it open, but not before she placed an innocent yet concerned expression on her face.

It had been a little disconcerting to discover that Brody's room was not only on the same floor as hers, but also right across from it. She assumed the bachelor would be separated from the girls to avoid any hanky panky, though it wouldn't have been too hard for some determined contestants to find his separate quarters and infiltrate the premises.

As she looked across the hall and waited for Brody to emerge, she couldn't help but thank her lucky stars that he'd been up planning events with her father last night, leaving his room blessedly empty and free for her to roam about and enact part one of her plan. Her father really needed to consider putting locks on the doors. All sorts of people with nefarious intentions could do anything if they really wanted to.

She allowed herself a wicked smile, but quickly reached for that mask of innocent concern as Brody came flying out of his suite wearing nothing but a towel around his waist and appearing ready to throttle the next person he saw. She had to swallow hard at the surprising sight of his sculpted chest, well defined abdomen, and broad shoulders. They were spectacular to behold—even if they *were* tinted a deep shade of green.

Midge had found it convenient that he used body wash rather than regular soap. It was also helpful that his toothpaste had been in the shower along with his shampoo and face wash.

He was quite the primper for such a manly individual.

"Knightly," he shouted.

"Brody, what on earth happened?"

He turned to look at her in surprise and then gave her an ugly glower.

Midge studied her handiwork and did her best to keep her expression acceptably horrified.

He let out a feral growl, exposing his perfect porcelain teeth. Well, under normal circumstances they would have appeared porcelain, but at the moment they were dark purple. His normally jet black hair was now a shocking shade of blue. She noticed that some of the blue dye had managed to create spots along his chest and shoulders. He looked, Midge thought, absolutely perfect.

"It's like staring at a strange mash-up of The Hulk and Body-Builder Smurf." Midge said in awed tones. "I had no idea we were dressing up as one of the Avengers today. Can I be Black Widow?

He took a menacing step forward, but she was too mesmerized by the satisfying results of her sabotage to feel intimidated.

"How can we film today with me looking like this? Who in their right mind would put dye in my toiletries in the first place?"

Midge raised an eyebrow, giving him a coy look. "I'm sure it was simply someone interested in helping you with your image. You have to admit, this is quite an improvement."

Brody's eyes narrowed and he took another step forward.

"What are you saying, Midge?"

Her eyes widened coquettishly.

"Why, I'm simply offering up a possible answer to your question. Though I do have a few words of advice to go with it."

"And they are?" he asked through purple-gritted teeth.

"This particular individual will probably stop being so helpful as soon as you eliminate her from the show."

Brody's eyes bulged. "You...?" he choked.

She yawned, demonstrating her total indifference to his emotional state and her sheer boredom with the entire ordeal.

"Well, I'd better go get ready for the day. Wouldn't want to miss out on all the fun."

She spun around, allowing a wide grin to take over as she entered her room. She turned around just before shutting it and took in Brody's incoherent spluttering. She let him see her wicked grin for the first time, and his eyes narrowed even further.

"Half a cup of lemon juice and a few teaspoons of vinegar," she suggested in a cheery tone.

"What?"

"Scrub, scrub, scrub."

She closed the door in his face, allowing herself a good laugh in the process.

Midge took a victory lap around her expansive suite, humming the theme song to Rocky. She even threw in a few punches for good measure.

Success. There's no way he's keeping me here now.

Instead of getting ready for the day, she headed over to her laptop and turned it on with a happy sigh. She doubted The Hulk would be filming anything anytime soon.

Now that round one of her plan had been executed with some imaginative flair, it was time to find out a little more about Felicia Davenport.

BRODY

Brody stood gaping at Madelyn's closed door like an idiot with a mental disorder.

She'd sabotaged him and wanted him to know it was all her doing. He'd never expected this reaction from her. He assumed she might be upset at being tricked into staying on the show for a few hours, but then she would calm down and see the situation for what it truly was. A handsome billionaire intent on making her his own. He was a catch, wasn't he? He could have any woman he wanted. No one had ever turned him down, turned him away or...turned him green and blue...and purple.

Bottom line: no girl had ever put up so much resistance at the idea of dating him, sending him on a merry chase that was sure to drive him crazy in the long run, and before he knew it he was grinning, grinning at the closed door and still looking like a mentally disturbed moron in the process. His grin widened further. He couldn't believe her nerve, her fighting spirit, the lengths she had taken—and might possibly continue to take—to get eliminated.

If she thought she'd discourage him then it was clear she had no idea who she was dealing with. He was a predator and Madelyn Knightly was his prey. The harder she fought and the longer she ran the more compelled he would feel to chase her until she was good and caught—until she understood how he truly felt about her—and then he would make Madelyn Knightly his.

With one final shake of his head, he entered his room and ordered up some lemon juice and vinegar from one of the staff members. Madelyn may have won this round, but there were several more to go, and he intended to be the victor in the end.

MIDGE

Midge's research into Felicia's background turned out to be quite fruitful.

Finally.

The daughter of a rich senator from Virginia, Felicia had been kicked out of every private boarding school the senator had managed to place her in, probably by greasing the hands of certain school administrators if her pitiful academic career was any indication.

She might have felt sorry for the way Felicia's parents had handled her childhood if the young lady in question hadn't behaved like a heinous wench. She had a penchant for dating wealthy men, most of whom ended up dealing with one scandal or another around the time they were involved with the frightening debutante. Midge wondered if the airing out of those scandals had anything to do with Felicia. It couldn't be a coincidence.

She concluded that Felicia needed more investigating and decided doing something illegal might prove absolutely necessary if she intended to protect Brody from any further damage—er, that is, if she intended to nail this girl as Felicia most definitely deserved.

Taking her focus from her laptop, she dove into her monstrous handbag where any and every item imaginable tended to disappear and then reappear a few months later. Fortunately, a small pocket existed within the lining of her purse where her cell phone currently rested.

"Hello," said a sleepy voice.

"Lisa." Midge glanced at her wristwatch and cringed. Midnight her time meant three in the morning for Lisa.

"I'm so sorry. I didn't realize how late it was."

"Didn't realize—shouldn't you be getting home today?"

Midge snorted. "I wish." She quickly explained her current predicament. "I'll be on the show until Brody finally decides to let me go."

"You're kidding yourself if you think that man has any intention of ever saying goodbye to you. I saw that YouTube video of you guys making out. Sweet Heavens, it was hot! I can't believe you never told me you actually knew the guy."

"I don't know the guy. This whole thing has been a mistake."

"Or it's just plain fate. You don't seem to recognize how everything is coming together on your behalf."

"Lisa, I'm staying long enough to save him from his own bungling. To do that, I need some help from you. I'm interested in one of the contestant's backgrounds. Are you in the mood for a bit of sleuthing?"

"Really? You told me hacking computer systems would eventually land me in jail where I'd become some lonely woman's new prison wife."

"Harsh. I seriously doubt I put it quite like that."

"You described my future wife in vivid detail, right down to her buzzed head, tattooed forearms, and alarming chin hair."

Midge bit down on her bottom lip. "Are you telling me my speech actually convinced you to turn from your criminally lucrative ways?"

"Of course not, but I *did* spend the rest of the week checking to see if any unmarked vans were following me."

Midge rolled her eyes and then moved to the mini-kitchen to grab a bottled water from the fridge.

"Are you willing to help me out with this or not?"

"Who are we talking about, here?"

"Felicia Davenport. You know anything about her?"

"Only what the tabloids report. She accused Brody Prescott of breaching his company's privacy policies. It tanked the guys credibility."

"Yeah, well, she is one of the contestants for this season's show, and I'm trying to figure out her angle here."

"It's interesting that she, of all people, would be pursuing this reality TV series," Lisa mused.

"I know, right? She attacks the guy's image, and now she wants to be his wife? It doesn't make sense."

"Maybe Prescott's involved in something shady. How well do you know this guy?"

Midge considered skirting the details but decided Lisa would need the entire picture. She did her best to make her two pre-show run-ins with Brody sound as inconsequential and meaningless as possible.

"You're in love with Brody Prescott," Lisa squealed.

So epic fail on that.

"That's not at all what I said."

"Of course it is. Why else would you want me to dig up dirt on this woman? She's full of crap and you want to save your man by discrediting her claims. Bravo and brilliant. I'm super excited to start working on this."

"Lisa, you didn't hear a word I said. I simply want her to pay for her behavior. Plus, I don't like the idea of that woman ruining my father's show."

"Whatever. I'll start looking into her relationships with these other wealthy guys and check into her finances. Should make for some riveting reading."

"Just be careful, Lisa. Otherwise, that fictitious future wife of yours could become a full blown reality."

"I'll call you when I've got the goods."

Midge signed off and headed to bed. As she climbed under the cool, crisp sheets her thoughts returned to the handsome billionaire. He might be a ladies' man, but he'd still managed to build a business over the years and make it a success. She hadn't forgiven him for imprisoning her on the show, or for being so darn underhanded about it, but she didn't want him to lose everything he'd worked so hard for. What would the fallout do to his mother?

Yes. That's it. Blanche Prescott was a good, honest woman. She didn't deserve to watch her son's good image get dragged through the mud again, and that Felicia chick seemed more than capable of repeating history.

Having convinced herself that her desires to expose Felicia had nothing to do with her feelings for Brody, Midge finally fell asleep.

CHAPTER 15

Midge

The previous day ended up being a bust due to Brody's impromptu, full-body scrub down. She might have felt guilty for destroying her father's carefully planned schedule, but she figured he had it coming. Let his world get turned upside down for once. See how he liked it.

This day brought with it a full scheduled itinerary, signaling that Brody no longer resembled The Hulk.

What a shame.

Midge hadn't seen Brody since the previous morning, and anticipation coiled within her gut. She didn't necessarily want to see him. No, absolutely not. She wanted to see if he was still angry and how she might use that to her advantage. She wasn't scared to prod and push this particular bear until he yielded. It was better to focus on that than the atmosphere in the room.

Being surrounded by superficial beauties and cold, sterile cameras set Midge's nerves on edge. The air was heavy laden with floral shower gels, shampoos, and copious amounts of perfume, preventing her from inhaling enough oxygen to keep the room from tilting side to side. Either that or she was poised on the precipice of some monstrous panic attack.

As Les Lassiter and her father entered the room, the tittering and obnoxious laughter came to a screeching halt.

"Ladies, you all look lovely this morning. I'm sorry about the shooting delays from yesterday. We ran into a few technical issues we were forced to deal with," Les said.

Her father gave her a meaningful look. She returned it with an innocent smile.

Seriously? What was he gonna do? Kick her off the show?

Doubtful.

He couldn't even take away her trust fund at this point now that he was contractually obligated to hand it over so long as she abided by the terms and conditions set forth in her contract. And isn't that exactly what she was doing?

"I want to congratulate you on making it through the first round," Les said as her father moved to the side of the room and gave a few instructions to one of his crew. "We're going to continue on with the schedule and introduce our first group date."

"Oh, I hope I'm included in this first date," Charlene said, squeezing Midge's arm and bouncing in excitement.

She was so excited, in fact, Midge could have sworn the beautiful brunette caught some serious air in between each bounce. She oozed peppy cheerfulness. After the last two days Midge had suffered through, she was hardly in the mood to sit by someone so utterly enamored with her nemesis.

Annoying.

She turned her attention to Les as he whipped out a white envelope and paused to allow the cameras to catch the bubbling laughter and excitement. She figured the collective anticipation of the group allowed for her to shrink back and present her normal show of disinterest for a few precious moments.

As soon as the contestants were announced and left for their date, she would go upstairs and wait for her father to inform her that Brody had decided to cut her loose. She smirked—nearly allowed herself a wicked chuckle—as she remembered her creative genius where Brody's food coloring debacle was concerned.

Ha!

I am so going home today. I can already taste Giacomo's overpriced chocolate croissants.

Midge was so focused on the image of Brody, barreling out of his room, awash in green, blue, and purple food dye, she failed to grasp what was happening until her name was called.

"Congratulations," Charlene said, squeezing Midge's arm again—the girl had one monstrous grip on her. "I can't believe we're both going on this group date with Brody. Only eight other girls were called. I think those odds are much better than dealing with nineteen other women, don't you?"

Midge stared at Charlene, completely aghast, and then looked up to see other girls with expressions ranging from congratulatory to outright vengeful.

Felicia Davenport's looks being on the vengeful side.

"I guess it's no surprise you were called, though," Charlene whispered as Les continued on with his instructions.

"Why would you say that?" Her question came out sharper than she intended, but Charlene didn't seem to notice. Her obvious excitement between bounces kept her a bit preoccupied.

"Because," *bounce,* "he's already made a huge show of chasing you, what with that kiss on YouTube and all." *Bounce.* "Most of us girls got wind of it and watched it in Cambria's room." *Bounce.* "We had no idea you two dated before the show."

She couldn't believe this. How could she still be in the running after the stunt she'd pulled?

Midge let out a low moan and slumped back in her chair. "We didn't date before the show. That incident was...well...it was a one-time deal."

"Didn't look like that to me, but I think you're sweet so I'll try not to hate you for kissing my future hubby." *Bounce.* She gave Midge a friendly smile, and Midge couldn't help but smile back, deciding that being in Charlene's presence might not be such a trial after all.

The room became too quiet around her, the atmosphere filling with anticipation, and Midge turned her attention to the front of the room where Brody walked in, standing before them in dark jeans and a simple, navy blue tee. He looked absolutely amazing, seemingly unaffected by the drooling females.

His piercing blue eyes shot directly to hers and held her gaze. Her breath caught in her throat and a slow blush bloomed in her cheeks, causing Brody's eyes to darken just a little. A small hint of a smile graced his full lips.

His gaze moved to assess the rest of those assembled, and with its release she finally found the presence of mind to take in some much needed oxygen.

Bad. Her supercharged reaction to this billionaire was very bad. So round one hadn't been as effective as she'd hoped. Fine. Round two was sure to do some damage, or at least annoy the heck out of her father. Either way, someone had to pay for her continued presence here, and why not the two men who had manipulated her into staying?

Brody still wanted her there? So be it. Things were about to get nasty.

"As you all know, I enjoy hosting charity events in support of great causes such as Smile Train, Children International, and funding for cancer research. I've worked very hard to arrive at where I am today, but I never forget my roots or the struggles my mother and I went through when we lost my father to cancer. I now have the means to help others in similar situations, and it is something I love to do. I hope my future wife has similar interests in her community and in bettering the lives of others. So this group date is going to involved a trip to the Hawaii Children's Cancer Foundation in Honolulu, where we will be visiting children suffering from various forms of cancer in the hope that we can brighten their day and lift their spirits."

From a PR standpoint, this date was pure magic in demonstrating the kind of man Brody Prescott wished to portray himself as. From a personal standpoint, it made it that much harder for Midge to emotionally cut herself off from admiring this frustrating bachelor any more than she already did. The quickest way to Midge's heart was selfless caring for the needs of others.

Oh, Brody Prescott had his faults, but did he have to have so many admirable qualities that tended to override anything objectionable about him or his personality?

Brody caught her staring at him, and she averted her eyes, horrified that her soft, doe-eyed expression had probably been observed. He'd completely undone her cool aloofness with a simple suggestion of good will.

"We'll be leaving in twenty minutes, so I suggest you ladies grab whatever it is you think you'll need for the day, and meet me on the yacht scheduled to take us to the mainland."

Excited voices rose in volume as Brody left the women to collect themselves for the group date.

She noted Felicia following Brody's retreating form with a gaze that suggested she wanted nothing more than to spear him against the wall and demand she be brought along for the ride. She turned around and caught Midge's eye before Midge could look away.

"I suppose you think you hold some kind of allure for someone as mature and worldly as Brody Prescott, but if I were you, I'd consider backing down. I'd just hate to see you set yourself up for failure once he directs his attention on me."

She folded her arms across her chest, allowing her blood red nails to tap lightly on her forearm.

Midge noticed a camera to her left moving toward them. She let out an internal sigh of frustration. Just as her father had hoped, Felicia was ready to start the first round of meltdowns and drama, and Midge just had to be right in the middle of it.

She didn't feel like rising to the bait, but she knew her father would expect it, and any fans from the YouTube video would be eagerly waiting for her to defend her budding relationship between Brody and herself. Clamping down on her natural instinct to simply walk away from the conflict she ponied up and prepared herself to play the part.

"Right, because he looked so eager to include you on this group date. Oh, that's right. You didn't receive an invitation. Must have something to do with those slanderous accusations concerning his company's privacy policies."

Felicia's eyebrow twitched and then settled, letting Midge know her verbal jab had hit its mark. Felicia studied her fingernails, behaving as if Midge's comment didn't concern her.

"Water under the bridge, my dear. He knows it was a complete misunderstanding, and since then we've kissed and made up."

"I highly doubt that. The only person in this room who's had the undeniable pleasure of kissing Brody is me." Midge leaned forward as if ready to impart some monumental secret. "You can YouTube the kiss for confirmation, and I'd just love it if you would subscribe to our channel."

Felicia's eyebrows narrowed, while her nails dug into her forearm.

She shoots, she scores.

"This isn't over, you little impostor."

Felicia turned on her heel and exited the room, her hair barely clearing the door frame as she passed. Midge absentmindedly wondered what would happen if her hair ever managed to collide with the frame. The detailed carvings at the top would probably end up with one mighty indentation.

Midge's father mimed his applause from the corner of the room.

"Perfect," he mouthed, sending her a proud papa bear smile.

She shook her head in disgust and reluctantly willed herself to move one dragging foot in front of the other toward the main hall. She fought for a possible out to this group date, not because she was opposed to visiting sick children in a hospital. On the contrary, she loved volunteering for activities like that, but she knew watching Brody in that kind of environment would completely undermine her attempts at detachment. She did *not* want to spend any extra time with him and risk more opportunities for bonding with the insufferable man.

No surprise she was the last person standing in the hallway. The crew and contestants had already flown out the front door. She felt a hand latch onto her arm and quickly spin her around.

Brody stood before her with a cheeky smile on his face. He appeared annoyingly well rested. Not a hint of anger graced his perfectly chiseled face.

Curse the man!

Her heart caught in her throat as she took in his freshly washed hair—no longer blue. A dark lock curled just above his forehead. The navy blue of his casual shirt brought out flecks of gray in his cobalt eyes.

Would she ever get used to her initial reaction to him?

"Unhand me, Judas." Her delivery was more forceful due to how shaken she was to see him sans righteous outrage. She checked the area for cameras and then leveled him with a glare once she was certain they were alone.

His smile deepened, which made her slant her eyes and wrench her arm from his grasp.

"Still angry that I kept you on the show, I see."

"How observant of you. I suppose the food dye probably clued you in."

"Look, Madelyn, I know you're upset with me—"

"Upset? I get upset when my computer crashes and I haven't saved my latest additions to my manuscript. I get upset when I'm drinking hot cocoa and I realize that Giacomo accidentally added skim milk to it instead of cream—although I'm nearly positive he does this on purpose. I get upset when I'm in the middle of my manuscript and find that I've written my protagonist into a corner. Those are legitimate reasons for getting upset. When someone—I'll refrain from dropping names here—refuses to disqualify a contestant due to selfish, egocentric desires, I am beyond upset. I'm...I'm...absolutely..."

"Still upset then."

Brody inched closer and placed both hands on her shoulders. The movement stopped her embarrassing stutters, but the tingling sensation shooting through her arms was an unwelcome reminder of the feelings she'd allowed herself to develop for him. After the stunt she'd pulled, she was supposed to feel like the victor. Cool. Calm. Collected. Yet Brody was the one behaving as if he'd already won. He should have been angry. Why wasn't the gorgeous bachelor seething with fury?

"Midge, I couldn't let you go. Don't you understand my reasons for keeping you here? Don't you see how much I need you?" He gave her a soul-searching look which only succeeded in upping her level of anger.

"Oh, yes. I'm indispensable when it comes to advising you on how best to survive this rat race you've landed yourself in."

Confusion wiped the smoldering look from his gaze.

"Midge, that's not at all—"

"Save it." She shrugged him off and took a step back. "I dislike this game you've been playing. Don't pretend you want me here for more personal reasons. It's plain mean, and I really thought you were better than that." She turned around and ran up the stairs, heading to her room for her purse.

BRODY

The yacht was enormous. Brody hardly understood how this great monstrosity could be called a yacht when it nearly passed for a small cruise ship. He'd been instructed to wait in the dining area of the ship so the cameras could roll as the girls walked in and noticed the elaborate luncheon prepared for them.

He found the thought of food unappealing, considering the turbulent flutterings in his stomach as he waited for Madelyn to walk through the door. He could have done without the group date and the extra people attending what would have otherwise been a fairly romantic luncheon with the only girl he cared about.

Brody's thoughts whirled in confusion as he thought of Madelyn. How had she misconstrued his feelings for her into something completely different? It definitely explained the dye in his toiletries. He thought back to Knightly's clear warning about her inability to trust easily. This was obviously a manifestation of that particular insecurity. He had to push through it and convince her of his genuine interest and affection.

Glancing around the room, he took in the windows on either side that opened up the vast expanse of ocean. He admired the magnificent swells and shifts of its frothy blue water where ocean met skyline. It seemed the waves were doing their best to reach the sky and offer it a few loving caresses, intent on joining its endless expanse. Or maybe it was coaxing the sky to join its watery depths below.

He felt very much like those waves, reaching for something as glorious, pristine, and inaccessible as Madelyn Knightly. He doubted he deserved her, but he didn't care. He needed her, he wanted her, and he wasn't above admitting that he was selfish enough to pursue her regardless of how undeserving he might be.

Les Lassiter and Corbin Knightly entered the room with two cameramen behind them. Brody suspected those two were thick as thieves, plotting the best way to drum up a little drama on the show.

"Okay, so remember what we discussed yesterday," Corbin said, rubbing his hands together in what looked like anxious anticipation. "One of the angle's of this show is going to be about this developing relationship between you and Midge. It may be a group date, but I want her with you for most of the time on this one. Do your best to give attention to the other women, but we need to see this obvious connection between you and my daughter."

"I haven't got a single problem with that idea. You talked to Madelyn about this, didn't you?"

Knightly glanced down at his nonexistent wristwatch. "They'll be here any second people. Roll 'em."

"Knightly?" Brody took a step toward the director's retreating figure, apprehension clawing at his stomach as he realized none of it had been discussed with Madelyn. He did *not* look forward to her displeasure.

Charlene stepped into the room first, full of smiles and air kisses. He did his best to hide his disappointed grimace as he turned on his killer smile and held out his arms to greet her.

"This is amazing," Charlene said as she gave him a rather enthusiastic hug.

"I wish I could take credit for the ship, but I'm merely a passenger," Brody said.

He continued to greet his "dates" with their exuberant hugs, wishing for all he was worth that Madelyn would arrive so he could enfold her in an embrace that actually meant something to him. He was in the middle of another long, enthusiastic hug from a young, petite thing by the name of Cambria when Madelyn stepped in appearing a bit too resigned to her fate. He noted heat creep up her cheeks and her eyes narrow as she took in the last second of his embrace with Cambria.

Is she jealous?

As he stepped toward her, he took note of her stilted smile which failed to reach her eyes. Without giving her a chance to avoid it, he scooped her in his arms, reveling in her acceptance of his attentions even though he recognized that the cameras were rolling and she didn't have much choice.

"It feels so good to hold you," he whispered next to her ear. He thought her body shivered slightly at his proximity, and his grin widened. She placed her hands against his chest and applied some pressure, but he only allowed her to remover herself an inch or so, just enough to look up at his face.

"I would think you'd had your fill of holding women this afternoon, and with so many willing partners." Her tone was light and airy, but he noted the bitter edge to it.

She was definitely jealous. He could barely contain his triumphant grin.

Perhaps he'd put that knowledge to good use and teach her a little lesson for that ridiculous prank she'd pulled on him.

He heard a throat clear and realized the room had become rather quiet. Turning around, he saw many of the girls had taken seats at the table and were watching him and Madelyn with speculative looks on their faces. Some he might have labeled calculating. A few disgruntled looks of jealousy graced other faces at the table, all directed at the girl in his arms.

He cursed himself for unwittingly painting a target on her back.

"Ladies, we're going to have a quick little luncheon as we make our way to Oahu." When he reached for her hand, he noticed a large bandage on her palm and quirked an inquiring brow. She shook her head, indicating she didn't wish to talk about it at the moment.

He couldn't imagine how she'd had time to sustain an injury since they'd parted company not twenty minutes earlier.

He guided Madelyn to a seat beside him.

Once seated, she discreetly pulled her arm from his and rested it on her lap. A muscle in her jaw twitched, the only sign of her obvious displeasure at the situation. Otherwise, she was the perfect picture of an excited contestant.

As the meal got started and chatter began to lighten the tense atmosphere, he found himself answering far too many personal questions and doing most of the talking.

"Do you have any pictures of yourself as a little baby?" Cambria asked.

"You'll have to ask my mother," Brody answered. "She's the one who has my pictures and Little League Trophies. She documented my most embarrassing moments, waiting for the chance to share them with some unsuspecting date."

"She did that often?" Madelyn asked. It was her first question during the lunch, and it quite delighted him that she had finally started participating.

"I rarely brought girls home to my mother in high school or college. I never really dated."

"I don't believe that for one second," Charlene said. "You must have had thousands of girls chasing after you."

"I can honestly tell you I didn't."

"Well, when it comes to women, do you have a type? Do you love brunettes?" Charlene gave him a winning smile which he couldn't help but reciprocate. She was actually quite delightful, and he might have been interested in pursuing her if he hadn't already been captivated by the woman seated next to him. He noticed Madelyn shift uncomfortably in her seat, appearing unhappy with his interest in Charlene.

Perfect.

"I am always interested in an attractive brunette," he said, making Charlene blush a rosy color. The other girls in the room let out silly giggles. "I'm also a fan of beautiful blonds," he directed his look at Cambria, enjoying the heat that rose to her cheeks as well. "And lately, I've found myself thoroughly intrigued by redheads, especially ones with curly hair and just a smattering of freckles."

He turned to Madelyn, giving her a tiny smile, and like a stealthy predator, he slowly brought his hand up and snatched her glasses off her nose. Madelyn let out a surprised gasp.

"What a coincidence, Madelyn," he said, staring at the bridge of her nose and giving her a wink. "Freckles. I do believe I'm in love."

The rest of the girls let out more silly giggles at his playfulness.

"May I have my glasses back, please?" Her lips quirked into a genuine smile, and his own widened in response.

"Only if you promise to put them in your purse so I don't have to go searching for those freckles again."

"Fine. I shall concede to your demands during lunch, but after that they go back on."

"As you wish." He handed the glasses to Madelyn and watched as she put them in her purse and met his look with a rueful grin.

"You'll be the death of me," she muttered under her breath.

Funny. He felt the same way.

CHAPTER 16

Midge

The group date had gotten off to a rough start when Midge went back to her suite to grab her purse, reached in for some lipstick, and cut herself on something sharp. When she'd dug into her purse, she'd found her small pocket knife open and much sharper than she remembered. She couldn't imagine how it had snapped open like that, but the gash in her palm was deep and painful. She'd had to hurriedly disinfect the area, bandage it with the staff's first aid kit, and then rush to the boat.

Fortunately, she didn't think she needed stitches. Unfortunately, it took a while for the pain to subside into a dull throb. It was an annoying nuisance that failed to distract her from Brody's unwanted attentions or the delectable smell of his aftershave. Rather, the throbbing in her hand acted as a soundtrack for the frustrating circumstances she found herself in.

She had to admit that his unguarded answers to everyone's questions, and the charming way in which he delivered them, prompted her to ask one of her own to which she immediately chastised herself. She needed to manage an air of disinterest toward Brody without the cameras picking it up. No small feat in the world of acting, something she was in no way proficient at.

Appearing completely engrossed in the charismatic billionaire while feigning indifference that she in no way felt was a serious drain to the emotions, not to mention her own mental state.

And the darn hand just keeps on throbbing.

The boat couldn't have docked fast enough in her opinion, and by the time everyone disembarked she found herself starved, having been too keyed up to do anything other than move her food around her plate.

There were two limousines awaiting the unorthodox dating party. Midge hardly paid attention to where Brody headed, praying that everyone else would hold back to see which limousine he deigned to grace with his presence and pile in after him. She just wanted a quiet moment to herself, her thoughts, and the increasing pain in her hand so she ambled toward the closest one and collapsed within it, firmly closing the door behind her.

She closed her eyes and hoped for silence but was disturbed by the opening of the door. She kept her eyes shut, hoping to dissuade anyone from talking to her.

"Driver, you can proceed to the hospital without waiting for any other contestants," said a low voice.

Midge sat up straight, turning in surprise as she beheld Brody sitting next to her, a thin frown turning down the corners of his mouth.

"What happened to the other contestants?" she asked.

"They're in the other limo. I thought you and I could take this limo by ourselves so we can talk for a few moments."

Midge opened her mouth to let out some scathing remark, but her eyes suddenly caught the lens of the camera across from them.

Great Heavens above, this was not the kind of escape she'd had in mind. Quickly plastering a smile on her face she turned to Brody and said, "How fortunate for me. Why do I get the special treatment and not some other contestant? This is a group date, after all."

Brody leaned over and took her bandaged hand in his, examining it.

"That's very true. However, I didn't kiss any of those girls before the start of the show, and I feel like we need to finally take the time to clear the air on that score. I'm a little surprised to find you here, especially after that smack you gave me."

Midge's discomfort level increased ten-fold. She was not about to acknowledge that kiss or the unsettling affect it had on her on national television. Her personal life was being invaded enough at the moment. She also felt this nagging suspicion that her presence here wasn't as much of a surprise to Brody as he let on. Still, she supposed they *did* need to clear the air since the viewers would be wondering why they hadn't discussed their previous history the very first day.

But she didn't want to.

"I...uh...Brody, I do want to discuss this at some point, but I'm a little distracted at the moment." She held up her bandaged hand and gave Brody a tremulous smile.

Immediate concern flashed across his features.

"Madelyn, what happened to your hand?"

She couldn't believe she'd just played the sympathy card to avoid the conversation.

He began unwrapping the bandage, taking note of the blood seeping through the two ineffective Band-Aids.

"I always carry a Swiss Army Knife with me just in case I need it for something. My father gave it to me when I was twelve, and I never leave anywhere without it. For some reason it was open when I stuck my hand in my purse."

"This looks deep. I think we need to have a doctor look at this when we reach the hospital."

"That's not necessary." She attempted to pull her hand from his, but he refused to relinquish it. "I'm sure it will be fine once the bleeding stops."

"I think it needs stitches. We're definitely getting this looked at. You don't want it to become infected."

"But—"

"Let me take care of you, Madelyn." His eyes pleaded with her. He reached into his pocket, revealing a granola bar and placing it in her good hand.

"What's this for?" she asked in surprise.

"You didn't eat anything on the yacht, and now I know why. Your poor hand must be throbbing."

She watched mesmerized as he placed two tender kisses on the tips of her fingers, and then lifted his eyes to ensnare hers.

"I didn't want you to go without any food while we were at the hospital."

She swallowed the ball of emotion lodged in her throat. It was simply too much. He had noticed her lack of appetite. He was concerned enough to grab a snack for her in case she needed it. Brody Prescott was making it very difficult to despise him at the moment.

"Thank you," she whispered as one traitorous tear escaped down her cheek. She blamed it on the pain in her hand and the unexpected duration of her stay on the show. Brody's kind gesture had nothing to do with it. Nothing.

He reached his hand up to catch the tear with an upturned finger.

"You are so welcome, Madelyn."

His lips hovered inches from hers and he studied her face with those beautiful eyes of his. She felt he saw far more than she wanted him too, but failed to tear her gaze away. Just as it seemed like he might close the distance and grace her lips with his, the driver spoke up from the front.

"We've arrived at the Cancer Foundation, Mr. Prescott."

Midge blinked her eyes, bringing herself back to the present, cursing herself for becoming distracted enough to forget that the cameraman was filming absolutely everything.

How had he managed to so thoroughly entrance her with a few simple words and a small act of kindness? She was supposed to be discouraging him from keeping her on the show, not encouraging some kind of rapport with these supercharged interludes.

Her submarining was being submarined!

"Let's get a doctor to take a look at your hand."

Brody opened the door, stepped out, and helped her from the limo, guiding her through the hospital doors.

One numbing shot to the hand and ten stitches later, Madelyn said thank you to the grandfatherly doctor attending her and accepted a prescription for a few pain killers.

Madelyn considered taking one or two for the first day, but decided she would be able to handle any lingering pain after that. Growing up with her mother's various addictions had convinced Midge that it was never a good idea to become dependent on anything...or *anyone* for that matter.

Brody had wished to stay—for moral support—but her father insisted he make the rounds with the contestants and visit the children who were expecting him. He only relented once Knightly agreed to personally deliver Midge to Brody's side.

"What are you, my jailer?" she asked her father after Brody reluctantly disappeared with Charlene trailing after him.

Her eyes followed their retreating forms as an unfamiliar pang of jealousy struck her hard in the gut. She did not like Charlene's arm tucked neatly within Brody's.

Her father gave her a smirk and wrapped a loving arm around her shoulder.

"You like him, Midge girl, and don't even try to pretend you don't. You can't fool your father."

"I'm not trying to fool anyone. He's here for a specific reason, and so am I. Neither of which entails a serious relationship."

"You're delusional if you think this guy isn't into you."

Midge leaned her head against his shoulder and sighed. "You and Brody are cut from the same cloth. It's all about business and the bottom line with you two. I have to love you because you're my father, but I don't have to put up with Brody's ambitious behavior. I'm not his pawn in this."

Knightly turned her to look at him. "Of course you're not his pawn. If I'm not mistaken, you mean much more to him than that."

"Save it, Dad. Let's talk about something else."

Knightly studied her for a few more seconds and then shrugged his shoulders as if to say, "Women!" Grabbing her elbow as the doctor finished up, he helped her stand and guided her down the hall.

"You know, I always wanted to take you to Hawaii for one of my trips. Can you imagine the fun we'd have had learning how to hula dance?"

Midge let out a soft chuckle. "Please. You and I both know the only one doing any dancing would have been me. Your true joy in life is to put me in the most embarrassing situations and then turn the camera on. Pure torture, Dad."

"It was never meant to be torture, Midge girl. I just wanted to hold on to you and your childhood for as long as I possibly could. Those cameos of yours are memories I get to revisit whenever I miss you."

Midge gave him a surprised glance. "If you ever miss me you know where I live. Come by and visit sometime."

"I believe I'll have to take you up on that offer, and soon. It's nice to know you still keep that pocket knife I got you all those years ago." He turned her to face him and planted a kiss on her forehead, a rare show of affection that nearly brought tears to her eyes. "Brody should be in one of these rooms along this hallway. Go find him while I check on some administrative garbage."

Midge nodded and watched as her father quickly headed in the opposite direction. The entire conversation had been unusual. The damage his high-handed ultimatum had done six years ago hadn't been remedied, but she thought that perhaps this was the first step toward healing.

Her musings distracted her from noticing she'd opened up a storage closet instead of an actual hospital room. Staring at the shelves of hospital supplies, she let out a self-deprecating snort and shook her head at her own silliness. Just as she went to shut the door, she felt a hard shove from behind which sent her sailing into the closet. She lost her balance and used her hands to catch her fall. A sharp stab of pain alerted her to the possibility of split stitches, but she didn't have enough light to assess the damage once the door slammed shut behind her.

Midge didn't feel ashamed to admit that the dark terrified her. She stood up on shaky legs and inched her way to the door. Sliding her hands across the surface, she finally located the knob and turned it.

Locked.

What in the world? It hadn't been locked before. She slid her hands along the sides of the door and finally felt the outline of a light switch. The neon fluttering of the stilted light gave her a modicum of peace as she surveyed the small storage room and then returned her focus to the doorknob, looking for any clues as to how to unlock it, but it appeared that the lock was on the outside, meaning someone had intentionally locked her in.

Which made absolutely no sense. Why would one of the hospital staff push her into a closet and then lock the door? She began to beat the wooden door with her good fist while screaming at the top of her lungs.

"Madelyn," she heard from the other side of the door. "Why is this door locked?" The knob jiggled under Brody's grip, and then he banged against the door.

"Yes. It's me. I'm here."

"How on earth did you get locked in? What is this, anyway?"

His voice sounded highly amused at her predicament. She might have thought this was payback for the prank she'd pulled on him earlier, but she doubted he would have done anything this cruel. He would never have pushed her so forcefully as to cause her injury.

"I was looking for some extra bandages and the door closed and locked itself behind me," she said, deciding to keep what had really happened to herself.

His chuckles drifted through the door, making her both annoyed and slightly amused at his reaction.

"I'm going to grab one of the staff to get you out of here," he shouted. "Oh, wait. Excuse me, do you have a key to this room? My girlfriend got herself locked in there."

Girlfriend? Over my dead body.

The door abruptly opened, and Brody stood with his arms held out, fully expecting her to rush into them. "Consider yourself rescued, young lady. I believe your hero deserves an appreciative kiss."

She quirked an eyebrow at him, taking note of the cameraman standing behind Brody.

"Is that so? Then I suppose it would be unthinkable to deny my rescuer his just rewards." She turned to the male nurse with keys dangling from his hands. Grabbing his face, she planted a soft lingering kiss on his lips and then stepped back. "I thank you from the bottom of my heart for unlocking and then opening such a heavy, unmanageable door."

The young man gave her a shocked look and then his lips broke into a delighted smile.

"If there are more of you ladies locked in storage closets, I vow to never take a sick day ever again."

Midge smirked at Brody and headed toward the next room. She paused long enough to look back at Brody and take in his annoyed grimace, the chuckling cameraman, and the smitten male nurse.

"Are you coming, Mr. Prescott?"

Then she sailed into the room, ready to visit her first child of the day.

Ah, sweet victory. How I've missed you.

"What is your favorite fairy tale?" Midge asked. "Perhaps I can read it to you." She was seated on a chair near the bed of an eleven-year-old girl named Claire. Claire had several books at her disposal, a collection of fairy tales that every child had been given, donated by none other than Brody Prescott. His charity work was just one more item that made him difficult to resist.

The young girl's hazel eyes sparkled at the question. She pointed to a large picture hanging on the wall across the room. Midge studied the child-like rendition of a prince chasing a young princess down a long staircase. At the bottom of the steps, a glass slipper stood waiting to be discovered.

"Cinderella?"

Claire nodded her head, but leaned close to her as if to whisper something important.

"It's a Cinderella fairy tale about you. I saw your kiss with Mr. Prescott on the internet. It was really romantic."

"Oh!" Midge's face took on a whole new shade of scarlet. "Well, I can certainly read Cinderella to you if you'd like."

Claire had lost her hair due to ongoing chemo treatments, and her skin was pale and translucent, but the beauty of her face and the sweet hope tucked within her expression gave her a courageous appearance. That courage, seemingly misplaced in her current circumstances, gave Midge the desire to pull her close and hold her for as long as time might permit. Perhaps that wonderful fortitude would rub off on Midge and see her through something a million times less daunting than the ravaging affects of cancer. It certainly humbled her to be in Claire's presence.

"Can you pretend to be Cinderella instead?"

Midge didn't know quite how to respond to that.

"If she gets to play Cinderella can I be the prince?" a gruff voice asked.

Midge glanced up as Brody strode into the room with a cheeky grin.

Claire clapped her hands in delight. "Yes. That's what I want. You're the handsome prince who sweeps her off her feet."

"Well," Midge still hesitated, uncertain as to how this should play out. "Do you want me to read Cinderella's part and Brody can read Prince Charming's?"

"Give me the book, and I can narrate. Then you two act out everything I say."

She had a very bad feeling about this, but one look at the excited expression on Claire's face was enough for Midge to agree to anything so long as it brought Claire the happiness she deserved.

"All right. I think Brody and I can act out a scene or two." She stood and walked to the middle of the room. "Do you think Mr. Prescott's acting skills will be up to par?" she asked Claire in a teasing tone.

"You two won't be acting at all since you totally love each other already." Claire's pronouncement had Midge raising two bemused eyebrows while Brody let out a hearty chuckle.

"I do believe the young lady has a point, Madelyn...darling."

Claire let out an infectious giggle, and Midge shook her head at the term of endearment he threw in, finding it difficult to stay cross with him for taking advantage of a situation that was clearly making Claire's day. She figured he hadn't finished paying her back for the prank she'd pulled on him.

"Once upon a time," Claire began, "there was a girl who lost her mother at a young age. The loss left Cinderella and her father completely devastated." Claire continued the narrative giving Midge instructions to kneel in grief at the side of her bed.

"Like this?" Midge asked.

"Yes, but you should be crying. You just lost your mom, silly."

"Oh." Midge let out a few soft wails and sniffed, wiping away imaginary tears.

"Seriously? It's your mom we're talking about. This isn't even believable. A little more crying would be nice. You're devastated, remember?"

Midge let out a few more high-pitched wails and threw herself across the foot of the bed, adding a few sniffs and hiccups in for good measure.

"So much better," Claire said, patting her head.

"Glad you approve." Midge peeked up at Brody when she heard a muffled chuckle. His eyes danced in merriment.

"Cinderella's father decided it would be best to remarry, but the woman he chose was cruel in spirit and cold at heart, and her daughters followed in her footsteps." Claire set the book down, and gave them both a disgruntled look. "Such a bad idea. You have to wonder if he married the first desperate widow he came across. You'd think he would have done a background check or something."

Midge buried her face in the covers so as not to laugh while Claire continued her narrative.

"Within months of marriage the father passed away—probably poisoned by his psycho wife."

Midge's head shot up. "Does it actually say that in the book?"

"Cinderella was put to work as a slave in her own home...blah blah blah..." Claire flipped the pages and scanned them before stopping at a page and slamming her finger down.

"While she spent her days cleaning, she grew beautiful of form and face. She was kind and loving to everyone she knew. She also had the loveliest singing voice and always sang while she cleaned." Claire grabbed Midge's arm. "Okay, now you have to sweep the floor and sing "'A Dream Is A Wish Your Heart Makes.'"

Midge gave her a suspicious look as she pretended to sweep the floor. "Isn't that Disney's version of Cinderella? I don't think that song is in your book."

"If Claire says it's in the book then we best comply with her wishes, don't you think?" Brody's smile was all innocence.

Midge glanced at Claire and noticed the exuberant way she clasped her hands to her heart, a sweet dimple gracing her cheek.

She continued sweeping while she sang her own rendition of the song. After finishing up the last chords, she took a sweeping curtsy while Claire and Brody applauded her performance.

"I didn't know you could sing," Brody said. His appreciative glance was difficult to ignore.

"Hush, Charming. It's not your turn to talk yet." Claire flipped through her pages while Brody mimed the process of zipping his lips shut.

"Cinderella wants to go to the ball...her stupid step-mom won't let her... fairy godmother comes...here is the dress...okay, now she is at the ball. Charming, you're going to see her and fall madly in love. Then you ask her to dance."

Brody paused for a moment to take in Midge, his eyes widened in feigned surprised, and then he dramatically raised his fist to his chest. Rushing over, he grabbed Midge's hands in his and brought them to his lips while Claire let out a few more giggles.

"I'm madly in love with you which means you have to dance with me."

"No! No!" Claire shouted between fits of laughter. "That was terrible. You can't tell her you're madly in love with her before she even knows you. Do you want to freak her out?"

"In fairy tales everyone falls in love at first sight."

"Get to know her first or she'll think you're a psycho."

Midge chuckled. "Oh, believe me, this type of approach is normal for our dear Prince Charming."

"You wound me, madam." He raised another fist to his chest and staggered back as if someone had stabbed him.

"Take it from the top, and this time try to be smooth instead of lame."

Brody pretended to be offended at Claire's assessment of his acting skills. He marched back a few steps, turned around, and began the whole thing all over again. This time he left out his declaration of love.

"I'm convinced there is no one else at this ball lovelier than you, miss. Would you honor me with a dance?"

"Oh, that was much better," Claire said.

"I would be delighted." Midge allowed Brody to lead her into a waltz while Claire hummed "A Dream Is A Wish Your Heart Makes."

"What is your name?" Brody asked.

"I am called Cinderella."

"What a lovely name. Most people refer to me as—"

"No. She's not supposed to know you're the prince until the end," Claire said.

"How is she supposed to fall in love with me if she doesn't know who I am?" he said.

"With true love's first kiss, silly. Haven't you ever read the book? Cinderella, you have to tell him it's time for you to go."

Midge placed the back of her hand against her forehead and sighed, "I'm afraid I must leave you now. My feet are killing me, and I haven't had a thing to eat."

"That's not at all how the story goes," Brody said.

"It makes sense, though," Claire said. "I mean, the prince dances with her the whole time and never offers her food or a chance to rest." She picked up the book and flipped through a few pages, shaking her head in disgust. "He doesn't even get her some punch. Rude much?"

"Actually, our handsome prince did give me a granola bar on the way over here." Midge pulled it out and opened it, taking a quick bite and closing her eyes to savor it.

"You've totally redeemed yourself, fair prince." Claire clapped her hands in approval.

"You still haven't eaten that thing? We've been here for nearly an hour."

"I was getting stitches. I can't eat while someone is sticking a needle and thread in my hand."

"Nauseating," Claire said in agreement.

"Now that I've had a bite of my snack I think I would like some punch," Midge said.

"Are you serious?" Brody asked.

"You heard the woman. I have some water in this pitcher over here." Claire indicated the small pitcher and glass that looked untouched.

"Your wish is my command."

Brody dashed to the pitcher, poured the water, and rushed to her side. Midge delicately sipped the water—making sure to lift her pinky finger in the process—and set it down on the nearest table.

"I do believe it's time for me to leave before I turn into a pumpkin."

"This is not at all how the scene plays out in the book or any of the movies for that matter," Claire complained. "Cinderella needs to rush to the door, and then Charming has to chase after her, stopping her before she is able to escape."

"I'm pretty sure she gets away in the books," Midge said.

Claire thumbed through the pages and looked up. "Not in *my* book."

"Fine." Midge did her best to delicately run towards the door. Just as she placed her hand on the doorknob, she felt Brody grab her around the waist and spin her to face him.

"You'll not get away from me, Cinderella. There are still two waltzes, an 'Electric Slide', and 'The Macarena' to contend with. Not to mention a possible encore of 'Cotton-Eyed Joe.'"

"Totally off script, but I'll allow it," Claire said. "Now, Cinderella has to protest."

"If you don't allow me to leave your little island post haste, I'll be forced to do something absolutely horrific, and if you think food coloring is bad you ain't seen nothing yet."

Claire grunted in frustration. "You guys are terrible at ad-libbing. Prince Charming, how are you going to respond to that?"

"There isn't a single thing you could threaten me with that would scare me more than the thought of you permanently walking out of my life."

"Wow. That'll do. Cinderella, you should definitely be swooning by now but fighting super hard to resist his charms, even though we all know it's a lost cause. You've already fallen for him."

Midge didn't like how her words hit so close to the truth, but seeing as how she had no way out of her current predicament she continued to play her part to perfection.

"You couldn't possibly want me to join this world of yours. I'm just a college student with lofty goals that have yet to come to fruition. I wouldn't fit in with you royals."

She'd planned on saying something having to do with being home by midnight and then that came out. What in the world was wrong with her? Brody's playful expression grew serious as he moved his hands to the small of her back and pulled her to him.

"You're not new to this classy scene, nor are you someone who is terribly impressed by it. You're kind, honest, ambitious, selfless, funny, and you genuinely care about other people. I love life when I'm living it with you. I don't want you to go. Please stay."

Midge swallowed hard. "You could have anyone at the ball. I can't believe you would want me. At least, not for the right reasons."

"Believe it, Madelyn. Believe that my reasons are always right where you're concerned."

Midge had no idea what to say to that. She wanted so badly to believe him. To believe that his motives were pure, but she remembered what she'd overheard and didn't know what to do. Just as she was about to throw caution to the wind and allow herself to place her faith in the affection Brody offered, she heard a slight whirring noise to her right. Out of the corner of her eye she noticed the crewman manning the camera through a connecting door. She had no idea how long he'd been there, but she figured it had been from the moment Brody entered the room.

Her heart nearly broke as she realized that this had all been a show. Of course, it had started out as merely make-believe, a way to entertain a young girl who deserved something fun and meaningful to lift her spirits, but it had taken such a serious and personal turn. Yet the farce had never ended, she simply hadn't been able to separate fiction from reality.

"Now you kiss her, Charming," Claire said in a hushed voice.

Midge caught her breath, knowing full well there was absolutely no way she could deny Brody a kiss. It was part of Claire's Cinderella recreation.

Brody didn't hesitate as he dipped his head and brought his lips to hers. She intended it to be a short, light kiss on the lips, but Brody had other ideas. He pulled her flush against him and deepened their kiss, demanding more than she'd planned to give. The kiss completely bypassed her mental resistance as the heat of his mouth and the possessive power of his arms took swoon-worthy to a whole new level. With her thoughts on stand-by and her lips fully participating in the rhythm and cadence of his affections, she wholly lost herself to Brody Prescott, completely forgetting the reasons against such a compromising situation and only recognizing everything that made her all for it.

He finally ended the kiss with a soft sigh and moved back to study her face, possibly checking for her reaction.

"That was pure perfection. Just as good as the kiss on YouTube," Claire declared.

"So glad the reenactment was a success," Midge said in a breathy voice. She pulled herself out of Brody's embrace and walked over to Claire, completely ignoring the rolling cameras. She bent down to give Claire a hug and then reached for another book.

"How about we tackle *The Princess and The Frog*, and this time I'll read it to you?"

"Oh, I love that fairy tale."

Midge snuggled close to Claire and began reading the book. It was the best distraction she could find under the circumstances. As she continued to entertain Claire with her best impression of a frog prince, she felt the heat of Brody's gaze on her. He pulled up a chair next to the bed and leaned close to her to see the pictures.

When he lightly wrapped his arm around her shoulder, she nearly lost track of where she'd been reading. She quickly recovered when Claire made a comment about the slimy consistency of a frog's skin, and seriously who would ever want to kiss *that*?

Despite Brody's distracting presence, Midge felt more content than she had in a very long time. Without realizing what she was doing, she gently laid her head against his shoulder and continued reading the fairy tale.

CHAPTER 17

Midge

Disaster!

That's the word that continued to repeat itself in Midge's mind as she finished her shower, toweled off, and dressed in some comfortable jeans and an American Eagle tee.

She'd managed to outfox Brody and the crew by taking a taxi back to the yacht and hiding in one of the cabins as they sailed to the island. She didn't have the fortitude necessary to smile on camera and pretend that her heart wasn't breaking after the events of the day.

Midge sat on her bed furiously typing away on her laptop, writing nothing but pure drivel, yet unable to collect her thoughts enough to make the chemistry between her main characters sizzle rather than fizzle. The complete and total panic she felt at the idea of she and Brody kissing one another on camera...again...did not afford her much focus.

She flopped back on her bed and massaged her temples muttering "There's no place like home. There's no place like home," under her breath, but no matter how much she wished it, she was most definitely stuck on an island filming a reality TV series with a guy she shouldn't be falling for.

Then there was the problem of that kiss.

Maybe, considering the circumstances the kiss was given in, she could still leave despite Brody's promise to only kiss someone he was serious about. No one would expect him to deny such a heartfelt request from a young cancer patient, and no one would hold him accountable if he didn't continue to pursue her afterward. She could still be safely eliminated without it reflecting badly on Brody.

There was no hope for it. She would need to brave a confrontation with him, and perhaps appeal to his sympathetic nature. Maybe saying please would do the trick.

Without thinking her actions through, she wrenched open her door and marched across the hallway to his. She wrapped a knuckle on his imposing door and expelled a nervous gust of air.

It opened, revealing Brody in all his male glory, bare from the waist up. His thunderstruck expression at her attempt to seek him out matched that of Midge's as she threw a hand over her eyes.

"Do you always come to the door without a shirt on?" She kept her hand firmly planted across her eyes and even glued them shut for good measure.

"I do once I've checked the peep hole and made certain that the love of my life is awaiting me on the other side."

"Hilarious, Brody. Go put a shirt on before I have an anxiety induced coronary." She broke down and opened her eyes, sneaking a glance between her fingers at the magnificently chiseled lines of his chest and stomach. Her thoughts tumbled around within her brain like clothes in a dryer set to high heat.

Sweet maple syrup was followed by *holy chest and abs, Batman* as she took in a deep breath and reluctantly squeezed her eyes shut, completely disgusted with her pathetic lack of willpower.

"Not the reaction I was hoping for, Madelyn, but I'll admit that such chiseled perfection might be difficult to take in for the very first time." The tease in his tone was irresistible. She found herself swaying toward him even though her eyes were still covered. She snapped her spine straight and gave up all pretense of not looking, removing her hand and placing both fists on her hips.

"This is the second time I've viewed such chiseled perfection, as you so humbly put it, only it looks a little different when it isn't bright green." She shook her head as he wiggled his eyebrows in a playful gesture.

"Overwhelmed are you? Not to worry, my dear. I'm happy to walk around with my shirt off if it will help you get used to my manly perfection."

"I can't have a serious conversation with you when you're half dressed. Go put a shirt on or I'm locking myself in my suite."

He shrugged his shoulders in a nonchalant manner. "Come on in, and I'll throw a shirt on."

Even though Midge wanted to protest, she thought it better to have this conversation in the privacy of his suite rather than in the hallway where anyone could hear.

He stepped aside, allowing her to walk past him. Her bare shoulder brushed against his chest and she nearly stumbled in her haste to put some distance between them. She thought she heard a low chuckle from Brody, but chose to ignore it. Once he closed the door, she felt as if she might have just allowed herself to walk into a trap, but Brody, as promised, went immediately to his dresser and pulled out a dark green t-shirt which, unfortunately, accentuated his beautiful biceps. Midge was beginning to wonder if she should ask him to wear an oversized paper bag.

When he turned to look at her again, his entire demeanor went from playful to hungry. The longing she sensed from him struck her with such force she had a hard time convincing herself that she was simply projecting her own emotions onto Brody.

"Madelyn, what happened at the hospital was—"

"You need to eliminate me tonight," she cut in, not wishing to hear him say that the kiss was all for show and had meant nothing to him.

His eyes widened in surprise and then flattened with anger. "That's not going to happen and you know it. I thought we were past this. I thought you understood my intentions are—"

"I understand why you need me here. Believe me. I get the angle you and my father are working on, but I'm telling you that I am not the right girl to feign a relationship with."

He rubbed a frustrated hand through his hair which made him look boyishly adorable.

"You are so stubborn, Madelyn. I've told you why I want you here and you're not hearing me. I don't know how your impression of my 'angle' as you put it has become so skewed, but you aren't leaving this room until we work it out."

"Nothing you have to say is going to change the fact that I can't act. I can't pretend to feel something on screen and then behave as if I feel nothing off screen."

He crossed to her in two strides and placed his hands on her shoulders, urging her to maintain eye contact.

"Are you suggesting you actually feel something for me?"

Midge gazed at him in horror. Is that what she'd said? Why hadn't she thought through this little speech of hers before barreling in when she knew how discombobulated she became around him?

"I'm suggesting that I'm a bad fit for this role, and I want you to eliminate me tonight so I can get back to my novel, my friends, and my completely perfect life!"

He inched closer, eyes dark with desire, forcing her to acknowledge that perhaps he felt a certain chemistry when he was around her. Well, she wasn't about to delude herself into thinking that whatever attraction he may or may not be feeling would be strong enough to inspire a lasting commitment.

"I don't think that's what you suggested at all." He bent his head forward and softly kissed her forehead. "I think you were hoping that what we feel when people are pointing cameras at us is something we can continue feeling when they're not."

Midge made a barely perceptible shake of her head, but that was all the denial she could muster. Words were beyond her at this point. No amount of willpower could compel her feet to take one single step away from Brody

Prescott. Just as she was certain that there would be no escaping the gravitational pull of Brody's lips, a loud knock sounded at the door, causing her to spring away while Brody let out a few expletives.

"Cocktail party in one hour, Mr. Prescott," came a gruff voice from the other side.

"Thank you," Brody said. His voice sounded husky with pent up emotion.

Midge took the opportunity to maneuver herself around him. "As I said before, Brody, I need to be eliminated tonight. It would behoove you to pick some other girl to schmooze on TV."

She reached the door and opened it just as Brody's voice stopped her in her tracks.

"I'm not eliminating you, Madelyn. Ever. I don't care how long it takes for you to believe that there is no angle when it comes to you, but I certainly can't do that if you're not here."

"You need to let me go," she said. She kept her back to him as she felt him approach.

"Never," he repeated, whispering against her neck.

She stiffened her back and cleared her throat. "Never say never, Mr. Prescott. You'll find I'm quite tenacious when I've set out to achieve something, and getting eliminated from this ridiculous show is no exception."

He placed both hands at her waist and spun her to face him. His intensity made breathing a real challenge. "I think you'll find I suffer from the same drive when it comes to getting what I want."

She pulled herself away, anger burning low and steady as she faced off with the only other human being on the planet who was quite possibly more stubborn than her father.

"Game on, Mr. Prescott."

"If you call me Mr. Prescott again, I'll be forced to kiss you to remind you of how familiar we really are with one another."

She had no doubt he would follow through with his steamy threat...or was it a challenge?

Midge decided she wasn't about to stick around and find out. She exited the room, huffed across the hallway, and slammed her own door behind her.

The infuriating bachelor had given her very little choice.

This night's cocktail party was going to be a memorable one. She'd make certain of it.

FELICIA

"Did anyone see you sneaking into my room?" Felicia asked.

Liz shook her perfectly curled hair as she eased herself into the room and took up residence in an overstuffed chair near Felicia's hot pink bed, an amenity Felicia had insisted upon. She always traveled with her own bed sheets and comforter, and hot pink was, according to her, completely empowering.

"How soon can we expect little miss Madelyn to turn tail and leave the show?"

"Well..."

Liz's hesitation made Felicia want to wrap her hands around her inept employee's neck and squeeze. Catching Felicia's murderous look, Liz hurried to explain.

"I thought for sure she would cut herself on her pocket knife badly enough to bow out of the group date. I had it sharpened and then left it open in her purse."

Felicia's eyes widened at the young girl's stupidity.

"You thought she would reach into her purse and cut her hand badly enough that none of the medics on sight would have the medical know-how to stitch it up?"

Liz hesitated before answering, most likely sensing a trap, but not entirely certain how to proceed. "Well, not in time to leave for the group date."

"If the cut had been deep enough to warrant serious medical attention, the group date taking place at the hospital would have been quite a fortuitous solution, allowing the medics to rush her to the same locale as Brody and those lovely little cameras. Correct?"

Liz's face blanched a sickly hue as she recognized her mistake. "Look, I'm sorry. I didn't know where we were headed before I planted the knife. I was lucky enough to get a look at the list of people going on the date."

"Which reminds me, was it totally out of the realm of possibility to slip my name in there while you were taking a peek at it?"

"The list was typed," Liz said in an angry huff. "What did you expect me to do? Rush over to Knightly's computer and retype the stupid thing?"

"It's what I'm paying you for."

"In my defense, I was able to push her into a supply closet and lock her in."

Felicia drummed her nails on the oak dresser to avoid storming over to the worthless girl and causing her some major bodily harm.

"Did she remain locked in there for long?"

Liz's eyes dimmed. Felicia let out an exasperated groan. She reached for her phone sitting on the dresser and turned it to face the stupid girl. She shoved it in her hand and waited as Liz played the YouTube video of the Cinderella reenactment between Brody and Midge. The more she watched, the more her frame appeared to cave in on itself.

"I had no idea she had that much alone time with Brody. They...certainly put out that footage fairly quickly."

"They revealed this scene early as part of a teaser for the next episode. Do you have any idea how many people commented on this particular teaser? It's all the rage on social media. The public is enamored with the idea of Madelyn Knightly and Brody Prescott falling in love with each other."

She slammed her fist against the wall, nearly sending a framed painting careening off its hooks.

"Do you have any idea how difficult it is to sway public opinion when they've found someone to cheer for? Now we have another romantic scene for all the world to see, made even more endearing due to the fact that it was all done as a last request by some sick kid on her deathbed."

"She has cancer, but I think the chemo is helping her fight it. Her chance of survival is high."

Felicia's eyes bulged as she attempted to rein in her anger. After running through a few breathing exercises she'd learned from her therapist she took a few steps toward Liz and achieved a brittle smile.

"Did you manage to do anything to scare her enough to leave this island for good?"

Liz gulped and shook her head. "I can't figure Madelyn out. I don't think she really wants to be on the show. I'm not really sure what her angle is."

"Isn't that something you should know by now?" The calm way in which Felicia delivered her question had Liz leaping to her feet.

"I'll do a little more snooping and see what I can find out."

Felicia said nothing, simply watched her pathetic P.I. slink out of the room with her tail between her legs. She sighed in frustration, so put upon by the complete and total incompetence of people in general. Could nobody execute a plan as flawlessly as she? No, of course not. She may have had a pretty face, but her calculating mind was a well-guarded secret. Nobody ever suspected a pretty blond to be smart enough to pull off the kind of manipulative, diabolical feats she had achieved.

Another opportunity for Brody to eliminate that little upstart would be tonight, but she highly doubted the man would take it. Not after the way he'd kissed her.

She had been so close to finally attaining her ultimate meal ticket and grabbing a man she could actually love in the process. She was not about to let her plans come tumbling down around her because the man she wanted to marry had stupidly grown attached to an absolute nobody.

BRODY

Though Brody was surrounded by beautiful women willing to shower him with the kind of attention most men would give their right kidney for, he was completely distracted. The only woman he wanted attention from still hadn't arrived at this very important, *very mandatory,* cocktail party.

He knew she was desperate to leave, but he hadn't thought she would simply refuse to show. If his presence wasn't enough of a motivator, surely her trust fund still held some sway. Or maybe she was so repulsed by him that her trust fund and future financial security weren't enough to tempt her to spend time with him.

That thought nearly compelled him to flat out leave the room and go in search of her. He pinched the bridge of his nose and wondered if he had simply become an unwanted suitor, or worse, an annoying stalker whose obsession with Madelyn was reaching a whole new level of unhealthy.

The thing that kept him going, that urged him to refuse to let her go—when normally he could take a hint or an obvious rejection if he had to—was his absolute certainty that Madelyn wasn't completely ambivalent toward him. She felt something when they were together. The way she returned his kisses with impassioned ones of her own could attest to that.

He couldn't let her go until the misunderstandings, the pretenses, and her fears where he was concerned were resolved. If she wanted to deny him after that...well, it would be painful, but he would let her go if that was truly her desire.

But it wasn't.

He felt certain of that.

He also felt certain that developing a relationship with Madelyn on a reality TV series was one of the biggest mistakes he'd ever made, but without the show, she didn't have a shot at her trust fund, and since it was important to her it was important to him.

Where is she?

He cast his eyes around again while Charlene chatted on about a couple of her purebreds and how the mongrels had won several dog shows over the last few years. He could have done without the detailed play-by-play of the various tricks they'd had to perform.

He noticed a door opening and heaved a sigh of relief as Madelyn's head peeked through. Then he watched her confidently glide into the room wearing the same jeans and American Eagle tee he'd seen her in just an hour ago. She wasn't wearing her dress, she didn't have a lick of make-up on, her curls were thrown into a casual ponytail, and she'd put on those annoying glasses, refusing him full visage of her adorable freckles again.

In short, she looked beautiful.

Her challenging smile shined brightly as she stared at him, and then she walked through the room—ignoring the shocked whispers of the other contestants—out the double French doors and onto the veranda, plopping herself down on a wicker chair and whipping out a book from a purse that looked like it'd been made from an old pair of jeans. She stuck her nose in it and appeared to become engrossed in the novel.

He nearly laughed at this latest ploy to get kicked off the show. The only thing about her appearance that truly aggravated him were the glasses, and not because he didn't like them. Quite the contrary. Her look screamed sexy librarian whenever she had them on, but she knew he wanted to see those freckles.

It was another ploy at annoying him, and it was working. How dare she deny him visual access to her beautifully sun-kissed cheeks? And the ones that were dusted across her nose were completely hidden. Nope. That was absolutely the last straw. She could dye his shampoo fifty shades of purple if she wanted to, but those glasses were about to be introduced to the nearest garbage can.

"Charlene, would you excuse me for one moment?"

"Oh, of course." She gave him a mildly annoyed look, but quickly schooled her features into a contrived smile. "Just don't be gone for too long."

Brody hardly registered that last comment as he walked over to Stacey who was hovering behind several crew members.

"I'm going out to talk to Madelyn. Can you make certain that no other contestants or crew try to encroach on my time with her?"

Stacey gave him a conspiratorial nod.

"I'll play goalie like Beckham on steroids."

Appreciating her enthusiasm, he thanked her and crossed the distance to the double doors, swiftly closing them behind him. Taking note that Madelyn had chosen to ignore his approach, he decided he'd have to get her attention in a more juvenile fashion. He walked to her side, knelt down, and plucked the offending spectacles from their snooty perch atop her nose. Her stunned expression was too adorable for words.

"Excuse you! I need my glasses back if I'm going to finish my current chapter."

She held out her hand, palm up, and waited for him to relinquish the stolen goods with an expectant air.

"Absolutely not." He held them up and squinted through the lenses. "No prescription. You don't even need these things. They seem like a convenient article to employ when shutting people out. How am I supposed to admire your freckles if I can't see them?"

With a smirk, she reached into her bag and pulled out another pair of glasses with frames the width and breadth of the Titanic. Now her emerald eyes looked as if they were being magnified several times over. She was absolutely delicious.

"Sounds like a personal problem to me, Brody. Now if you'll excuse me, I'm simply dying to discover if Mr. Darcy and Ms. Elizabeth Bennet are finally going to clear up their latest misunderstanding and resolve their ridiculous issues."

"Sounds like a fairly familiar problem. Is Elizabeth Bennet as contrary as you are?"

"This coming from a man who preaches love and commitment when his history with women reads like that of a serial dater with an obsession for females who are blond, buxom, and Botoxed."

Ignoring her verbal barb, he gently retrieved the second pair of glasses from atop her nose and took great pleasure in snapping the blasted things.

Madelyn gasped in horror as she ripped the two halves of her glasses from his grip.

"I *cannot* believe you did that!" She lifted them up to inspect the damage. "Do you have any idea how much these glasses cost me?"

"Judging from the cheap material they were made from, I'd say five bucks tops. Did you buy those offensive things at Wal-Mart?"

"They were ten dollars, thank you very much, and it doesn't matter where I bought them. You owe me some money, Mr. Prescott."

"Go on the next one-on-one date with me, and we'll call it even."

"That'll be difficult to do since you're going to eliminate me. Tonight." She said that last part through clenched teeth and snapped her book shut with some seriously scary force. "I'd appreciate it if you would return the pair of glasses that you *haven't* destroyed like some caveman throwing a temper tantrum."

His grin widened. Brody knew he shouldn't push her buttons, but he wasn't about to let her win this round, and he loved watching her get riled up whenever he teased her.

"I'll return your glasses on two conditions?"

"Two? Don't make me take them by force, Brody."

"Oh, I think I'd like that very much."

Madelyn rolled her eyes heavenward and let out a groan. "What are your conditions?"

"First, you have to promise to keep these glasses in your purse. I don't want you hiding behind them ever again."

"I'm not hiding behind them!"

"Second, I want full access to those freckles for the rest of our lives."

She spluttered in confusion. "Full access? In what way? For the rest of our lives? I can't promise that."

"I'm allowed to kiss those freckles whenever I please."

"That will be a little difficult to live up to once we go our separate ways, don't you think?"

"Who said anything about going our separate ways? Promise me, Madelyn, or..." he pulled the glasses from his pocket and dangled them in the air, "this monstrosity goes in the garbage disposal."

In a crisp, clear voice filled with venom she said, "Fine. Now give me back my glasses."

"I want to be allowed to take full advantage of our deal."

"What, right now?"

"You agreed that I would have full access to those freckles whenever—"

"Yeah, I got it the first time. Fine."

She leaned forward and clenched her eyes shut as if she expected his kisses to cause her pain.

He let out a soft chuckle and cupped her chin, tilting her face toward him and placing a light kiss across the bridge of her nose. Then he hovered his lips above her cheekbone just under her eye and placed a gentle kiss across those adorable freckles. He let his lips softly graze her skin back and forth, and then he moved to the other cheek and administered the same affections there.

He noted their breathing had become slightly labored, and he couldn't help but take full advantage of this situation. He moved to her lips and captured them with his. His satisfaction grew as she immediately accepted his kisses and responded with heated ones of her own. Their combined heat and fervor grew to a nearly inappropriate level as he pulled her down from the chair and into his arms, rejoicing in the feel of her hands in his hair and the possessive hold she had on him.

All too soon they broke away from one another, gasping for air. Brody took note of her panicked look as she realized that she was sitting in his lap. She quickly scrambled to her feet, smoothing out her shirt and her mussed hair.

"That shouldn't have happened," she muttered. "You're only supposed to kiss contestants you're serious about."

Brody got to his feet. His frustration with her refusal to see reason where both of their feelings were concerned caused him to act out in yet another childish way.

"This is exactly why I have no intention of eliminating you, Madelyn. You may behave as if there is nothing between us, but your kisses would suggest otherwise."

He took her last pair of glasses in both hands and with great satisfaction broke them in half, reveling in the crisp snap it afforded.

Madelyn gasped. "You promised to give them back to me."

He reached out and placed them in her hand, allowing his lips to linger next to her cheek.

"And so I have. Don't you ever cover up those freckles again." He smiled as she shivered at his close proximity. "See you at the diamond ceremony, Madelyn."

And with that, he walked away confident in the knowledge that he had made his point perfectly clear. There was no way she could assume he didn't feel anything but an all-encompassing fire when she was near him. With any luck, they'd be discussing their future together after the diamond ceremony concluded.

Mission accomplished.

CHAPTER 18

Midge

*After the diamond ceremony is over, I'm packing my bags and flagging the
nearest sailboat out of here. Trust fund or no trust fund!*
Anger burned within Midge's breast as she watched that cocky
playboy stroll away from her, clearly convinced he'd handled her like he would
some pesky little gnat threatening his endgame. And her glasses! True they
weren't expensive, but they were a deliberate rebellion against her father's
insistence that she fit into the same visual mold as every other female in
Hollywood and a great way to avoid attracting attention. Besides, out of all the
pairs she owned, they were two of her favorites. The thickest, widest set of
glasses she'd found to hide behind. Such injustice would not go unanswered.
He must have assumed that fake little show of affection was going to convince
her to back down and play nice, but she wasn't about to forget the words he'd
uttered to her father or his real reason for keeping her around. She bit her lip
and angrily dug into her bag, pulling out her third and final pair of glasses she'd
brought with her on this trip and studying them with perverse satisfaction. He
might insist on breaking them in half as well, but at least they would be broken
on her terms with one final act of defiance. And if he thought she was going to
accept his rock encrusted flower, he was in for one massive surprise.

BRODY

Brody spotted Madelyn as she ascended the riser and took her place between
Cambria and Charlene. The first sign that his besotted and willing future

girlfriend was neither besotted nor willing occurred when she caught his eye and made a deliberate show of reaching into her denim purse and pulling out yet another pair of offensive Coke-bottle glasses that were even thicker and wider than the previous two he'd taken great pleasure in destroying.

Just how many pairs of glasses did this girl own?

She slowly lifted them to her face and put them on, giving him a wide grin in the process. Forget not being able to see her freckles. He couldn't even see Madelyn. The darn things covered the entirety of her face. She may as well have been wearing a brown mask. She mouthed something to him which he failed to catch since he was so distracted by the way the glasses made her emerald eyes bug out like they would in a 3D movie.

He noted Cambria and Charlene giving her curious stares. Her father stood in the back corner trying to catch her attention, directing her to take them off. He looked nearly apoplectic. Brody might have found the entire situation amusing if his sense of foreboding hadn't gnawed its way into his gut. He had the awful feeling that perhaps his latest interlude with Madelyn had not given her the impression he'd intended. Looking back on it, he supposed breaking her glasses, ordering her about, and behaving like a caveman probably hadn't been the best way to win the girl over.

In his defense, he'd never had to work so hard at convincing a girl to go out with him. He'd never had to work so hard at convincing a girl he was actually interested in her, and now he wasn't so sure that the trust fund was going to keep her here as he had suspected. From the furious look in her eyes—made that much more apparent by the bizarre 3D effect of her spectacles—she was in full-on battle mode. What if she planned on rejecting his rose...rejecting him?

He couldn't allow that to happen, but he wasn't sure what kind of measures he might need to take now that the filming had started.

With a sickness in his stomach, he recited the names of the girls who were staying and gave them each a flower, frantically formulating a plan that might keep her here, which meant he was announcing her name last instead of first like he'd originally intended.

Finally reaching the point where Madelyn and four other girls stood waiting for either a rose or a refusal, he softly called out Madelyn's name.

She stepped from the riser and crossed the short distance between them. She stood firm and resolute just a foot from him, waiting for his question and the opportunity to give him her answer, one he knew would send her flying home and out of his life forever.

He reached over and gently removed the glasses from her face, reveling in the sparkling green of her glorious eyes. She didn't appear at all surprised that the glasses were now in his possession. In fact, he thought she'd been expecting such a maneuver.

"Never cover that gorgeous face of yours, Madelyn. God never intended anything so beautiful to go unnoticed."

He saw a little of that steady resolve waver as his heartfelt words penetrated that impervious wall of hers, but then they hardened ever so slightly, and he knew he would have to follow through with his plan.

"Madelyn, will you please take this rose and allow me to get to know you better?"

She gave him a glacier smile that froze him to the very center of his heart. With a vindictive gleam in her eye she opened her mouth, no doubt ready to give him what would probably be some scathing rejection. Brody discreetly slipped the toe of his left foot into her right instep, causing her to lose her balance and stumble forward into his arms, making it look as if she was accepting him with an eager embrace.

He wrapped his arms around her and twirled her in the air, letting out a forced chuckle.

"I'll take that as an exuberant yes." He kissed the top of her head and set her down. From her expression, it looked as if she was still trying to figure out what had transpired.

"Cut!" yelled Knightly in a harried voice. "Perfect, everyone! All the contestants who are staying can retire to their rooms for the evening, but we need to film Brody's last few moments with the contestants who have been eliminated." As the group dispersed, Knightly walked over to Midge and wrapped a shoulder around her. "I'm glad you're still playing the good sport, despite your questionable attire tonight. Seriously, Midge girl, what happened to the stylist I sent up to your room earlier this evening?"

Midge glared daggers at her father, and then leveled her killer glower at Brody, causing him to internally wince. He'd probably managed to do some serious damage to their fragile relationship after manipulating her like that. Was the damage irreparable?

"I was making a statement," she said. "One that had very little affect on my intended target." She wrenched her glasses from Brody's clutches, turned on her heel, and exited the room, leaving Brody to wonder if he would find her suite empty the next morning. Perhaps an overnight vigil was in order. He'd gone this far with his obsessive/borderline psychotic behavior. Why not add a stakeout to the mix?

MIDGE

Midge did some angry pacing once she settled back into her room for the night and reviewed the last few minutes of the diamond ceremony, still uncertain as to how it had all gone so wrong so fast.

How in the world was she still here?

She'd put the glasses on and earned an irritated look from Brody which had been awesome. Then she'd mouthed the words, "You're going down," mainly to instill the fear of God into him. He'd have to wonder just what she planned to do once he called her name. From the pallor of his skin, she'd felt certain he'd received the message.

"Two points for me!" she said, sarcasm bleeding through her syllables.

Then she'd marched right up to him, ready to tell him to jump off a cliff, and somehow she'd managed to lose her footing and literally fall into his more than accommodating arms. Something had tripped her up—or rather *someone*. She was stuck on this show for another round.

Her cell phone jingled loudly in the silence of the room and she nearly let out a startled shout.

She reached into her purse and grabbed her phone, flipping it open without checking to see who her caller might be.

"Hello?"

Her greeting was met with dead silence.

"Hello?" she tried again.

She heard heavy breathing, and then a disjointed voice carried over the line.

"You need to leave the show before something terrible happens to you."

"Excuse me?"

"That injury to your hand is going to seem like a paper cut compared to what comes next. Leave the show or else."

The line went dead before she could respond. She pulled back the phone and checked the caller ID.

Blocked.

Someone had deliberately left her knife open, hoping she would cut herself and miss the group date. Someone wanted her off the show. Enough to threaten her with bodily harm. Enough to make good on those threats. If only her tormentor knew she'd already been trying to get kicked off the show. Apparently, she wasn't the only one trying to submarine her TV time, and she had a fairly good idea who that someone might be.

It would seem Felicia Davenport was playing for keeps.

Midge stared at her phone and looked to the corner of her room where her suitcase sat, waiting for her to exhibit some common sense. If she packed up her things and left in the middle of the night this would all be over. No explanations. No questions asked. But Brody, despite his infuriating ego and bossy manner couldn't be left alone to deal with some unhinged contestant, especially when that unhinged contestant was Felicia Davenport.

Resigned to her unfortunate fate, she turned her back on the inviting suitcase and flung herself on her bed, dialing Lisa's number and praying that her friend wouldn't kill her for waking her up in the middle of the night.

"I hope this doesn't become a thing," Lisa said in a groggy voice. "I'm a huge fan of twelve hours of sleep...in a row."

"I'm sorry, Lisa, but I need you to see if you can trace a phone call for me."

She recounted the threatening phone message and the suspicious events of the day, including her brief time spent in a locked supply closet.

"I'm all over it, Midge. I think it would be a good idea to let your father or Brody in on your predicament, especially since blood has already been drawn. You're not safe there."

"I'll think about it. I have a hunch as to who might be behind this, but without anything solid to go on, I doubt either one of them will believe me. More than likely, they'll assume this is another prank or pathetic attempt at getting legally eliminated from the show."

"Another attempt? How many times have you tried to convince Brody to kick you off the show? And how?"

"Do you remember our prank wars from a few summers back?"

A happy chuckle flitted across the line. "Oh, you are so naughty. Don't tell me you stole his clothing, including his unmentionables, and sold them on eBay. Actually, considering his rising-star status that might be a very lucrative prank to pull."

"I didn't really have the time or the resources to start boxing and shipping clothes off to destinations unknown. I went for the old food-coloring-in-the-toiletries ploy."

"Effective. I bet that held off shooting long enough to annoy your father. I take it Brody wasn't annoyed enough to let you go, considering we're having this discussion several hundred miles apart."

"Nope. I'm still here for reasons I don't fully understand, but maybe if we get some solid proof that I've got some crazy stalker making threats on my life, I can convince both Brody and my father to target some other contestant for Brody's happily ever after and get the heck outta dodge, and we can get rid of any possible threat to Brody's safety in the process." The thought of Brody with any woman other than herself made her blood boil. Like she had any claim on him to begin with. "Have you found some dirt on Felicia yet?"

"She's covered her tracks well, but I'm starting to see some inconsistencies in her finances. She's in debt up the wazoo, forking over money faster than I can fork in a jumbo-sized cookie, and you know how talented I am at inhaling one of those. She received some major deposits within the last five years that were inconsistent with her current employment—since she's never had a job— and delivered sporadically."

"Keep working on it. Something tells me her dirty little secrets might shed some light on my current predicament."

"Will do, but please be careful. I'm interested in your happily ever after, not some depressing funeral procession where I'm asked to give your eulogy while I try to assuage my overwhelming guilt by admitting to everyone assembled that I knew you were in danger from the get-go and did nothing to notify the authorities."

"What authorities? I'm on an island."

"With some sociopath. Nice set-up for a horror flick."

"Except this is supposed to be a romantic reality TV series."

"That's what makes it so creepy," she whispered.

Midge chuckled. "Okay, keep me posted, and I promise to tread carefully."

After hanging up she glared at her laptop and wondered if she should try squeezing out a few paragraphs. She gave up on the idea and decided sleep would help her forget that she was sitting in a mansion on an island where America's most eligible bachelor currently resided.

And maybe she'd be able to forget about her most recent kiss with Brody.

Yeah. And maybe someday Lisa would set her up on a date with someone who didn't live with his parents or receive a monthly stipend due to good looks, nice hair, and the right last name.

BRODY

Brody stared at the king-sized bed in his suite. For the first time in his life he dreaded going to bed all by himself. He didn't want to sleep on one side while the other half lay empty.

She was still here. He'd made certain of that when he'd tiptoed next door and listened to her muffled voice as she spoke to someone on her phone. At least she hadn't fled the mansion in one angry huff. Still, he planned on camping out next to her room for the rest of the night.

Rubbing some tension from his neck, he reached in his back pocket and pulled out his cell phone. It might be nothing. Madelyn accidentally locking herself in the closet was a plausible enough story to believe, but the fear lurking behind her bright green eyes and the way she'd glanced to her cut hand gave Brody an unsettling idea, a possibility that she hadn't been completely forthcoming with him, and he wasn't about to complacently accept her explanations when his gut was telling him something wasn't right.

"Gregg, I need you to look into someone's background for me," Brody said in a whisper.

"Do you have any idea what time it is?" Greg said, clearly annoyed..

"You're an insomniac, Gregg. You can't tell me you were sleeping when pacing tends to be your forté."

"I might have just managed a miraculous recovery."

"For as long as I've known you, you've been wound tighter than Tina Turner in concert. I'm concerned about Madelyn. I think someone might be targeting her, and considering Felicia Davenport is here, it wouldn't be a stretch to point the finger at her."

He quickly shared his suspicions concerning possible threats to Madelyn's safety.

"We've already done some extensive background checks on her since her recent stunt with the tabloids. Nothing came up on our radar," Gregg said.

"I think Felicia is adept at covering her tracks. If she has a history of deviant and possibly violent behavior, I doubt there's any history of it with the police. I need you to hire someone to take a look into her background."

"It could be nothing, Brody. Ms. Knightly probably *did* accidentally lock herself in that closet. Maybe she was trying to get away from you."

"I've got a feeling, Gregg. You know how these feelings tend to pan out."

"To the tune of several billion dollars." Gregg let out a tired sigh. "Okay. I'll get started on it right now, but Brody, if you really think Felicia might be dangerous, you should consider eliminating Ms. Knightly as soon as you can."

Brody immediately dismissed that thought, selfishly, he knew, but he couldn't protect the woman he cared for if he wasn't close to her, and there was no guarantee that Felicia would leave Madelyn alone once she left the show. What if something happened to her while he was stuck here, playing a farce and pretending to enjoy the dates he went on when the woman he wanted wasn't even on the same island anymore? He was here for Madelyn, and if it came right down to it, he would leave with Madelyn if he thought he couldn't protect her. For now, it was just a feeling with nothing concrete to go on.

"Just find out if Felicia is dangerous, and we'll go from there."

"Will do. Get some sleep for me. Heaven knows mine will be sporadic."

"At best."

Brody threw his phone on the bed and walked over to his window, opening it to let in the balmy breeze sweeping in from the ocean. No matter what he discovered, he wasn't going to let Madelyn get away from him again.

Okay. Maybe that did sound like the musings of an obsessive stalker. Not wanting to analyze his behavior any further, he threw himself into the routine of getting ready for bed, wishing with all his heart that Madelyn was sharing it with him.

CHAPTER 19

Midge

"Today we're going to be introducing something new, something that hasn't been done on any other dating show. We are going to try something called The Date Challenge," Les Lassiter declared, flashing is Colgate smile and blinding the contestants in the process.

Boring.

Like she cared if she won or lost a date challenge here. Midge gave her father an indifferent glance and focused her attention on the open windows across the room. A small bird, colorfully bright against the morning sunrise, infused in her a desperate longing for freedom. If only she could take flight and escape the perfumed odors in the room.

"The Date Challenge is an opportunity to compete for a chance at a one-on-one date with Brody Prescott this week. We will offer up a challenge pertinent to Brody's specific needs for his business and personal life, and he will choose his date from the group that excels in this challenge. Essentially, we'll be breaking you off into four different groups, and since there are fourteen contestants left, two of the groups will have four members."

There was a slight groan at the unfairness of the situation.

"If you ladies will follow me to the kitchens please, we can continue further instructions there."

The contestants rose in one perfectly choreographed perfumed wave and followed Les out of the main meeting room with the crew hot on their heels. Upon entering the kitchen, which incidentally looked like the cooking set from Cupcake Wars—*hmmm cupcakes*—Midge crossed to the cooking area assigned to her and faced the front doors as everyone else took their respective places.

Brody Prescott came striding into the room with a confident air and commanding presence. She swallowed hard as a tight ball of desire coiled within her. Her pulse jumped when his eyes sought out and found hers, pausing long enough to send ripples of tension along her spine. The small hitch of her breath caught his notice, and his lips curled into a smug smile.

Curse that blasted man!

"This particular challenge is going to test your ability to embrace other cultures," Brody stated.

Midge did her best to avoid flinching when his gaze flicked back to her once again before moving to scan the rest of the ladies assembled.

"Due to the widespread success of my business, I entertain sponsors from all over the world, and I do my best to make them feel as comfortable and welcome as possible. My future wife will need to be familiar with the details and customs of these countries in order to perform her duties as hostess to the best of her abilities. These challenges have been set up to test those abilities."

Brody strode to the middle of the kitchen. He was surrounded by various cooking stations. With hands clasped behind his back and his head held high he played the part of an intimidating CEO to perfection.

"The social gatherings I host will always serve cuisine that my guests are comfortable consuming. Though I don't expect any of you ladies to actually cook for these events, you will need to become familiar with dishes that may not appeal to your particular palate or preference. So as not to offend my guests, you will need to acquire a taste for them either way. For this challenge your group must prepare a specific meal, pertinent to the country given to you in each of your group's envelopes, and then you must eat a serving upon completion."

Midge's glance shifted to the white envelope at the center counter of her group's work station, wondering what country they had been allotted. She hoped undercooked octopus wouldn't be their challenge for the day. Chewing the legs on those suckers was like tearing into rubber. When she'd traveled with her dad to Japan for a particular location shot, she'd been subjected to the nasty meal and forced to eat the entire thing. Her father had been proud of her for finishing her meal. He still remained ignorant to the fact that she had purged herself of the ugly mess after excusing herself to use the strange Japanese bathroom, a precarious adventure in and of itself.

"The first group to successfully cook and eat their meal will be the winners and candidates for a one-on-one date with yours truly." Brody flashed a pearly white smile. "Ladies, you may begin."

A slight blond girl in her group lunged for the white envelope and ripped it open with her sharp nails. They looked a little like talons to Midge. She made a mental note to cook a safe distance away from the lethal things, and then the young lady turned and she recognized Cambria.

"Okay. Our country is China," Cambria shouted.

Midge let out a stifled moan while the two other girls jumped up and down in excitement. She nearly let out another one when she heard the girl behind her say, "I just love Panda Express."

Clueless, the whole lot of them.

Cambria continued to jump up and down until she finally took the time to read the dish assigned to them.

"We have to prepare a dish of shanghaied cicadas." She glanced up at the rest of the group. "Is cicada like a type of vegetable?"

Seriously?

Silence met her stupid question. Midge scrunched her forehead in defeat. Apparently, the burden of enlightening the group fell to her.

"Cicadas are bug-eyed locusts, sweetie. We've been asked to prepare a dish of cooked locusts and eat them."

"That's crazy," another girl exclaimed among the squeals of disgust.

The disgruntled moans from the other groups made Midge wonder what kind of other culinary atrocities had been doled out. For her part, she considered cicadas pretty low-key compared to what they could have been assigned. She didn't mind them, either. If you could get past the legs and wings they tasted a bit like lobster tail with about the same consistency.

Even better than their dish choice was the idea that none of these girls would be willing to put their perfectly polished digits on a cicada, dead or alive, let alone eat one. Her group had zero chance of winning this challenge. Which meant zero chance of going on a date with Brody.

Perfect.

Her mood brightened at that thought.

"Okay, ladies. Let's get to it." She turned to Cambria. "I assume we have a recipe to work with?"

Cambria let out a nervous laugh and handed the envelope over. "You aren't seriously going to make this, are you?"

"Well, I generally prefer crickets and grasshoppers to cicadas, but I'm flexible."

She tried not to snicker at the looks of revulsion on Cambria's face as she opened the freezer and pulled out a large mixing bowl with her name taped to the front. She then moved to the counter and took the lid off. Inside, she beheld frozen cicadas.

Appetizing.

At least she was getting an entertaining reaction from the ladies in her group. She figured she might as well make the best of it.

Midge pulled out another folded sheet from the envelope and read the ingredients.

60 FRESHLY EMERGED CICADAS
2 tsp. sea salt
4 tbsp. organic anise seeds
2 tbsp. soy sauce

4 cups salted sherry wine
4 cups rice wine
Some celery for garnish
20 cloves of mashed up garlic
Turnip greens and parsley for a garnish

She dutifully gathered her ingredients together, placing them on the counter. She paused for a moment as she felt all eyes on her and turned to see that the three other girls in her group were watching her with interest.

"You know, it wouldn't hurt any of you to at least try to prepare it. No one says you have to eat the dang things, but it might be a fun story to tell at social gatherings."

She let that sink in as she turned around and filled her silver pot with the salted sherry wine. She then dumped the entire bowl of cicadas into the wine and used a mixing spoon to ensure they were completely submerged. Then she added the anise seed.

"Can I work next to you?" Cambria asked. She offered Midge a tentative smile. It surprised her. This girl seemed to be afraid Midge would refuse her company.

"Of course you can. My name is Midge."

"I thought it was Madelyn."

"My friends call me Midge," she responded automatically. She didn't miss the happy look that swept across Cambria's face.

"I'm Cambria."

"I know. It was easy for me to remember because I thought was pretty."

"Thank you. My mother thought it was the perfect stage name for a girl on the cusp of Hollywood success."

"On the cusp of—you were a newborn when you received this name, correct?"

Cambria let out a rueful chuckle.

"According to my mother, a person's career begins at birth."

"Sounds like our moms attended the same PTA meetings."

"You ladies look like you're having fun. Can I join in?" Charlene moved up to Midge's right and began filling her pot with salted sherry wine.

"The more the merrier," Midge said. "I'm just going to set this on the burner." As she moved toward the oven she nearly tripped over someone's foot. She stumbled forward and regained her footing, but her momentum caused the sherry wine to slosh all over her shirt.

Well, isn't this lovely? Now I smell like my mother.

"Are you okay, Midge?" Cambria asked.

"No worries. My clumsiness is a health hazard I'm used to." She set her sherry soaked cicadas on the burner and turned on the gas stove.

Okay. These babies need to boil for six minutes.

"How is it you seem to know your way around cicadas?" Charlene asked with a smile.

Midge had to laugh at that.

"Honestly, I've never cooked an insect a day in my life, but I did quite a bit of traveling with my father, and you wouldn't believe the things I had to eat just so I wouldn't offend any of his clients or business partners. Cicadas are actually pretty tasty."

Cambria gazed upon her in awe and something akin to hero worship. "You've traveled to Italy, then?"

Midge laughed at her expression and moved back to the counter, beginning the tedious task of smashing twenty cloves of garlic.

"Italy, China, the gorgeous countryside of Ireland. I've lived a charmed life in many ways, I guess."

"I've only ever lived in Los Angeles. This is the first time I've left California. It's been a little scary for me."

Midge suddenly understood this young girl's suspicious lack of confidence. Traveling for the first time anywhere was bound to attack your comfort zone. Cambria and Charlene went to put their cicadas on the stove and then returned to participate in garlic smashing tedium. Midge noticed the other girl in their group begin to pull her own pot out as well. Her name failed to come to mind.

"So what do you do when you're not competing with a group of girls for a billionaire husband?" Charlene asked.

Midge snorted. "I'm an author, actually. I'm nearly finished with my first manuscript and plan on submitting it to a few agents and publishers I've had my eye on for a while."

Charlene's eyes lit up with interest.

"What do you write about?"

"I'm a hopeless romantic, so I stick to the romance stories with happily ever afters."

"That explains why you're here then," Cambria stated. The fierce smashing of her mallet hilariously contrasted against her diminutive personality and slight figure. "It's hopelessly romantic to join a dating show where you're fighting for the attention of a man you admire and hope to fall in love with. I bet this gives you all sorts of material for a good book."

Midge looked at her in surprise.

"That's not a bad idea at all, Cambria. It's not why I'm here, but it's definitely something to consider."

"I can't believe we have to do this by hand. Where's a food processor when you need it?" Charlene grumbled.

"Why are you here, then?" Cambria brought her mallet down again and bits of garlic sprayed in several directions.

"Cambria, you're beating that garlic like you would an enormous insect," Midge said, ignoring the question.

"Exactly."

Charlene and Midge laughed at Cambria's exaggerated smashing technique and went back to smashing their own garlic.

"I'd better check on my cicadas." Midge made her way back to the stove, but became disconcerted when she noticed that her burner wasn't on.

I swear I turned my burner on. That's so strange.

She shrugged her shoulders and lit her gas burner again. She decided to stand there and wait for it to finish before wandering back to the other girls. As much as she enjoyed making friends, she really didn't want to go into detail about her personal reasons for being there. She also didn't want to get too friendly with any of the women vying for Brody's attention.

It doesn't matter. I shouldn't care who gets that man's attention.

Just then the man in question came into her line of vision. She watched him as he scanned the room, dispassionately taking in the movements of the other women. She was going to have to warn him about that. He couldn't look bored out of his mind on national television. Not if he wanted to uphold this new image they were creating for him.

Wait a second. Why do I even care? No way am I giving him more reason to keep me here.

Only when his eyes met hers did he demonstrate a hint of emotion. They took on that hungry, smoldering stare he'd used on her in his bathroom and at the restaurant—and everywhere else now that she thought about it.

Oh, give it a rest would you?

That come hither look wasn't about to work on her this time, especially when she stood next to a pot of boiling cicadas. Nothing like the smell of simmering bugs to effectively wreck any and all romantic inclinations. She turned her back on him as a subtle way of demonstrating he held zero power over her. It was also a pathetic attempt at proving to herself she was immune to his charms.

What a challenge.

Once her bugs had boiled and the rest of her garlic looked like a pulverized, pasty liquid, she heated up a pan of mashed garlic, soy sauce and sherry. Within minutes it thickened into a yucky brown color but the smell was divine.

The next step involved skewering her boiled cicadas with little bamboo sticks and then arranging them on a large oval platter. She took great satisfaction in stabbing each cicada, visualizing Brody as she did so. The crunching sound only added to the fun of the activity.

I am so sadistic.

Midge took the brown mixture and scooped it into the middle of the plate and then added her parsley and celery in a way that made the brown heap look like a dirt mound amongst foliage. She speared the cicadas into the dirt mound so they appeared to be crawling out of the earth just as she had seen it arranged in Shanghai.

"The instructions don't tell us to make our platters look like that," Cambria observed.

"Oh, this is just how I've seen it served before, but you can arrange your bugs any ol' way you like."

Cambria's nose scrunched up at the reminder of what they were preparing and then she began arranging her plate exactly how Midge had.

"Now what?" she asked.

"Now we eat them. Five of them is the prescribed number, and thank Heaven's for that. I can't imagine having to eat sixty of these suckers."

"No kidding," Charlene said. "Why on earth did they have us make so many?" Her look of disgust as she surveyed their platters was comical. Midge would probably be the only one eating the creepers. Best to get it over with.

She grabbed one, thanked her lucky stars it had been de-winged and then took a bite, managing to get half of it in her mouth. The cicadas were soft-shelled, another bonus for her because she wasn't one to prefer super crunchy exoskeleton.

It definitely had that taste and texture of lobster tail without the fishiness, and the sherry, anise seed, soy, and garlic gave it some added kick. Not bad at all so long as you didn't look at the eyes before you popped it into your mouth.

Kill me.

Midge dutifully finished her first one off and went in for a second.

Cambria and Charlene studied each other as if to say, *You game?* Then they both picked up a speared bug and went for it.

Midge felt exceptionally proud of her little protégés.

"I think I might be able to choke down the rest of these so long as I can chase it down with something fortifying," Charlene said.

"That's crazy. These things are totally delicious," Cambria said.

Midge turned to her in surprise as the young girl grabbed two more and began munching on them as if they were candy bars.

"I bet I can finish my five before you, Cambria," Midge challenged.

"You're on, girlfriend."

"You three are disgusting," said their fourth group member. Midge still fought to place her but failed to. "Please remember to dip your tooth brush in some rubbing alcohol and scrub your mouth once you've finished. Oh, and don't breathe on me."

Midge stifled a laugh and almost choked on her fourth cicada. She and Cambria held up their last bug and gave each other a challenging look.

"Do it. Do it. Do it," Charlene began to chant. Other groups took notice and soon the cameras had zoomed in on them.

With a nod, Cambria and Midge shoved the last cicada in their mouths and furiously chewed away. After a few moments they swallowed and tapped their hands on the counter at the same time.

"I believe it was a tie," Charlene stated.

Most of the contestants and the crew whooped and clapped in a congratulatory fashion, but Midge happened to notice one contestant in particular who didn't seem to be thrilled with her success.

Felicia stood at a station to her right with her arms folded across her chest. Midge imagined that the snarling vixen wished to go for her throat, but there were too many witnesses present. She'd have to check Felicia's background for possible signs of homicidal activities—and lock her door and windows morning, noon, and night.

She responded to the acidic stare with a wide smile of her own and turned her attention to the group surrounding her. Cambria's exuberant smile and Charlene's friendly arm around her shoulder warmed her heart just a little.

Okay, so maybe making a few friends wasn't completely taboo.

BRODY

Brody surreptitiously watched as Madelyn involved herself in an eating contest with another girl from her group. He couldn't figure out how she managed to look so sophisticated in a t-shirt and blue jeans. It was attractive and completely distracting. She was the only person he wanted to look at, but he was supposed to be surveying the progress of everyone in equal measure.

Tedious.

He hadn't worried about Madelyn's reaction to the challenge. He'd done his research on her and figured cicadas would be the least of her worries, but he was pleasantly surprised when she seemed to take charge of her group and rally them into trying something new and challenging.

She was a born leader, yet so unassuming at the same time. Lead by example, as his mother frequently reminded him. Madelyn appeared to be a natural at it.

He also took a few moments to enjoy the predicament Felicia found herself in. He'd made certain to give her group something she was sure to detest. Smalahove was a Western Norwegian traditional dish made from sheep's head. She didn't even have to cook the sheep head or singe the hair off it and scoop the brains out as required for preparation. It came ready made since the process was time consuming. No, all she had to do was heat up the head in the oven and prepare the mashed rutabaga and potatoes to go along with it.

The fact that she had mentioned her immense dislike for all animals in general, though she was referring to keeping pets, had merely added to his delight in giving her this particular assignment.

When Felicia had opened the freezer and squealed at the frozen sheep heads peeking out from sightless eyes, he'd been hard-pressed to contain his laughter. There was absolutely no way she'd consider eating something like that let alone preparing it. No chance of a date with that walking death trap.

He continued to admire Midge from a distance as she gave her teammates hugs and then grabbed a cicada and carefully placed it on top of a crew member's head, creating a cacophony of laughter as the young man did his best to dislodge it from the top of his cranium.

She certainly knew how to play to an audience, commanding everyone's attention as if she reveled in it, though he suspected that to be far from the truth. He couldn't wait to spend some alone time with his tempting little librarian. Fortunately for him, he wouldn't have to wait too long.

CHAPTER 20

Midge

L adies, I'd like to thank those of you who gave this challenge your best despite the unusual cuisines you were asked to cook," Brody said.

The contestants in the room let out some nervous giggles and a few murmured comments. Midge kept her eyes locked on Brody with a feigned look of interest.

"The goal was to choose someone among the group who won the challenge, but only a few of you from each group actually attempted to eat your meal once it was prepared. So the winner will have to be chosen by determining who finished the challenge first."

Midge glanced around the room, wondering who amongst the girls in the other groups had finished their challenge first.

"There was actually a tie for first place so there will be two one-on-one dates. One with Cambria Kessler and the other with Madelyn Knightly."

Everyone in the room let out happy cheers, whether forced or genuine was anyone's guess, but Midge didn't even notice, trying to come to grips with the fact that she'd managed to land herself some alone time with Brody after all. Though her initial reaction was to utter a blatant refusal, she had the presence of mind to keep her mouth shut and paste a smile upon her face.

"The first date will be this afternoon with Madelyn. I'll pick you up at four o'clock sharp."

She realized she needed to say something since their collective audience looked at her with an expectant air.

"I'll be waiting," she managed.

Brody gave her a knowing smile, sensing her discomfort and no doubt finding it humorous. She'd done such a fantastic job of sabotaging him and then avoiding him, and now he had maneuvered her into a position impossible to run away from, and on national television. She was going to have to play nice and behave herself instead of ranting and raving at him like she wanted to.

In the meantime, she'd have to convince her heart that a date with Brody Prescott meant absolutely nothing to her.

Nothing at all.

⌾

A sharp knock sounded at Midge's door, causing her to jump a little and jar the laptop on her desk.

"Midge, it's Stacey," came a muffled voice through the door. "Brody is waiting downstairs for you, and the film crew is ready. You'll have two crew members plus your father and me going on this date with you."

She pinched her eyes shut and chewed at her bottom lip. Then she stared forlornly at the empty page on her laptop. She'd spent the last few hours attempting to ground herself in work-related material. The romantic interests in her novel had one last obstacle to overcome, filled with hilarious misunderstandings, an interfering best friend, and a naughty rival of the female variety.

She knew exactly how she wanted the next few scenes to take shape. At least she had before she got stuck here on this island with a handsome billionaire intent on coercing her into the role of fake girlfriend. Now her turbulent thoughts were wholly centered on how to prevent herself from feeling anything while being in Brody's presence.

Should have been a no-brainer since she loathed and despised him.

Yep. She totally hated him. She hated his soft, silky hair and the way it felt when she stroked her fingers through it every time he kissed her. She hated his lips and how demanding they were when pressed against her own. Oh, and she most definitely hated his confident and aggressive nature. The way he pulled her to him without so much as a by-your-leave and forced her into such passionate consuming exchanges of affection, making her feel like she was the most desirable woman in the world.

Yeah. She really hated that.

An indifferent attitude was going to be her best line of defense against his irresistible charm.

"Midge? Are you in there?"

"Yes," she shouted. "I'm coming." She jumped off her bed, placing her laptop to the side, and went to open the door.

Stacey stood smiling and exuberant in the entryway.

"I am so excited to see you and Brody interact on this date."

"I'm glad that you're coming along on this particular shoot." In Midge's opinion, women and moral support went together like chocolate and chick flicks.

"Yep. Your dad was impressed with the confrontation I caught between you and Felicia. He said it was exactly the kind of petty cat fight he'd been hoping for."

Midge rolled her eyes. "Well, glad to have the old man's approval. I mean, why would American viewers enjoy something culturally educational when they could watch high-strung females lay claim to a man who's not interested in any of them?"

Stacey chuckled. "I'm sorry, but Brody is most definitely interested in you. That kiss on YouTube was something else. I'm seriously hoping for a repeat of that during this date." She let out a wistful sigh.

"That isn't going to happen, Stacey. He's made it quite clear he will only kiss someone he is seriously intent on pursuing."

"Whatever you say, girlfriend. But if I were the betting type, I'd wager fifty bucks that those lips of yours get ambushed before the end of the day." She wiggled her eyebrows suggestively. "Let's get this show on the road. I'm itching for some romance."

Midge let out a bereaved sigh and closed the door behind her.

Following Stacey through the massive mansion gave Midge's anxiety just enough time to take root and tear through her confidence while simultaneously fueling her self-doubt. She had to remain emotionally distant even if she appeared cold and inaccessible on television. It was the kind of behavior her father had always preached against when it came to camera time. An audience needs to find you likable, lovable, and even vulnerable in order to relate to you. Bare your emotions, leave your heart on your sleeve, share the most personal traumatizing aspects of your life—a real sob story that will appeal to viewers—and your TV success is a guarantee.

Her distant behavior wasn't going to win her any fans or followers, but she wasn't here for that. She shouldn't have been here at all.

As she reached the top of the staircase she took note of the two cameramen on either side with Brody in the middle. Her father was just beyond the action, viewing everything from a director's standpoint, critically assessing facial expressions, atmosphere, and emotional dynamics.

She allowed her eyes to fall on Brody. His hungry stare sent heat to her tummy, blossoming out and causing a traitorous blush to rise to her cheeks. He took note of it and gave her a winning smile.

It infuriated her.

Why did he have to look so gorgeous? His casual wear, khakis and a sports t-shirt, gave him a boyish appearance.. She had no idea what activity loomed upon the horizon, but she sincerely hoped it would afford her a little breathing room in Brody's presence.

As she reached the bottom of the staircase, he held out his hand to her. She hesitated to take it. One touch from him would be enough to undo her resolve. Instead, she tucked her hands into her pockets and gave him a polite smile. Brody's smile slowly faded, and a predatory look replaced it. She nearly shivered, receiving the impression that she had somehow issued a challenge he intended to accept.

"Cut," her father yelled. He stood up from his seat and walked over to her. "Midge, what was that? You looked like you were descending the staircase to your death. When Brody offers you his hand, the polite thing to do is take it."

Midge turned to him, giving him a fiery glare. "I'm pretty sure I made it clear how I felt about being here. You said I would be eliminated the first round and you lied. Do you really think I'm just going to pretend to pursue a proposal of marriage here?"

She sensed Brody shifting next to her and thought she heard him chuckle. His amusement at her discomfort only fueled her anger.

Her father ran his hands through his hair in exasperation. "We don't have time for this, young lady. You know exactly how you're supposed to behave on camera. I've trained you much better than this. It doesn't matter how you're really feeling. I need you to do some acting for your old man here. This is important."

"Right. More important than your daughter or the fact that her private and personal life is now going to be aired on TV. And you," she pointed her finger at Brody, "are just as much responsible for this uncomfortable predicament as my father. I don't understand why I've been singled out to go on this date. Aren't you supposed to be spending time getting to know the girls you're intent on pursuing?"

"What makes you think I'm not intent on pursuing you?" Brody said.

"Excuse me?"

He had the audacity to look amused, wholly unruffled by her behavior. Exasperating man!

"He's right, Midge. The idea of you two as a possible item is flooding social media sites. Viewers all over the world have fallen in love with the idea that you and Brody shared a special connection before the show. We've already created a great marketing spin and backstory for you two."

Midge felt horrified.

"Backstory? You've fabricated history between Brody and myself?"

"Fabricating history was completely unnecessary. We already had so much to work with." Her father smiled, rubbing his hands together in delight. He looked like a Star Wars fanatic attending his first convention. "After that YouTube video came out we just had to capitalize on it. We leaked a Cinderella-type story to the press. It's a good thing the paparazzi follows this billionaire everywhere because we have some nice footage of you two in the restaurant. He helps you with your shoe, asks you to dance, chases you out of the restaurant and stops you before you can leave, kissing you in the hopes that he can convince you to stay."

"The paparazzi picked up all of that?" Midge felt as if the air had just thinned around her.

Her father ignored her and continued on. "Once you make your escape, he is determined to find you no matter the cost. He searches to no avail and becomes discouraged, believing this mystery woman he has fallen for will never be found. He reluctantly agrees to be the bachelor on *Marry Your Billionaire*, and low and behold you just happen to be one of the contestants on the show. American viewers are eating this up, Midge girl. You have no idea how many followers you and Brody have."

"Followers? You've had less than a week to get this information out and we already have followers?"

She was all about keeping a low profile and had never desired to be one of her father's puppets on camera. She couldn't believe he had exploited her like this.

It shouldn't have surprised her, though. With his director's hat on he never did think in terms of familial loyalty. Daughter or no daughter, this was simply how her father operated.

"Am I to understand that I'm now the audience favorite? I'm the one the viewers are hoping Brody will pursue? Isn't that supposed to be decided after he spends time with other contestants?"

"You've already had off-camera time with him, Midge, and it was explosive. We're catering to the wants of our viewers and they want to see you and Brody falling in love."

"But now you have no show. If everyone believes that Brody favors me over the other girls why would they stick around to see how this ends?"

"Well, of course your relationship with Brody isn't the only relationship we'll be highlighting. He's going to pick two other girls he finds just as interesting, and we'll craft a beautiful fairy tale romance around them as well. We'll slowly develop these relationships as the season progresses while he eliminates others who aren't quite as popular with our viewers. The audience will be on the edge of their seats wondering which girl Brody will pick. They'll be just as torn as he is by the end of it."

She swallowed hard at this pronouncement. There was no way she could pretend to fall in love with this man without actually falling in love with him. Her heart was beating wildly, her breathing came in sharp and raspy as she felt herself lose control of the situation.

A warm, steadying arm wrapped itself around her waist. She peered up into Brody's eyes and saw worry and concern. The idea that he had noticed her distress and come to her rescue managed to calm her breathing and slow her heart rate, even though he was basically the cause of it

He might have been a manipulative jerk, but she'd take the support he offered her—regardless of the reasons behind it—if only to get through the next few hours.

"That's it," her father said, motioning to the two of them. "That's exactly the kind of connection and chemistry I want to see. I knew you wouldn't let me down, Midge girl."

Midge snapped out of the hold Brody's smile had over her and took a discreet step away from him while her father shouted more instructions to his crew.

"I suppose this farce is going to help your image then? Eventual wedded bliss?" she said, avoiding his gaze.

"Isn't that exactly what you told me to do when we met at Café Canapé? I'm simply following your directive."

She glanced at him and caught his rakish grin.

Her rueful one fought against a grimace.

"I believe I told you to pursue one woman you were actually interested in."

"Precisely."

She peered up at him questioningly, but the sound of her father's voice rang through the air.

"Midge, I want you to take it again from the top of the stairs. Descend the staircase with an engaging smile rather than the dread you exhibited only moments earlier." He approached her side and whispered, "Just remember, there is a trust fund in it for you. Play your part and do your best."

"I really don't care about the stupid trust fund," she hissed.

"But I bet you care about finishing your degree, don't you?" Her father nodded triumphantly at her continued silence and then walked back to his chair.

She swallowed her anger at this new manipulation and rushed up the stairs, doing her best to cool her temper, steel her emotions, and pull her face into the appropriate expression demanded of her. Two more steadying breaths and she turned around to face her fate.

"Roll cameras," her father shouted.

BRODY

Brody did not like the way Corbin Knightly had managed his daughter. Madelyn deserved to know exactly what angle Corbin had taken with the media attention his shared kiss with Madelyn had received, and instead of allowing Brody to take her aside and explain the circumstances, her bungling father had broached the subject about as tactfully as Kanye West.

He felt proud of her for standing up to her father and hated to see her like this, but trapping her on the show was the only thing preventing her from running away. He needed to prove to her that there was nothing to fear from him, nothing to be wary of. His intentions were pure, sincere, and genuine when it came to the way he felt about her. He just had to convince her of it and woo her into feeling the same way.

She took a moment to regain her composure and then turned to face them. The transformation completely astounded him. Her easy smile when she locked eyes with him, her eager steps as she descended the stairs, and then the accepting way in which she placed her hand in his made him feel as if he'd just encountered a different woman. Her acting skills were superior. The adoring look she gave him made his breath catch in his throat. This was the reaction he wanted from her off-camera. He wanted and needed it to be a reality instead of a fabrication.

He couldn't help but respond to her behavior whether genuine or scripted. Brody enfolded her into a warm embrace and planted a soft kiss on her forehead.

He felt her arms tighten around him ever so slightly, and she pulled back to look at him, a smile teasing the corners of her full lips.

Heaven help him. He wanted so badly for this to be real.

CHAPTER 21

Midge

I couldn't stop thinking about you after you left the restaurant," Brody stated.

Midge broke from her intense admiration of the various trees and plant life surrounding them to bear the full onslaught of his penetrating gaze.

Aware that he was attempting to create a serious moment between them, she moved to her default setting of dry sarcasm. A truly juvenile defense mechanism.

"I should hope not. That smack I gave you was meant to be memorable," she said.

His lips twitched in amusement.

"Just as memorable as that kiss you gave me."

"If I remember correctly, you stole that kiss. I was in the process of fleeing the scene."

"And if I remember correctly, you eventually participated."

Midge rolled her eyes. "You took me by surprise. You ought to be ashamed of yourself. Kissing women you don't even know."

"I regret nothing."

The teasing glint in his eyes made her smile in response. She quickly turned her attention to the scenery. It was better than staring at Brody Prescott's mesmerizing eyes.

"After you jumped into that taxi, I spent the rest of the night cursing myself for letting you go. I didn't even get the chance to grab your phone number. Do you have any idea how relieved I was to find out you were on the show?"

He sounded so sincere, but his words to her father while they conversed in Knightly's office flitted through her mind.

I can just use her as a valuable resource for coaching me through this series. Or perhaps I can use her as a shield to avoid the advances of Felicia Davenport.

She would do well to remember that this exchange between them, this date, was simply a farce, a way to further his career. But it was difficult to merge what she knew to be true with what she felt within her heart, especially when he said exactly what she wanted to hear and gazed at her as if he meant it.

Pure torture.

She was an idiot to stay and put herself through such an emotional hurricane.

Trust fund. I'm sticking around for the trust fund. My last semester of college certainly isn't going to pay for itself.

Midge swallowed a nervous ball of emotion at Brody's expectant air. What did he want from her? A declaration of her insane attraction to him? Though it terrified her to consider it, it might be liberating to be candid concerning her feelings for him without appearing too vulnerable in the process. Everyone present figured this was all for Brody's image either way. No one would take her words or actions seriously, including Brody. Of course, there were American viewers to consider.

Nothing more vulnerable than an entire nation knowing how much you admire someone as out of your league as Brody Prescott.

The small canoe they shared slowly meandered along a scenic 3.5 mile portion of the Kohala Sugar Plantation's irrigation system. The activity known to tourists as "Flumin' da ditch" was an exciting educational tour through pristine rain forests filled with trees like the awapuhi, albizia and guava. The tour took tourists through ravines, waterfalls, and romantic tunnels.

The helicopter flight from their private island to Waimea-Kohala airport had been a thrilling experience to say the least. Then Brody had surprised her with this relaxing activity, one she would have enjoyed more if cameras weren't following right behind them.

Generally, when fluming the ditch, you had a guide with you, but her father had retained special permission to keep this particular tour a little more intimate.

"Did you think of me at all?" he asked.

Midge forged ahead, knowing these little admissions of her own heart were going to cost her.

"It's difficult to think of anything else after a handsome stranger draws you into a waltz, chases you out of a plush restaurant, and then kisses you like you're the only woman for him."

"And then you smacked me."

"A girl must play hard to get," she answered coyly. Then her expression grew serious as she allowed herself a moment to drink in his handsome features. "It felt like a fairy tale."

Brody rested the oars on their pegs and leaned forward, taking her hands in his, their knees slightly touching.

"Our fairy tale, Madelyn?" He lifted her hand to his lips and held her eyes as his warm lips massaged her knuckles.

It amazed her that such a small gesture could make her face sting with heat. He made a simple kiss on the hand positively blaze with seduction.

"Midge, my friends call me Midge," she said in a strained voice.

"I want to be more than your friend, Madelyn." His words were convincingly sincere. A repeat of what he had said in his bathroom.

This man was good. He didn't seem to need any coaching at all.

Of course he doesn't. Not in this area. He's an accomplished playboy, Midge. Pull yourself together!

"But you're still a stranger," she whispered.

He reached a hand up to brush away a lock of curly hair along her forehead and softly caressed her cheek.

"I can remedy that."

She couldn't help the shy smile that graced her lips, but she pulled back to ease some of the tension she felt building between the two of them. His presence was simply too overwhelming. She couldn't have him touching her as well.

"Have you been to Hawaii often?" she asked.

"Enough to know some of the folklore and legends concerning the area. What about you? Have you traveled here before?"

He seemed a little disappointed at her change in subject, but didn't try to touch her again. Thank Heavens for small mercies.

"Believe it or not, this is my very first time."

"Really? I would have thought your father's business trips would have brought you here before now."

"Nope. I suppose you'll have to educate me on the Hawaiian folklore."

Brody pondered this for a moment. "I think I have one you might enjoy."

Midge settled back in her seat to listen.

"This particular legend has to do with a beautiful plant called the Lehua Blossom that grows on Ohia trees. The legend states that Ohia and Lehua were young lovers. Ohia was a handsome man, and Lehua was considered the most beautiful girl on the island."

"Oh, I like this legend already," Midge said.

Brody gave her a smile and continued. "There's nothing more beautiful than people falling in love with one another, but as so many love stories go, the lovers were met with opposition in the form of a jealous rival. Pele, the volcano goddess set her sights upon Ohia and coveted him for herself. When Ohia refused Pele, she became vengeful and turned him into an ugly, twisted tree."

"Vengeful women. They can certainly do damage to one's love life."

"Pele ignored Lehua's desperate pleas to change him back, but the other gods sympathized with her plight. They weren't powerful enough to reverse Pele's magic, but they could turn Lehua into a beautiful flower and place her on the tree so that the lovers would never again be parted from one another. It is said that as long as the flowers are never plucked from the tree, the sun will continue to shine, but when a flower is taken from the tree, rain begins to fall like tears from the sky. Lehua still cannot bear to be parted from her husband Ohia."

"That's so tragically beautiful."

"It is a bit sad to think of anyone being separated from the person they love."

"I think a good love story is always like that, though. Two people who care for one another must face obstacles and challenges to come together and remain inseparable. Sometimes the challenge is getting them to fall in love with one another or even admitting to that love in the first place."

"Yes, I'm familiar with that particular challenge." Brody raised his eyebrows suggestively.

"I doubt any woman has ever found it difficult to fall in love with you, Brody."

"That sounds particularly ironic coming from the woman who turned tail and ran after I gave her the kind of kiss meant to make her feel like she was the only woman for me."

Blast the man and his pointed remarks. How had the conversation been brought back to their potential relationship so quickly?

His words and expression had rendered her speechless. Her father probably wanted her to wax eloquent at this point and spout off romantic nonsense to please his viewers.

She kept her eyes glued to the scenery surrounding them and willed herself to breathe.

"Why did you run from me, Madelyn?"

She hesitated, wishing she could be anywhere but in a canoe with Brody.

"My response to you caught me by surprise. I honestly don't remember entering the taxi or the long ride home. I just remember thinking about the time we spent together. I didn't believe I would ever see you again."

"Yet here we are."

"Yes. I imagine this is a bit confusing for you. You have fourteen women left, all of them here to date you, and you have to choose only one to spend the rest of your life with."

"I'm not confused, Madelyn. I know what I want."

There was an open invitation there to ask what that might be, but Midge didn't think she could bear to listen to him utter the words she wanted to hear when she knew it would be a lie and little else.

"Do you feel like running from me now?"

With the intensity of his look disarming her defenses, she could do nothing but answer with complete and total honesty.

"Yes."

"Why?"

"Because I like you too much."

He stopped rowing and held her gaze. "Well, there's no way I'll let you run from me now."

"We're on an island. I probably wouldn't get very far."

He chuckled. "I'm an excellent runner, Madelyn. I'm not afraid to chase you, and there are no taxi's to contend with now."

His words both frightened and thrilled her. This date needed to end as soon as possible. She didn't think she'd be able to take much more of his attention if she had to fight so hard against her own natural response to him.

The canoe soon brought them to an open area where a small dining table flanked by two chairs held a simple white candle. With the sun barely beginning to set, washing the dining area in golden light, Midge couldn't help but feel like the very gods of Hawaii were determined to undermine her resolve. Brody alighted from the canoe and reached for her hand, pulling her onto dry land.

Once they were seated she felt more at ease. At least she had a table blocking his carefully orchestrated advances.

A waiter suddenly appeared out of nowhere, causing Midge to wonder if her father was some kind of magician. After he took their orders, he offered them something to drink.

"Just water with lemon for me, thank you." Midge thought she heard her father's mild sigh of reproof somewhere beyond the line of cameras, but she ignored it as she ignored his employees.

"I'll have a piña colada," Brody said, handing the waiter their menus. "You didn't want something more substantial to drink?"

"I'm not much of a drinker," she stated. She figured she may as well bring this abnormality out in the open if they were really going to play at getting to know one another. "There's alcoholism on both sides of the family, and I figure if I can't eat chocolate responsibly then alcohol and I have no future together."

Brody barked out a laugh that made it seem as if he were not only surprised, but highly entertained by her explanation. She thought she heard snickering from the crew which nearly made her smile. Her father's frustration at her inability to blend in at social functions didn't seem to bother his coworkers.

"So you've determined what your level of alcohol consumption will be due to your personal addiction to sweets."

"Everybody has to draw a line somewhere."

She noted the way Brody's eyes took on a happy glint as if he wholeheartedly approved of her behavior. She wasn't used to it, approval that is.

"Some might say that social drinking can hardly be labeled abuse."

"Maybe they haven't accidentally had too much to drink and then woken up in the morning with one awesome hangover only to find a stripper by the name of Roxy sleeping beside them. Walk of shame, Brody."

He gave her a contemplative nod. "So you don't think a glass of wine every so often is acceptable?"

"If a person is capable of that, then I don't see a problem with it. I'm only telling you what *my* limits are. I'm not interested in losing control like that. For me, the answer to your question is simple. I won't go there. Not even once."

"That conviction must have brought you some serious flack from friends and peers."

"You have no idea. Yet at the end of the day, I was heading home for a restful night's sleep while they were vomiting their guts out in their parents' hydrangea bushes. I get that people like to drink. I'm not pushing my lifestyle choices on anyone. I'm just saying I've never seen alcohol truly benefit anyone in my family. It just begets more of the same problems they're trying to hide from." Midge took a sip of the water the waiter placed before her and leaned back in her seat. "I'm assuming your thoughts on the subject differ from mine."

"Actually, no. When I was sixteen my best friend Casey and I were in a terrible car accident due to a drunk driver who ran a red light."

Midge immediately sat forward in her seat, hands clenched tightly in her lap.

"I'm so sorry to hear that. Were you both injured?"

Brody looked off to his right away from the cameras and toward the crashing sounds of the waves hitting the shore. She wondered if she should have changed the subject. It was such a personal thing to discuss, and every word was immortalized on camera. Their lives laid bare for all to see. She wanted to protect him from the public's intrusive scrutiny, but she knew this was the kind of exposure he needed to repaint his image. It was his decision to allow this magnifying glass to scrutinize his character and personal history, after all.

His gaze returned to her, a deep sadness embedded within his expression.

"Casey didn't make it."

Midge's hand shot forward across the table and grasped his, squeezing it to show support. It was an instinctive reaction to soothe away the ache of his loss rather than a desire to play to the cameras.

"That's awful. I'm so very sorry, Brody."

He rubbed his thumb along the curve of her hand and glanced to her, clearing his throat. "It was a long time ago, but there are certain lessons given in this life a person can't afford to ignore. I learned that our choices will always bleed into other people's lives whether we wish that to be true or not. I'm sure the man who killed Casey never imagined that his drinking that night would be the cause of another person's death. He didn't have a problem with alcohol abuse. He just made a bad decision when he was under the influence and now he's in jail for manslaughter. I just remembered thinking that it would never be me. I can't ever be that person. I never wanted to be the one causing damage to another person's life whether emotional, physical, or mental. So yeah, I can understand your take on alcohol. I'm not much of a drinker myself."

For the first time in her life, Midge felt like a perfectly normal human being rather than the weirdo her parents and peers had always hinted at. If Brody really was the person he presented at the moment, she definitely wanted to get to know him more, purely for the sake of his image, of course.

"So what drew you to the world of online dating? I assume there is a good story behind that."

Brody released her hand as their food arrived. Once the waiter left them he answered her question.

"I was extremely tired of the losers my mom dated. She met most of them through friends and coworkers, but other guys she brought home for dinner were men she met on the internet. Wash outs, the whole lot of them. From a business standpoint, my mother helped me discover a need that single women everywhere experience. How do you find decent men to date? How can you assure yourself that the men you meet aren't psychopaths? I figured if women were experiencing this problem then men most likely were as well. So my purpose for developing the company was two-fold. I needed to protect my mother and reassure myself that the men she dated were fully vetted before she ever brought them home, and I had a great market in which to start a flourishing business where people searching for a safe online dating community would have the opportunity to find legitimate dating opportunities. The idea grew from there."

"Foolproof."

"Well, there were several starts and stops along the way. It didn't happen overnight, but now I can honestly say it's become a huge success."

This was good. She needed to make sure she focused on the positive aspects of Brody's business and what it meant to him.

"So tell me about the people you've helped."

Brody took on a delighted, almost boyish grin as he reached into his pocket.

"I can do better than that. I have a few pictures of friends and family members who tried the online dating program in its infancy."

He opened up a small wallet and pointed to a few pictures held within. She flipped through four pictures of happy, smiling couples on their wedding days.

"That first picture is of Dan and Joan Williams. Dan was one of my old bosses who ran a landscaping business. He was divorced at the time my business got off the ground, and I asked him if we could use him as a guinea pig. He hated the idea at first but soon changed his tune when he got a look at the profiles of the pretty women on our website."

Midge chuckled. She studied Dan's red hair and twinkling blue eyes. His wife, Joan, was a tall, slender beauty with blond hair wrapped in an elegant up-do. Their shared happiness was unmistakable. Midge sensed the cameras closing in and tried to shift a little so the crew could get a good view of the pictures. These precious insights brought Brody one step closer to a more favorable image. The sooner that was established the better.

"They must have been very much in love."

"They still are. They've been married now for about nine years and have two kids. They send me a Christmas card every year with their family picture included. It wasn't easy, though."

Midge glanced up. "What do you mean it wasn't easy?"

"They were both wonderful people when they met, but each of them had survived a messy divorce and that can cause a lot of heartache. They knew they liked one another. There was definite chemistry between them, but they had to decide to take the time to get to know and trust each other. They began as friends and eventually their friendship became the roots for the love that blossomed between them. Everyone is going to fall in love at their own pace. These two just needed time to let things simmer a little."

Midge studied Brody's features and found a refreshing amount of heartfelt sincerity as he discussed his business and the people who benefited from it. He was humble and unassuming in the way he discussed his thoughts and feelings. She quite liked this side of Brody Prescott.

"So you've kept a few pictures of the people you have helped?"

He gave her a soft smile and scratched the back of his head as if embarrassed to answer her question.

"These are just a few of the pictures I have. To be honest with you, I've kept every single picture a couple has ever sent to me and pinned them on my office walls. The walls are pretty cramped. I've had to place them on other walls in other offices. My secretary isn't sure how she feels about the wallpaper."

"I don't believe it," Midge said, awarding Brody a rare smile.

"I would be more than happy to show you someday."

"I just might take you up on that."

"I sincerely hope you do."

Uh oh. He had that look in his eye. The one that shot fire to her cheeks and turned her knees to jelly. She felt fortunate to be in a seated position.

"I believe I just made you blush, Madelyn."

"Don't get too excited about it. Redheads blush easily."

"Do they? I suppose I'll have to experiment with that."

Midge allowed her mouth to quirk into a half smile. She shook her head in chagrin and took another sip of her water. She was simply too keyed up to eat.

"Thank you for not running away from me this time."

She shrugged her shoulders and gave him a playful smile. "It's a small island. I'm sure you would have found me eventually."

"Does that mean I've caught you?"

"Maybe."

His smile made her heart feel so light.

CHAPTER 22
Brody

B rody knew he was laying it on thick with Madelyn, stating his obvious interest with little preamble and even less tact, but if what her father stated about Madelyn's trust issues was true then he felt it imperative that he dispense with the slow approach. Not that he'd utilized the slow approach even once since the moment he'd met her.

"Madelyn, I know that the situation we find ourselves in is a little unorthodox, but I hope you know that with you, I will always be sincere, whether on or off camera."

A flash of sorrow flitted across her face, but then her expression smoothed into a half smile as she acknowledged his comment.

"Thank you, Brody. Sincerity in this situation will definitely eliminate any misunderstandings or trampled feelings. I only hope that once you've acquired what you came here for that you will be kind enough to release those contestants with whom you feel there can be no future. It would be hard to drag this out any longer than necessary. Most women are going to find themselves very attached to you."

"I think you're exaggerating my appeal with the ladies, but I promise I won't trifle with anyone's affections, especially yours."

He understood her meaning and almost sighed in frustration as he realized that she fully believed him to be performing for the cameras. Why she believed he had kept her here to begin with, he couldn't fathom. He'd done everything short of declaring his undying love and proposing to her on the spot, but he was definitely going to find out what she believed his ulterior motives were...off camera.

Until then, there was another way to drive home his sincerity, and it was an idea that Madelyn was wholly responsible for.

"Would you like to take a little walk with me? There's a nice path we can take toward the beach."

Her eyes lit up with interest.

"I'd love to see more of the surrounding area."

Brody stood quickly and offered his hand to her, helping her from her chair. He tucked her arm in his and marveled at her slight hands and slender fingers. His large frame dwarfed her own, yet he knew, despite her small build, Madelyn held the ferocity and strength of an Amazon warrior. He'd been on the receiving end of that fighting spirit more than once and looked forward to facing off with it again.

They meandered down a well laid path and came to the rise of a small bluff overlooking the sandy beach and crystal blue ocean below. Standing there with Madelyn and drinking in that moment with her arm in his gave him more clarity than he had ever before experienced. He knew he cared for her, wanted to be near her and continue getting to know her, but he'd never felt so much contentment with any other individual by his side. It was peaceful, simple, and one hundred percent right. He cleared his throat to take that next step in convincing her of his sincerity and hopefully winning her trust and her heart.

MIDGE

With the soothing sound of lazy waves lightly breaking against the shore beneath them, Midge could almost forget the camera crew and her own father positioning themselves for that perfect shot. That kind of attention made her insides curl with anxiety, but the enormous man beside her lent her some added strength and comfort without him even realizing it. She drew from that quiet strength he held, something she would never acknowledge vocally, though the irony of depending upon him to get through the rest of this date wasn't lost on her. She became so relaxed with Brody by her side, she rested her head against his arm without thinking about it. His soft voice broke the peaceful silence of the moment.

"I want to kiss you, Madelyn."

She balked and took a step back, her peaceful calm dashed to pieces.

"You made it very clear that you would only do that if you were serious about the girl in question."

"I am."

Okay, she understood that the American viewers were interested in their supposed love story, but she had no intention of pursuing a fake engagement with Brody. It would emotionally destroy her. She'd already formulated other ways of getting herself kicked off the show, and being publicly kissed by Brody would mess that up.

After declaring he would only do such a thing if he were completely serious about a contestant on the show, eliminating her would seem callous and further his image as an incorrigible playboy. He wouldn't be able to let her go... and he *had* to let her go. She had no intention of seeing this series through to the end, not when her heart was so thoroughly invested in the billionaire standing before her.

"You've just begun to get to know everyone. There are still fourteen girls here that you haven't gone on single dates with. Perhaps you should...give yourself some time to process...everything."

He reached for her hips and pulled her to him.

"I don't need to process anything. I know how I feel."

"You have a date with Cambria tomorrow. You may feel differently after spending time with her."

"I think Cambria is very kind, but I don't feel quite so strongly about her as I do about you. Tell me to cancel the date, and I will."

"You can't cancel it. That's why you're here. To get to know these other women."

"I'm here to find my wife."

"I know that, but—"

"Why should it take an entire season to determine which woman is the best fit for me?"

"Don't let the producers hear you say that," she hissed.

"What are you afraid of, Madelyn?"

Rejection. Humiliation. Being used as a pawn in this game you and my father are playing. Getting my heart broken.

She stood stock still, incapable of voicing her thoughts on camera. Refusing to allow herself that much vulnerability when Brody was using her to repair his image and help shield him from Felicia's spiteful publicity.

"If you can tell me you don't have serious feelings for me yet, I will refrain from kissing you...for now."

Midge hesitated, aware of her father and the crew hovering around them, holding their breaths, waiting for her to give Brody that perfect answer.

Under normal circumstances she was strong enough to fight against handsome men who were interested in her for all the wrong reasons. She didn't allow anyone to take advantage of her, and never revealed her true feelings for any man, especially someone like Brody Prescott, but then she had never had feelings like these before, and she had never been in a situation where she could act on those impulses under the guise of pretense.

"Can you tell me you don't feel this like I do?" he pressed.

Midge allowed all of her defenses to crumble and let go of her guarded expression. It was terrifying.

Closing her eyes for a moment, she took a deep breath, and then opened them, allowing her true desires to shine through, allowing herself some vulnerability.

"I can't tell you that. I don't *want* to tell you that, but I'm not so sure it's a good idea."

"Why?" His hands slowly slid to the small of her back and pulled her forward, pressing her against his chest. She tilted her head back to maintain eye contact with him.

Tell him, she admonished herself. *He'll never suspect it's the truth.*

"Because I'm...I..." she faltered. *Because I care too much for you, and you're gonna break my heart.* "I just think it would be best if you kept your options open for now."

"Cuuut!" her father yelled.

Midge took a step back from Brody and his smoldering gaze, waiting for her irate father to approach. It obviously wasn't the way he'd wanted that scene to play out.

"Kept your options open? These are not the words of a woman who came here to find true love. Midge, there was so much build-up right there. How could you let the tension between you and Brody dissipate like that when Brody did all the work to bring you guys to that perfect moment?"

Midge shook her shoulders and fortified herself for combat.

"If Brody kisses me now, he makes a very clear statement to the audience that he is going to keep me around for awhile, and that isn't what we agreed to. It was one thing for him to adhere to Claire's wishes and kiss me at the hospital. No one will fault him for that. But if he kisses me right here, right now, then he's making a very pointed statement, a declaration that no one will be able to ignore. I won't be eliminated for the rest of the season. He can't just kiss contestants left and right and then eliminate them. We're trying to get away from the playboy angle, am I right?"

Brody took her shoulders and forced her to face him.

"Madelyn, is that what you really think this is all about? I'm not interested in angles or public perception."

"I heard you," she shrugged in an attempt to mask the acute stab of pain near her chest.

"What are you talking about?"

"Midge, we don't have time for this. We're on a tight schedule here, and I'm pretty sure I made it clear that you're here for the long haul. You are Brody's future. Your established connection before the show and the viewers' approval of that connection has sealed the deal here. You'll be the last woman standing no matter what. So kiss this guy already and make your viewers happy."

"Knightly, you're giving your daughter the wrong impression." Brody turned to Midge. "This isn't a fake romance."

"Of course it is," Midge said. "Don't you remember the job offer you gave me at the café? I refused it then, and I'm refusing it now. If you need three girls to eventually narrow it down to, fine, but I don't need to be one of them." She turned to her father. "I have fulfilled more than my share of the contract, and I am willing to stick around long enough for Brody to develop stronger feelings for three other girls, but that can't happen if he kisses me."

"Madelyn, you have completely misunderstood my intentions here, and that job offer was my lame and rather crass way of hitting on you. I thought I had to present it as employment rather than an extended invitation to dinner considering how unimpressed you were with me."

"Stop lying to me," she shouted. "I know exactly why you need me here, but I have no intention of getting engaged to you to further your image or to field off Felicia's advances."

She watched Brody's face blanch in understanding. Now he knew that she'd heard everything. How would he deny his motives now?

"You took that out of context, Madelyn."

"Save it. I'm here because I need to graduate from college, and my father is holding my trust fund hostage. Now that everyone's true motives are on the table, we can stop with this game and be honest for a change."

"Here's some honesty, Midge. If you don't see this thing through with Brody to the very end of the show, you can kiss your tuition money goodbye." Knightly waved away one particular cameraman who had inched his way closer to the argument. "Stop filming this, people. We can't use any of it for the show. We need them to be falling in love, not discussing their relationship like it's a business transaction."

Midge tried another tactic. "My contract states—"

"That you don't leave until you're eliminated. Brody, do you plan on eliminating my daughter any time soon?"

"Absolutely not, but Madelyn you need to understand why I—"

She shot her hand up to stop whatever manipulative, cajoling argument he intended to use to sway her into believing he saw her as anything other than an opportunity.

"Don't." She drew in the pain she felt at her father's callous behavior and Brody's ulterior motives. Neither one of them would see how badly this affected her. Ever. "I'm here to get my trust fund back, and you're here to save your company." She drew in a deep breath and lifted her eyes to his. The concern written on his face sliced at her frail emotions. This on-screen kiss could not happen. Not when she still planned on getting eliminated. "If you want me to be the girl that sees this thing through with you to the end of the series then you're going to have do things my way, and kissing me on this first one-on-one date is not a good idea. Not when you still have so many girls to eliminate."

"Midge, it's what the viewers want," her father said.

"And they'll get it, but not right away. You want more viewers, and Brody needs to restore his credibility. If I have no option to leave the show then you're going to do things my way in order to facilitate both of those goals; otherwise, I'll be so uncooperative you'll be forced to send me home."

"I'm listening."

Midge took note of Brody's glower, but she ignored it and turned her attention back to her father. If anyone had the right to glower it was her. Brody was getting everything he wanted.

"You know better than anyone how to keep people coming back to watch one more episode. You've got to create suspended tension with no resolution. Make them come back each episode, anticipating that next kiss between me and Brody, but never delivering it until there are only a few contestants left. That same tactic should apply to any other women you want him developing a relationship with. Wait until there are only a few weeks left, and then he can kiss whoever he wants."

Hopefully by then, she'd have found a way off the show.

"The build up of sexual tension," he said. "Sounds like a fabulous idea to me. And what's your angle for Brody?"

Midge glanced at the handsome billionaire, surprised to see him barely concealing his anger.

"He can continue to get to know the other women, but in his personal interviews he will make note that he's taken a special interest in me and a few other girls. When each girl fails to catch his attention, he will kindly eliminate them. That way he appears to be taking this seriously and he is given more time on camera to allow his personality, character, and convictions to shine through. He also appears kind and honest in his dealings with women by cutting them off when he realizes he doesn't feel as strongly for them as he does for the last three girls standing."

"Brilliant, Midge. This is why you should have come to work for me. Your talents are wasted behind that laptop of yours."

Her father turned away before she got the chance to deliver a scathing remark. He always got the last word in.

"Let's take it back right before Brody brings up the kiss. We'll shoot that part later." Her father commenced shouting out orders and camera jargon while the crew regrouped and moved into their previous positions. She felt someone clamp a hand on her arm and pivoted to face Brody's enraged glare.

"What is your problem, Prescott?" She ripped her arm out of his grasp and took a step away from his tempting physique.

"You haven't given me a chance to explain myself or my intentions where you're concerned. You insist on believing that I have absolutely no feelings for you."

She sighed heavily, lifting a hand to rub the tension from the back of her neck.

"Brody, you can stop this now. The cameras aren't rolling yet. There's no reason to play to my ego now that I've agreed to stay."

He surprised her by grabbing her shoulders and roughly pulling her against his chest.

"I don't know what I'm going to have to do to get you to believe that I'm here for you and no one else, but I'll say it over and over again until it sinks in."

His hands slid down her arms and then moved to the small of her back, holding her to him with no room for escape, and escape was most definitely what she wanted and needed.

His hungry gaze held hers as he continued. "I am here for you, Madelyn. I don't want anyone but you, and I may not be allowed to kiss you on camera just yet, but you're not going to prevent me from kissing you when those stupid things aren't rolling."

His arms tightened more firmly about her waist and his mouth descended to meet hers in a fervent collision of lips, warm and soft while one of his hands came up to hold the nape of her neck when she attempted to pull back. She let out a breathy moan which he took advantage of by deepening their kiss and exploring her tongue with his.

Completely lost in his kiss, Midge explored the clean feel of his shaved jawline as she used her other hand to rake her fingers through his silky hair, fully participating in yet another stolen kiss from Brody Prescott.

BRODY

She felt so good in his arms, especially when she relaxed against him and stopped putting up such a useless fight. Her lips were soft and warm against his, and the warmth of her touch sent his mind reeling with thoughts better left unexplored for now. He didn't truly feel exultant in this latest battle of wills until Madelyn's hands began exploring his hair, her soft fingers flitting lightly against his chin. When she parted her lips even further and allowed him to delve deep into her mouth, he knew she was his. She couldn't possibly ignore what was happening between them now.

He slowly tapered off the intensity of their exchange by softening his kisses and then taking his lips and lightly sucking and kissing the corner of her top lip as he took his fingers and traced soft circular patterns on her lower back.

He pulled back just enough to look Madelyn in the eye, feeling satisfied to see them slightly glazed. Her lips were delightfully red and swollen. Her eyes focused a bit as she let out a shaky breath and bit her bottom lip, a nervous gesture on her part that he found to be utterly irresistible. He couldn't stop himself from leaning forward and placing a soft kiss on her lower lip and then softly tugging on it with his teeth for good measure, eliciting a satisfying gasp from the gorgeous creature in his arms.

He pulled back again and watched her as she tried to pull her emotions together. Her defenses were down, and he wanted to keep them that way.

"From now on, Madelyn, no one bites that bottom lip but me."

Her eyes widened in surprise, but she didn't attempt to move from his grasp or slap him this time. An encouraging bit of progress.

"Please tell me someone captured that on film," Knightly shouted, breaking the spell of his shared kiss with Madelyn. "No? You're all fired."

Madelyn's eyes came into sharp focus at the sound of her father's voice. The hardening of her features clued him in to her fortifying resolve to shut him out. Before she was able to mentally and emotionally talk herself out of what he knew she felt for him, he tilted her chin and brushed a light kiss on her lips, capturing her attention long enough for her to look at him openly without any walls blocking out the sincerity of his next sentence.

"I'm here for you, Madelyn. Whether you're willing to believe me or not, I want you now, and I'll want you after this show is over."

"Why are you doing this to me? You don't have to convince me of anything. My performance will be just as believable without your false attempts at winning me over."

He sighed heavily at her stubborn refusal to believe him. Then he brushed his thumb against the high ridge of her cheekbone and placed a soft kiss against her forehead, moving to rest his own forehead against hers and drawing her in closer, he whispered, "I won't give up, Madelyn. I know you don't trust me, but I won't stop showing you or telling you how much I care. Eventually, you're going to believe me."

Her back went rigid and she stepped away from him. He was shocked to see a tear slide down her cheek.

"One thing *you* can believe, Mr. Prescott, I won't be holding my breath."

Brody ground his teeth in frustration. Did he need to grab her and shower her with his affections again to get his point across? He would gladly do it, but she didn't seem to place much trust in these public displays of affection. Private ones with absolutely no cameras around would be a better strategy. He was hardly against that tempting idea and planned to put it into play every chance he got.

"Let's film the ending of this date without the heavy kissing that no one seemed bright enough to capture on film."

Brody sighed as Madelyn took her place by his side and plastered on an interested expression at whatever he was supposed to say next. He wanted this circus act to be over and done with so he could have Madelyn all to himself.

CHAPTER 23

Felicia

How could you let this happen?" Felicia nearly screeched. Her hand grasped the miniature camcorder which showed her unauthorized footage of the passionate kiss Brody exchanged with Midge during their one-on-one date together. It didn't matter that it hadn't officially made it on the series because it was simply a matter of time before Brody made his intentions toward that little minx public on the show, and where would that leave her? Eliminated. Alone. Rejected once again by a man she was determined to have for herself.

"It was risky enough for me to sneak out of the mansion and follow them. There were too many crew members around to do anything other than film the progress of their date," Liz stated in exasperation.

"I'm paying you good money to sabotage this interloper's film time and relationship with my future husband. What, if anything, have you accomplished thus far?"

Liz's affronted look annoyed Felicia. She wasn't nearly as efficient as promised. Felicia wondered if she would have to start sabotaging Madelyn Knightly herself, but she never liked getting her own hands dirty. It was always best to let others do her work and possibly hang themselves in the process.

"I've opted to take it to the next level," Liz stated. "With the nasty surprises I have planned for her, I can't imagine she'll voluntarily stay for too much longer. I've recently discovered she doesn't have much of a reason to be here."

"What do you mean?"

"I have it on good authority that the only reason she agreed to be on this show was because one of the contestants canceled and her father asked her to fill in. She was supposed to be eliminated that very first night, but Brody wouldn't have it. It would seem he is interested in her and plans on keeping her here. Madelyn doesn't seem too thrilled about that idea."

"Doesn't seem too thrilled? Are you kidding me? Were you not watching what you filmed? I don't care what she says, her reaction to Brody's kiss would suggest she very much wants to remain here, hoping for something more permanent with him."

"Well, I still say she'll be an easy nut to crack. Leave it to me and she'll be walking away from the show within the week."

"I want her gone by the next elimination round. Do you understand me?"

Liz gave her a serious nod. "I did the background check you wanted. She's clean. No sex tapes, scandalous affairs, or any criminal records that might have been hushed up by her father. She doesn't even drink. Squeaky clean, that one, so blackmail is going to be out of the question, not that I think it will come to that."

"What are her interests?"

"She's an author, currently writing her first novel and nearly finished with her degree."

"Find out more about that. Specifically who is funding her college education. It could be her wealthy father, or maybe she has a sugar daddy we can expose on television."

"I'll look into it."

"See that you do."

As soon as Liz left her suite, Felicia threw the camcorder through the air and smiled as it slammed against the wall with a satisfying crack.

Madelyn Knightly could be Mother Teresa herself for all Felicia cared. No one was invincible. Everyone had a weakness. She would sniff out that weakness and bury her in it.

MIDGE

After the end of her one-on-one with Brody, Midge immediately grabbed Stacey and convinced her to fly back to the island with her before the rest of the crew, her father, or even Brody could stop her. Her father and Brody were too distracted, plotting the next group date to notice her stealthy withdrawal from the premises.

As they landed on the private airstrip and then disembarked from the helicopter, Stacey turned to Midge with hands on her hips and a disgruntled look on her face.

"What?" Midge asked.

"I can't believe you didn't want to wait for Brody. This guy has practically asked you to marry him, and you're shooting him down as if handsome billionaires in hot pursuit are a dime a dozen. What is wrong with you?"

Midge let out a despondent breath and tugged on one of her red curls. "Stacey, I know Brody can be charming and convincing when he flashes you that intense, soulful stare, but this whole thing is a charade. He holds no more interest for me than he does Felicia."

The girls walked over to one of the Jeep's waiting for the crew's return. Stacey got in the driver's seat while Midge rode shotgun.

"Look," Stacey said, turning the key in the ignition, "I know you think you're being played and used, but I honestly believe Brody is into you. You can't fake the kind of chemistry you two have because it's still there when the cameras aren't rolling. I really think you should let down your guard a little and give the guy a chance."

Midge considered Stacey's words carefully, but in her heart she knew what she knew. She had a lot to lose if this thing went south. Previous experience had taught her that men with money, power, and prestige acted in accordance with what served their own assets and interests best. Did she believe that Brody was good at heart? Of course, she did. His integrity with his company, his astounding work ethic, and his devotion to his mother were all aspects of his character that she greatly esteemed, but she knew Hollywood. She understood what bad press meant for a businessman like Brody, and he had a lucrative business to keep afloat.

In the end, Brody would do what was best for his company, his family, and himself, and who could blame him, really? Midge certainly didn't. Hadn't she come on the show for selfish reasons? She was also taking care of numero uno by making sure her own college fund didn't remain dry and barren. The free exposure as an author was a big draw as well.

In the end, the difference between Midge and Brody was their level of commitment to one another. She feared she might give up almost anything simply to help protect him and further his career, and she also feared that he would allow that and then leave her emotionally wrung out and abandoned once his image was restored and the show was over.

If she had to play along, she wanted to protect herself in the process, and those kisses weren't helping one iota.

Never again.

"Hello? Are you still with me, Midge?" Stacey gave her a soft nudge in the side.

"I'm here. Sorry. I was just considering what you were saying. I don't plan on lowering my guard, Stacey, but I do promise to avoid Brody when we're not shooting. That should dispense with anymore uncomfortable confrontations."

"I don't mind the confrontations. That's how I know you two aren't faking it. If you held little or no interest in one another, those confrontations wouldn't even happen, and they certainly wouldn't be as explosive as they are. It's pretty yummy, actually. I wish we could film that and put it on the show."

Midge shook her head but had to chuckle at Stacey's contagious, upbeat attitude.

"I forget that on-set there are eyes everywhere, including yours."

"Oh, and don't think I'll be closing my eyes anytime soon. Camera ready, that's me!"

As they pulled into staff parking, Midge turned to Stacey and gave her a grateful smile.

"Well, it's been a very long, grueling day. I think I'm gonna hit the hay."

"Yes, it must be so difficult to be ravished by Brody Prescott. I pretty much hate you, by the way."

"Ha! So what's on the schedule for tomorrow?" Midge asked as the girls got out of the Jeep and walked along the beach toward the mansion.

"They'll be filming Brody's date with Cambria, I believe, and the day after we're flying to our next location for the following week of shooting. Your itinerary should be on your bed by now, so just prep yourself. You'll be able to take it easy for the next two days since you already went on a date with Brody."

"That's a relief. I need to get some work done on my novel."

"Romance?"

"Of course."

"Is Brody Prescott the main character?"

"You're never going to let this go, are you?"

"Never. I'm convinced you two are meant for one another. Your love will rise above the challenges. The bright flame of your passion will never be extinguished. Your—"

"Before you continue to wax eloquent about my severely disturbed love life, I think you should consider writing romantic fiction, Stacey. Your talents are wholly wasted here with my father."

"Mark my words, Midge. Brody Prescott is the billionaire for you."

Midge smiled at Stacey's tenacious personality. She was like a dog with a bone once she got an idea in her head. Brody seemed to be of the same persuasion when it came to ideas he intended to pursue. She sincerely wished he wasn't quite as tenacious as Stacey, but in reality he was worse.

Much worse.

Midge grabbed the doorknob to her suite just as someone touched her on the shoulder.

She startled at the unexpected contact and turned to find Brody glowering down at her. His eyes were dark with repressed emotion and a muscle twitched in his jaw.

Would nothing go her way today? She cursed herself for wasting so much time talking to Stacey when she could have holed herself up in her room, with Brody Prescott safely on the other side of her door.

She arched an eyebrow in an attempt to collect her scattered emotions.

"Can I help you, Mr. Prescott?"

"Brody," he corrected. Then he took a step closer, backing her up against the door. "Why did you take off like that? We hadn't finished our discussion."

"Our argument, you mean?" Midge discreetly reached for the doorknob behind her and nearly sighed in relief as the cold metal slid comfortingly within her fingers. "I think we covered all the crucial topics for today." She slowly turned the handle.

"Madelyn, we were nowhere near close to working out this misunderstanding between us. I want you to trust me."

"This isn't a conversation to have in the hallway. There's always going to be someone listening in."

Midge glanced around, feeling certain a crew member would sniff them out at any moment. She couldn't believe Brody had managed to get away.

"Fine, then we'll discuss it further in your suite."

"We will not be discussing it further, period. I said my peace, and I'm done talking about it." She pushed the door open, backing into the room and slamming the door shut in his face. Only it didn't work out quite like she'd hoped. Unfortunately, the persistent bachelor planted his foot inside the door and entered the room, shutting it with much less force than she'd used.

"Get out of my room."

"No."

It was one word, but stated with that husky voice and calculating calm it made her blood throb within her veins. Why did he continually have this affect on her? She would never get used to it, nor would she ever get enough of it.

Enough of him.

Midge pushed against his chest, attempting to force him toward the door even though she really wanted him to stay.

Traitorous feelings!

"I said, get out of my room."

"And I said, no." His arms circled her body and pulled her against his chest. She should never have initiated contact. What a colossal mistake.

Midge tilted her head up to let out an angry retort, but the deep blue of his eyes caught her attention and made her say something entirely different.

"I've never seen eyes as blue as yours. Are you wearing colored contacts or were you just born with eyes meant to melt the most cynical hearts out there?"

Those blue eyes widened in surprise and then darkened with desire.

"Twenty-twenty vision," he said in a low voice. "Though they're only useful to me if they've managed to melt your heart, Madelyn."

Her hand lifted of its own volition. Her fingers lightly traced his eyebrow and then brushed along his cheekbone to the underside of his jaw. He turned his face into her hand and planted a soft kiss there. Then another at her wrist.

Her skin tightened and tingled at the contact while her blood heated within her veins. She blinked herself out of the stupor his magnetic gaze had captured her in and moved to pull away, but his arms held her locked and secure against him.

"You need to let me go."

He let out what sounded like a soft growl. Midge didn't expect that possessive refusal to make her feel wanted or desired, but it did.

"Never," he ground out.

Stalemate.

Unless she could distract him with some other topic and extricate herself from his grip.

"What are you going to be doing on your date with Cambria?"

His jaw tightened. "Why would you bring that up? It isn't what I came here to talk to you about."

"It's either that subject or more tales of Hawaiian mythology and folklore because I'm not interested in discussing anything that has to do with you, me, or our fabricated relationship."

"You seem to think you have a choice at the moment, but I have you trapped in my arms in your own suite."

"I'll scream."

He lowered his lips until they were hovering over hers.

"What makes you think I'll give you the chance?"

He crushed his mouth against hers in the most electrifying kiss yet. Without anyone present his kisses took on a whole new level of heat and intensity with no sign of him letting up or letting go.

Though Midge had done her best to mentally prepare herself for another round of Brody's sizzling affections, she nearly lost herself in the powerful pull he held over her, and then she realized that was exactly what she needed to do if she wanted to remove herself from the situation before she willingly gave as good as she got.

For the first time during one of their kisses, she threw her arms around his neck and fully engaged herself in the kiss while discreetly directing him backward and in the direction of her large bed. His surprise, yet eager acceptance of her capitulation released some of that tension in his arms. Once she positioned him exactly where she wanted, she managed—with great difficulty, considering how much she was truly enjoying this impromptu kissing session—to rip herself from his grasp by giving him one mighty shove backward which caused him to fall flat onto the mattress with a loud grunt. She ran to the bathroom, to what she hoped would be her safe haven against Brody's relentless pursuit of her.

She slammed the door just as Brody took inventory of the situation and jumped from the bed.

The door locked with a satisfying click, but the lock was flimsy at best. Nothing as sturdy as a deadbolt, but surely he wouldn't be so barbaric as to—

The door fairly shook with the brunt force of Brody's...fist? Shoulder? What exactly was he using to batter against the door?

Midge took one step back as it shook yet again.

"Madelyn, this is completely childish. We could have talked this out and cleared up this ridiculous misunderstanding between us by now," Brody said in a calm voice that belayed his intermittent hits against the door.

Midge did her best to stifle a laugh though her grin was unavoidable. Much to her dismay, she actually enjoyed the fact that he hadn't given up on her. Which was ridiculous. Like any man, he would let her go just as soon as he got what he wanted from the relationship.

She shook her head to dislodge the irrational thought, fortifying her resolve to avoid succumbing to Brody's charms or his currently attractive caveman persona.

"I'm afraid I'll have to pencil you in some other time, Mr. Prescott. Do feel free to speak with my secretary."

"Not good enough, Madelyn."

Midge looked behind her, trying to remember if there had been a window in the bathroom.

"I'm afraid it will have to be. I'm planning on taking a bubble bath now, if you don't mind."

"Not at all," he said in a casual tone. "Do you need someone to scrub your back for you?"

Her eyes sparkled at the mischief in his voice, and her mouth turned up into yet another smile despite herself.

"I'm a big girl, Brody. I believe I can manage."

"It would have been rude of me not to offer. I certainly could have used some extra help while scrubbing off the green food coloring you doused me with."

Midge couldn't help but let out a loud laugh. She came near the door and rested her head on it, imagining Brody might be doing the same thing.

"You had it coming, you know. Forcing me to stay on the show was bad form, Brody. You have no idea what else I have planned for you."

"I'm not eliminating you, Madelyn." His voice was low and alluring. "Do your worst, young lady. I never give up on what I want."

His bold declaration sent butterflies directly to her stomach. The wide grin on her face shouldn't have been there. His pursuit of her shouldn't have amused her and delighted her the way it did, but there it was.

Brody Prescott was a force of nature, an unyielding tsunami upon the normally smooth waters she'd been treading for so long, and she wondered how on earth she was going to stop him. She didn't know, but after scrutinizing the top of the door and noticing a small window just above it she figured she'd found a way to momentarily throw him off. She moved to the cabinet to her right and opened it, grabbing her body wash—appropriately dubbed Morning Mist—and then moved to stand on the sturdy end table next to the door.

"And you'll find that lingering by my bathroom door when you are entirely unwanted will carry severe and immediate consequences."

With that, she lifted up the small window and stuck her body wash out the opening. With a churlish grin she squeezed the bodywash, hoping it would hit its mark and letting out a triumphant laugh when she heard Brody's outraged response.

"What...? What is it with you and body wash? Madelyn, don't think for one second I won't make you pay for this."

Her skin fairly tingled at all the ways she figured he would make her pay, and then she chastised herself for actually looking forward to it. With one last chuckle she jumped from the table and moved to the door.

"I'm afraid your threats have bored me, and now I think it is you who needs a nice bubble bath. Shall we continue our little spat tomorrow?"

"Oh, you can count on it, minx."

She snorted and turned around, laying her hand on the counter near the sink and facing the mirror for the first time.

She couldn't help but let out a bloodcurdling scream at the sight that met her.

BRODY

Brody was about to leave Madelyn's suite—he couldn't do much with body wash dripping from his hair and shoulders—when he heard Madelyn's ear-piercing scream.

The fear and panic lacing her voice had him turning and bolting for the bathroom without pause. He threw his massive frame against the door and broke through on the first try, sending the door ajar on its hinges. He barely spared a glance for the damage he'd caused as he took in Madelyn, his Madelyn, staring in horror at the bathroom sink and the dangerous looking snake coiled in a sinister S shape, getting ready to strike. He reached her side and pulled her to him, attempting to get her as far away from the snake as possible.

She held her hand to her chest, cradling it. He turned her to face him, fearing the worst. His fears were soon realized as he saw blood oozing from two puncture wounds on the skin between her thumb and forefinger.

Madelyn's gaze was bright with unshed tears and her cheeks were a chalky white color.

"It bit me," she whispered.

CHAPTER 24

Midge

Midge stared at the menacing snake while Brody pulled her back against the bathroom wall and encouraged her to sit on the tile floor.

"Madelyn, look at me. Madelyn!" His terse command and the panic that laced it snapped her out of her shock. She flicked her eyes to his, noting his worry and concern.

"It's fine," she said, though it was far from the truth.

"It isn't fine, sweetheart. That bite is already starting to swell."

She heard him curse as he whipped out his cell phone, barking orders to someone about medical assistance and security. His voice hardly penetrated her thoughts due to the coiled snake peeking out over the top of her bathroom sink. How had that snake managed to make its way into her bathroom? Considering recent events, she doubted it had slithered in of its own accord.

Another threat. This one much more sinister than the last. Her tormentor's actions were escalating to an alarming level of lethal. Her immediate inclination was to blame Felicia since the pariah was more vindictive than any woman she had ever encountered, and that was saying something considering the people she knew in Hollywood. Women like her were all about winning the prize. She was like a child with a shiny new toy: only interested in it if she couldn't have it, and then pulling her hair and throwing tantrums if she didn't get what she wanted.

Midge imagined this stunt was the precursor to one mighty tantrum.

Stacey came running into the bathroom, surprising Midge with her presence.

"Are you also running security, Stacey? My father isn't paying you what you're worth," Midge croaked out. Her attempt at brevity fell short as she winced in pain. Her hand throbbed at the puncture site.

"Don't I know it," she said, kneeling down next to Midge and inspecting the bite mark on her hand. She glanced behind her to the snake still coiled and hissing in the sink. "That's a Brown Tree Snake." She shook her head and gently lowered Midge's hand to the floor, instructing her to remain still until the medic could get there. "Aggressive little monsters, but their venom isn't lethal. They're sending head of security up here to get rid of the snake."

Brody finished his phone call— which had actually seemed more like a yelling match with whoever was on the receiving end—and gently took her by the shoulders, slowly lifting her to a standing position.

"Do you think it wise to move her?" Stacey asked.

"We need to get away from that snake, and Madelyn can't be comfortable on the floor. Let's prop her up on her bed."

"Okay, but make sure to keep that hand below her heart. The venom may not be lethal, but everywhere it spreads it is going to cause serious discomfort."

"What in the world do you have in your hair?" Stacey asked.

"Body wash." Brody's reply sounded distracted and a bit offhand.

"Is this a new form of foreplay?" she mumbled under her breath.

Midge noted Stacey's raised eyebrows, but didn't have the energy to explain away her little prank.

She gingerly followed Brody's lead as he placed a hand on the small of her back and guided her out of the bathroom. The throbbing pain reached her elbow and didn't abate in the slightest. With gentle care, Brody lifted her, cradling her in his arms with her good arm propped against his chest. He then crossed the short distance between the bathroom and bed and lowered her down, making sure to prop up several pillows, fussing over her like her father used to.

The silent tears that slowly slid down her cheeks were in direct response to Brody's considerate attention and the realization that she craved such loving care.

"How did that snake get in here, Stacey?" Brody asked.

Stacey pointed to the window across the room.

"Her window was left open, and there are several tree branches hanging within slithering reach. It most likely made its way into her room through there."

Midge didn't correct Stacey's assumption, still lacking the proof she needed to point the finger at Felicia. She did her best to block out the pain so she could focus on the conversation and possibly add her two cents in where she could, but the throbbing took up her attention.

A medic arrived shortly, elbowing Brody out of the way. She expected Brody to retreat a few paces, but he surprised her by circling around the bed and taking his place next to her on the other side. He encouraged her to lean back against his shoulder, and for once she didn't fight the physical contact or his attentions.

As Stacey explained what kind of snake had bit her, Midge began to experience some dizziness and then a strange tingling started in her chest, tightening every time she took in a breath.

"Brody, I'm having a hard time...I can't seem to catch my breath," she wheezed out.

She heard a flurry of activity as Brody frantically barked orders at the medic. He spoke to her, but his words were muffled by the pounding in her head and her desperate attempts to pull air into her lungs.

Her last conscious thought before she blacked out was how badly she wanted to erase the panic and fear from Brody's expression.

BRODY

"She's not breathing. What's happening to her? I thought this snake bite couldn't kill her," Brody shouted. He held Midge's face in his hands, and his heart squeezed as he took in her blue lips and the dark circles under her eyes.

"She's having an allergic reaction to the toxin in her system," the young medic explained. He dove into his bag and grabbed what looked like a big pen, moving much slower than Brody would have liked and behaving much calmer than the situation warranted.

The medic jabbed the pen into Midge's thigh and within a few seconds her chest expanded as she gasped for air. Brody felt like he could finally breathe with her even though she'd only stopped breathing for a few moments.

He pulled her against his chest as she clung to him with her good arm. He noticed it shook from the trauma she'd endured.

"You scared me. That scared me." Brody kissed the top of her head, reveling in her nearness and rejoicing in the rise and fall of her chest against his. "You're never allowed to stop breathing again, do you understand me?"

She surprised him by letting out a shaky laugh. "I think we're both in agreement on that."

He marveled at her ability to find some humor in the situation when the women he was acquainted with would have dissolved into hysterical bouts of wailing and moaning. She pulled back to lean against the pillows, giving him a genuine smile, one without the usual wariness or distrust she had manifested thus far. He moved her to lean against his chest, figuring he needed to get in as much physical contact as he possibly could. He hated to take advantage of her vulnerable emotions, but if she was willing to let him in, he wasn't about to throw such a rare opportunity away.

She momentarily tensed as his arm circled around her, but then she relaxed into him again, her head resting just under his chin, and for the first time in his life he felt like he was exactly where he was supposed to be. Here, holding Madelyn. And miracle of miracles she hadn't pushed him away as she was so apt to do.

MIDGE

After giving her something through an IV to counteract the effects of the venom, the medic left her with instructions to notify him if anymore symptoms developed. She nodded wearily and closed her eyes for a brief reprieve.

Held in Brody's arms, Midge found it possible to relax a little. It made her very sleepy...and very happy.

Once the medic left, she waited for Stacey to get back to her other duties, but Stacey seemed to be bouncing around in an anxious sort of way.

"Stacey, are you okay?"

"I'm just a little nervous, that's all. The security guy they have coming to dispose of the snake is absolutely dreamy. I figure there isn't any harm in seeing if he needs help, but I'm always so darn tongue tied whenever I'm around him. Oh, and I am absolutely distraught over your painful snake bite. Nursing you back to health is my number one priority. It makes me look like a nurturer. Right?" She gave Midge a winning grin and strutted over to her.

"Naturally."

Stacey startled when her cell phone rang. "Hey Mr. Knightly...yes, Midge is doing fine, but...okay, yes...I'll let them know."

Midge furrowed her eyebrows, feeling certain she wasn't going to like whatever her father had to say.

Stacey appeared apologetic as she said, "Your dad wants you guys to reenact this entire thing for the cameras when you're up to it."

Midge's eyes widened. "Are you freaking kidding me? What does he mean reenact it?"

"Absolutely not," Brody said.

"Please, you guys," Stacey urged. "I know this is a crappy thing to ask you to do, but if I can't convince you to reenact the snake bite scene, I'll suffer the wrath of your father."

Midge screwed her face into a grimace. "What will this entail?"

Stacey smiled and sat down on the bed. "We won't actually film the snake bite. We'll just have a camera outside your door with screams coming from your room." She paused for a moment, clearly thinking something through. "What if Brody hears the screaming, bursts from his bedroom, and breaks into yours?" She glanced back at the bathroom door on its hinges. "Did you do that, Brody?"

"Well..."

She gave him a speculative look. "Just what exactly were you doing in here, anyway?"

Midge turned to him, wondering how they were going to explain themselves.

"It's like you said," he shrugged. "I heard Madelyn screaming and came to her aid. I can't resist a beautiful damsel in distress."

Stacey glanced to the door again and grinned. "Yeah, I definitely want to see that happen. We'll also need you to reenact the allergic reaction."

"My father is out of his mind." Midge said.

"Individual interviews will follow."

"Of course they will."

"When you've recuperated from your ordeal."

"Mmm hmmm."

A loud knock at the door announced the arrival of the head of security.

Talin Rhodes was a thickly built individual who barely cleared the bedroom door due to his gargantuan height and expansive shoulders. His light blond hair was cropped close to his head in a military style haircut, and he looked to be in his early thirties. Midge would have known that body-building lug anywhere.

"Talin." She held out her good hand as he hurriedly crossed to her side and took it in his own. "I didn't realize you were still working security for my father."

"I was looking into joining Taylor Swift's cavalry, but your father made me an offer I couldn't refuse, so I decided to stick around. Plus, there was the possibility of tormenting you again."

Midge smiled, remembering the little pranks he'd played on her when she had worked for her father. He'd behaved like an older brother in that respect. One of the few men in her life who enjoyed her company without expecting anything in return.

"You were unbearable, Talin, even though I got you back several times for all the pranks you pulled."

He chuckled. "I learned a thing or two from your ingenuity, but mainly I just wanted to be around you."

His eyes and words conveyed a meaning Midge didn't quite understand. Unclear as to why the atmosphere had become so heavy—or why Brody was all of a sudden radiating tension—she released Talin's hand and settled back into Brody's arms, ready to change the subject.

"So have you been dubbed the official snake catcher?"

He nodded and walked back to the door, retrieving a long stick with a noose hanging from the end.

"I'll have him out of here in no time, Midge, and then you and I can talk about old times for a little bit."

"Unfortunately, Madelyn is supposed to be resting after her allergic reaction to the bite," Brody said. Though his words were civil enough, Midge noted the bitter undercurrent they floated upon.

She thought she saw Stacey break into a small smile, but the twitch of her lips soon smoothed into a clear expression.

Seemingly unperturbed, Talin nodded and said, "I'll catch up with you after your nap then." Turning his eyes on Brody he said, "You've got some goop in your hair, bro."

Midge noted Brody's nostrils flare and his lips thin. He accepted a few tissues from Stacey to try and wipe away the generous amount of body wash still stuck in his hair.

Midge caught the satisfied smirk on Talin's full lips and narrowed her eyebrows as he entered the bathroom. Too tired to analyze the strange animosity between Brody and Talin she attempted to relax a little further. Within no time, Talin had the snake bagged and ready for...well, wherever he planned on taking the nasty reptile.

"See you soon, Talin." Midge said.

"You can count on it." He gave Brody an unflinching stare, some form of communication passing between them that thoroughly puzzled her, and then offered her a teasing wink before heading out the door.

"Dreamy, that one. A total bad boy, too. Just my type, really." Stacey sat down on the edge of the bed and fanned herself with her hand.

"I don't like him," Brody said. "I think he's got a thing for you."

Midge couldn't help but crack up at that pronouncement. Brody raised his eyes in surprise.

"You don't believe he's into you?"

"Of course not. I hardly believe that *you're* into me. Now the head of security is sporting a crush? Be serious, Brody. I've known Talin since I was sixteen."

"I *am* being serious. I'm seriously concerned that I'll be fighting off every male on the island in order to keep you for myself. I'm not opposed to it, but I'd rather not waste time with shows of male bravado when I could be kissing you instead."

Midge gulped as the cobalt blue of his eyes turned a shade darker at the thought.

"Pretty sure that's my cue." Stacey said. "Maybe I'll give stalking Talin Rhodes a try." She rushed out of the room before Midge could convince her to stay. The last thing she wanted was to be left alone, on her bed, with the man she was falling in love with.

"Brody, I think it's time for me to get some sleep."

"Sounds amazing. I could do with a catnap myself."

Her eyes widened. "You aren't seriously considering sleeping next to me, are you?"

"What better way to protect you from any further snake bites than to keep you here in my arms?"

"This is ridiculous. The window is closed. There won't be any other snakes in my bathroom, though there seems to be one in my bed." She gave him a pointed look.

"What if you have trouble breathing again?"

"I'll be fine."

"I'm staying, so accept it and let me hold you while you sleep."

Too tired to argue she merely nodded her agreement and allowed herself to ease back into his arms.

"This is only happening because I'm too exhausted to make another run to the bathroom to lock you out."

"It's not like there's anywhere for you to sleep comfortably in there."

"Don't even think about kissing me while I'm sleeping."

"Like you'll even know now that those pain meds are in your system, but I promise to be on my best behavior."

"Fine. We'll call a truce for now, but once I wake up, you're in for it."

She felt Brody's warm lips press against the side of her temple as he whispered, "I'm looking forward to it."

LIZ

Liz grabbed her cell phone and dialed Felicia's number, a number she hated about as much as she detested Felicia Davenport and her insulting, condescending behavior.

"Is she leaving or did you manage to screw up your latest attempt at harassing the girl into submission?" was Felicia's curt greeting.

Liz bit her tongue. Hard. As much as she despised taking Felicia's verbal abuse, she wasn't about to behave like her snarky self or take a defensive stance. Best if Felicia continued to consider her a pathetic tool in her arsenal rather than a potential threat. Because that's exactly what Liz intended to be. A threat to everything Felicia was fighting for. It wouldn't do to tip her hand and lose the obscene amount of money Felicia was paying her. Not until her own perfect plan fell into place.

Felicia Davenport wasn't the only contestant here with her eye on Brody Prescott.

"The snake was taken care of by security, but I haven't heard anything about her leaving the show."

"So now she has a small snake bite. Boo hoo. I should have hired Osama Bin Laden to terrorize the tramp."

"Not just a snake bite. Apparently she had a rather nasty allergic reaction to the venom." That bit of information hadn't sat well with Liz. She'd intended to scare Midge, not cause a potentially fatal situation. That's why she'd chosen that particular snake rather than something truly lethal.

"An allergic reaction that failed to do anything other than scare her. Pitiful. Are you even trying, Liz? Am I really going to have to take matters into my own hands?"

"No." Liz tamped down her panic at the thought of Felicia doing anything truly harmful to a girl she'd grown to respect. Liz's behavior toward Midge wasn't personal. It was business. Felicia Davenport needed to pay for the wrongs she'd committed. She needed to know what it felt like to have everything taken from her. She needed to lose, and she needed to lose big. "I've finally figured out why Midge has stayed on the show. Her daddy wrote up a contract stating that if she stays until Brody eliminates her she gets her trust fund back. If she leaves before that she gets nada."

"How much are we talking here?"

"I don't know the particulars, but I'm guessing millions are at stake for Midge. She really needs this money. Her scholarship dried up and she has no way to fund her last semester of college."

"Well, wouldn't it be interesting to see what her adoring fans think once they find out little miss Madelyn's reasons for being here have nothing to do with her love for Brody and everything to do with cold, hard cash?"

"My thoughts exactly," Liz agreed.

"Leak it to the press in a few days. We're changing our location to Rio de Janeiro in two days. I want reporters in Brazil ready to pounce on her once they smell blood in the water. If Brody wants to save his image, he'll have no choice but to cut ties with Madelyn once she's no longer the viewers' favorite."

Felicia hung up on her, which ticked Liz off. It shouldn't have angered her so much when Felicia's crimes against Liz's family were so much more monumental and devastating in nature, but it was just one more item to add to her valid list of reasons for ruining Felicia's life.

It was a shame Midge had gotten in the middle of everything. She and Brody seemed to have real chemistry despite their personal reasons for being on the show. In another life, another time, she imagined she and Madelyn Knightly would have been wonderful friends. Unfortunately, friendship—or any other relationship for that matter—hadn't played a role in Liz's life for quite some time. No. Just a burning need to right the wrongs against her family and finally mete out the punishment Felicia Davenport so richly deserved.

If destroying Midge's credibility with Brody and the American viewers helped her accomplish that…so be it.

BRODY

Brody strode into Talin Rhodes' office with a great deal of reluctance. He didn't like the man due to Talin's obvious interest in Madelyn, but he knew the security guard would be an extra layer of protection for what he feared might be stalking his girlfriend...soon to be girlfriend. His thoughts turned to her as he considered the information that Gregg had discovered about Felicia Davenport. It was all suspicion and conjecture, of course, but he thought if a certain tabloid received the slanderous information they might publish it, forcing Felicia to leave the show. He doubted Corbin Knightly would allow that kind of bad press for his show, but he would appreciate the scandal it caused. More scandal equals more viewers.

However, there was no question that Madelyn was in serious danger as long as Felicia remained on the show. The incident with the snake took on a whole new menacing feel as he realized that she was probably responsible for the attack...and possibly anything else that may have happened without his knowledge. It would be just like Madelyn to suffer in silence without confiding in anyone, especially if she felt he wasn't someone she could turn to with her problems.

Stepping into Rhodes' small office, he felt the other man's eyes assessing and dismissing him. He doubted the head of security had scored as many kisses with the blushing librarian as he had.

I'm behaving like a jealous frat boy.

Regardless of the unspoken challenge between the two, they needed to work together to protect Madelyn.

"You mentioned a concern about Midge's safety?" Rhodes started as he motioned for Brody to take a seat.

"I think, due to my obvious interest in Madelyn, and Felicia Davenport's obvious interest in me, Felicia might be targeting her in an attempt to get her off the show."

"Do you have any proof to substantiate your claim?"

"No, just a string of disturbing coincidences that occurred in Felicia's past." Brody then proceeded to share what Gregg had told him about Felicia's marital background.

Rhodes remained silent for a few moments as he digested the information. "I can't arrest her or force her to leave the show."

"I'm working on that angle at the moment. What I need from you is upping security where Madelyn is concerned. We need to know where Felicia and Madelyn are at all times. We need more cameras near the door to her room and also the window in case someone tries to let something more deadly than a snake into her suite."

Rhodes leaned his desk, steepling his fingers together and allowing his chin to rest atop them. Brody felt his eyes considering him for a few uncomfortable moments and then Rhodes spoke the words that had no doubt been on his mind since yesterday.

"If you hurt Madelyn, I won't hesitate to beat you black and blue."

"Not that it's any of your business, but I plan I asking her to marry me." He let that sink in as Rhodes continued his unflinching stare. "If you cared about Madelyn like that, why didn't you do anything about it before the rift happened between her and her father?"

Rhodes leaned back and rubbed his tired eyes. "She was too young when I first started working there, and even though I doubted the age difference would have been a real issue for her, I thought she deserved someone better than me, plus it was a serious conflict of interest for me to date Knightly's daughter."

"And now?" Brody pressed.

"Let's just say that if you don't snatch her up and marry her, I will. I won't hesitate a second time."

"Understood." Brody stood up and left Rhodes' office, feeling a bit discomfited by the man's serious interest in the woman he was falling in love with. So long as Rhodes helped to keep Madelyn safe, he would try not to worry about anything else.

CHAPTER 25

Midge

T he chartered plane descending upon a private landing strip just outside of Rio de Janeiro met with enough turbulence for Midge to grab the arm rests of her seat and once again curse her father, Brody, and the forces at be which seemed intent upon keeping her trapped in the most confusing situation she'd ever found herself in.

She had to admit, the view from the plane had been breathtaking once they circled close enough for Midge to catch sight of the imposing structures of Rio colliding beautifully with the dark blues and greens of the ocean water which gently caressed the white sands of the Copacabana beach. The last rays of sunset spread over the surface of the sea.

Midge couldn't help but feel overcome with excitement at the prospect of being in Rio again. She'd spent a summer here with her father when she was sixteen and had fallen in love with the culture, the people, and the wonderful language of Portuguese. She wasn't about to let her current predicament ruin the beauty of the city or color her previous experiences of her first visit to Brazil.

A slight tickle upon her neck made her feel as if someone was studying her from a distance. She didn't have to look up toward the front of the plane where her father and Brody were hashing out more details. She knew Brody was most likely pretending to listen to her father while attempting to burrow into her brain and extract her thoughts and feelings with his weighty stare.

She'd done a bang-up job of avoiding him after he'd stayed the night with her to "keep away the snakes" and "protect her virtue" while he was at it. She couldn't deny that sleeping in his arms after the traumatic events of the day had given her some of the best dreams she'd ever had.

Dang it.

Upon awakening, she'd found herself facing Brody with his arms wrapped tightly around her small frame and their lips mere inches from one another. Panic had quickly set in. She'd very carefully extricated herself from his embrace and hightailed it to the bathroom where she checked for snakes, locked the door, and jumped into the shower—a very cold, refreshing shower she dubbed as her own personal wake-up call. She remained in the shower even after she heard Brody tap lightly on the bathroom door and call out her name, inquiring about how she was feeling and letting her know he was going to grab them some muffins from the kitchen.

Once he'd left, she'd quickly dried off, got dressed, and made sure she was nowhere near her suite when Brody showed up with breakfast. It was easy to avoid him after that since his day was spent with Cambria on what was probably a perfectly romantic one-on-one date where he'd no doubt realized Midge wasn't even worth his time with Cambria in the picture.

And wasn't that just the biggest downer ever?

Like she cared.

Ha!

She probably owed him a huge thank you for coming to her rescue and staying with her all night after her run-in with the local wildlife, but she feared expressing her gratitude would result in throwing her arms around him and stealing a few kisses of her own.

Not an option for her. Not a safe one, anyway.

Getting on the plane and making sure Charlene sat on one side of her and Cambria sat on the other had also been a strategic maneuver to avoid Brody's annoying talent of getting her alone with him no matter where they were. Avoidance had been her number one priority up to now, and from the stormy expression on his face it was obvious he knew exactly what she was up to and didn't like it one bit.

Too bad. She was in survival mode, and she'd given him fair warning that their truce would end after their impromptu sleepover.

Disembarking from the plane put a glitch in her plans. As she brushed past Brody toward the exit, he grabbed her arm and detained her while the other contestants, too excited to notice the thrumming tension between them, hurriedly left the plane with their phones at the ready, taking selfies as they got the scenery behind them just right.

"I need to speak with you for a moment," Brody said. Obviously not a request. Midge gave Charlene and Cambria a pleading look which they misinterpreted as a plea for privacy. Giving her sly nods and not-so-subtle winks they disembarked with the rest of the girls, leaving her alone on the plane with a seething Brody Prescott.

Traitors! Weren't they competing for Brody's love and affection? What the heck was wrong with them?

"I'm a little tired from the trip, Brody. Do you think we could save our chat for the cocktail party later this week?"

His jaw tightened at the obvious suggestion that they not see each other until then. Just then her father stuck his head back in the plane.

"Midge, you and Brody can take a private limo to the hotel. We need more footage of you two together. Viewers like Cambria, but surveys show that they are anxious to see you and Brody thrown together a little more."

Brody slipped an arm around her and propelled her forward. "I think we can handle a little more alone time together."

"Fabulous. I'll leave you to it. Don't hold back on my account." Her father gave them an amused look and wiggled his eyebrows suggestively.

Traitor! What kind of a father sanctioned hanky panky in the backseat of a limo?

Her father, of course.

Sweet maple syrup!

Midge kept her mouth shut as Brody led her down the steps from the plane and into a waiting limo to their right. She caught sight of a few contestants glaring at her just before she allowed Brody to help her inside. It was so painfully obvious he favored her she almost wondered if some of the contestants were ready to voluntarily leave the show since being here was such a colossal waste of their time.

Once the limo pulled out of the landing area, Brody got right to the point.

"You're avoiding me," he whispered. She figured he didn't want the camera to pick up their conversation and he must have turned off his mic.

She surreptitiously moved to flip hers off as well.

"Yes."

He reached for her hand and brought her fingers to his lips, kissing the very tips of them and then leaning over and placing soft kisses along her jawline. She gathered he was trying to play to the camera, but the affect his actions had on her prevented her from achieving clear, rational thought. Her blood heated as his lips drew closer to the spot between her jawline and her earlobe.

"Why?"

She nearly shivered at the warm breath upon her neck. To continue playing to the cameras, she copied his actions and began her own line of kisses along his jaw. Once she reached his ear she whispered, "You're a dangerous opponent, Mr. Prescott. I'm currently giving myself some time to regroup."

"Not allowed. Do you really think I'll hold back when your defenses are down?"

She pulled away to look at him and noted the stormy intensity of his gaze, the way his eyes raked across her face as if he was trying to commit to memory every angle, every line, every single detail to sustain him and spur him forward. Okay, he either found her one of the most attractive females in the Universe or he was one of the most skilled actors she'd ever come across.

Probably the latter.

She had to get out of this limo.

"Stop that," he whispered.

"Stop what?"

"Planning your escape. Resistance is futile at this point."

Midge's brain was quickly becoming an incoherent pile of mush. She knew she wasn't supposed to allow him these privileges, not yet anyway, but she couldn't remember why.

"You're not allowed to kiss me yet," she murmured. It was a pitiful last attempt at preventing what was quickly becoming inevitable.

He placed his fingers just under her chin and began guiding her lips to his.

He'd been absolutely right. Resistance *was* futile, especially because they were on TV and breaking away from his skilled seduction clearly wasn't an option.

Just before he administered another one of his thrilling kisses, a sharp rap sounded on the partition between them and their driver.

"We've arrived at the Windsor Marapendi, Mr. Prescott."

Midge broke away from him.

Close call. Much too close.

She swiftly flipped her mic back on before disembarking from the limo.

Their lodgings were located just opposite the gorgeous splendor of the Barra da Tijuca beach at the Windsor Marapendi, and she might have taken in the grandeur of the place if she hadn't been so distracted by Brody's magnetic presence at her side.

Still in a daze, reeling from the abrupt change of avoiding him to nearly devouring him, she hardly paid attention to her surroundings as they checked into the hotel together and followed a clerk to her room. She allowed Brody to unlock her door for her and hardly registered the cameraman's presence as Brody leaned close and placed a kiss on her forehead.

"I'm just across from you, so if you need anything let me know."

She nodded, half drunk from his affections as he placed another lingering kiss on her cheek and pulled away, looking rather triumphant and smug as he crossed the hall, opened his door, and turned to give her one last smoldering stare.

"Good night, Madelyn," he said, though it was obvious he would have gladly joined her for another sleepover if she'd suggested it. "I'll see you tomorrow."

"Tomorrow," she said, nodding like a crazed bobble head with zero brain capacity.

He smiled and shut the door behind him. She took a few steps back and, miracle of miracles, managed to shut her own door without drooling in the process.

Once she had the benefit of a buffer zone between Brody and herself, she finally snapped out of whatever crazy spell he'd woven around her and sagged against the door.

"What just happened?" she said.

Midge braced herself for Brody's arrival as she waited with the rest of the contestants for the day's activities to be announced. The meeting room within the Windsor was quite stunning with art and decor that represented the free and passionate spirit of the people of Brazil.

She caught Felicia giving her the evil eye from across the room and couldn't help but give her a friendly wave as if they didn't just absolutely loathe one another. Felicia's narrowed eyes and clenched jaw shouldn't have made Midge feel so smug at that moment, but they did. For someone as calculating and cold as Felicia, she broadcasted her anger easily enough.

Les Lassiter made his arrival with his normal toothy grin. Brody was right on his heels.

"Today," Les began, "we've got another wonderful date challenge for you, which is going to get you out of this hotel and interacting with the friendly people of Brazil." A round of applause began, building the already anxious energy within the room. Midge had to admit she was excited to see the sights and experience the bustling city all over again.

"As many of you know, my company seeks to bring people together, fanning the flames of that love and passion that so many people find difficult to discover on their own," Brody said. His gaze swept over Midge, almost suggesting that their relationship certainly didn't suffer from that issue. "It takes passion, enthusiasm, and an appreciation for what romance is all about to run this company and make it the success it has become, and I've never encountered more passion, enthusiasm, or romance from any other culture than I have from the people of Brazil. Today, we're sending you on your own individual scavenger hunt so you can have the opportunity to capture that for yourselves."

An excited murmur swept through the room. Not even Midge could find a single thing to be upset or nervous about with the anticipation of interacting with the locals of Rio.

"We're passing around an envelope with a list of activities you need to capture on digital camera. The young lady who is able to capture the most items on her list by the time ten o'clock rolls around will be the winner of the next one-on-one date."

Cambria and Charlene giggled in excitement as they were handed their cameras and envelopes. Midge quickly accepted hers and turned to her friends as a new plan presented itself. She'd lost her cool with Brody the previous night. That couldn't happen again.

"I think we should work together, don't you?" she asked them. "We'll get these items checked off much faster than anyone else and then one of you can decide who gets the one-on-one date with Brody."

"You don't want to win the challenge?" Charlene asked.

"I've already had my chance," Midge stated with a shrug.

"Well, in that case we should just be helping Charlene, since I've had mine as well," Cambria said in excitement.

"That is so nice of you guys," Charlene squealed.

These girls constantly surprised Midge with their kind and giving nature. This was a competition, after all, but it seemed like Cambria and Charlene were more than happy to do what was fair rather than act cutthroat about the whole thing, a refreshing departure from what she was used to.

"All right, ladies. You have ten hours to complete your scavenger hunt. Show up back here with your camera and list intact," Brody shouted above the chaos of the room. "Ready, steady, go!"

Midge, Charlene, and Cambria looped their arms together and took off with one purpose and goal in mind: to make Charlene the winner of this latest date challenge.

Midge smiled and gave herself a mental pat on the back as they exited the hotel and started walking down Avenida Lúcia Costa.

Truce over, Brody Prescott.

It really was a perfect plan.

○

"First on my list...we need to capture the Brazilians' enthusiasm for food. How am I supposed to do that?" Charlene asked as the girls continued their walk amidst curious glances from people on the street.

Midge figured the sight of a man following them with a huge camera on his shoulder might seem a bit peculiar.

"I know exactly where to go, ladies," Midge volunteered. "Let's grab a taxi and head over to Ipanema Beach."

Midge hailed a taxi, and once the girls piled in she gave the taxi their desired location. "Playa de Ipanema por favor."

"Tudo bem, senhorita," the young man responded. He couldn't have been more than twenty, with creamy mocha skin and wild curly hair. He gave the girls an impish smile and a wink, eliciting laughter from them as they headed to their destination. Once they arrived and exited the vehicle she turned to the driver and said, "Pode esperar aqui até a gente volta?"

"Sim, sim. Vou te esperar aqui."

"Muito obrigada."

Midge turned to see a mixture of surprise and respect in Charlene and Cambria's expressions.

"What?"

"I didn't know you could speak Portuguese," Cambria said, wrapping an arm around her shoulder.

"It's very basic. Just stuff I learned when I lived here with my father while he was filming *Samba Heat*."

"That movie was amazing. I decided I wanted to become a professional ballroom dancer after that." Cambria started dancing her way across the warm sand as Midge and Charlene followed.

"Did you?"

"Of course not, silly. My mother enrolled me in acting classes and that was that."

"Is that where you get your dramatic flair?" Charlene teased.

Midge smiled at their playful banter as she led them along the beach, weaving her way through gorgeous Brazilian women taking in the warmth of the sun.

"Did you see that? Some of those girls are topless," Cambria squealed.

"Just go with it, sweetie. Indecent exposure isn't really a thing here." Charlene winked at a well muscled man who gave them a wink as they walked by. As a result, he failed to see the volleyball headed toward him and got knocked square in the head.

"You're a hazard to the male population here, Charlene," Midge said in a wry tone.

Charlene placed her hands on her hips and gave them a little shake. "Yes I am, and don't any of you forget it."

Midge suddenly wished they had worn bathing suits and sarongs for the occasion. Her yellow sundress was cool enough, but she felt like joining in on the next volleyball game.

"Where exactly are you taking us, Midge?"

"Over here. Some of the best food in Brazil can be found in these barracas."

Midge led them to Barraca do Uruguay, a food stand that specialized in made-to-order sandwiches. She remembered coming here almost every day with her father during his lunch break and grabbing a sandwich or two. They would sit and enjoy the warmth of the sand and the salty sea breeze as he talked about previous visits to Brazil or his plans over the next few days.

She missed it. She missed those talks with her father when he asked for her opinions and valued everything she had to say. A lump formed in her throat as she considered how difficult it must have been for him to discover she had no interest in joining his business after everything they'd shared together. She'd managed to only see her side of things rather than wondering if perhaps her father had wanted her to work with him, not to control or dictate her choices, but to simply continue that connection they shared.

She swallowed down an unexpected lump of emotion took a bite of her delicious chicken sandwich. After they took pictures of themselves ordering and eating their food they decided to tackle something else on Charlene's list.

"Brazilians are passionate about their soccer. Capture an image of you playing street ball with the locals," Charlene read.

"Easy," Midge responded. "You can literally go into any neighborhood in Brazil and find children willing to play a game with you. Let's check off a few more items on the list here before we go searching the neighborhoods."

After taking several pictures of themselves on the beach with various locals, volleyball players, and vendors they headed back toward their taxi.

"So, Midge," Cambria began, "I hope you don't think I'm trying to butt into your business or anything—"

"Even though that's exactly what we both want to do," Charlene said. Cambria elbowed her in the ribs and continued.

"There's obviously a really deep connection between you and Brody, and so far I haven't heard you say one thing about it. At least not to me, anyway. What exactly do you feel for him?"

Midge became painfully aware of the cameraman trailing them. She bit her bottom lip as she realized changing the subject wasn't going to be an option."

"I care for him a great deal more than I thought I would," she said, surprising herself with her honesty while simultaneously worrying about Brody seeing any of this footage.

"I feel like there's a 'but' hovering at the end of that statement," Charlene said.

"Well, it's complicated. I mean, obviously you both are here for Brody. You've already gone on a date with him, Cambria. You know how charming he is, how easy it is to fall into conversation with him and drink in every word he has to say."

Cambria nodded in enthusiastic agreement.

"Preach, girl. That man is too tempting for his own good."

"You see. You've already become attached to him, and Charlene, I'm sure you've enjoyed your conversations with him during the cocktail parties."

"He's scrumptious. That's all I've got to say on the subject. Any woman who doesn't fall under that man's spell is either dead or gay, and even then I'm thinking there's room to negotiate."

"So we all begin to care for him, and we have to do it in a way where we can protect ourselves in case he sends us home, which is insane. I can't understand why any of us agreed to this kind of heartache. It's completely masochistic."

Cambria laughed at that.

"But don't you think Brody is worth it? I've always been of the opinion that anything worth loving and worth loving well is also worth hurting for if it comes to that."

"You think a man is worth that kind of pain?"

Cambria thought long and hard about it and shrugged her shoulders.

"I suppose we could simply avoid men for the rest of our lives, but it seems to me that eternal loneliness is more painful and permanent than a few heartaches on the road to finding the person you're meant for."

"Why are you suddenly spouting out sage words of wisdom? I thought you got your degree in Fashion Merchandising. Now you're Gandhi?" Charlene said, in a good natured tone.

Cambria sniffed and turned a haughty look on them both. "Make fun of me if you want, but at the end of the day I'll have Brody all to myself while you girls are still hiding behind your own shadows afraid to give your heart to anyone."

"Well, I do believe we've just been challenged, Midge. Are we prepared to open our hearts and chase after the same guy?"

"Isn't that what we've been doing?" Midge asked wearily.

Charlene smiled and put both her arms around Cambria and Midge and said, "Suckers. That's what we are. Lovesick fools."

CHAPTER 26

Midge

T he rest of the day flew by in a blur of sights, sounds, and sweets as the girls continued to sample the city's culture, monuments, and all the food they could get their hands on. By the time eight o'clock rolled around, they had managed to cross several items off their lists, though they were nowhere near close to finishing all the tasks.

But there was one item in particular that Midge assured her friends they absolutely had to participate in.

"Get a picture of yourself dancing with a local at a street festival," Charlene read. "What's a street festival? Is that like Carnival?"

Midge laughed. "Not even close, but they are so much fun either way. Something amazingly special about Brazilian people is their unapologetic love and expression of music. They will literally sing and dance anywhere and everywhere, and street festivals are a perfect way to experience that. Let's head over to Lapa and check out the night life."

Their driver whisked them away to Avenida Mem de Sá, and then got out and actually joined them. Midge figured the sweet sounds of rhythm and samba music wasn't anything the young man could deny himself.

Grabbing Charlene's hand, he immediately led her into the tightly packed crowd and began dancing with her, much to the young girl's delight.

"Hurry, Cambria, you have to get a pictures of this," Midge said, laughing as the atmosphere of the festival lightened her spirits even further. She watched in amazement as people of all ages danced and sang to the music coming from a large street band on a makeshift stage in the middle of the street. It wasn't long before she and Charlene were swept up by friendly young men interested in dancing with two girls who were obviously tourists. Following her partner's lead, she allowed herself to get swept away, grateful that there was no language barrier when it came to dancing.

As the band wrapped up the last notes of the samba, she felt a tap on her shoulder and turned, surprised to discover Brody Prescott wearing a sultry smile. The street lights illuminated his features, making them appear more angular and defined. It sent her heart racing in a way that had nothing to with exertion from her previous dance.

"Posso dançar com ela?" he asked, directing his question toward the young man she'd partnered with.

The curly-haired boy gave them both a smile and then spun her in and right out into Brody's accommodating arms just as the music picked up again. Brody led her into a fast cha-cha and then dipped her low, causing a throaty chuckle to escape her lips before he lifted her back into his arms.

Midge surveyed the area, wondering if anyone from her father's crew had managed to penetrate the crowd of people, but it appeared that the dancing hordes were too cramped for camera and crew to follow. Relieved with this brief reprieve, she flipped her mic off and motioned for Brody to do the same.

"I had no idea you could dance like this," she shouted above the music.

He brought her closer to him and rested his lips against her ear.

"There are so many things you don't know about me, Madelyn, but I definitely plan to fix that."

They continued to dance amidst the crowded streets. Midge felt relaxed and peaceful for the first time since she'd joined the show. She couldn't think of anything more exciting—or dangerous for that matter—than spending time at a street festival dancing with this handsome man. Every look he sent her and every touch and caress of his hands caused tingles of electricity to thrum through her veins. That, combined with the lulling rhythm of the music and the celebratory atmosphere of the people around her, made her feel as if she was in some protective bubble, floating in a dream she hoped to never wake from.

As the music came to a close and the audience applauded and cheered, one of the street musicians announced their intention to slow things down a bit.

"Esta é a música de Djavan," he shouted.

The crowd let out uproarious cheers of approval.

As the familiar strains of the melody washed over Midge it brought with it a flood of emotions connected to her previous visit here and the time she'd spent with her father.

"Dad and I used to come to these street festivals all the time. He loved it when they played music by Djavan," Midge said.

She noted Brody inching closer to better hear what she had to say.

"What happened between you and your father? There seems to be quite a bit of tension in your relationship."

Midge bit her lip, trying to understand just how she'd allowed six years to pass without fighting to fix her relationship with Corbin Knightly.

"He loves me. I know he does, but his career has always come first. I was with nannies when I was a baby and then a toddler. My poor mom did what she could, but her addictions got the best of her early on in their marriage, and he never did get her the help she needed. I used to think it was because he didn't care, but I wonder if he was just as clueless as everyone else when it came to finding the right rehab facilities and the right words to motivate my mother to clean up her act."

Midge felt Brody slide a hand around her waist as the sweet sounds of *Faltando um Pedaço* played across the street. The song was about missing a piece of your heart or maybe even a piece of yourself. It was a song she easily related to since she felt that most of her life had been spent searching for what was missing.

"I was lonely. I don't think I've ever really admitted that to myself, but it was the truth. My father was too busy filming movies all over the world, and my mother was too high to notice me. When I was six, Dad planned a trip to Ireland for one of his projects. It was the last straw for me. I threw the kind of temper tantrum any diva would be proud of."

Brody let out a husky laugh. "I imagine that got his attention."

"It did. He hadn't really had to do much parenting up to that point, and I distinctly remember him saying he would be more than happy to take me if he didn't think I'd be so bored. For me that was the answer, the key to everything. If I shared his interests, if my world revolved around what was most important to him, then I wouldn't be alone anymore. So he took me to Ireland, and we were inseparable after that. I was home schooled quite a bit, but I didn't mind it. Not when I had so many amazing adventures with my father to look forward to. He taught me everything he knew about film and production, budgets and sourcing...everything necessary to prepare me for a partnership in his company once I was old enough to carry that responsibility, but something neither one of us counted on was the fact that I would love writing stories more."

"He couldn't see that maybe that would have been an asset for his company? Think of the screenplays you could write, or new and inventive ideas for reality TV." He wiggled his eyebrows teasingly.

Midge just stared into the swaying mass of people dancing to the haunting strains of Djavan's music.

"When I told him what I really wanted to study, the look on his face was terrible...like I'd gutted him. He said he wasn't about to pay for my education or continue to fund my elaborate lifestyle if I wasn't going to stick to the plan, insinuating that I spent money carelessly or that I might only care about money rather than my relationship with him."

Midge swallowed hard, remembering how insulted she'd felt. How could he even hint at her being as shallow and unfeeling as that. "It hurt me. It hurt to think he assumed I had ever cared about the money or his financial support. I wanted his emotional support. I wanted to believe that he loved me and saw me as an individual with brilliant ideas and goals worth pursuing, but in that moment he proved to me what I'd always feared: if my interests didn't center around his career and around the world he had built for himself then I wasn't worth his time or his company. It wasn't worth it to him."

Brody nodded.

"Maybe your dad was afraid if you didn't stay completely involved in his life and his world that he might lose you. Maybe he feared your love was conditional based on his past experiences and not due to any bad behavior on your part. Is it possible you two simply misunderstood each other's motives, Madelyn?"

She turned her attention to him, surprised by his candid response.

"I suppose it's possible, but we've never really talked about it. Both of us were too stubborn to see the other's point of view."

"Well, maybe it's time to put that misunderstanding to rest. Talk to him."

"Maybe." Midge gave him an appreciative look. "Who needs a therapist when Brody Prescott's in the vicinity?"

"I think a better question to ask is, who needs to go looking for love in all the wrong places when Brody Prescott is the obvious choice?"

"Well, you are the only man on the show. That limits my options considerably," she teased.

Brody brought a fist to his heart, behaving as if she'd just wounded him.

She gave Brody a playful push. The music changed to another Djavan song and she clapped her hands in excitement.

"Do you know this song?" Brody asked.

Midge nodded as she swayed to the music, allowing Brody to bring her in for a slow dance as he said, "I would love to hear you sing along."

The song was a favorite of hers, one most Brazilians knew by heart. As the vocalist began to sing, everyone in the crowd joined in.

"What is the song called?"

"Se.... It means, if." Midge sang along with the crowd, allowing the wonderful music and the voices of the people of Rio to take her back to a time when her life had been less complicated and much more fulfilling. A time when her father could do no wrong, when her heart didn't belong to a man she feared she could never trust, and a time when her future had appeared so clear and promising.

"Can you tell me what the song is about?"

Midge nodded. "I can loosely translate it for you." She waited for the song to repeat before she began. "Djavan wrote about a girl who is being very indecisive in regards to her feelings for him. He says: You say that you don't know if you're saying no, but you also aren't certain if you're saying yes. You know when it is a yes, let it come from the heart."

"Beautiful," he said under his breath.

Midge nodded as she continued to translate.

"You know that I only think of you. You say you live to think of me. Could be, but if that's true you need to let go of the part of you that says no. Free the wildness inside and burn with passion. It won't hurt you to decide. Just say yes or say no. But you love to say if."

Midge felt Brody's eyes burning with intensity as they rested upon her features. The more she translated the song the more she realized how applicable it was to their situation. She was definitely hovering between a yes and a no, but the situation was far more complicated than any song could put into words. If she crossed that threshold and gave her heart to Brody she had to be positive it was a sure thing. All she knew for certain at this point was his obvious attraction and regard for her, but did it go beyond the lights and eyes of the cameras? Were his feelings as serious and enduring as hers?

She tried to cast aside her troubled thoughts as she continued to translate the song.

"I take it seriously, but you continue to pretend it isn't. You say so many things, I'm afraid to believe. It makes me feel the kind of cold that comes from a southern winter. You want this to be zero-on-zero, but I want one-on-one. I don't know if you want my warmth and love. Saint George please lend me your dragon. It would be easier to learn Japanese in Braille then for you to decide if our love can be or not."

Brody chuckled under his breath at that. "Sounds like a man truly frustrated by the indecision of a woman. I can very much relate."

Midge glanced up at him, spurred on by a spike of anger at his insinuation. "Can you? Because I find that I can very much relate as well. You're hinting at my being obscure in my feelings for you when this is just a game to you. Am I supposed to give you my heart both on and off the screen when I have no idea if you're saying yes, no, or if?"

Midge tried to pull herself away, but Brody's firm grasp reeled her even further toward him. He rested his forehead against hers. "On camera or off camera, I will always be saying yes, Madelyn. Am I going to have to learn Japanese in Braille to have any hope of deciphering what your intentions are now that I've laid mine bare? Or can you give me a yes and simply allow me to love you?"

Love. He'd said the word love. Like it was that easy. Faced with this pointed question, Midge didn't know how to respond or even how to begin to trust in what he offered. His words to her father kept replaying over and over in her mind, completely contradicting what he claimed to feel for her now. The idea of taking that leap into waters unknown and most likely treacherous in nature left her shaking in his arms, terrified to make that call only to drown in the process.

A new song began, more up-tempo in nature, and the moment passed, but Brody kept her close to him, refusing to move along to the beat of anyone else's drum.

"It was a beautiful song, Madelyn."

"More beautiful in Portuguese," she admitted, letting out a soft breath.

"Some things weren't meant to be said in any other way or in any other language."

"The issue of whether one can love another or not seems to be fairly universal, no matter which country you find yourself in. Do you leap or do you fold?" He regarded her intently as he lifted her fingers to his lips and softly kissed each of them. "Seems to me the solution is also a universal one."

"Leap?" she whispered.

"It's the solution I'm hoping for."

She thought he might pull her in for a kiss, and at that very moment she knew if he did there would be no hesitation on her part. Fortunately, a sharp cry to her right interrupted their charged moment.

"Brody, I didn't know you came to hang out with us!" Charlene shouted over the din of the music. She grabbed Brody by the hand and pulled him towards her. "I'm just gonna borrow this cutie for a moment, Midge. My turn for a dance."

Midge smiled in relief, ready to be freed from Brody's demanding presence, but her heart let out an involuntary pang as she watched Brody hold Charlene in his arms, leading her into a samba.

Cambria sidled up to her, shaking her cute little fanny the whole way. "I think I've decided that I'm never leaving Brazil. Not even for Mr. Brody Prescott," she shouted. She did a few hip bumps with Midge and then grabbed her hands and began dancing with her.

Though Midge appreciated the interruption, she knew she wasn't going to be much fun anymore and decided the best thing to do was hail a taxi back to the hotel and let Cambria and Charlene have their time with Brody. She tried to convince herself that her decision wasn't a ruse for simply running away from him. After communicating her plans with Cambria, she set off down the street and away from the more crowded areas to search for a taxi.

Within minutes the heavy weight of someone's stare fell upon her shoulders, tracking her movements. She couldn't dismiss the sensation. She stopped and allowed her eyes to peruse the area, not entirely certain of who she was looking for. A quick nudge on her shoulder had her nearly leaping out of her shoes in fright. She turned and found herself facing nothing more threatening than a small, barefooted boy holding out a note for her.

"Uma mensagem para a senhorita," he said in a scratchy voice.

Midge's eyebrows narrowed at this, but she accepted the dirty paper and handed him a few reais in the process.

Her eyes widened and then narrowed in anger as she read the brief note written in red ink.

YOU DON'T BELONG HERE.
LEAVE NOW OR YOU'LL BE SORRY.

Midge folded the piece of paper into a tight square and clenched her fist around it, nearly grinding her teeth in the process. Did Felicia really believe she would simply cower in a corner and let these threatening messages send her packing?

Did Midge want to be here? No. Was she falling in love with Brody? Yes. It made more sense for her to heed the threats and leave since both her body and emotions seemed to be in danger of potential harm, but she was more interested in getting to the bottom of Felicia's game and protecting Brody from that woman's dangerous obsession. Angry at the world in general, but also with herself, she grabbed a taxi and headed back to the hotel.

CHAPTER 27

Brody

As Brody prepared himself to enter the hotel's meeting room and announce the winner of the one-on-one date, he couldn't help but feel a huge amount of frustration that Madelyn hadn't been the one to win the challenge, and the thing that bothered him most about the entire ordeal was his lack of knowledge where her feelings were concerned. He didn't know if she'd really given the scavenger hunt everything she had or if she hadn't cared at all and entered the challenge with absolutely no intention of winning it.

Instead, Felicia had won the damn thing, though he knew she'd cheated. There really was no way that any of the contestants could have finished every single item on the list in time. There were simply too many to fit into one day. After arguing with Knightly that morning over disqualifying Felicia and going on the date with Charlene, who had finished a close second, he was in a seriously frustrated mood.

Knightly had insisted Felicia needed to have her moment. He wanted their time spent together to end in one massive blow-out just like Knightly had hoped it would when he first signed her for the show. So now Brody had the distinguished honor of essentially starting a fight with Felicia by asking the hard questions concerning the measures she took to slur his good name.

Brody really wasn't interested in the inevitable confrontation and subsequent meltdown he knew Felicia would subject him to.

"America needs to see Felicia as she really is, which will further cement your glowing image in their eyes," Knightly had instructed.

"I thought we were focusing on Madelyn," Brody had argued.

"Felicia has been leaking a story to the press about how you're torn between her and Midge. She says she isn't getting the right amount of attention required to solidify her claim on you. You need to nip this in the bud now, Brody."

"Does that mean I get to eliminate her at the end of the week?"

"Of course not. You know Rhodes wants her here to keep an eye on her activities."

Brody sighed as he reviewed that less than satisfactory conversation in his head before squaring his shoulders and entering the meeting room with immense trepidation.

"Isn't this wonderful, Brody? A private candlelight dinner on the beach is just the thing we needed to revive that spark between us," Felicia crooned as she took a small bite of her dinner salad.

Brody couldn't have felt less turned on by Felicia's presence than if a long line of Brazilian men had come parading by wearing nothing but Speedos. He nearly gagged just thinking about it.

"Felicia, I did want to continue to clear the air between us. Some of your explanations concerning your involvement in maligning my image didn't really hold much water."

"Why whatever do you mean, Brody dear?" Felicia lifted a leg under the table and strategically rubbed her foot along the inside of his calf muscle. Brody retreated a little with a pained smile fixed upon his features.

"That friend of yours who told you such inflammatory information couldn't be found anywhere, and after doing some private investigating of my own it would seem that the story was fabricated entirely by you. Now my only question is why? If you care for me as you say you do, then why would you allow my clients and prospective clientele to assume that I would ever tread on my company's privacy policies?"

Brody knew why, of course, but Knightly insisted upon a full unveiling of who Felicia Davenport really was, and he intended to follow through with the plan no matter how unappealing he found it.

Felicia set down her fork, scrunching up her nose a tad and then allowing her full lips to pout in what he assumed was her alluring attempt at looking sad and repentant.

"I was hurt by the way you brutally turned me down when I invited you into my home for drinks."

"As I recall, I politely declined your invitation for drinks due to an early morning meeting I couldn't cancel. I'd hardly call that grounds for slandering my name on tabloids and social media."

Brody watched as Felicia's grip on the table perceptibly tightened. Her hand began to turn white due to the amount of effort it took to control her temper. He waited with anxious anticipation as she did her best to control what he assumed would be one mighty outburst. To his dismay, she took in a deep breath, patted her enormous hairdo into place, and reached across the table, taking his hand in hers. The temptation to recoil in disgust nearly overwhelmed him.

"I suppose I was so devastated to think that someone as wonderful and brilliant as you would reject me. I behaved poorly and tried to blame my actions on other people."

Brody watched in fascination as her jaw ticked in the corner. She wasn't used to having to explain herself, apologize for anything, or even beg someone for forgiveness. Watching her squirm under the lights and scrutiny of the cameras surrounding them was almost acceptable payback for her vindictive actions so many months ago.

Almost.

He kindly patted her hand like a father might with his child and then pulled it out of her reach. Her eyes flashed in anger, but she deepened her smile and offered him an imploring look.

"It seems a bit extreme to go to such measures in order to get a man to notice you. Are you certain you were truly interested in me or in my money? Some women can become unhinged at the thought of losing such a lucrative meal ticket."

He was pushing her buttons, baiting her in the hope she might break through that thin exterior of calm and collected poise and unveil the she-devil he knew existed.

Unfortunately, Felicia had much more control than he or Knightly had anticipated. A brittle smile spread across her face as she leaned forward a little more, making certain that the rise and fall of her cleavage was on full display for Brody's benefit. He kept his eyes glued to Felicia's overly made-up face, refusing to give her the idea that he might enjoy sampling her wares.

"Brody, when I look at you I don't see money at all. I see a good man worth pursuing, someone I can easily see myself falling in love with."

So she wasn't going to take the bait and rise to the occasion. He almost glanced past Felicia and the bright lighting of the set to glare at Knightly and ask, *Now what?*

"Well, if that's the truth, Felicia, then I'm honored you think so highly of me."

He lifted his glass and toasted to her health. It was going to be a very long, very trying date.

MIDGE

Midge paced her hotel suite, waiting impatiently for Brody to return. She'd been miserable at dinner with the other contestants. It didn't seem prudent or even rational to worry for Brody since her father and several members of the crew were filming his date with Felicia. It was silly to think that the vixen might try to hurt him when her target was clearly Midge. But she was convinced Felicia Davenport was a dangerous woman, threatening her at every turn yet lurking in the shadows behind anonymous phone calls and menacing notes.

Midge stopped short as a new realization came to her. How could she have been so stupid as to never consider it? Felicia hadn't been on the group date in Honolulu. She wasn't there to push Midge into the closet and lock the door behind her. She worried her lip between her teeth, wondering if that incident actually had to do with Felicia or if perhaps Felicia was the puppeteer behind all of this. What if she had her own little puppet doing the work and she was pulling the strings?

The thought sent a shiver down her spine. Midge didn't have a clear picture of who her enemies were and even less chance of protecting herself. Her heart nearly leaped out of her chest at the sharp rap at the door. Midge distractedly moved to answer it, but the only thing she found on the other side was a small white box the size of her palm. She bent down to pick it up, looking for something that might hint at who had sent it.

On top of the box she found a small card with a floral design on the front. The words *Thinking of You* were written in a precise hand that looked masculine. Surprised that Brody would have a gift delivered to her in the middle of his date with Felicia, she quickly untied the bow at the top and pulled back the lid.

What lurked beneath left her completely immobile. Resting within the white folds of sparkling tissue paper was one of the ugliest spiders she'd ever seen, and certainly the ugliest of this particular species.

A Brazilian Wandering Spider was one of the most venomous spiders you could run into anywhere. This one was black as night with strips of silver along the spindly legs and a humongous, grayish-black abdomen. It's sinister eyes glared up at her from its perch.

She knew enough about them to know that any sudden movements might encourage the spider to jump at her and bite, but as she continued her frozen staring match she realized the spider's stillness wasn't quite normal, especially after unearthing it from the box like that. She slowly set the box down on her dresser, taking hasty steps away.

It had to be dead. That spider would have jumped at her the moment she opened the lid if it had been alive. Her father had made certain she knew all about the various types of animals and insects in Brazil before they had moved there for the summer.

She still remembered her lessons and knew exactly what this spider was capable of. The fact that it remained motionless convinced her even further that some sick, deranged person had killed the thing and delivered it to her door.

Why? How exactly did this further Felicia's agenda other than working as an intimation tactic. Midge glanced to the lid she still held in her hand. Her eye caught some writing scribbled in red on the inside of the lid.

THINGS ARE ABOUT TO GET VERY NASTY FOR YOU.
LEAVE NOW!

If she'd had any doubts about whether or not Felicia had an accomplice, they no longer existed now. Felicia couldn't have left her date with Brody to deliver this delightful present at her door. Someone else had done it for her.

Things were definitely escalating toward violence. True, the spider was dead, but Midge hadn't missed the fact that her tormentor could have used a number of harmless spiders to send the same message. Instead, the most venomous one sat dead in that box, The distinction wasn't lost on her. Felicia Davenport was out for blood.

BRODY

After such a grueling evening with quite possibly the most appalling woman on the planet, Brody needed a good cleansing, a way to revive himself, to give himself the wherewithal to continue his crazy plans of wooing Madelyn while essentially pretending to date several other women.

His cell phone rang just as he headed into his suite. He groaned when he recognized the number.

"Mother, I'm surprised you're up right now? Isn't it the middle of the night in L.A.?"

"Brody, why in the world did I just see teasers of you and Felicia Davenport on my TV tonight?"

Brody rubbed a hand through his hair as he sat down on his expansive bed.

"That was fast. I just barely went on the date with her."

"You may as well have gone on a date with a barracuda. At least the creature gives you the courtesy of looking you in the eye when it strikes. This woman is a sneaky little black widow."

"Mom, Knightly and I were trying to draw Felicia out and create a scene to enhance ratings."

"She didn't really rise to the occasion then, did she?"

"No. She's smarter than that, something I wouldn't have said after the first hour of meeting her, but I've found Felicia Davenport to be a fatal combination of stealth, beauty, and smarts."

"This entire charade is ridiculous, Brody. You and Madelyn are obviously perfect for each other even if she *is* still fighting it a little bit."

"You can tell she's hesitant from the footage?"

"Well, I may not have spent much time in her presence, and it may not be obvious to anyone who has never met her, but it's obvious to me that she's putting on a show for the cameras. What's the matter, sweetie? You still haven't managed to charm her yet?"

"I hit a snag when she overheard me saying something to her father that she took out of context." He explained what had happened and how she had misunderstood him and then waited to see if his mother had any suggestions for him.

"Well, you certainly screwed this one up, didn't you?"

"Your criticism is not exactly helping me, Mom."

"I'm just giving it to you straight. Can you really blame the girl for being gun shy around you when she heard you say one thing to her father while you pretend to feel something completely different when you're filming?"

"I'm not pretending to feel anything, but I'm beginning to wonder if she is."

"You need to go have a talk with her. Clear up this little misunderstanding once and for all."

"Now?"

"No, Brody. How about you continue to let her assume you're using her for all the wrong reasons."

"Right. So I'll go talk to her now."

"Clever. I've always thought you were the smartest billionaire on your block."

"Thanks, Mom."

MIDGE

Midge jumped at the knock at her door, unclear as to whether or not she should grab the lamp and use it as a weapon in case the next delivery involved something not only lethal but living.

"Who's there?" she called out in a faint voice.

"Madelyn, it's Brody. I know you may not want to speak to me right now, but we really need to talk."

Relief swept over her as she rushed to the door and opened it. She drank in his gorgeous eyes and the sharp edges of his cheekbones and jaw as she motioned for him to come in.

"What's that in your hand?" he asked pointing to the lid she still had a death grip on.

Midge stared at it for a moment, at a loss as to how to explain the threats she'd been receiving.

"Oh, it's just a lid to one of my jewelry boxes." She quickly strode over to the dresser where the lid's other half and its hideous occupant stood just out of Brody's field of vision. She reminded herself that the stupid spider was dead and wouldn't jump out at her if she placed the lid over it. Once the box was closed, she returned to Brody's side and folded her shaking hands in front of her. She hadn't been prepared to see him so soon, especially after her initial scare, which she hadn't quite recovered from.

"What can I help you with, Brody?"

He studied her closely for a moment, looking as if he were about to ask her something and appearing to change his mind.

"I missed you," he stated.

The simple yet honest ring to that statement left her searching his expression certain she would find some underlying reason behind his words, but all she saw was uncompromising sincerity. She had to say it. She had to understand why he was still playing the part even when there was no one filming them.

"I heard what you said to my father, so why are you still pretending?"

He lifted a hand to her hair and sank his fingers into the soft curls at the side of her temple. She wanted to close her eyes and allow herself to revel in the feel of his fingers tugging gently on her hair, but she left her features blank and did her best to hide the way he affected her.

"As I stated before, you took what I said out of context. If you'd continued to eavesdrop just a little longer you would have heard me explain to your father that you are the reason I am on the show in the first place."

Midge's eyes widened in disbelief.

"What? That isn't true at all. You were already planning on it when I met you and your assistant at Café Canapé."

His eyes danced in remembrance.

"Right. We met. You intrigued me. You knew who I was and that information didn't impress you in the slightest. You weren't afraid to tell me the truth and show your disdain for my terrible behavior and inappropriate suggestion that I pay you to date me—which was my bungling attempt at tricking you into spending more time with me—and you put me in my place in a way that no one ever has before. You were completely uninterested in my money or my connections, which might have given you some publicity as an author." He removed his hand from her hair and cupped her cheek, drawing her face just an inch closer to his. "There was no way I planned on doing the show after finding a woman as interesting and remarkable as you. I went to your father's office to personally inform him that I wanted to bow out gracefully. I had every intention of searching the city for you. Imagine my surprise when you showed up at Knightly's office just before I had the chance to cancel on him."

Midge's eyes widened. "You...you were in the other room? Please tell me you didn't hear everything that was said."

Brody shrugged. "It wasn't my fault your father didn't shut the door."

Midge's eyes narrowed, not fully believing in his innocent expression.

"So you knew exactly who I was, and you overheard my father bribing me to be on the show."

"That's right."

"Why didn't you just cancel on my father, either way? You found out who I was. You didn't have to do this. You didn't have to continue on with the show."

"How else were you going to pay for your last semester of college? I wanted you to be able to get your trust fund back, but I also wanted you to feel like you had earned it. From the little I know of you, Madelyn, I recognize that your independence, your ability to fend for yourself is important to you." He moved his hand to the nape of her neck and moved her just a little closer. "If I'd canceled the show, it would have pushed production back while they scrambled for a new billionaire. And with my luck you might have become interested in the guy. I couldn't risk it."

Midge's defenses weakened, especially after he admitted to doing this show so she could get her trust fund back. It was probably the nicest thing anyone had ever done for her. The most amazingly thoughtful gesture.

"Now, I could have called the whole thing off, pursued you, and offered to pay for your tuition, but you wouldn't have accepted that, and you might have been completely offended by it or believed that I was trying to pay you off for dating me and helping me with my image instead of recognizing that I'm interested in simply being with you and nothing else. So this was my solution, though I would have pulled out of it at the restaurant if you had given me a reason to think that my attentions were welcome. Slapping me in the face forced me to pursue you in an environment where you couldn't get away from me so easily."

He gave her a wolfish grin that sent tingles shooting along her spine.

He knew her so well. He understood her personally instead of labeling her as Corbin Knightly's daughter. She could hardly wrap her brain around the possibility that this man wanted her with no strings attached.

"So you came for me. You're here for me." She thought if she said it out loud it might make the idea of a handsome, wealthy billionaire interested in her even remotely believable, but it didn't. Not one bit, yet what exactly did he have to gain by telling her this when she had already agreed to play along.

None. She could see no reason why he might go to these lengths to convince her of his interest unless he truly *had* followed her onto the set of *Marry Your Billionaire* to pursue a relationship with her.

And didn't that just beat any and all fairy tales out there?

Still, years of duplicitous and thoughtless behavior from the opposite sex, and even close friends, had managed to fuel her insecurities to the point that she didn't know how to trust him or what to believe. That fear held her in check and prevented her from simply accepting the possibility.

"Brody I..." she let out a shaky breath. "I don't know how to believe you."

"Do you *want* to believe me?"

She hesitated before throwing herself off that precipice where life gets messy and experiences can hurt.

"Yes. I want to believe you."

The smile he gifted her nearly blinded her with its brightness.

"That's all the encouragement I need, for now."

CHAPTER 28

Brody

B rody swore his heart stopped beating as he waited to hear Midge's response to his question.

"Yes. I want to believe you."

The relief he felt at that one simple concession nearly brought him to his knees, and the happiness that came immediately on its heels produced the first real smile he'd been able to give in a long time.

"That's all the encouragement I need, for now."

She bit her bottom lip in a nervous gesture, the one he found absolutely adorable. He considered kissing her to commemorate this first step toward a possible future together, but man-handling her hadn't really earned him too many points, and he didn't want to push her too far too fast, destroying this tentative trust she had reluctantly bestowed. Instead, he slowly moved forward and enfolded her tense frame in his arms. He sighed in relief when she rested her head against his shoulder and relaxed in his embrace.

It irked him that he'd had to spend the evening with Felicia when all he could think about was the previous evening of dancing with Midge. She had taken off so quickly, making her escape when he was distracted with Charlene. Before he knew it she was gone, and his heart had hollowed in the wake of her absence. She seemed to be forever running from him, and the anxious ride back to the hotel afterward was made more desperate with this irrational fear that she wouldn't be there when he arrived.

That one moment of desolate worry made it clear to him that his feelings had grown from beyond interested to absolute. He wanted no one but this beautiful girl he held in his arms. This angel who was willing to face some deeply rooted fears in order to give him a chance. He wouldn't fail her. He would be everything she wanted, needed, and deserved.

"So what now?" she asked.

"Well, I think eating should be our next order of business. I could go swipe some food from the kitchen, and we could have a little picnic here. Spend some time together without any cameras getting in the way."

"We just had dinner," she teased.

"But we didn't have dessert."

She pulled back to look at him, and her lips twitched at his subtle, flirtatious comment.

"I'm not really hungry, Brody. I'm more sleepy than anything else."

"Another slumber party sounds good to me."

He noticed her give a nervous glance in the direction of her jewelry box, sending a red flag his way and making him wonder why she had been so jumpy and nervous when she'd answered the door. Okay, so Madelyn had never really and truly relaxed around him, but her behavior lately had been filled with a strange amount of anxiety and nervousness that had absolutely nothing to do with him.

"You know what? I think a slumber party sounds like a fantastic idea."

Now he *knew* there was something wrong with Madelyn. She may have stated she wanted to trust him, but that didn't mean they had arrived at the point where she willingly gave in to his flirtatious suggestions.

"But only sleeping, Brody," she warned, pointing a finger in his direction to emphasize her warning.

"Of course. What else could I have possibly meant by that?" He flashed her a cheeky grin.

She shook her head. "Just wanted to lay some ground rules."

"You're not comfortable with me then?" he prodded.

"It isn't that. I just feel like I can't trust myself to...think clearly when I'm with you."

He grinned at that admission.

"That works to my advantage."

"Don't I know it. That's why we need to establish the rules now before I get any more muddled in the head than I already am." Her rueful smirk said it all. She wouldn't run from him anymore, but he would need to tread carefully. She was like a frightened bird ready to take flight at the slightest provocation, and yet her backbone was made of steel. She was an irresistible combination of feminine vulnerability and courageous strength.

"If it makes you feel any better, clear thought tends to escape me when I'm around you. You're not alone in that department. I'm simply reacting to how I feel when I'm near you."

He released her curls and caressed the side of her neck just at the base, allowing his thumb to brush against a pulse point where he felt it leap underneath his touch.

"Brody, I'm not good with relationships. I'm used to dealing with ulterior motives rather than refreshing honesty, but I do care for you. I just think we need to take things slow so I can get to know you like I should have allowed myself to right from the beginning."

Brody brought his hand down, resisting the urge to kiss her again. If she wanted to take things a little slower then that's exactly what they would do. The very idea that she was even considering it made his heart palpitate with worry that he might somehow mess this up.

"How about we make it a movie and dessert slumber party. I can go get some movies from my room while you order up some sweets."

Her smile brightened at that, giving him some curious warm fuzzies.

"I think that sounds like a fun date to me."

Brody nodded, taking note of the strain in her smile and her furtive glances toward the box on the dresser.

Something was definitely wrong.

"I'll just go freshen up while you grab supplies for our slumber party then," she said.

"Sounds like a plan."

He reluctantly let her remove herself from his grasp. As she strode toward the bathroom, she skirted the dresser where the box sat. He nearly asked her outright what exactly she was afraid of, but he held his tongue, afraid to pry if she wasn't willing to mention it. He heard the shower turn on and immediately tried to fill his mind with pure thoughts instead of the ones the normal guy in him had conjured up.

Brody had every intention of leaving the room and getting the movies he needed, but Madelyn's nervous behavior prompted him to walk over to the dresser and investigate her jewelry box a little further.

Nothing could have prepared him for the spectacle that met his eyes. He gasped at the gigantic, ebony spider that sat stiffly amongst the white tissue paper in the box. He studied it for several seconds, wondering why on earth Madelyn would keep a pet spider in such a tiny box. As he moved to quickly secure the spider within the box, he noticed red markings on the inside and read the message.

He sucked in a breath at the implied threat and the realization that this spider no more belonged to Madelyn than Brody belonged to Felicia.

Someone was threatening the woman he loved, and he suspected it had been going on for quite some time, surely long enough for Madelyn to confide in someone. So why hadn't she confided in him?

He studied the arachnid further and eventually concluded it must be dead, though that didn't change the fact that it had been sent to threaten and intimidate his girlfriend. He quickly grabbed his cell phone and began taking pictures of the spider and the threatening message, fully intending to send everything to Gregg and Rhodes. He wanted that handwriting analyzed and the spider identified. If its venom was as deadly as it looked then he feared that his sweet Madelyn was in far more danger than he'd first suspected.

Once he finished, he returned the lid to its original position and hurriedly walked out of the room even though he desperately wanted to remove the entire thing and throw it out the window. Madelyn would know he'd been snooping which might ruin all the progress he'd made in the last few minutes. He'd allow her to think he didn't know what was happening for now, but it didn't matter if Madelyn wanted his protection or not. He was going to get to the bottom of this situation and protect his future wife from the crazy person threatening her.

Hopefully, she'd come to trust and confide in him soon.

MIDGE

Midge walked out of her bathroom dressed in light pink cotton pajamas and stole a glance at the horrible box on her dresser. She had no intention of getting rid of it since she wanted to hold onto it as evidence, but she felt uneasy sleeping in the same room with the dead creature. It was partly why she had jumped at Brody's suggestion to stay with her tonight.

She couldn't help but smile as she sat down on her bed and for the first time in years acknowledged to herself that she might be worth a man's interest after all.

Brody knocked lightly on the door and then entered the room. He wore flannel pajamas that made him look adorably boyish. The reality of him being here in her room for a sleepover made her wonder if he would expect more from her than she was ready to give.

He must have noticed the worry on her face because he sat down on the bed and folded his hands in his lap.

"Madelyn, I hope you're not worried about my expectations for the evening. I promised you we would take things slow, and I have no intention of doing anything you're not comfortable with."

Midge let out a breath through puffed cheeks and moved toward the bed.

"I suppose I should probably let you know where my stance is on intimacy just in case it bothers you enough to send you running into another contestant's arms."

Brody smiled engagingly. "There's no chance of that. Spill it. What's on your mind?"

"I kind of made myself a promise that I wouldn't...I wouldn't...why is this so hard to explain to you?"

Brody must have decided to show her a little mercy with his next words.

"You're a virgin."

"Yes."

"It's nothing to be ashamed of, Madelyn. It's actually quite commendable."

"I'm not ashamed, I'm just used to plenty of censure from men when they find out."

"Why are you a virgin?"

"What do you mean?"

Brody took her hand in his and rubbed a thumb along her palm.

"Madelyn, you're a very desirable woman so the decision to remain a virgin must have been yours and yours alone. So why have you decided to remain a virgin? Why wait?"

"I just can't give all of myself like that without becoming attached to the person, but casual sex doesn't seem to be a huge deal to most people. They're just having fun with nothing tying them to one another, but I can't wrap my brain around that concept. It just seems like someone is going to get their heart broken eventually. Obviously, that's part of dating and relationships, but giving that much of yourself to someone who doesn't value it seems crazy to me." She gripped Brody's hand and prayed he wouldn't laugh at her as she continued her bumbling explanation. "I'm not very experienced. The few times I've kissed a guy, I was doing it because I cared, but he was doing it because kissing me felt good. Nothing more to it than that. I've watched countless relationships and marriages fail because of this cavalier attitude toward something I view as exceptionally special. I guess what I'm saying is, I'm looking for someone who thinks that sex is as special and sacred an experience as I do. I'm the minority here. I get that. What works for me isn't going to work for most other people, but I'm willing to wait until I find someone who respects my decision."

Brody nudged her shoulder in what seemed like an effort to get her to look at him. Once his eyes captured hers, there was no escaping that kind and caring expression.

"I respect your decision, Madelyn, and contrary to what you might believe, I'm not quite as experienced as you think."

"I find that hard to take in."

"Oh, I'm no virgin, but I learned the hard way how painful it can be when you give all of yourself to someone who doesn't truly care."

"A previous relationship? I didn't think you had many of those," she teased.

He chuckled and pulled her close to him.

"Believe it or not, I actually had a relationship last several months. Her name was Rita Harper, and I thought the world of her. I was even planning on introducing her to my mother."

"Several months of dating and you hadn't introduced her to your mother yet?"

He laughed at her surprised expression. "I think that deep down I had a feeling something wasn't right, but I liked her so much, and the physical aspects of our relationship were addicting, I didn't do much thinking with my head. It was all hormones."

Midge swallowed the uncomfortable emotions that thoughts of Brody with another woman produced.

"Then one day, I overheard her talking on the phone to her other boyfriend."

"She was cheating on you?" Midge couldn't even fathom that.

"She was scamming me. She and her boyfriend planned on cashing in on half of everything I owned once she married and then divorced me. It was a hard lesson to learn, but I figured out who the gold diggers were fairly fast after that."

Midge shook her head and wrapped her arms tightly around his torso, resting her head against his chest.

"That's terrible. I'm so sorry you had to go through that."

He stroked her arm and planted a kiss along her hairline. "I'm not. Some lessons are best learned through mistakes that might seem massive at the time. Hard learning is the best learning. The great thing about life is the opportunity for growth and then eventual change. I learned it was better to tread carefully and hold onto that part of me until I could find someone who would love and appreciate me. Not my money. Just me."

Midge tilted her head back to look at him.

"I don't think many women would find it difficult to love someone like you."

"Except for mousy, redheaded librarians who refuse to allow themselves to get caught."

Midge swatted at him as he ducked and jumped to the other side of the bed.

"What's the deal with those glasses of yours?" he asked.

Midge laughed at the abrupt change in subject. "I originally began to wear them to avoid my father's endless attempts at setting me up with the most spoiled, self-absorbed playboys on the planet."

Brody leaned back against the pillows and gave her a quizzical look.

"Why would your father set you up with playboys?"

"He didn't realize they were that terrible. Most of the guys he set me up with were sons of his friends, connections, and other acquaintances. He wanted me to get out more and make friends my own age since I was always on set with him. One day when we were shooting a movie in Chile, one of the producer's sons showed up and wanted to meet me, but I wanted to avoid the entire ordeal."

"You knew what was coming?"

"Oh yes. First the elaborate activities, then the expensive gifts, and finally a delicious dinner filled with dancing, dessert, and debauchery."

Brody shrugged. "That doesn't sound too terrible."

"It might have been flattering if their expectations hadn't been so high. Once they did those things for me, they expected something in return. At the end of the evening, I was treated like a high class escort, and when I wouldn't put out they became pretty incensed. So when this guy came on the set, ready to wine and dine me, I panicked and grabbed some glasses from the prop table to hide behind."

"Did it work?"

"Like bug repellent."

Brody chuckled. "He couldn't see the beauty underneath a pair of measly glasses? I certainly did."

Midge swallowed at the hungry look he gave her. "Well, in all fairness to him, they were New Year's Eve glasses and extremely oversized. The frames were covered in confetti, glitter, and streamers."

"I would have loved to have seen that. I don't mind your glasses, Madelyn. I just can't see your—"

"Freckles. I know." She leaned forward. "Can you see them now?"

He took her offering and trailed his lips lightly across the bridge of her nose and along her cheekbones, planting a kiss next to her earlobe where an errant freckle had taken up residence. She shivered at the sensations his attention evoked.

"No more hiding?" he asked.

"No more hiding."

"I think," he whispered, "that we should start this movie before I break my promise to control myself when I'm around you."

Midge nodded and moved away, but not before she leaned close and gave him a soft kiss on his cheek.

"So what are we watching?" she asked as they settled back on the pillows.

He lifted a DVD with Drew Barrymore on the cover.

"Does *Ever After* sound good?"

"It sounds perfect."

CHAPTER 29

Midge

Midge thought taking a limo to the private airport was overkill, considering she didn't feel like much of a celebrity, but her father absolutely refused to consider taxi cabs as part of their last hurrah in Brazil. And, of course, Brody managed to get her neatly tucked into a limo without allowing anyone else to enter but him.

She didn't mind it so much now that she was willing to admit she'd misunderstood those words spoken between Brody and her father in Hawaii.

The evening after their slumber party, she'd suffered through one more cocktail party followed by another diamond ceremony, but this time the suffering came from not being able to spend the entire night with Brody.

She'd been allowed fifteen wonderful minutes with him where they'd spent their time getting along rather than being at odds with one another as they had during previous ceremonies. He wanted her to trust him, and she had taken that leap of faith, accepting the olive branch he'd kindly offered.

He'd literally shown up to the cocktail party with a small branch from the Ohia tree with a Lehua blossom attached to it. She didn't know how he'd managed it since they hadn't been in Hawaii all week, but a billionaire's resources were vast and deep.

She'd approached him on the veranda, wearing the last set of glasses she'd brought with her, waiting for his usually irritable reaction, wanting to tease him a little bit. He'd taken in the coke-bottle glasses and shook his head ruefully, pulling out the small branch with the flower and extending it to her.

"I thought we called a truce," he stated.

She remembered the legend behind the branch and its flower, and didn't miss the deliberate way he had left the flower attached to the branch, it being an extension of the Ohia tree. Lehua and Ohia, never to be parted again.

She took the glasses off and broke them in half, enjoying the delighted look on his face as she pocketed her last pair of glasses and reached for the branch and its lovely flower.

"No more hiding," she'd said, allowing her lips to curve into a full smile without any fear or reservations.

He stood and lightly traced his knuckles against the softness of her cheeks, taking a long moment to rub along the light dusting of freckles on her cheek bone.

"No more hiding," he echoed. His voice was gravelly, filled with an emotion she couldn't accurately describe.

Finally accepting one of the diamond roses when offered to her instead of seething with fury that he still hadn't conceded defeat by eliminating her was a new experience. Though in truth, she considered the unassuming Lehua blossom and branch more valuable than the diamond encrusted rose she'd accepted for the third time. The rose was something he offered to all of the remaining contestants that night, but the Lehua flower meant something particular to her and Brody, a sweet understanding and a wonderful moment of discovery that they both shared.

Three more contestants were eliminated, leaving eleven left in the running, including Felicia Davenport. Midge knew without a doubt this had more to do with her father's interference than Brody's personal wishes.

Now they were sitting in a limo together, driving to the airport. Brody's musky cologne tickled her senses, making her want to bury her nose in the crease of his neck and wait with anticipation for those arms to enclose protectively around her small frame.

She restrained such impulses, still unsure in the newness of their fragile relationship and taking note of Brody's distracted air.

"I think your obvious favoritism where I'm concerned is beginning to grate on the other contestants' nerves," she said, reaching for some subject to discuss.

He blinked his eyes as if to dislodge a few worrisome thoughts and then his handsome smile transformed his face into an expression she wanted to look upon for the rest of her life.

"I'm not going to ignore you simply because other contestants might get jealous. I'm here to find someone special, and I have."

He reached for her hand, dwarfing it in his own and giving it a loving squeeze. She noted the worry lines around his eyes and the deep shadows which seemingly had appeared overnight.

"Brody, is something troubling you? It doesn't look as if you slept well."

He let out a heavy sigh and leaned against the seat, taking her with him as he wrapped his arms around her.

"I've just been a little worried that another snake might find its way back into your suite. I'd sleep easier if you were sharing the same room with me."

Midge's body heated at the thought.

"You truly have nothing to worry about. I promise to check my window every morning and night once we arrive in Germany. I'll be hyper-vigilant for any and all things reptilian."

"Ah, then I suppose you've done an impressive job of avoiding Felicia Davenport."

"Like I would a hotel room on prom night."

He chuckled at that and planted a kiss on her head. Ever since their night filled with movies and popcorn, he'd been especially careful with any physical affection, taking things slow just as he'd promised. She kind of missed his more aggressive nature, if she were being honest with herself. His thoughts must have run along the same vein.

"Madelyn?"

"Yes?"

"Can I..." he expelled a breath. "Does this truce, this agreement we've made to take things slow allow for me to take liberties that any red-blooded boyfriend would take?"

"I'm more than a little surprised that you're asking when you usually just dive right in," she teased.

He lifted her chin so that their eyes locked together.

"I was hoping a humble request for permission might get me a little farther than throwing you over my shoulder and taking you to my cave."

Midge felt a delighted smile take form before she could stop it. Not that she wanted to.

"Yes, Brody, I'd like it very much if you would kiss me."

He crushed his lips to hers the moment the words were out, molding her body to his as his hands slid along the contours of her back. One arm snaked around her as the other found the back of her neck and held her firm and steady against his lips.

She allowed her fingers to explore the sharp edges of his jaw, holding his face in her hands and moving them back to lightly feather her fingers through his hair. A soft moan escaped his lips and they pulled apart for a moment. He rested his forehead against hers and ground out a frustrated sound.

"We need to get to the airport now before I do more than kiss you."

Breathless, Midge could only nod in agreement as they clung to one another and fought to get their emotions under control. He only released her once the limo eased into the private hangar where their plane awaited to take them to Germany.

"Saved by the tarmac," Brody grumbled as he opened his door, exited the limo, and then turned to help Midge step from the vehicle. "I need to discuss a few details of our next shoot with your father. Save a seat for me on the plane?" His question held a hint of uncertainty, possibly wondering if she was going to turn tail and run from him as she usually did after he gifted her with one of his mind-blowing kisses.

Eager to reassure him, she lifted herself up on the tips of her toes and gave him a soft peck on the cheek. "Consider it saved."

She turned to walk away, but not before taking note of the smoldering look in his eyes. Smiling to herself, she quickly headed to the plane with the rest of the contestants.

"I saw you in the limo with Brody again," Cambria said, grabbing her arm and giving it an excited squeeze. "That's like five times that he's ridden alone with just you, isn't it? So exciting."

"He's definitely singling you out," Charlene said, coming up on her other side. "I'm totally devastated for myself, but I think you two make a great couple."

"You mean you guys don't want to tear my eyes out and possibly push me down a flight of stairs?"

"Oh, we totally do," Cambria said.

"Yeah. We're plotting something evil, but we need to behave like we're happy for you to throw you off our trail."

Midge looked from Cambria's innocent expression to Charlene's teasing one and then the women began to laugh.

They were a few feet away from the plane when out of nowhere several reporters with cameramen trailing them surrounded the three girls and started asking questions in accented English.

"Madelyn Knightly, is it true that you only came on the show to get your trust fund back?"

Another reporter followed up with, "Isn't it true that you were never here for Brody and have no interest in him at all?"

"Where did you hear this?" Midge asked. Her stomach took a nose dive, causing her to feel clammy all over.

Cambria and Charlene moved a few steps away from her.

"What are they talking about?" Cambria asked, suspicion evident in her tone.

"It's nothing," Midge said as she tried to move forward toward the plane.

Another reporter stepped in front of her, blocking her path, flinging question after question at her with the vicious force of a hale storm.

"You're really in it for your daddy's millions and possibly Brody's. Does your boyfriend have any idea that he's been duped into believing you care for him?"

"I need you to move out of my way, please."

She tried to inch forward, but the reporters surrounded her, closing in and cutting her off from Cambria and Charlene, who, to their credit, were doing their best to worm their way back in, pushing people out of their path to get to her. Midge felt the air leave her lungs as the questions and accusations continued to pummel her.

She was a gold digger, a liar, and a fake. She hadn't joined the show for the right reasons. She didn't have Brody Prescott's best interests at heart. She'd tried to avoid this kind of slanderous exposure all her life. Being the center of attention with the camera exposing her faults, her weaknesses, her secrets, basically her entire life was a nightmare she'd repeatedly awoken from during her teen years. Nothing was sacred or represented factually when viewed from the public eye.

She reached up to her face, getting ready to push her glasses higher onto the bridge of her nose when she remembered that she wasn't wearing them anymore.

No more hiding. Isn't that what she had decided? She didn't think she could follow through with it. She couldn't parade her life on live television and expect to be understood any better than she had when meeting people in private. Misunderstanding Madelyn Knightly was all anyone ever tended to do.

Just as she was ready to slump to the ground and curl up into a tiny ball she heard a familiar voice yelling for people to move back. Brody's supportive arm circled around her shoulders, giving her the strength necessary to meet the reporters' glares head on.

"None of you are authorized to be here, and you're especially not welcome if your intention is to harass the contestants," he shouted.

One of the more tenacious reporters shoved his mic in Brody's face. "Mr. Prescott, were you aware that Ms. Knightly only came on the show to retrieve her trust fund from her father so she could continue to finance her reckless lifestyle?"

"Reckless lifestyle? What are you talking—" Midge started, but Brody pulled her to him and cut her off.

"No comment. You all need to leave before you're arrested. Security has been called."

"Mr. Prescott, how can you defend someone who is clearly here for money rather than love? What if she intends to steal your billions as well?" The reporter reached out and grabbed Midge's shoulder, tugging on her clothing as he said, "How will this lowly college student afford her fancy clothes and party lifestyle if she doesn't have the money to fund it?"

Midge watched in complete shock as Brody gently pushed her aside and then snaked a fist out, clocking the reporter square in the face. The man went down like a heavy sack of moldy potatoes.

"I think the real question you should have asked yourself is how I might react if you touched my girlfriend."

With that, he put his arm around Midge's shoulder and herded her toward the airplane as the other reporters continued to shout out the same questions and accusations, albeit from a healthy distance.

Midge allowed Brody to situate her in a comfortable seat at the very back of the plane and then ordered her some lemonade as he began rubbing her arms and shoulders, intuitively aware of the numbness settling in with the shock of the encounter.

"Your first run-in with the paparazzi is never easy, Madelyn." He accepted the drink from the stewardess and lifted it to Midge's lips, encouraging her to take a sip.

"It's not my first," she barely managed to get out.

"You're right. I'd imagine you've had quite a few run-ins with the media considering who your father is. The sugar will help with the shock. Even though they didn't physically attack you, I've found that words are powerful enough to do some serious damage to your mind and body."

Midge accepted the drink and allowed the cool liquid to wash away the bile creeping its way up the back of her throat.

"I never wanted this," she choked out. "I've never wanted any of this attention. I...it's my worst nightmare."

Brody took her in his arms and rubbed his hands along her back.

"I don't know how those reporters got that information, but I promise we will find a way to set this right. It's simply a misunderstanding. Information twisted to make you look bad. It's what the media does."

"I know." Midge nodded. She knew only too well how powerful the media's words could be, and how capable they were when it came to destroying not only someone's image, but someone's life with just a few misrepresented facts and subtle suggestions. Her mother was a casualty of this and the perfect example of someone who hadn't succeeded in handling the constant press, rumors, lies, and public humiliations. She self-medicated and ruined her life in the process.

"I just can't believe this is all public knowledge now. No one is going to believe I actually care for you."

She hardly realized what she'd just confessed until Brody squeezed her hand and lifted it to his lips for a soft kiss.

"You care for me, Madelyn?"

Apprehension gripped her, wondering if Brody would laugh at her for admitting how she felt or if he would simply stop pursuing anything with her now that he had won her affections, her worst fears realized.

Somehow he understood the need to reassure her, stroking her cheek as he said, "I hope eventually you'll see that caring for me will never be a mistake, not when all I can think about is holding you in my arms and taking care of you for the rest of our lives."

She blinked her watery eyes at the underlying meaning behind his words, unable to formulate a response at the magnitude of it all. His jaw went slack at just how candid he had been and he backed up a little, giving her an apologetic look. "I'm sorry if I come on too strong most of the time. I can't seem to hold back anything when you're near me." He quickly stood, failing to meet her gaze. Midge's heart nearly broke in two as she fought to produce the words necessary to reassure him that his admission hadn't frightened her. It had worked as an antidote for any fears or insecurities she'd been holding onto in regards to their budding relationship. And hadn't he called her his girlfriend in front of the cameras and publicly acknowledged his interest in her while defending her against their harassment?

Brody had tirelessly worked to convince her of his feelings for her, coming on the show for her, chasing her all the way to Hawaii and then Brazil. Every word and action had proved time and again that he cared for her and only her. She wasn't a passing fancy, a publicity stunt, or a play for more Hollywood connections. He wasn't interested in Corbin Knightly's daughter, he was interested in Madelyn Knightly, and that was all there was to it.

"I'm going to discuss this situation with your father and see what he wants to do about it."

He moved to leave, still refusing to make eye contact with her. She quickly reached across the seat and grabbed his hand.

"Brody, if you plan on taking care of me for the rest of our lives, you should know that my favorite movie ever made is *The Count of Monte Cristo* with Jim Caviezel, and that I absolutely have to be eating chocolate chip cookies with popcorn while I watch it."

His eyes flashed to her in surprise and then the most wonderful smile broke through his stormy expression, like a burst of sunlight through an overcast sky.

It wasn't a declaration of her true feelings for him, she knew, but she didn't know if she was ready yet to simply blurt out that her feelings for him involved a long-term commitment beginning with a white dress and ending with "until death do us part".

"That's good to know." He squeezed her hand and released it with a wink, turning to walk down the aisle to where her father was being apprised of the altercation by a few crew members.

Cambria sneaked into the seat next to her and Charlene stood in the aisle.

"You okay?" Cambria asked.

"I'll be fine. I guess it was naive of me to assume that my private affairs would remain private once I joined the show."

The girls remained quiet for a moment. Midge felt their burgeoning curiosity concerning the accusations leveled against her, but before she had a chance to defend herself, Cambria placed a hand on her arm and spoke.

"Look, Midge, I have no idea why you decided to come on the show—whatever your reasons it's really none of our business—but I don't believe that you feel nothing for Brody. It's obvious you care for him as much as he cares for you." She let out a sigh of regret, and Midge felt a little sad at the thought that Cambria had grown attached to Brody, though she could hardly blame anyone for doing something smart like that.

"It doesn't matter how this all started. What matters is that you're here for the right reasons now. So no judgments from this corner," Charlene added.

Midge felt tears prick the backs of her eyes as she took in two women who, for all intents and purposes, she probably should have been at odds with. Their situation didn't exactly encourage budding friendships, but they were developing nonetheless. She couldn't help but feel grateful that Cambria and Charlene were so supportive.

"Thank you. I'm glad you didn't let the reporters sway your opinion of me."

"I just wish we knew who leaked that information to the press. Your father would most likely have them kicked off the show for good. Less competition for us," Charlene said. She smirked at her own joke.

Unfortunately, Midge had a very good idea who might have leaked that story to the press. This move had Felicia Davenport written all over it.

BRODY

"I think the best way to approach this possible catastrophe is to meet it head on," Knightly stated.

Brody hardly heard what the man was saying, his thoughts focused solely on the sweet reassurances Madelyn had gifted him. Instead of shutting down and freezing him out, she had given him a reason to believe that his serious pursuit of her was something she wanted.

"Brody. Brody, I just asked you a question!"

Brody ripped his thoughts from his sweet librarian and focused on the situation at hand.

"I'm sorry, Knightly. I'm worried about Madelyn."

"So am I. So let's make certain her reputation isn't dragged through the mud by this obvious breach of privacy. I think you and Midge need to have a 'tell all' segment where you sit down with Les and air this whole thing out."

"You want us to admit that she came here strictly for her trust fund?"

"Well, obviously her behavior toward you has warmed up considerably, as I knew it would. So in this case, honesty is going to be our best policy. Deny it and no one is going to believe you, but admit to Midge being resistant and then you finding her here and winning her over...well...its the stuff of fairy tales, Prescott. It's the best way to handle this situation."

"Do you think Madelyn will agree to this?"

"Of course. Just because Midge hates the spotlight doesn't mean she can't handle it. The only reason she broke from me, my company, and Hollywood in general is because of what it did to her mother."

"What do you mean?"

Knightly shook his head as if regretting his decision to open his big mouth.

"I did love Celeste, Midge's mother. I loved her very much, but my ambitions and my career took precedence, and I didn't see how the limelight combined with Celeste's insecurities worked to wear her down until it was too late. She was doing drugs and abusing alcohol, refusing to get the help she needed or even being willing to accept help from me. Eventually, she overdosed, and we weren't able to resuscitate her before the lack of oxygen did some serious damage to parts of her brain. She hardly recognizes us when we visit her." He ran his hands through his hair and let out a tired sigh as he puffed out his cheeks in frustration. "Midge saw it all, though. Everything. And even though I took her everywhere with me to get her away from the influence and dysfunction of her mother it still had an adverse affect on her. The closer she and I became the more others gravitated toward her to get to me. She has a lot of reasons to hate the entertainment industry, but that doesn't mean she wouldn't have been an enormous success if she had ever decided to pursue it."

Brody refrained from commenting on the other reasons Madelyn had broken ties with the industry or even why she had been involved in her father's work to begin with. These two definitely needed to sit down and communicate a little more concerning their past hurts and disappointments.

"You think she can pull herself together enough to give an interview about her personal life and feelings where I'm concerned?"

"She's tough, my Midge. She'll do it, if not for herself, then for you."

"I can't help but feel like this entire situation is all my fault. Madelyn is going to have to face some of her worst fears, and all because I wouldn't eliminate her."

"Do you believe in destiny?" Knightly asked, peering at him with an intensity that belayed the offhand way in which he'd asked the question.

"I believe our own decisions create our destinies for us."

"Then make these next few decisions with Midge count, Brody. She's so close to letting go completely and putting her faith and trust in someone who actually deserves it. I need you to put your faith and trust in her and her abilities now."

Brody nodded. "I can manage that."

Knightly smiled. "Good. I suppose as far as a son-in-law goes, you'll be tolerable."

Brody raised his eyebrows. "So glad you approve."

MIDGE

Midge sat in a chair next to Brody with her hands clenched at her sides and her stomach churning in a bubbling meld of anxious agony. She understood the necessity of this interview, and as far as TV interviewers went, Les Lassiter seemed to be relatively harmless, but she was still sitting in front of the lenses of several news cameras in a studio in Germany rather than standing behind them. She felt Brody reach for her hand as they were given the "On Air" signal.

She whipped out the smile and confident air that she'd perfected for the cameras and squeezed Brody's hand, but the fear and anxiety still lurked just below the surface.

"We're here tonight with owner and CEO of Shackled and Loving It, Brody Prescott. Brody and Miss Madelyn Knightly, have agreed to discuss some of the more personal issues recently revealed on the show. Thank you both for joining me today."

Midge and Brody murmured their thanks for being invited.

"Madelyn, there are vicious rumors circling around that you only came on the show to secure your trust fund from your father. Is there any substance to this sensational news?"

Midge took a deep breath and forced herself to let go of all thoughts of privacy, pride, or self-preservation. Time to face her phobias and be done with it.

"The rumors are one hundred percent true, Les." She heard a gasp from the studio audience and waited for the initial commotion to settle before continuing on. "You see, I walked away from my trust fund several years ago to pursue a career that didn't necessarily align with my father's own designs for me. I felt that with my scholarship and my own initiative, I could make my way in life without my trust fund."

Les gave her a friendly nod of understanding. "If you were intent on making your own way in life why is the trust fund on the table now?"

"Well, as fate would have it, the funding for my scholarship dried up at the same time my father had a cancellation on the show. He was in a bit of a bind, Les, and he needed someone to fill in. He offered me a solution to my worrisome scholarship issue if I agreed to be on the show for one day."

Les's eyes narrowed in thought as he uttered his next question. "Mr. Prescott, were you aware of this arrangement between Corbin Knightly and his daughter?"

"I knew right from the beginning, and I had even been instructed to eliminate Madelyn that very first night. She never intended to pursue a relationship with the bachelor of this show and had no idea that I was the one who would be starring in it before she signed on to do the show."

"My plan was to go for a day, and then leave with the rest of my college education fully funded," Midge explained.

"Well, obviously that isn't what happened. Care to explain why Madelyn is still on the show, Brody?"

"As you are aware, I had the opportunity to get to know Madelyn before the show started, and no one can discount the moments we shared at Club 23. I'd already signed a contract with the network at that time and felt powerless to pursue anything with her. So naturally her arrival on set was a bit of a surprise, and I had no intention of eliminating her no matter what my instructions entailed."

Les smiled at this bit of information. "And what was your reaction to this, Madelyn?"

"To be perfectly honest with you, I'm not quite comfortable with cameras pointed in my direction. The thought of being a permanent fixture on a reality TV series left me feeling very uncomfortable."

"Well, that certainly never came through on screen."

"Does that mean my acting skills are going to win me an Oscar, Les?"

The audience let out some amused chuckles, allowing Midge to take in a deep breath, relaxing her shoulders in the process.

"It took me a while to get used to the idea that someone as powerful, successful, and handsome as Brody Prescott might be genuinely interested in me, but once I realized how truly sincere his pursuit of me was, it didn't take long before I decided that staying around and seeing what might happen between us was not only the smart thing to do, but what my heart dictated I absolutely had to do."

"So even though you came on the show for an entirely different reason, you are staying for the right ones now."

"Exactly."

Midge turned her gaze to Brody and found him staring at her with a delicious look of hunger on his face. She thought it very lucky that they were surrounded by so many people. She never would have stood a chance against him with that look in his eye if they were the only two people in the room.

"Many media hounds have claimed that Madelyn's intentions are underhanded. That she's merely interested in my money. I want to make it clear that I always knew why she came on the show but was determined to change her mind and convince her to give the idea of 'us' a chance. She's never been anything but wonderfully candid in her thoughts and opinions where I'm concerned. So I hope that people will see Madelyn for the amazingly honest and forthright individual I know her to be."

Midge gifted him a smile of thanks, allowing him to take her hand and lift it to his lips. His soft smile peeked out around her knuckles. The audience let out some ohhhs and ahhs in response to his sweet words.

Les's own smile became indulgent as he allowed them their moment of affection.

"Now how many more contestants are left on the show, Brody?"

"I believe we are down to eleven," he replied.

"And how do you feel about this, Madelyn?"

"Well, obviously I'm not thrilled about him dating other women while he is dating me, but he came on this show to find the best possible chance at true happiness, and if he needs to explore those options with other women then I would rather he do that now than always wonder if he might be missing out on something or someone when he is with me."

It was one of the biggest lies she had ever told in her entire life, but she knew it was the response the viewers were looking for. In truth, the thought of Brody dating anyone but her made her teeth grind in outrage.

Revealing that Brody had come on the show just for her would essentially end the series halfway through the season. She knew he had to continue on with this farce and make an effort to get to know the other contestants, but she couldn't wait for the nonsense to be over so they could have a chance to date one another under normal circumstances where emotions and situations weren't so overly charged.

"Brody, have you been able to decide who you'll be eliminating during next weeks diamond ceremony."

"Three more girls will be going home, Les, and when that happens I will wish them all the best of luck and hope that they find someone who truly makes them happy."

"I take it that Madelyn is someone who will continue on through the next round?"

"While I'm not at liberty to confirm or deny that information, I'm hoping that my actions will speak louder than my lack of words."

Brody stood and grabbed Midge by the hand before she had the presence of mind to feel embarrassed about what happened next.

With a wicked grin on his face, he pulled her to him, and gave her a blush-worthy kiss.

The audience's applause and approval proved that they had successfully weathered that potential scandal, but Midge barely registered the noise, too caught up in the delicious sensations his kisses evoked. It was a bold declaration of his feelings for her.

"Well, I guess that answers that question. Stay tuned for the next installment of *Marry Your Billionaire* as we discover just who's going home and who is still in the running."

CHAPTER 30

Felicia

F elicia Davenport was sick to death of seeing Brody and Midge lip-locking on national television. She reached for something else to throw against the wall and realized that there wasn't anything left in her suite that hadn't been decimated through her rage-induced temper tantrum. The small hotel they were all huddling in until Midge and Brody finished their interview was absolutely awful, adding insult to what she perceived as one monumental injury.

"I am completely over your uncanny ability to fail at every single thing you do, Liz. It seems like every time you work to tear Brody and Madelyn apart they grow closer together, and the viewers love her even more now than they did before the interview."

Liz winced and drew away as Felicia took a menacing step toward her.

"I had no idea she would actually tell the truth. Most people, when backed into a corner like that, will deny everything, making them appear guiltier in the process. All she had to do was deny it, and then I could have leaked that contract to the press as proof of her deception. Going for the truth was absolutely brilliant."

"You should have seen that coming. Did you really think little miss, 'I don't have a police record, I don't get drunk ever, I'm a virgin so stop undressing me with your eyes' was going to suddenly turn into someone with zero morals?"

"Everybody does what they can to save their own butts. Self-preservation is primal and instinctive no matter how high your ideals might be. Besides, I believe leaking this information to the press was your idea."

Felicia chose to ignore that last comment. "Well, clearly we've run into the one human being on this planet who doesn't operate like a normal self-obsessed individual. If she can't be bought, blackmailed, or beaten into submission then it's better if we completely erase her from the competition."

Liz gave her an apprehensive stare. "What...what are you planning on doing?"

"I'm taking matters into my own hands, dear. Your employment with me is terminated. I want you eliminated by the next diamond ceremony."

Liz held up her hands in alarm. "Now wait a second. You promised me no one was going to get hurt in this venture, and I've found another in with Madelyn. She's nearly finished an entire manuscript that she's been working on for months. I've created a virus and emailed it to her computer. Once she opens her mail, the virus will infiltrate her computer and give me access to her files. I can make a copy and wipe her hard drive so that she has nothing left. Do you really think she'll continue to stay on the show if you threaten to print her own work under a pen name? There's no way she'll give up her shot at being an established author. It's what she's been working toward for six years."

Felicia gave Liz a pitying look and shook her head in disgust. "You haven't been paying attention, have you? Do you see the way they kiss one another? The way she looks at him when she thinks no one is watching her? She is in love with him, Liz. That little upstart, that nobody, is in love with the man *I'm* supposed to spend the rest of my life with, and she will easily give that manuscript up for a shot at Brody and his billions."

"I've already sent the virus, Felicia. Just give me this one chance to take care of it without things getting messy. I'll film the encounter. We'll get it all on tape and prove to Brody that Midge is more concerned about her career than she is about whatever relationship she may have been willing to pursue with Brody."

"One more chance, Liz, and then we do things my way."

Liz swallowed hard, sweat lightly glistening down the side of her temple, causing Felicia to glare at her in revulsion.

"Get it set up as soon as possible and then go take a shower. Scrub your skin with lye soap if you have to because you stink of failure."

Liz quickly grasped for the door knob behind her and left the room.

MIDGE

Midge sat in her suite, doing her best to recover from the emotional ride of the interview while being placed into the terrifying position of having to bare her soul before Brody, a studio audience, and national television. The person to blame for this, she knew, was Felicia Davenport. Midge's trepidation where Felicia was concerned grew with every jab. She had to wonder just how far the crazy debutante would go to get Midge off the show, and without some kind of proof tying Felicia to the threats there was nothing Midge could do except prepare herself for the next assault and hope she was able to gather more damning evidence in the process.

She grabbed her laptop, deciding to throw herself into the mind-numbing world of romantic interludes and happily ever afters since her life at this point definitely needed more of that. A note popped up on her screen, giving her notice of a new email from her father which she found odd. He never emailed her. In fact, she was pretty sure he didn't even know her email address. The subject heading read: About The Trust Fund. She rolled her eyes, hoping that he hadn't found a way to renegotiate their terms with more strings attached.

She opened up the email only to find herself looking at a blank screen. She snickered as she realized her dad had emailed her *before* remembering to add whatever attachment he'd intended to send. The screen flickered for a moment, went black, and then came back on again.

Hmmm. Is the battery ready to die?

She quickly grabbed her cord from her bag and plugged it in. Confusion engulfed her as she noted that the battery for her laptop was fully charged. Shaking her head at its bizarre behavior, she began edits on the rough draft of her novel, but found it nearly impossible to concentrate.

Closing her laptop in frustration she climbed into bed and considered knocking on Brody's door to see if he was interested in a late night game of Phase10 or maybe Yahtzee. Anything to keep her mind from racing with worry. Of course, if she asked him to distract her he might take measures that would leave them both fighting not only for breath, but for a little bit of control.

Letting out a frustrated groan, Midge rolled over and grabbed her phone from the nightstand, uninterested in attempting to fall asleep while her mind leapt to all sorts of ugly scenarios Felicia might be planning to throw at her. She needed some answers and she needed them now. She quickly grabbed her phone and called Lisa.

The ringing on the line continued until Midge wondered if perhaps Lisa had put her phone on silent to avoid Midge's poorly timed phone calls.

"What up, lady?" Lisa asked.

Midge wondered at her chipper tone, but decided it might be best not to know what she'd been up to all night.

"Things are beginning to get a little hairy over here. Have you found out anything new concerning a certain psycho contestant?"

"Well, I was going to save this for tomorrow considering how seriously creepy the information I have to relate is. I wouldn't want to keep you from your sleep. I'm considerate like that."

Midge ignored the verbal jab. "That bad, is it?"

"You have no idea. Felicia Davenport could school a mob boss or two. Of course, this is all speculation on my part since nothing has ever been pinned on her and certainly no charges were ever filed, but I'm assuming that's simply because she's fabulous at covering her tracks."

"Just tell me," Midge said with zero enthusiasm.

"She started collecting husbands, it would seem."

"Husbands?"

"Well, more specifically their fortunes. This girl is a big spender. She can't seem to live within her means, and her daddy cut her off at the age of twenty due to her elaborate spending and delinquent behavior. He had to pull her out of a few scrapes that would have landed her in jail for possession of cocaine."

"She doesn't look like a user. I don't see any of the signs." And boy did Midge know how to spot those signs. Her mother had given her one heck of an education in that department.

"Felicia's careful. She wasn't stupid enough to use the products she pushed."

"Are you saying Felicia Davenport was some kind of drug dealer?"

"No, nothing so trashy. Her crimes are a bit more refined and sophisticated in nature. It was just a way for her to make some extra money so she could buy those ridiculous pairs of shoes she seems to think make her legs look good."

"They *do* make her legs look good."

"I know, but I'm trying to be disparaging here since physically there's not a dang thing wrong with her."

"Right. So what happened once she was cut off?"

"She got creative and started schmoozing married politicians. The first man she targeted was Senator Kincaid."

"Neal Kincaid? Didn't his wife pass away under mysterious circumstances several years back?"

"I'll say. It was five years ago to be exact. Gloria Kincaid's car brakes went out during her drive to visit her mother in Ohio. She took a sharp curve too quickly and as a result went right over a cliff."

"That. Is. Awful. That must have been terrible for the senator."

"He took it hard, I suppose, but he was having an affair with Felicia Davenport at the time so I'm sure he had her to turn to during his time of grief." Lisa couldn't hide the disgust in her voice, and Midge had to agree. How completely inappropriate to find solace in the arms of your mistress over your dead wife.

"It would seem that Felicia was tired of the affair remaining a secret, and since the wife was now out of the picture she wanted to make it public."

"No way he'd go public. It would hurt his credibility with his voters."

"Right? He's in his fifties. Way too old for a twenty-year-old. Dating someone that young is going to raise several eyebrows, so he agrees to marry her. They got hitched about two months after the wife died."

"Two months? How did marrying Felicia help him avoid a scandal, and why don't I remember this? I don't generally follow which senators are dating whom, but that would have made some headlines."

"He agreed to marry her in private and allowed her to live her expensive lifestyle so long as she agreed to keep their marriage and interactions private. Put her up in a house in L.A. and kept her comfortable for a year, after which she promptly filed for divorce. Her lawyer swindled quite the alimony bundle for her, and she lived off that until Kincaid died of a heart attack a few months later and willed everything to his illegitimate son whose mother was the senator's secretary."

"Sweet maple syrup. He had an illegitimate son?"

"Yep. Everything was kept quiet, but Felicia no longer had any monetary support, and clearly hadn't seen another heir apparent in the mix. So she moves on to some corporate big wig with some well-played investments in the stock market. Randall Ramsey."

"Wait a second. Didn't he and his entire family die in a house fire a few years back?"

"Three to be exact."

"Felicia strikes again?"

"Someone's catching on. Apparently his wife died several years ago and he'd been raising his two kids on his own ever since."

"Yes, but didn't he get remarried to a woman named Lilith?"

"Yep. Lilith Davenport. AKA Felicia Lilith Davenport."

"Cheese and crackers!"

"You said it. They hadn't been married for even three months before that house fire hit. Lilith Davenport happened to be away on business when Ramsey and his two teenagers burned to death in the inferno."

"I can't believe this. So she made certain to get rid of any possible heirs to his fortune in one fell swoop. This woman is heinous. How have the police not caught on to her?"

"She had a solid alibi, which means she wasn't working alone. I doubt this woman ever does her own dirty work, but again she wasn't counting on someone else getting the bulk of Ramsey's fortune."

"What? There was another illegitimate kid in the mix?"

"No. Apparently, Ramsey was a die-hard fan of donations and everything went to St. Jude's and various other charities that preserve endangered species or work to solve world hunger. I guess he wanted his kids to earn what they lived on. Wasn't planning on giving them a hand out. Good guy, really. Such a shame he burnt to a crisp."

"Seriously? How tactful, Lisa."

"You know what I can't figure out? If she really is behind these deaths, and I think she is, she should have been smart enough to check the wills. These plans have been so manipulative and elaborate. Cunning, really, and I hate to give her credit for being smart when I'll never physically be nearly as pretty as she is, but I have to wonder how she could overlook something as important as her husbands' beneficiaries."

"Maybe they changed their wills last minute. Any way to check on that?"

"Of course, and brilliant idea. Why didn't I think of that? Anyway, the trail of blood, murder, and mayhem continues," she intoned dramatically.

"Are you saying there are more husbands involved?"

"Just one more. Sasha Putin, an internet marketing guru she met while on vacation in Europe. Net worth was in the millions, not quite the big fish she usually targets, but desperate times call for settling for millions, I guess. Married him within a few months of meeting him, and this time when he passed away—after an unexpected stroke at the ripe old age of thirty-five—she inherited quite the fortune and spent several months in Europe spending it."

"She must have gotten wise with the will there."

"Either that or she simply found a way to forge a new one. He did have extended family, after all, but everything went to her. Currently, her funds are nearly non-existent. You'd think with all the money she finagled she would have wised up and invested it. She could have lived off the interest alone quite comfortably, but why should investments and banking cross the mind of a seriously deranged serial killer?"

"Probably not as riveting as marriage and murder. Did she change her name with that last marriage?"

"Nope. Stayed the same. She wasn't even under investigation since the coroner claimed the stroke stemmed from natural causes, whatever the heck that means."

"It means she found an untraceable toxin to kill him with. I doubt anyone had a reason to test for toxins in his system."

"She's really refined her whole process. To be honest, I'm both frightened and morbidly fascinated by this woman. Of course, now she's living on credit and targeting her next victim."

"Brody," Midge said on a strangled puff of air.

"Brody, and anyone else who gets in her way. Crap, Midge, I didn't even take into account his interest in you. You have several kisses with him plastered on national television—nice cameo at the hospital and the interview by the way. Fabulous acting on your part—and it's obvious he wants you since he refused to eliminate you when he knew he was supposed to."

"Yeah, I think Felicia's already started working on getting me out of the picture. Between my injured hand, my small stint in a locked supply closet, the snake bite, and the spider, I think it's safe to say she's working on attaining husband number four and dusting the competition in the process."

"Wait, I missed out on the snake and the spider. What the heck has been happening over there?"

Midge quickly summarized the events surrounding Felicia's last few attempts at threatening her.

"You have to tell someone, Midge. You have to tell Brody. You're both targets now, and there's no way this can end well for either one of you."

"I agree that I need to be careful, but so does Felicia. She's on national television. Her movements are in the public eye right now, and she can't afford to get caught bumping off the competition. I have a feeling she's been working with someone here on the show. Is there any chance you can start investigating the backgrounds of the cast and crew? I just don't think Felicia would risk pulling any of this off on her own."

"Email me a list of names, and I'll get on it right away."

Midge considered her options and then she wondered if they might not turn the tables on Felicia. "She can't afford to have her previous marriages and the circumstances surrounding everyone's deaths come to light. Any chance you can get this research leaked to the tabloids?"

"Consider who you're talking to. I'm all over it. I'll give them so much smut and conjecture these tabloids won't know what to do with themselves."

"Perfect. That might just keep Felicia at bay while I try to figure out how to keep Brody safe."

"From what I can tell, he's safe until he actually marries the wench."

"Yeah, but he has no intention of marrying her, and who's to say that someone as deluded and crazy as Felicia won't retaliate in a very lethal way if she decides she can't win him over? She's already struck at his company. She'll go for the jugular next time."

"You could just leave...*with* Brody. You're kidding yourself if you think there's nothing there between you two."

"I'll admit recent events have convinced me that Brody isn't playing around with my feelings, but I intend to proceed with caution."

"Proceed with—seriously, Midge? Who talks that way about the process of dating? Date the guy and enjoy yourself. You analyze things way too much."

"Just work on wrecking Felicia's image and see if you can get anything concrete to pin on her. Maybe we can land this heinous woman in jail where she can't hurt anyone else."

"Can do. Stay safe and be sure to tell Brody about what we've discovered. He needs to know how to protect you."

Midge hung up the phone and shook her head.

Advising Brody of the danger they were both in would cause him to go on a rampage. He was a good man and wouldn't sanction death threats of any kind by anyone in the group. But if they tipped their hand and Felicia got wind of it she might bolt before Lisa was able to find solid evidence that pinned Felicia to any of the murders.

And Midge had no intention of allowing Felicia to continue to endanger anyone else ever again.

Midge stared in awe at the magnificence of Sababurg Castle, the original Sleeping Beauty Castle from the Brothers Grimm Fairy Tales. The castle had fallen into ruin many years previously, but parts of it had been restored into a romantic hotel with a restaurant, café, and theater. Rising up from a cluster of trees in the middle of the Reinhardswald Forest, the two massive towers and broad turrets made Midge feel as if she'd landed in the very heart of fairy tale land.

"Apparently, this is the very castle the Brothers Grimm frequented and modeled their story of Sleeping Beauty after. At least, that's what many locals believe." Brody's lips were right next to her ear as the limousine drew closer to the impressive structure.

Midge shivered a little at the proximity of his lips near her ear.

"This castle is absolutely stunning, but it doesn't look a thing like the castle from the Disney movie."

Brody smiled.

"Disney is prone to take liberties when it comes to their versions of fairy tales, and I'll never complain about that since I secretly watched every single one of those movies with my mom on the weekends as a teenager."

Midge let out a delighted laugh.

"You spent the weekends with your mother watching Disney movies?"

Brody looked around the limo, feigning wariness at possible eavesdroppers even though the cameraman was sitting opposite them, recording every gesture they made and every word they spoke.

"If you ever accuse me of such unmanly things in public, I will fervently deny it and immediately turn the conversation to football stats and extreme sports."

Midge shook her head, unable to picture this manly billionaire in raptures over Disney fairy tales.

"Disney's Sleeping Beauty Castle was inspired by the Neuschwanstein Castle in Bavaria," he continued.

"How do you even know these random factoids?"

"My business is romance, Madelyn. It pays to know my fairy tales." He reached for her hand and helped her out of the limo. "Plus, I really like to read."

"Good to know, Brody Prescott."

Looking at the castle from a distance was one thing, but it was even more fascinatingly beautiful to stand right in front of it and take in the various colored stones of the castle turrets and the trellised vines covered with pink roses, snaking their way all along the walls' surfaces. There were roses everywhere. It was the most vibrantly colorful display she'd ever seen.

Upon entering the lobby, the fairy tale feeling lessened only slightly as the more modern feel to the area set in. With only seventeen rooms in the entire hotel, Midge wondered how the contestants and the crew were going to manage to stay there. She imagined she would have to bunk with one or more of the contestants.

The rooms were all nestled in one of the larger towers with a spiral staircase leading up to the very top where even larger more elaborate rooms were on display. Midge was surprised when Brody led her up the staircase and handed her the key to one of the biggest rooms available. She caught her breath as she opened the door.

"This room is sick," Cambria whispered, behind her.

"Does that mean you're bunking with me?" Midge asked.

Brody grunted as if he weren't at all pleased with the sleeping arrangements, but what exactly did he expect? That her father would willingly put them together as if they were already on their honeymoon? Not likely.

"I'm in the room to the left. You girls take a few minutes to get settled and then head back down to the lobby for more instructions."

Midge nodded as she continued to study the decor of the room. The large four-poster bed and its elegant bedding matched the light creamy peach coloring of the carpet and draperies on the windows. A rounded table with detailed floral etchings on the legs of the table and chairs sat in one corner while on the other side a bathroom with a jacuzzi held an inviting rose scent. There was beautiful artwork depicting the local countryside adorning the walls.

"I'm so stinking jealous of you two," said Charlene as she joined them in their room and spun around to get a three-sixty experience of the decor. "I'm stuck in a room with Felicia Davenport of all people. How did I get the short end of that treacherous stick? Don't be surprised if you find a third bunk mate in your bed tomorrow morning."

"My sincere sympathies," Midge said.

"Can you believe this place? I already feel like a princess and I've been here less than ten minutes. It makes me want to grab a handsome looking stranger and begin waltzing with him."

Midge chuckled as Cambria spun around the room in the arms of her invisible Prince Phillip while singing, "I know you. I've walked with you once upon a dream..."

"Better keep an eye on that one," Charlene said. "Cambria's all about taking little souvenirs to commemorate each step of our journey."

"Yes, I'm sure the proprietors of the hotel wouldn't be too thrilled to find that the table, chairs, and four-poster bed are missing once we vacate the premises."

"You've got me all wrong," Cambria said as she continued to twirl upon the creamy carpet. "I'd pillage the doilies and artwork first."

Les, Brody, her father, and the crew were already waiting for them as they entered the lobby. Midge dared a glance in Brody's direction and couldn't help the smile that tugged at the corners of her lips as he mouthed the words *I miss you* before having his attention diverted by a question from Les.

Once the entire cast had gathered in the lobby, members of the crew began handing them large envelopes with their names printed on the front.

"Ladies, Brody has something wonderful planned for this evening's entertainment, another group date challenge that I think you'll all find extremely exciting."

Brody stepped forward as all attention moved to him.

"Thank you, Les. My company offers a sister site that provides fun dating ideas and helpful feedback to make the dating process a little less daunting. I've used these ideas from this site to host several group dating functions for many of my clients, friends, and family members. Something I've found to be a regular hit is a murder mystery party."

"Awesome. I've only been to one of those things, but it was so much fun," Charlene said, adding her usually excited bounce at the end.

"For this event, we're using a fairy tale theme entitled, *A Happily Never After Murder Mystery.* Your character assignment and a list of characters are in the envelope given to you. We expect you to study your personal role and arrive tonight, at the desired location and time, completely in character and wearing your appropriate costume. The stakes for this are high ladies because at the end of tonight's party the winner will have won a date with me, and three girls will be going home before the next diamond ceremony tomorrow night."

There was a collective gasp throughout the room at the revelation of this extra elimination round.

Midge didn't allow the anxiousness that everyone else adopted to permeate her psyche. For once, she didn't wish to be eliminated, but more importantly she was putting her faith and trust in this truce she and Brody had established.

"We'll see you ladies tonight," Brody said.

Midge caught Brody's eye one last time before departing for her room. The tingles his smile gave her should have been illegal.

CHAPTER 31

Midge

"A rial Font? That's my character's name?" Midge said when she opened her envelope.

Cambria leaned over to read Midge's character description printed next to a photo of her.

"Oh, that's clever," she said with a bounce. "They've made a nod to your profession as an author and you're playing the role of Ariel from *The Little Mermaid*! Oh, look! Les gets to play Hans Christian Philanderson. Hilarious!"

Cambria grabbed her own envelope and sat down to read over the different characters.

"Who do you get to be?" Midge asked as she scrolled her eyes down the list of faces and names.

"Rap-Pun-Zel. Apparently, I spend my days locked in a tower thinking up lame puns to rap about. How incredibly stupid. I love it."

Midge grinned and continued down the list of names and character assignments.

"Looks like Felicia got handed the role of the See Which. Is she blind as a bat or something?"

"Talk about type casting," Cambria mumbled as she pulled out more materials. "That narcissist can't see anyone else but herself. Charlene is Snow Fright. According to this, her character is afraid of huntsmen, forests, old women, and red apples. Can't say that I blame her. Apples freak me out."

Midge eyed her askance. "I'm going to pretend you didn't just utter that last comment. I really don't want to know what caused you to develop such a strange phobia."

"Fair enough."

A loud knock at their door interrupted their perusal as Charlene breezily sailed her way through their door wearing the most awesome Snow White ensemble ever created.

"What do you think, ladies? Too cliché?" Charlene spun around and then struck a cheesy pose.

"OMGoodness, I want your costume. Where did you get it?" Cambria said.

"They've got everyone's costumes down the tower on the bottom floor. You guys come with me and I'll show you where to go."

"Go ahead without me. I'm going to study this, and then I'll come down and find you in a few minutes," Midge said.

She sat down on the bed and allowed herself to relax a little once Charlene and Cambria left. Sometimes Charlene's energy was a little overwhelming, and there was simply no way to tone the bouncing down.

She pulled out the invitation to the party and read it to herself.

"Come one, come all, ye fairest in the lands. Prince Alarming, the last bachelor to be found in all of the fairytale kingdoms is throwing a ball in hopes of uncovering his one true love and living happily ever after. Who will the lucky girl be?"

Midge studied the beautiful pink roses adorning the corners of the invitation. A gorgeous picture of the Sababurg Castle surrounded by lush, green forests remained fixed at the top center between the roses. The rest of the invitation was written in flowing gold script.

"Fancy," she said and then picked up her suspect list. "Arial Font spends her days pining for love and fulfillment just below the surface as she buries herself deep within the pages of human love stories, only coming up for air when it's time for a new book. Though she's comfortable on land, she feels like a fish out of water when faced with any type of dancing. Two left feet you see, courtesy of the See Which who is also vying for Prince Alarming's attentions. Hans Christian Philanderson and the Brothers Dimm have threatened possible changes in regards to everyone's fairy tale endings, and it is absolutely imperative that Arial seek out her own happy ending with Prince Alarming before Hans and the Brothers have the chance to ruin her story."

Midge snorted at the silliness of the premise, and then realized that this tongue-in-cheek theme fit in well with other murder mystery parties she'd attended. She might as well throw herself into the character and simply enjoy the party.

She reached for more materials within the large envelope and accidentally bumped Cambria's purse off the end of the bed. Sighing, she knelt on the floor and began returning the spilled items to Cambria's flashy gold bag. Her hand froze as she noticed a small square box that looked nearly identical to the one she'd received in Brazil.

It was ludicrous to think that the box had anything to do with Felicia or the recent harassment, but her trembling hands betrayed her.

With shaky fingers she lifted the box and let out a short puff of air as she

MARRY YOUR BILLIONAIRE   271

found it completely empty. Shaking her head at herself she went to place the lid back on the box only to discover red markings on the inside of it.

THIS IS YOUR LAST WARNING BEFORE THINGS GET HAIRY.

Midge stared unseeing as the red words blurred together, causing her to blink back tears she hadn't realized she'd been shedding. She knew Felicia had a partner on the side, executing her directives to avoid suspicion for herself while simultaneously giving her plausible deniability, but never in a millions years would she have suspected someone as sweet and kind as Cambria to have fallen in with someone like Felicia. Was Cambria planning to fill this box with something even nastier than the Wandering Spider and leave it for her to find?

Or was it possible that Midge hadn't been the only one targeted by Felicia? Cambria, from what Midge had observed, had hit it off with Brody on their date, and they seemed to get along with one another fairly well, though she'd never noticed anything more than a friendly interest from Brody where Cambria was concerned. Was it possible Felicia hadn't seen it that way and sent something awful to Cambria? If that were the case, then why was the box empty?

Was Charlene being targeted as well? She and Brody got along wonderfully even though they hadn't had their own one-on-one yet.

It was nauseating to think that her friends might be in danger while simultaneously wondering if Cambria was Felicia's sidekick in all of this.

The box was empty. Why else would it be empty unless Cambria planned to fill it with something...something living and breathing...and extremely deadly this time.

Laughter carried up the tower steps. She hurried to replace her roomies' items and returned the purse to the exact spot it had previously rested.

She couldn't label her friend a traitor until she had more evidence, but she also needed to be on her guard tonight. It couldn't be a coincidence that she and Cambria were sharing the same room. How easy would it be for Felicia's minion to do something to her in her sleep?

She quickly moved to the door and headed down the spiral stairs in search of her friends and her costume. Tonight, she not only had to play the part of Arial Font, she had to pretend she didn't suspect Cambria's involvement with Felicia.

There was no other way to handle the precarious position she now found herself in. She'd simply have to be on her guard tonight and play her many different parts to perfection.

The party was held within the courtyard in the middle of the castle. The fairy tale decor that covered tables laden with delectable foods enhanced the ambiance of the occasion. The crew was dressed in footman attire while the contestants were dressed to the nines in their respective character ensembles.

Even her father was getting into character by playing the role of one of the Brothers Dimm along with Talin Rhodes.

Talin caught her eye and swiftly made his way over to her, bobbing around enormous hoop dresses and servants carrying platters of appetizers for the guests.

"Midge, you look amazing in that emerald contraption," he said as he wrapped his arms around her and brought her in for a big bear hug.

Her dress was made of sparkling green sequins in an effort to imitate the color and texture of a mermaid's fin.

"Your tailored clothing seems to fit you in all the right places, but I think you're supposed to address me as Ms. Arial Font," Midge teased. She accepted the quick kiss he planted on her cheek and then stood back, noticing as she did that Talin kept hold of her hands.

"Do tell me all about yourself, Ms. Font."

"Well, apparently I'm here to fight for Prince Alarming's hand in marriage since there seems to be no other bachelors available."

"Au contraire, my dear lady," he huffed in an injured tone. "Even though I spend most of my time writing stories about captive princesses and evil queens, I am still unattached, as it were, and completely available to star in my own happily ever after with one of you lovely ladies." He wiggled his eyebrows suggestively.

"The plot thickens, I see. In other words, though Prince Alarming is purported to be the only bachelor available, the Brothers Dimm are here on a mission of their own matrimonial pursuits?"

"Indeed we are, much to Hans Christian Philanderson's dismay—" Talin broke off and choked down a laugh. "I honestly can't take that name seriously. Did you read his character profile?"

"Oh yes. Hans seems to be dallying with many of the key players in these fairy tales." Midge tapped a finger to her chin in thought. "I hate to spread nasty rumors, but I do believe the identity of one of these ladies must be Rap-Pun-Zel."

Talin and Midge made a great show of not so subtly observing Cambria over the throng of people dancing. She was currently laughing at something Brody had to say.

"It would appear that the young woman in question is moving in on your intended. What makes you think Rap-Pun-Zel has been having an affair with our dear Hans?"

"What else could she possibly be doing up in that tower of hers?"

"Good point." Talin gave her a wide grin, dropping all pretense of remaining in character. "I've missed you, Midge. I would have come to catch up with you sooner, but my work has been busy, and every single time I get a free moment that bloodhound of yours is always sniffing around your skirts."

Midge's eyes widened in surprise. "You mean Brody? Talin, even if I *am* in conversation with him, you know you can come and talk to me anytime you want to."

"Somehow, I don't think your boyfriend appreciates it."

"I think he's under the mistaken impression that you're interested in me."

"Who says he's mistaken?"

Midge let her curious gaze flit to Talin's features. She was about to delve deeper into his comment when another loud laugh from Cambria pulled her attention away. She studied Cambria's friendly smile and open demeanor. Was it all one big act?

"Talin, I wonder if I could talk to you about something."

"Shoot."

"I think I have a stalker on my hands, and I was hoping you could look into the situation without letting anyone else know."

Talin was immediately on alert. "What exactly has been happening?"

She quickly went through the events at the hospital, then went over the snake incident, the threatening messages, the spider, and eventually her findings in Cambria's purse.

"Why didn't you bring this to my attention sooner? My job is security, Midge. It falls on me to protect you, and I can't do that if I don't know about the threats to your safety."

"At first I thought it was a hoax, a pathetic attempt to scare me into leaving, and you know how I feel about being manipulated."

"Yes, I'm fully aware."

"I don't have concrete proof that Felicia is involved, and I don't know if I'll be able to get that since I think she has an accomplice."

"And now you're wondering if Cambria is the accomplice."

"As much as it pains me to admit it, yes. I need proof, Talin. If Felicia is the one pulling the strings here, we need to tread carefully because she is dangerous. If we spook her, there's no telling what she might do to any contestants who threaten her chances with Brody."

"I'll start looking into Cambria's background and see if she's another victim or possibly the perpetrator. I don't like the fact that you're sharing a room with her. As much as it pains me to suggest this, you might consider bunking with Brody tonight."

"That's not happening, but I'd like to know what you have against Brody. He's a fairly decent guy."

"Exactly. You think he's decent, and I'm beginning to think I never had a chance."

Midge bit her lip as understanding washed over her.

"Oh, Talin, I'm—"

"Don't you worry about it, Midge." He placed a comforting hand on her shoulder and brushed his fingers across her cheek. "I've always known you were a long shot. I'll start my investigation and let you know what I find out. You be careful."

He squeezed her hand and walked back through the guests, mingling with a few contestants and no doubt getting their character backstories.

"You were certainly chummy with Dimm over there. I hope he didn't capture your attention before I have a chance to possess it permanently, Ms. Font," Brody said as he wrapped an arm around her waist and pulled her against his chest.

She spun in his arms to face him, a teasing smile on her lips. "Why, Prince Alarming, always thinking the absolute worst in every situation when nothing could be further from the truth."

"Dimm may be a few chess pieces short of a set, according to his character synopsis, but Talin Rhodes knows exactly what he's doing, Madelyn. Do you have..." Brody puffed out his cheeks on an exhale and rubbed the back of his neck. "I hope you don't have feelings for this guy because I have no intention of backing down now that we finally seem to be on the same page here."

Midge quirked an amused brow. "And if I did have feelings for Talin Rhodes, exactly what would you do about it?"

"Revert to my caveman ways and carry you off to my room in the top of the tower. I'll go Mother Gothel on you and lock you in there for good measure. Your hair doesn't grow too quickly, does it?"

"Not unless I have a special spell on hand."

"Then there'd be plenty of time to convince you I'm the only man you'll ever need."

Midge's look softened as she took in the tension near the corners of Brody's eyes.

"Brody, we've called a truce, and I've decided to see where things will go between us. I'm not interested in doing that with anyone else but you. Do you believe me?"

"Yes, I believe you," he said. A warm glow filled his eyes as he took a step closer.

Midge was about to remind him of where they were when a strangled cry was heard at the edge of the courtyard.

Stacey flung herself dramatically to the floor, though it looked as if she had nearly tripped on her servant's gown. She flung a hand to her forehead and screamed, "Murder. Hans Philanderson is dead!"

Brody stifled a snort. "It would appear there are games afoot, Ms. Font. Stick with me, and I'll keep you safe."

"I'm counting on it."

Madelyn took Brody's hand and allowed herself to be led from the courtyard toward the vaulted cellar where Stacey pointed to Les Lassiter's body hanging on the stairs leading to the small stage.

There was fake blood on his chest and letters scattered everywhere, which upon examination proved to be love letters from various characters in the room.

"That looks so real," Charlene said as she moved closer to Les's body. "Is it Ketchup?"

Les opened his eyes and lifted his head to survey the mess on his chest.

"I think it's corn syrup dyed with red food coloring," he said.

"The food coloring strikes again." Brody's reference to her first prank had her giggling under her breath.

"Les, you're not supposed to be talking, you're dead," Cambria gently reminded.

"Right." He let his head sink back to the floor and allowed himself a dramatic moment to die all over again.

"My dear ladies, I'm afraid no one can leave the palace and return to their respective lands and kingdoms until this heinous murder has been solved and the culprit brought to justice," Rhodes said.

"I'm convinced the murderer is Ms. Font," Felicia said in a shrill tone.

"Now who saw that coming?" Charlene muttered under her breath.

"Ms. Font is anxious to find herself a husband, and Hans was insistent that her story end with her one true love choosing another while Ms. Font's soul was lost in the process," Felicia continued.

"This, unfortunately, is quite true," Midge said with a heavy sigh.

"No," Charlene shuddered.

"Yes," Midge reaffirmed. A smile pressed its way over her lips. There was no way she could maintain her character. The whole thing was just too ridiculous, but she couldn't deny she was having fun.

"I received a letter from Hans letting me know that my request for a change in circumstance had been approved, but not in the way I wished. He'd decided that I wouldn't die after all, and he would simply hand me over to Mother Gothel where I would spend the rest of my days in unwedded misery while coming up with new puns to entertain my roommate Rap-Pun-Zel."

"Why in the world would Hans want to keep you in a tower?" Cambria asked with actual curiosity garnishing her tone.

Midge threw herself on the floor in the middle of the cellar and shouted, "He wanted me for himself."

Horrified gasps echoed throughout the cellar while one lone chuckle from Brody carried across the room and tickled her senses.

"That can't possibly be right. He was sneaking me out of my tower every Friday night to see the lantern show in the neighboring kingdom," Cambria stated in mock disdain.

"Told ya," Midge mouthed to Talin who was biting his hand to keep from laughing.

She turned her head and caught Brody's tense look at Talin, surprised by the jealousy exhibited there. For the next fifteen minutes revelations, dark secrets, and surprising connections between the characters—apparently the

Brothers Dimm didn't actually have the same mother—were sallied back and forth as the contestants did their best to figure out who had motive, means, and opportunity for killing Hans Christian Philanderson.

The case finally broke when Charlene squealed in triumph, "I know exactly who killed poor Hans. The culprit is none other than Prince Alarming." She pointed her finger at Brody and waited for the murmuring to die down.

"That's ridiculous. What proof do you have?" Brody said, pretending to be affronted.

"You yourself admitted to being low on funds and needing to marry a wealthy heiress in order to continue your princely lifestyle. You discovered that I had been left a sizable fortune from my dead father."

"Your point?"

"You intended to announce our engagement tonight, but Hans found out about it and refused to rewrite my story unless you gave him fifty percent of my inheritance once we were married. So you stabbed him in the chest." Charlene walked over to him and reached her hand into his coat pocket, pulling out a sharp dagger covered in blood.

Everyone began clapping as Charlene gave a deep curtsy and received a hug from Brody for being the winner of the next one-on-on date with him. Midge wanted to be happy for Charlene. She really did, but two things were holding her back. First, she didn't want to have to share Brody one single moment longer. The very idea of him going on a date with Charlene made her insides feel raw and weak. Second, she didn't want Charlene to become the next target on Felicia's hit list.

Spotting the See Which by the stairs, she sauntered over and stood next to her.

"What do you want?" Felicia hissed.

Midge supposed the woman was feeling especially nasty tonight due to her failure in winning another date with Brody.

"I was just thinking how surprised I am that you weren't the one to guess the culprit. I mean, you've had so much experience with the subject matter in question."

Felicia's eyes widened for a mere second, but it was enough for Midge to see that her comment had not only hit home, but was completely accurate.

"I'm sure I have no idea what you're talking about," she said through clenched teeth.

"No? I'm sorry. I thought for sure I heard you mention that you had already attended several of these types of parties."

Felicia's eyes darted to Midge and the lamplight from the cellar gave them a supernatural glow.

Creepy.

"Unfortunately, we've reached that moment where Brody must say goodbye to three more contestants," Les said, still wiping red corn syrup from his chest.

"These eliminations are so tedious," Felicia said, fanning herself in boredom.

"You don't feel like your position on the show is tenuous at best?" Midge asked.

"Oh, don't you worry about me, Madelyn." Felicia flashed her teeth, reminding Midge of a tigress ready to bite. "Your father and I have come to a certain understanding. Believe me when I say I'm the last person Brody will be eliminating. See you later."

Midge's eyes flickered to her father. She wondered what on earth Felicia could have been referring to. Surely her father hadn't promised Felicia she'd be one of the final three in the running.

Once Brody announced the three women leaving the show, and all the hugs and goodbyes were said, Midge hurriedly made her way over to her father and pulled him into a small corner of the cellar for a private moment.

"Why does Felicia think she's going to continue to remain on the show right up until the very end?"

Her father cringed and looked away, doing his best to avoid her gaze. "I may have promised her some extra air time on the show if she promised to cause as many scenes as possible, which she has."

Midge shook her head in disbelief.

"Does Brody know about this?"

"No, but I honestly don't see what the big deal is. He obviously cares about you, and she'll eventually be eliminated during the last round."

"Dad, she is dangerous. The longer she stays here the more likely she's liable to—" Midge cut herself off abruptly.

He narrowed his eyes at her and stepped closer.

"More liable to what, Midge?"

"Nothing. I just don't like her." She bit her lip in frustration.

She had no proof, and she wasn't in the mood for her father to laugh at her suspicions when everything was pure conjecture on her and Lisa's part. If she showed him the latest threat there was a very good chance he would send her packing. How would she protect her friends and Brody if she wasn't here? Who would Brody propose to if she suddenly up and left the show? The thought made her ill one moment and then completely shocked her the next.

Brody was playing for keeps here. At the end of this show, he fully intended to propose to someone. Was she ready for that someone to be her?

BRODY

Brody, Talin, and Knightly gathered in the hotel manager's office later that night after Talin informed them he had something important to impart. As much as it pained Brody to spend any amount of time in the security guard's presence, they were both working toward a common goal, and he needed the man's skills, experience, and insight to protect Madelyn.

"Midge believes that Felicia is using someone else to deliver these threats," Talin said, after sharing the details of his previous conversation with Madelyn.

Brody pinched the bridge of his nose in frustration. It hurt to think that when she had finally decided to confide in someone, she'd confided in Talin.

"Talin, I know you wanted to keep Felicia on the show in order to catch her red-handed, but that doesn't seem likely if she's leaving the dirty work to someone else," Knightly said.

Brody had brought more of his concerns to the group immediately after he found the box with the spider in Midge's room. Brody and Knightly had thought it best to eliminate Felicia from the show rather than attempt to press charges of harassment since there was nothing concrete they could pin her with, but Talin had worried that Felicia's elimination would cause her to become more dangerous, and he wouldn't be able to keep tabs on her actions if she weren't present on set, but keeping tabs on her hadn't seemed to prevent Felicia's attacks. An accomplice definitely filled in a few blanks.

"I think at this point we're damned if we do and we're damned if we don't. Even with Felicia off the show, she still has an accomplice here working for her."

"What's the likelihood that it's Cambria?" Brody asked.

"I don't know, Brody. You've spent more time with her than any of us, and you certainly looked like you enjoyed it. What do you think?"

Brody felt annoyed at Talin's verbal dig, but decided now wasn't the time or the place to have a confrontation.

"I'd never pick her out of a crowd and label her Felicia's minion, but that might be what makes her so perfect. She isn't the obvious villain here."

"Midge is sharing a room with Cambria tonight," Knightly said. His voice held a hint of panic. "What are we going to do to ensure her safety?"

"She can bunk with me," Talin said. "Putting her with any other contestant is only going to endanger them both, and she'll be much safer with me in my room."

"If she's going to be staying with anyone, it's going to be me. She's my girlfriend, after all, and I think I'm just as capable of protecting her as you are."

"Right, because you've had just as many years of military training as I've had."

Brody scowled at Talin, ready to take this argument to the next level if he had to when Knightly interrupted.

"Personally, I'm not happy with the idea of Midge sharing a bedroom with either one of you. A father shouldn't be privy to such details, but I agree she can't stay in a room with Cambria if we aren't certain of the young woman's innocence. Brody, she'll stay with you in your room tonight, but I must insist that you sleep on the couch, or carpet, or possibly in the tub."

"I think I can manage that," Brody said, deciding it would be unwise to mention the other times he had spent the night with Madelyn.

"Fine," Talin muttered. "What are we going to do about Felicia? Has your man come up with anything in her background that we can possibly take to the police?"

Brody shook his head. "Nothing concrete."

"Then I think it is better to keep her on for now and observe her interactions with Cambria. At some point we'll catch her doing something underhanded, and hopefully we'll catch it on camera.

Brody nodded, though he was ready to eliminate Felicia and be done with it. In truth, he was ready to elope with Madelyn and leave the cameras, the spotlight, and the threats to her safety far behind them.

Unfortunately, he was contractually obligated to continue on with the show, and since he had no intention of proposing to anyone but Madelyn he couldn't eliminate her in order to protect her, and who was to say she would be safe without him by her side. He simply didn't know how far Felicia intended to take this.

Talin took off in a frustrated huff after that, and Brody sank back in his seat with worries of Madelyn's true affections for him plaguing his thoughts.

She shared a long history with Talin, and they were obviously very good friends. She trusted him enough to go to him when she was being threatened while Brody had tried to patiently wait for her to come to him, not wanting to force her trust or confidence, but fully expecting that their developing relationship would eventually nudge her in that direction. He had no idea what to make of her current actions.

"Talin is a big brother to Midge and nothing more, Brody." Knightly gave him a knowing smile. "Try not to get in your head too much over the guy."

Brody gave him a rueful chuckle and let out an uneasy breath.

"Is my jealousy that obvious?"

"Yes, but so is her affection for you."

"And you approve of your daughter remaining in a relationship with me?"

"Brody, I've done everything in my power to protect and provide for my daughter. I'm not saying I was always one hundred percent perfect at it, but I took her with me everywhere I went, tried to keep her out of the spotlight when it came to the media, and eventually, I put her through college even though I wanted to keep her close to me."

Brody's brows raised in astonishment.

"Hold on a second. Are you saying *you* were the one funding her scholarship?"

Knightly shrugged. "Of course I was. Madelyn only applied for one, and some other doofus with zero intelligence got it. She would have had no way to pay for her tuition, and after the fight we had where I behaved like a tyrant, she wasn't going to accept any help from me, so I had to do something to make her dreams a reality. I contacted some bigwig at the school and set up funding for Midge under the agreement that it would be presented to her as a scholarship."

Brody shook his head, marveling at Knightly's actions and gaining much more respect for him than he'd previously possessed.

"So why cut her funding now? Why not offer her trust fund to her after she got her degree?"

"Do you really think Midge would have accepted it? She needed a compelling reason to take it back, and I was groping for a way to become relevant in her life again. So I cut her funding and forced her to face me. I've spent the last six years giving her the space she needed to become her own person rather than Corbin Knightly's daughter. She needed that independence. She needed to get away from the Hollywood scene for a while, but I've missed her." He shrugged his shoulders again. "I just wanted my daughter back in my life again, Brody, but I've never been very good at communicating that to her."

"Are you ever going to tell her about the scholarship?"

"No. I won't take that accomplishment away from her. She thought she earned that tuition money, and in my opinion she did. I never did pay her for all the work she put in on my projects. I consider it back pay." He smiled unseeingly at a picture across the room. "I know she's upset that she was forced to come on this show and then stay, but like I said, I've done my very best to provide for and protect my daughter, and when it comes to what's best for Midge, I'm convinced the eternal solution to that problem is now going to be you. So to finally answer you, yes, I approve of your relationship with my daughter."

"I won't let anything happen to her, Corbin."

"I know you won't."

CHAPTER 32

Midge

C ambria and Midge stopped short in the entryway of their door. The navy blue cocktail dress Midge had planned on wearing the next night was lying on the bed in shreds.

"What in the world is going on? Who did this?" Cambria cried as she ran over to the bed and began gathering pieces of the dress into her arms.

Midge was stunned at the ferocity with which the material had been destroyed.

"I have no idea, but it looks like someone has some serious rage issues."

Midge surveyed Cambria's heartbroken expression and couldn't deny that it was very convincing.

"Why weren't my things ripped to shreds? It's almost like this was a targeted attack on you? I don't understand it."

"I've received a few pranks here and there that have led me to believe someone on this show wants me gone," Midge admitted with reluctance.

"I think we better get Rhodes in here and let him know what's happened," Cambria said. She immediately whipped out her phone and called him before Midge could comment on her surprise that Cambria actually had Talin's phone number.

Unfortunately, there was no way she could keep this quiet now that Cambria was involved. Talin arrived moments later with Brody quick to follow.

Midge cringed as his eyes took in the damage and his skin became blotchy with anger.

"Madelyn, you're staying in my room tonight," Brody said.

"Look, I'll admit this looks bad, but I really think it's just a prank."

"Just a prank? Are you really going to pretend you don't know what's going on here or should I leave the room so you can continue to confide in Talin?

Midge's jaw went slack and her eyes widened in surprise.

Talin eased himself over to Cambria and grabbed her by the arm.

"Midge, I think you and Brody have a few things to work out. Cambria, let's relocate you to a different room. Possibly mine," he said with a wink in an obvious attempt to lighten the mood. "I can come back and take a look at the damage in a few minutes."

He ushered Cambria out of the room as quickly as possible.

Brody slammed the door behind them and then turned to face Midge. His chest was heaving with the obvious anger and frustration he felt.

"Do you mind telling me what that was all about?" Midge said.

"I'm not the one responsible for explaining myself. When were you going to tell me about the spider and the threatening messages?"

Midge grimaced and bit her bottom lip.

"How did you find out about that?"

"I checked the box with the spider in it when you were in the bathroom."

Midge nodded, feeling relieved that he finally knew the truth.

"I should have told you about the threats, but I didn't because I knew you would overreact."

"Overreact? Your life is being threatened. Any reaction at this point isn't going to be nearly strong enough, and then you go and tell Talin all about it? Apparently, you trust Talin enough to worry about your safety, but you don't trust me."

"You are taking this the wrong way, Brody. I have no interest in dating Talin."

"Then why in the world would you turn to him as if he were your boyfriend?"

"He's head of security and he's a good friend. He was the obvious choice."

Midge bit the inside of her cheek, immediately aware that hadn't been the best thing to say.

Brody's eyes darkened and he took a step toward her.

"Is he the obvious choice now? Is he your only choice, Madelyn?"

She pointed a finger at him.

"That's not fair and you know it. I have been honest with you about my feelings toward you, Talin, and everything else you've ever asked me. I am only interested in you."

"Then why didn't you come to me the moment you knew you were in danger? Why go to Talin."

"Because I was afraid if I told you what was happening you would eliminate me from the show to keep me safe, and then I'd have to watch you proposing to some other woman who will never be capable of caring for you the way I do."

Midge gasped at her own admission fully expecting Brody to laugh at her or worse, admit that his feelings weren't as strong as hers, but her words seemed to ignite a fire within him. His eyes flashed then darkened and the hungry gaze of a predator set in as he crossed the distance between them.

"Good answer," he said before grabbing her roughly by the shoulders and devouring her lips with his.

She responded to his lips with equal passion, wholly immersing herself in the possessive feel of his arms wrapping around her and pulling her snug against his chest. He pulled back just enough to give them time to breathe and then he was kissing her again. Her lips, her cheeks, the freckles across her nose, and then back to her lips again.

"For the record, I would never have eliminated you from the show, not when I can get rid of Felicia instead and never let you out of my sight, and I'd certainly never propose to anyone else when I am completely and madly in love with you," he said once they finally came up for air. "You are rooming with me tonight."

"Yeah. I think that's probably a good idea," Midge agreed.

"Your father has given me strict instructions to sleep anywhere but in the same bed as you."

Midge snorted. "You've already discussed this with him?"

"Corbin, Talin, and I have been working on keeping you safe for some time, and even though I would much rather share a bed with you, I think I may need to take a cold shower and then stay safe in the bathtub for the rest of the night."

"How exactly will you keep me safe if you're in the bathtub and I'm on the bed?"

"A very good question. Perhaps I'll allow you to posit that one to your father."

Midge laughed. "Just hold me tonight like you did the last time, and we'll be okay."

Brody kissed the top of her head and snuggled her into his arms more securely.

"I think that's an excellent idea."

FELICIA

"How could you be so reckless?" Liz hissed as Felicia sat at the ornate vanity brushing her long hair. "We agreed that our next move was to blackmail Midge with her own manuscript, not shred her dress like some psychotic hell-cat."

Felicia's eyes narrowed into slits. She wasn't about to take any lip from this particular peasant.

"I lost my temper momentarily. Who cares? No one saw me go in their room."

Liz's grunt amused and annoyed Felicia.

"Have you downloaded Madelyn's manuscript?"

"Yes," Liz replied becoming all business. She handed over a jump drive and a large purse. "The drive has a copy of the manuscript, and the purse has a hidden camera embedded in the lining on the side. You'll need to keep the purse pointed in front in order to film Midge's reaction."

"Tell me again why I'm the one blackmailing her instead of you? I'll be caught on camera blackmailing a contestant."

"And you're worried Brody will eliminate you for it, I know. We've been over this several times. You are going to let him know that you suspected Midge's feelings were fake all along and you just had to do something to protect him. You can even lie and say you never really hacked into the computer and stole her manuscript. You were just bluffing to get her to confess. He'll see you did it for love and keep you on the show. Once she's out of the way, there's no reason to think he won't chase after you like he should have from the beginning."

"Yes, he certainly will, won't he?" Felicia studied her reflection in the mirror and then grabbed a tube of bright red lip stick and smeared it over her collagen-filled lips.

"This needs to be recorded and given to Brody before the diamond ceremony tonight. When is your one-on-one with Brody?"

"Right now. We're doing some rose garden tour and eating a light breakfast. You can confront her while I'm gone, and when I get back I will edit the recording and burn it to a disk for Brody."

"Just remember that you're going on a date with my future husband. Keep your claws to yourself."

Felicia took sick joy in the annoyed grimace that flitted across Liz's features. So much so that she had to dig the nail just a little bit deeper. "While you're at it, make sure to be the worst, most annoying version of Charlene Dubois you can be."

LIZ

Liz came out of Felicia's room so fast she didn't think to check the stairway to see if anyone was coming. Her shoulder bumped into someone and she let out a startled gasp, nearly losing her footing in the process.

"Charlene, are you okay?"

Brody Prescott held her firmly by the shoulders, helping to steady her as she slightly wavered.

"I'm fine," Liz said.

Responding to her alias was difficult when she was consumed with so much rage.

Brody looked behind her, noticing the door from which she had stumbled. "Isn't that Felicia Davenport's room?"

"Ah, yes. Yes it is, and unfortunately I got stuck rooming with the heinous cow. Worst roomie ever. She just flagged me down and asked that I bring her a mojito and some all natural fruit yogurt of all things. Since she's kind of scary, I decided to actually do it rather than ignore her."

Brody chuckled, his serious expression relaxing as he motioned for her to continue to walk with him down the hallway.

"I can understand that instinctive need to protect oneself in the presence of Felicia Davenport."

Liz smiled at his candor, enjoying the feel of her arm in his as he escorted her down the hallway. He may have had feelings for Madelyn, but she hoped that once Madelyn agreed to leave the show that he would see her as the best option left for him. After all, they had always gotten along great on the group dates and their personal conversations during the cocktail parties were easy and comfortable. He clearly liked her. Possibly as just a friend and nothing more, but great relationships always started off with great friendships. She could wait for him to come around so long as Madelyn was out of the picture...in a non-lethal way.

"Are you ready for our date?" he asked.

"Absolutely. I've been looking forward to this since the start of the show."

"You mean you're not sick of me yet?" he joked.

"I imagine I could probably throw out several compliments to convince you of my enthusiastic interest in you, but would you believe me or would you just assume that I'm after your money?"

Her question seemed to take him off-guard for a moment, and then he looked at her...really looked at her for the first time since she'd arrived.

"That's definitely an issue I always take into consideration. It's hard not to feel like a target for those gold diggers out there, but if you're saying that I'm interesting enough without my money then I am sincerely grateful for the compliment."

"Then I will simply say, you're welcome, and leave it at that."

"You're a good person, Charlene. I'm happy for this opportunity to get to know you."

It was a very promising breakthrough. Her plans were all coming to fruition—she simply had to stay the course. After months of working for Felicia, she had managed to get all the proof she needed to expose Felicia and her many crimes, especially the ones against herself and her family.

One more step left and then Midge and Felicia would be exiting the show for good, leaving Brody heartbroken, vulnerable, and very available.

MIDGE

Midge jolted at a sharp knock on her door. She'd spent all morning trying to cope with the idea of Brody on another date without her and she felt supremely insecure. Which was ludicrous considering his declaration of love for her the previous night, not to mention the wonderful feeling of waking up completely ensconced in Brody's arms this morning. Old habits died hard, she guessed.

What worried her most was her inability to return his declaration of love with one of her own. She'd overcome many fears simply by admitting that she cared for him, but what if it wasn't enough and his date with Charlene turned his head in a different direction?

Was he enjoying himself? Did he like Charlene? Were they laughing together, feeling comfortable and happy with one another? Insecurities as to her own worth and merit were something she would simply have to overcome day-by-day.

The sharp rap on her door sounded again with an impatient urgency that had Midge grudgingly moving off her bed.

She opened the door only to become fully alert when she saw Felicia Davenport standing on the threshold. She was dressed to the nines in white capri pants with a bright yellow shirt that looked as if someone had vomited gold glitter on the front, obviously a brand-name shirt that was valuable due to the label attached and not the design glued across it. Her Louis Vuitton bag was slung over her shoulder and possessively clutched to her side. Though her make-up was immaculate, her perpetual scowl and disdainful air completely marred the perfection of her features.

Was this it? Was this the moment when Felicia decided to do her own dirty work after all? It was just like her to attack with Brody out of the way.

Where the heck was Talin?

A spike of fear shot through Midge's core as she considered everything she had learned about Felicia's background, but she squared her shoulders and arched an imperious eyebrow, doing her best to fake boredom lest Felicia think she had actually managed to intimidate her.

"Seven in the morning, Felicia? Did you have to get up at three to put yourself together or do you tend to roll out of bed with three layers of make-up caked to your face?" It was nasty, she knew, but she couldn't help baiting the evil wench.

Felicia's eyes narrowed at the insult. "I would tread very carefully if I were you, considering I have something of yours which I'm sure you're going to want back?"

"Something of mine? I doubt that."

"Why don't you invite me in and find out?"

"Won't you come in?"

She opened the door a little wider and stood back as Felicia strutted into the room. Midge shut the door and stood silent right next to it just in case Felicia decided to surprise her by pulling out a gun from that monstrosity she called a purse.

Felicia didn't waste time mincing words. "I want you to leave the show today. Now."

Midge's eyes widened in surprise. "You think I would leave the show just because you demand it? Felicia, this god complex you have needs to be put in check. You're really not as important or powerful as you think you are, and your pathetic attempts at intimidating me haven't really panned out either."

Felicia's eyes took on a lofty glint, and Midge was sure the feline was about to unleash a trump card she wasn't prepared for.

"You'll leave the show today and cut off all ties with Brody Prescott or I'll publish your manuscript under my own name and use the connections I have to establish myself as the best selling author of...of...what is that little book of yours called?" she placed a finger to her chin and tapped it for a moment as if trying to remember something inconsequential. "*Forget Me Not.* Which, by the way, is the worst title ever. I'll probably have to change it if I want any hope of it succeeding in the entertainment industry."

Midge's insides began to curdle as the magnitude of Felicia's threat solidified within her brain.

"How could you have possibly gotten access to my laptop? I always put it in the safe, and it's password protected."

"Please. Do you really think I would do something as mundane as breaking and entering? I had a very sophisticated virus emailed to you. Once it uploaded onto your computer, I had full access to everything." Felicia pulled out a thumb drive and held it up to the light. "The only copy of your manuscript in existence happens to be on this tiny piece of technology."

Midge felt her mouth go dry. "You...you deleted everything from my computer?"

"Even from the hard drive. There's absolutely no way for you to prove that you're the one who wrote what is no doubt a sniveling, sentimental tale of love, loss, and second chances. Love conquers all, am I right, Madelyn? Did all of your naive ideals where love and marriage are concerned make their way into your pitiful novel?"

Midge didn't even acknowledge Felicia's insults, too intent on the thumb drive she dangled like a carrot in her hand. Months worth of work, sweat and tears had gone into the writing of that book. It was her first step to achieving everything she'd dreamed of, her concrete validation that she had truly joined the ranks of all authors everywhere, and now the only copy in existence was being held hostage in Felicia Davenport's blood-red claws.

"Now that I have your undivided attention, I expect you to pack your things, tell Brody you're no longer interested in what he has to offer, and fly away on your little charter plane to wherever you roost."

Midge felt her breathing become shallow as she considered what giving up Brody would mean for her happiness and her future.

"I tell Brody I don't love him and I never did, and in return you give me back my manuscript?"

"I'll mail it to your home address the day you leave the show," Felicia said, growing more confident by the second.

Madelyn wondered if she could pretend to feel nothing for Brody, then Felicia wouldn't assume she had the upper hand in this.

"But I *don't* love him, Felicia. I'll admit that he's extremely likable, but for you to think I'm still here due to any interest in Brody Prescott is simply ludicrous. I can't leave the show until Brody eliminates me; otherwise, no trust fund."

"I'm not an idiot. Every time you two are on camera together you positively glow with love and adoration. It's sickening."

Midge smirked at that. "I've spent years directing actors with my father. Do you really think I'm incapable of acting well enough to please an audience? I've even got you believing that something exists between Brody and me when it doesn't. I'm sorry, Felicia, but as much as I love the idea of publishing my first novel, I love my trust fund even more, and since Brody seems very interested in putting a ring on my finger, what do I need a book for when he's more than happy to offer me his billions. The benefits for pretending to love Brody far outweigh the loss of this one story. So you can take your thumb drive and leave my suite now. This entire conversation has been one big snooze."

Midge nonchalantly patted a hand to her mouth while she gave an over-dramatic yawn and prayed that Felicia would believe her bluff and even go so far as to throw the thumb drive at her in frustration. She didn't want to lose her hard work over the last year, but she didn't want to lose Brody either.

Felicia tapped her finger to her chin as she gave Midge a long, calculating stare.

"Well, I suppose if this manuscript means so little to you then I may as well flush it down your toilet right now." She moved toward the bathroom, and Midge couldn't help when her body stiffened in response.

Felicia's smirk spread across the entirety of her face. "Not so indifferent to the loss of your precious manuscript, are you? You see, I've done my research, Midge darling, and I happen to have it on good authority that you were the one to walk away from your trust fund six years ago. So I don't, for one second, believe any of the crap you've just spewed. You may want your trust fund, but you want Brody more."

Midge's façade began to crumble as Felicia called her bluff.

"You're going to tell Brody you don't love him and then you're going to leave the show."

"I can't do that. I can't lie to him like that."

"Of course you can. Repeat after me, Brody, I don't love you." Felicia clamped her hands around the thumb drive. "Or I'll just toss this in the toilet right now."

Midge held up her hands. "Brody, I don't love you." She repeated.

"And when people ask you why you left you'll say what?"

Midge's heart sank. "I never loved Brody Prescott."

"Exactly. You need to decide what's more important to you, Madelyn. Brody's love or your career as a respected author. Which is it?"

Midge couldn't answer, the bile burning the back of her throat was moments away from choking her. Felicia's eyes narrowed as she inched her way toward the bathroom.

Midge could control the course of her career, but she still didn't have complete faith in the strength of Brody's love. Was she willing to risk everything for a man who may or may not have been willing to commit to forever with her?

Midge took in a shallow breath, forcing herself to consider her own insecurities and fears and finding herself completely terrified at the possible outcome.

"Well?" Felicia said.

"My career." The moment Midge uttered those words she felt tainted and dirty. Surely, she would feel relieved at having come to a decision if that decision was correct. Instead, the pit in her stomach widened further.

Felicia nodded in satisfaction and placed the thumb drive back into the black depths of her purse. "I knew you'd see it my way."

Midge's thoughts began to race as Felicia made her way to the door. She couldn't do this. She couldn't walk away from Brody because she *did* love him. As much as her hopes and dreams of becoming an author were important to her, she couldn't imagine attempting any of that without Brody by her side.

"Wait," she said just before Felicia opened the door. Felicia turned around and tapped her foot in an impatient gesture. "I do have other pressing things to worry about at the moment."

"I won't do it. I won't forfeit mine and Brody's happiness for a three hundred page manuscript. I can always write another book, but I can never replace someone as amazing and wonderful as Brody Prescott. So if you plan on publishing that book under your name or destroying the only copy in existence, I suppose that's up to you. I love him. It's taken me far too long to get to the point where I can actually admit that out loud, and I can't give it up now. I can't give him up ever. Brody means far more to me than my success as an author, and if you had any concept of what true love feels like, you might have found your own happiness by now rather than lying and murdering others in an attempt to grab it."

Felicia's face drained of all color. "What did you just accuse me of?"

"Kincaid, Ramsey, Putin? Did you think no one would eventually put two and two together? I know far more about the skeletons in your closet than you realize."

"I would watch yourself and your next course of action. You're hardly a threat to me, but I assure you I'm more than a threat to you. I've just become your worst nightmare."

"Don't let the door hit you on the way out, Felicia. I'd hate for those butt implants of yours to explode."

Felicia ground out an oath and turned around, wrenching the door open and storming down the hall.

Midge let out a shaky sigh of relief as she closed the door and considered her next move. Her manuscript was gone for good. There was nothing she could do about that loss. She could recreate a similar plot with the same characters, but the labor of love in the journey of her creation wasn't something she would be able to capture again. She took a moment to mourn the loss of what felt like the death of a family member and then remembered what she had gained from that loss.

She knew she was in love with Brody, and though the realization came with insecurities and doubts as to how truly invested he was in their relationship, she knew she had more to lose by not giving into her feelings completely and letting their relationship take the course it was meant to. The only real obstacle preventing her from doing that had just walked out the door. Felicia needed to be dealt with as soon as possible. She picked up her cell and dialed.

"Lisa," she said as her friend let out a sleepy hello.

"It's called lunch time, Midge. People generally call their friends during the afternoon."

"Did you leak that information about Felicia to the tabloids yet?"

"I emailed one of their journalists." She let out a derisive snort on that last word, "I let him know I had some dirt on one Felicia Davenport. Let me check my email to see if he got back to me."

Midge impatiently waited while Lisa got busy on her laptop. A few minutes later Lisa came back with some puzzling news.

"He says that the information I have couldn't possibly match the dirt that was leaked to them two days ago."

"What?"

"They are running some story on Felicia today. Apparently, the story is so big that the local news has picked it up?"

"What?"

"Do you have a TV in your bedroom?"

"Not in Sababurg Castle. Even if I did, I hardly think I'd get L.A. news in Germany."

"Holy crap!" Lisa said. "Get on your laptop or cell phone and stream what's happening on L.A. Nine News."

Midge grabbed her laptop and did as instructed. An anchor woman stood just outside an enormous residence, vying for the attention of Senator Davenport.

"It has recently been discovered that Felicia Davenport, daughter of Senator Davenport and current contestant on *Marry Your Billionaire* has been tied to a string of suspicious deaths over the last five years. Though we haven't been able to reach Ms. Davenport with her own response to these accusations it would seem that there is enough circumstantial evidence to bring her in for questioning."

Midge watched the chaos of reporters and news crew attempting to get some kind of comment from Senator Davenport as he left his humble abode for work.

"I don't have anything to say to you people," he shouted. "My daughter and I haven't communicated with one another for several years now."

"Who leaked the story?" Midge asked.

"I'm as clueless on that front as you are, but I have to admit I'm thanking them from the bottom of my heart. There's no way she can stay on the show now that she's wanted for questioning by the police. You and Brody are in the clear."

Midge had to agree, though in the back of her mind she wondered if it was really that simple.

LIZ

Liz watched as Felicia stormed into the suite, spitting curses and threats that made even Liz's stomach feel weak. She'd been waiting for over twenty minutes for Felicia, wondering if their plan would indeed provide the results they both desired. From Felicia's volatile behavior the answer was most likely one resounding no.

"I take it she didn't go along with our plan?" Liz asked.

Felicia angrily dove into her purse and pulled out the thumb drive, holding it up in Liz's face and then throwing it across the room where it landed on the bed.

"I'm so furious. I actually went on a walk around the countryside to see if that might calm me down. I can't believe I thought nature would be more soothing than retail therapy. I told you this wasn't going to work, and now I've just tipped my hand in a big way. She has dirt on me from my past. I should have just killed her when I had the chance."

"Dirt? Felicia what are you talking about? You told me that there was nothing in your past that needed to be buried. Was that a lie?"

"Of course it was a lie. First rule of getting away with murder, Liz: never kill and tell."

Liz wondered what exactly Madelyn had discovered, but whatever it was, Liz had already leaked the most damning evidence to the tabloids, police, and news stations. It was simply a matter of time before Felicia's goose was good and cooked.

"We don't need to resort to killing her just yet. Depending on what was said, I can edit what you filmed to make it look as if Midge accepted your offer and chose her manuscript over living happily ever after with Brody. Let me see your purse."

Felicia nearly threw it at her in her anger as she stormed into the bathroom. Liz grabbed the purse and pulled out the tiny digital camera she had hooked to the front. She reviewed the footage quickly to make sure that Midge was not only heard but seen. She'd been half afraid that Felicia would wear the bag on the wrong side and end up filming her enormous plastic breasts by accident.

A loud knock at the door took Liz by surprise.

"Ms. Davenport this is security. I need you to open up at once."

Liz's heart went into overdrive as she realized that having anyone catch her here with Felicia at the moment was an extremely bad idea. Surveying her options, she quickly dove under the bed with the tiny camera tucked under her arm.

Felicia took her time exiting the bathroom which was the only thing that saved Liz from losing such a great hiding spot.

"Liz," Felicia called looking around, "where are you?" Grumbling she opened the door and moved back as the head of security, Talin Rhodes, entered the room with a few other security guys behind him.

"I'm afraid, Ms. Davenport, we are placing you under arrest as per the request of the LAPD. You'll be delivered into the hands of local authorities at the airport and accompanied by a plain clothes detective on your flight back to L.A."

Liz couldn't help but smile as she watched the carnage unfold from underneath the bed.

"What are you talking about? Do you have any idea who I am? Do you have any idea who my father is?"

Rhodes ignored her and spun her around, cuffing her hands behind her back.

"You'll regret this you glorified mall cop. I'll have your greasy hide handed to you by the most expensive lawyers in L.A."

Felicia continued to breathe out threats as Rhodes finished cuffing her and shoved her out of the room.

Liz expelled a huge breath. At least she didn't have to worry about Felicia doing something crazy like murdering Midge in her sleep. She hated to ruin Midge's happiness as she sought to attain her own, but if living on the streets through her formative years had taught her anything it was to take care of yourself.

Friends just weren't a luxury she could afford, and revenge on Felicia

Davenport was really the only thing that mattered. A shot at happiness with a halfway decent guy who could provide for her was also extremely appealing, and one more thing she was stealing from Felicia.

Sorry, Midge. It's time for me to finally have my happy ending.

She was about to pull herself out from under the bed when she heard the turn of the door handle. Holding her breath she watched as two bare feet came into view.

"Where is it?" said the young woman whom Liz recognized as Midge.

She held her breath, afraid to give away her location.

"Please tell me she left her purse here. Aha." Midge found the purse that Liz had dropped and began rummaging through its contents. She let out a grunt when she came up empty handed.

Look on the bed, Midge. It's on the bed, thought Liz.

At the very least, she could hope that her friend retrieved her manuscript since Liz intended to take away her future fiancé.

There. I'm not completely heartless.

Midge's footsteps inched further into the room, and soon she let out a triumphant squeal as she strode over to the bed, reached for the thumb drive, and then turned around and headed for the door.

Liz couldn't help but be grateful that Midge had retrieved her manuscript, though in truth she probably would have anonymously emailed it to Midge either way.

She could be kind when it suited her. Patting her pocket to assure herself that the small camera was still there, she inched her way out from under the bed and quietly slipped out of the room.

Now all she had to do was edit the video, casting Midge in the most unfavorable light, and hand it over to Brody. With any luck, there would be trouble in paradise by the end of the day.

CHAPTER 33

Brody

B rody sat in his room with his laptop on and his jaw hanging open.

"Did you leak this info to the press, Gregg?"

"I most certainly did not. If that information had been traced back to me it would make it look as if you hired me to discredit Felicia in the same manner she discredited you. It would hardly help the image we've worked so hard to salvage."

Gregg's nerves carried over the line. Brody could just picture his high-strung assistant pacing back and forth in front of his own TV, wondering if somehow this information *could* be traced back to him even though he hadn't reported any of it.

"Then who else knew about Felicia's background, and why release it now? Not that I'm complaining. It's been exhausting, having to work with Rhodes to keep Madelyn safe. Like I want that guy anywhere near the girl I love. With Felicia gone, I won't have to worry about any other pranks or possible attempts on her life."

"That girl has no doubt made countless enemies over the years. Anyone could have done enough digging and made those connections. I'm more inclined to thank the individual responsible and move on."

"Good point."

"Brody, there are a few emails I need you to look at. We have some new weddings set for next month. Two couples who met through the program have set their wedding dates for the end of the month and they contacted the company, wondering if you would accept an invitation to the ceremonies."

"You know the answer to that is yes."

Gregg sighed. "You don't have time to attend every wedding, Brody, especially when none of them is your own. This is half the reason you're not married. You never make time for yourself."

"Well, I think you'll be happy to know that progress has been made with Madelyn, and she has agreed to a truce."

"A truce? Are we talking about a relationship or a battle of the sexes?"

Brody smiled, reviewing Madelyn's particular brand of warfare. "She's giving me a chance, Gregg. Once she actually lets down her guard completely, I can't see this ending in anything less than matrimony. I certainly won't accept anything less."

"Considering her complete and total aversion to you from the first time you two met, I'd say I'm impressed with your rapid progress. It's also a bit heartwarming to think that money has nothing to do with it."

"Exactly."

"Well, carry on with the schmoozing and please take a look at those emails soon...as in right after we hang up."

"Fine. I'll get some work done."

Brody set his cell phone down and reached for his laptop. An afternoon filled with work-related emails didn't sound very appealing when all he really wanted to do was spend the rest of the day with Midge and reassure her of his feelings for her. Even though she hadn't mentioned it, the tension around her eyes had deepened when he left her to go on his early morning date with Charlene. He couldn't wait for this show to be good and over so he could get to the business of spending every waking moment with the girl he'd fallen in love with.

His lips quirked into a smile as he opened up his email account and started reading through his emails. A few were from his accountants, web designers, and people in other countries helping him to expand the company. A knock at the door broke his focus. He stood to answer, excitement filling him at the prospect of seeing Madelyn as he opened the door. Was she going out of her way to seek him out first? This was definite progress.

He was brought up short by the appearance of Charlene. Swallowing his disappointment, he worked to rearrange his features into a polite face.

"Charlene, what brings you here? Did I forget to tip the waiter?" He laughed at his lame joke and then swallowed away his mirth. She appeared extremely uncomfortable, shifting nervously from one foot to the next.

"I...Brody...I went back to my room after Rhodes arrested Felicia—"

"She's been arrested already?"

Charlene nodded. "Apparently, she's wanted for questioning. Can't say I'm surprised, and I'll certainly enjoy my room much more in her absence now that the police have arrested her."

"Much to everyone's relief, I'm sure."

Charlene gave him a weak smile and did a little more shifting.

"I'm being extremely rude. Come in, Charlene. You seem to have something you really need to tell me."

The look of relief on her face only furthered Brody's curiosity. Once the door had been closed, Charlene rushed to her explanation as if she felt she might back down if she didn't spit it out.

"I went to my room right after Felicia was escorted out of the hotel, and I was surprised to see Midge in my room when I got there. She grabbed what looked like a thumb drive from Felicia's purse and left in a hurry. I tried to pretend like I didn't see her do it. Anyway, she dropped the purse when she left, spilling its contents on the floor, and when I went to pick it up I found this DVD with your name on it."

Charlene offered him the DVD with a shaky hand and waited for his reaction.

The label on the front read *Brody Prescott*. His questioning eyes found hers as he tried to understand why she was behaving as if she felt reluctant to hand over the DVD. Then it occurred to him that she had probably watched it.

"You know what's on this, don't you?"

Great big tears welled in her eyes as she nodded. "I can't say that I'm surprised by what's on there, and to be honest I'm almost relieved because it makes me feel as if I might have a chance with you after all, but I don't want to see you hurt." She paused for a moment and let her tear-filled eyes weigh on him before she said, "But I think it's definitely going to hurt. I'm so very sorry, Brody." She leaned up to kiss his cheek and then she left the room.

With numb fingers he fumbled to take the DVD out of its case and place it in the player in his laptop. He watched it while tendrils of nausea made their way to his stomach. Felicia was blackmailing Madelyn with her own manuscript, and his sweet Madelyn was quite easily denying that she'd ever had feelings for him in the first place. Worse, she was happy to give up her manuscript and play along with this lie she had fabricated if it meant she got his billions in the end.

How could she? It didn't add up. It didn't make sense. This wasn't the Madelyn Knightly he'd come to love and respect. Had she and Knightly been playing him? Knightly was always looking to make the biggest splash when it came to ratings. Was it possible Knightly had been cunning enough to use Madelyn in order to get him to do the show?

Ridiculous. He was seeing conspiracies and mind games where none existed. He would go to her right now and talk to her. There had to be an obvious explanation for her response to Felicia's blackmail.

But what if there wasn't, and what if she simply rejected him right then and there, admitting that all she'd ever seen when she looked at him were dollar signs? He could hardly believe any of this was happening, and yet he had the proof right in front of him, falling from her very lips. Lips that he had kissed more times than he could count. Kisses that held meaning, that promised a certain level of commitment, trust, and love. How could she have not felt that love like he did?

He'd thought she was simply afraid to trust him, when in reality she hadn't felt a thing. She'd played him for a sap.

He was a fool. Such a lovesick fool. The answer to her affections had been staring him in the face for quite some time, but he was too in love and simply too stubborn to give up on what he wanted.

Brody was very much used to coming in second place while his money came in first. His fears of never truly being loved for anything other than his billions had followed him around like a stormy raincloud refusing to dissipate. He probably could have forgiven her for that, he could have forgiven her for anything if she had claimed to actually love him as well, but she wasn't even sure if she liked him.

It was like a knife to the heart, twisted to inflict as much pain as possible, and he wasn't sure how he was ever going to recover from it, but he thought anger might be a good starting point. Anger might be the best counterpoint to the pain that currently ran rampant through his system.

MIDGE

"I'm so nervous, I think my intestines are about to explode!" Cambria stated in a squeaky voice.

Midge grimaced at the visual Cambria's words brought to mind, but she had to smile at her behavior. She found Cambria's penchant for speaking the first thought that came to mind endearing. It gave her a kind of refreshing naiveté compared to Midge's experiences with people whose every phrase and comment were delivered with cold calculations and double meanings. She mentally berated herself for ever thinking that Cambria might have been in cahoots with Felicia. Then again, they still didn't know who her accomplice had been, and after trying for several hours during the afternoon to discuss it with Brody without ever being able to find him, she felt anxious to get his opinion on the subject and talk about Felicia's arrest.

"I'm feeling a little unsteady as well," Midge offered.

"I don't believe that for one second. You're Brody's favorite. Which makes me want to hate you, but I just can't. Your ability to eat cicadas without batting an eye made you much too likable for me."

Midge chuckled, wrapping an arm around Cambria's shoulders and giving her a squeeze.

"Anytime you're interested in bugs for breakfast just give me a call."

"Bugs for breakfast?" Charlene asked as she entered the courtyard. "Please tell me that's not on the agenda for tonight's cocktail party."

"No, we were just discussing some good times," Cambria said.

Charlene rolled her eyes. "If you can call bugs in your entrails a good time."

Charlene looked gorgeous in a black sequined number that hugged her curves and left very little to the imagination, especially with the thigh-high slit, revealing a nice side view of her leg. The dress was strapless, dipping low in the cleavage department. It was a daring look that left Midge feeling slightly dowdy, though she never would have considered showing that much skin.

Her turquoise dress had an empire waist with a mermaid tail skirt flowing out in ruffles and lace around her feet. There was a slit in her dress toward the front so she had room to maneuver, but it came to just above her knees. The scooped neckline came together at the back with a thin strap, leaving her shoulders and arms exposed.

Cambria looked like a frothy strawberry milk shake with whipped cream, but in a delectable way. She'd gone into full Cinderella mode with her dress, something definitely fit for a princess and a royal ball. It was also the perfect complement to her bubbly personality of which Midge felt certain she would miss once Cambria left the show, whether tonight or the next elimination round. There were only seven girls left with Felicia gone, and three more would be leaving tonight. The next week the remaining four women were flying home to meet Brody's mother and spend some time getting to know her and Brody's hometown.

Midge realized she didn't have any doubts about tonight. She knew how strongly Brody felt for her, and she was anxious to get the cocktail party started so she could speak with him again.

"So on a scale from one to ten, how nervous are you?" Cambria asked Charlene.

"Oh, I'm super nervous, like a nine nervous, but the date went really well so I am hoping the time Brody and I spent together will be enough to get me through this round."

Midge quirked a questioning brow in her direction. Charlene's expression was peaceful and serene.

Les entered the room at that moment effectively silencing the small group, and grabbing their immediate attention.

"Ladies, I know you were looking forward to the cocktail party tonight so you could spend some further time with Brody, but I'm afraid there's been a change of plans."

"Oh, no," Cambria moaned.

Les gave Cambria a sympathetic look before continuing.

"It would seem that Brody knows exactly what he is going to do tonight and feels that the cocktail party will not only fail to change his decision, but merely prolong the inevitable and cause everyone in the room more anxiety than is necessary. He's opted to cancel the party and move straight to the diamond ceremony."

Midge felt slightly relieved at this announcement.

"It'll be okay, Cambria," Midge said as she squeezed her shoulder.

After a few moments Brody entered the room. Midge felt like she could finally take in her first real breath of the day. She leveled her gaze at Brody, giving him a sincere smile and waiting for him to acknowledge her, but his gaze remained steadfast and resolute, pointing toward the back of the courtyard. Upon closer inspection his jaw appeared tense, a muscle bulged in his neck, and his fists were clenched at his sides. Something terrible must have occurred for him to appear so distraught. Midge feared that something had happened to his mother. She nearly rushed over to inquire about Blanche's health but caught herself. The glint of a camera in her peripheral vision grabbed her attention and reminded her of where she stood.

Brody's words and movements were stiff as he said, "I want you ladies to know that my decision tonight was based on the level of love, honesty, integrity, and compassion you have shown toward me and toward those you interact with. True affection and trust is important to me. It was easy to make this decision tonight based on my feelings for you and your true and sincere affections for me."

Brody grabbed a diamond encrusted rose and held it before him still refusing to make eye contact with her. Midge was utterly bewildered by the anger and tension pulsing about him.

"The first person I choose tonight is...Charlene."

Charlene let out a huge sigh of relief, walking over to Brody and folding herself into his tight embrace. Then Brody took their hug a little further. After Charlene accepted his rose, he clasped hold of her by the waist and brought his lips to hers, participating in a rather passionate exchange that didn't seem to surprise Charlene in the slightest but definitely bowled Midge over. She eagerly accepted his affections while Midge stood there reeling with this new development, attempting to hide the fact that she felt like she'd just been sucker punched, stabbed in the heart, and left for dead by someone she'd given more than just her trust.

Why is he kissing her? Why would he do this?

She felt Cambria squeeze her hand as the young girl let out a shaky breath and muttered, "Well, that was unexpected. I know he promised to kiss only those he felt serious about, but I thought he was only serious about you."

She could only nod in quiet bewilderment as their kiss ended and Charlene came back to stand in line with them. She looked thrilled by the change of events, and Midge certainly couldn't blame her for that. She glanced to Brody again, and this time he met her gaze with a smug, satisfied one of his own. The corners of his eyes were strained with bottled up rage, but he kept his composure, wiping the brief smugness from his expression so quickly that Midge wondered if she had imagined it.

Brody called out two more girls,—neither one of them Midge or Cambria —and gave them both what Midge considered overenthusiastic hugs and shared kisses on the cheek.

Her stomach continued its churning as Brody reached for the last diamond encrusted rose on the table and brought it forward.

"The last girl who has shown me what true love and genuine affection can do for a relationship is..."

Midge felt the sinking sensation tank to the bottom of her stomach as Brody's gaze fell upon her, filled with nothing but disgust and contempt. Then he turned his attention to Cambria and gifted her a beautiful smile.

"Cambria."

A collective gasp swept the room as crew, contestants and security alike reacted to this unexpected twist in the competition. Midge hardly felt the floor beneath her feet as despair, grief, agony, anger, outrage, and finally a numb kind of acceptance settled in while Cambria quickly glanced to her and then left her side, making her way in front of Brody and accepting his rose and another unsettling display of public affection. Brody made certain to make eye contact with Midge the moment his kiss with Cambria concluded.

Midge stared back at him as the shock and eventual numbness at such an unexpected betrayal set in. Cambria returned to the center of their group, and flashed Midge a worried look. Midge wondered if she was broadcasting the pain she felt, but she simply didn't have the emotional energy required to paste on a brave face in order to deal with this very public, very humiliating rejection after she had finally taken that leap of faith and trusted in him.

She'd actually believed in the love he'd so willingly offered, at least where she was concerned, but apparently she really had been part of the angle used to help his image and get ratings for the show. Did that mean her father knew about this? Not that he would have understood the emotional ramifications for her since he wasn't aware of her feelings for Brody, but still, had the public rejection been his idea for more ratings, and now she would forever be that poor girl who wasn't good enough for Brody Prescott?

And that wasn't even the part that hurt. No. His malicious rejection of her after gaining her trust hurt far worse. He knew her vulnerabilities and was aware of her fears on camera. He'd managed to hit her in the most vindictive way imaginable, and she had no idea why. She didn't believe Brody to be a cruel individual, but perhaps he had played her for a fool.

Brody came forward and reached out to embrace her as was customary for him to do with contestants he'd eliminated. His arms felt like liquid fire as they touched her, scalding her and wounding her at the absurdity of this interaction, adding insult to injury. Just before he released her she heard him whisper in her ear.

"I suppose you thought you had me wrapped around your little finger, Midge. Now it's time you realize that whatever was between us was little more than a publicity stunt. Thanks for playing along so nicely. Enjoy your trust fund."

Midge. Not Madelyn. The distinction couldn't have been any plainer, though most wouldn't understand its significance like she did.

His words effectively shoved that knife to the hilt embedding it deep within her chest. Midge's heart blackened and withered like a decaying flower in the midst of winter. Her devastation was so complete, she nearly fainted when he released her, wobbling for a moment and causing Brody to hesitantly reach his hand out as if to steady her, but then he pulled back and hardened his features. Midge's shock at this horrific turn of events was so complete she failed to notice the brief look of concern that crossed Brody's face as he studied her.

"Goodbye, Midge," he whispered, and then strode from the room.

CHAPTER 34

Midge

"I still can't believe Brody proposed to Charlene and passed up an opportunity to be with you," Lisa said as she passed a tray of Oreos to Midge and then seated herself on the sofa next to her.

Midge sighed, deciding that any more Oreos would be vomited up if Lisa insisted on rehashing the events of her failed attempt at a relationship with Brody Prescott.

She'd refused to watch the rest of the season, knowing full well that his choice would be between Cambria and Charlene. How had this inconceivable scenario reared its ugly head?

Her existence since the night she'd been eliminated from the show could be compared to that of a zombie going through the motions; never quite aware of its surroundings.

"There's a story there. Something happened to scare the guy. Something sneaky and underhanded," Stacey said as she grabbed the Oreos from Midge and sat down on the other side of the couch.

Stacey had been key in getting her out of Germany with her possessions and her sanity intact. After Brody's hurtful rejection, Midge hadn't been capable of making a single decision in regards to her welfare, and her father had requested that Stacey accompany her on the flight home.

Her father's anger at the situation had come as a complete surprise since she assumed that he had staged the whole thing, but apparently he'd been just as convinced as everyone else that Brody was sincere in his pursuit of her.

Stacey had gone from babysitting her to actually moving in, and Lisa had accepted the new roomie with amazing aplomb. Midge suspected that had much to do with a three-way split in rent.

Penny pincher!

"There's nothing sinister about Brody dumping me other than the way he went about doing it," Midge said. She really didn't want to listen to Lisa and Stacey analyze and dissect the entire extent of her relationship with Brody and its devastating demise. Not again, anyway.

"He loves you. I'm absolutely positive of it, but something spooked him, and I'm inclined to think it was Felicia."

"She'd already been arrested at that point," Lisa said, not for the first time this evening.

"I still think she got to him somehow."

"Guys," Midge's voice came out defeated and spent. "I can't listen to this anymore. Can we please drop the subject, and forget that I ever had feelings for Brody Prescott?"

"You're going to have to face him, you know. The cast's 'Tell All' live broadcast is this Friday. You'll be sitting with the contestants waiting to rehash the dirty, gruesome details of the entire series. It's going to be absolutely hellish, so consider our theorizing as part of your prep time for the cameras," Stacey countered.

Midge sank into the couch a little further and did her best to focus on *The Mindy Project*. Her mood needed a good dose of Mindy's irreverent and unapologetic behavior.

After watching one of these episodes she always felt empowered enough to tell herself that she was a dainty princess rather than a floating blimp getting rounder by the minute due to the exorbitant amount of Oreos she'd inhaled over the last two weeks.

Unfortunately, Mindy and Danny had finally come around to admitting their love for one another, which was a painful reminder of the love she wasn't sharing with Brody. She reached for the remote and changed the channel.

"They just solved their inner and external conflicts, enabling them to come together in love and happiness. How could you change the channel like that?" Lisa wailed.

Midge raised an eyebrow at Lisa's wording. "Have you been reading my Writing 101 books?"

"I was bored while you were gone. Dry reading, by the way."

"I need a breather from all things romance," Midge replied, vigorously flipping through the channels. She stopped on Channel 9 news, convinced that terrorists, petty thievery, and drive-by shootings would put her in an infinitely cheerier mood.

"A shocking update on the Felicia Davenport case," said the news anchor. "Despite the overwhelming evidence supporting the theory that Felicia Davenport murdered all three of her late husbands, Judge Griffin has deemed that Ms. Davenport is not a flight risk at this time.

"Her bail has been set for one hundred thousand dollars which was paid by her father. His team of lawyers have worked up a convincing case to dispute these three counts of premeditated murder. The case goes to trial in three months."

"That wench is roaming the streets of L.A. a free woman?" Lisa gasped.

Midge shook her head, unable to comprehend how Felicia's lawyers managed to get her out on bail.

"I'm going to call Rhodes and get him to set up some surveillance around the apartment," Stacey said, reaching for her phone.

"Why on earth would you do that?" Midge grabbed Stacey's hand to stop her.

"For two reasons. One: because Felicia was targeting you during the competition, and there's no telling what she'll do now that she's out."

"She was targeting me because I was a threat to her relationship with Brody, and she was targeting Cambria because the girl is so dang cute. Charlene's the one who needs the protection now."

"I doubt that Felicia will go after Charlene. She knows she doesn't have a chance with Brody at this point. Her vendetta against you may have started because of Brody, but it became personal lightning fast. Might have had something to do with those awesome insults you hurled at her throughout the series. Though I found it highly entertaining, was it really necessary to taunt the tramp?"

"I stand by my insults."

Lisa shook her head, a wide grin spreading across her face. "If she's gunning for anyone she's gunning for you."

"What's the second reason?"

"Rhodes is super dreamy." Stacey fluttered her lashes and fanned herself with her hand.

"I second that," Lisa muttered. "I wish you would have accepted his offer to have lunch with him last week, Midge."

"I've sworn off men. I think my track record speaks for itself."

"Ugh. These manly security guards and their rippling pectorals are completely wasted on you. Stacey, do you think we should invite Rhodes to our pity party tonight?"

Stacey whipped out her phone and started dialing. "He can offer security and entertainment at the same time. More bang for our buck."

"I'm going to pretend I didn't hear that. I'll see you guys tomorrow." Midge moved to stand up, but both Stacey and Lisa firmly pushed her back onto the sofa.

"Not a chance, Midge. We need to exorcise Brody's demon from your psyche, otherwise, you're never going to recover from such a publicly humiliating rejection," Lisa said.

Midge gritted her teeth. "No one ever puts anything quite as succinctly as you do, Lisa."

"Thank you."

BRODY

Brody's gut clenched in dismay as Gregg imparted the news of Felicia's release.

"I feel like the only way I'll ever be rid of that woman is if someone shoots her in the head."

Gregg slapped a hand to his forehead and then moved to close Brody's office door.

"When discussing the finer points of someone's murder, I'd appreciate it if you could avoid letting your secretary in on the gruesome details. It tends to give the wrong impression."

"Do we have any information to add to the case? Anything that implicitly ties Felicia to those murders?"

"Nothing. Everything I found was circumstantial, and I still have no idea who leaked that information to the press *or* the authorities. The only reason I'm telling you about this now is because I'm concerned about Madelyn."

Brody visibly blanched at the sound of her name. Nausea clawed at his insides and bile threatened to choke him. This physical reaction to the mention of Madelyn was something he hadn't prepared himself for. Her loss was something he felt as keenly as he would a lost limb or the death of a loved one.

He was grieving the loss of her love, of her presence in his life, and was furious with himself when the girl in question didn't give a fig about him or his feelings. All the while he had a wonderful girl like Charlene to hold on to, and he could hardly work up the enthusiasm to meet her for dinner tonight.

"Why..." he took a moment to collect himself before continuing. "Why on earth would you be worried about Madelyn? Why would you even mention her name?"

"When Felicia was asked by a reporter if she knew the identity of the person who had leaked the information she immediately blamed Madelyn Knightly for it."

Brody's brows drew together. "That's ridiculous. Madelyn didn't have the time or the resources to look into Felicia's background."

"She is quoted as stating that Madelyn Knightly had maligned and unnecessarily attacked her. From what we know of Felicia's background and temperament, I think it's safe to assume that Felicia will shut her up any way she deems necessary."

"You think Madelyn is in danger?"

Gregg nodded and then waited as Brody processed this new development.

"Why bring this to me, Gregg? Her welfare isn't my concern. She isn't my responsibility."

"You love her, and I believe she loves you."

"You saw the video."

"I can't help but think it was a huge misunderstanding. Consider the source. Charlene had a lot to gain by turning you against Madelyn."

"Charlene has been nothing but wonderful. Madelyn's denial of love for me wasn't edited. She said all of that, willingly, I might add, and a great deal more. I had the DVD checked for inconsistencies, and there were none."

"But maybe there was more. Is it possible you didn't receive the whole of what was filmed?"

"How could anymore footage of that conversation between Felicia and Madelyn negate what Madelyn clearly stated?"

Gregg shook his head, clearly discouraged, yet looking for some lifeline, some other contingency that he and Brody had failed to unearth.

"It's just...the look on her face, Brody. When those cameras panned to her face after you kissed Charlene—I've never seen anyone more shocked or more devastated. And then when you chose Cambria...you could see the disbelief register, the light leaving her eyes.

"Those dang cameras did a thorough job of capturing every single emotion she experienced when she realized you were sending her home, and I'm sorry, but those emotions would not have belonged to someone completely and wholly indifferent to you."

"She was simply embarrassed and upset that I rejected her first. Do you think I was willing to wait it out and hope that she wouldn't reject me once I was down on my knee begging for her to accept me?"

"You didn't even give her a chance to explain," Gregg tried again. "You never showed her the film. All she knows at this point is that you offered her love as a publicity stunt. You were never sincere."

"That's exactly what I want her to think. It's what she has to believe. She'll never know how much she hurt me. She'll never know what her cruel rejection did to me."

"No. I suppose she won't, but everyone else certainly knows what your cruel rejection did to her...even if you can't see it. You're a good man, Brody, but there were other, less hurtful ways of handling that situation. You should have given her a chance."

"I'll never believe that, and you'll never convince me of that."

Gregg sighed in defeat and handed over a piece of paper to Brody before moving toward the door. He stopped just before opening it to say, "You're not happy with Charlene. I hope you don't live to regret the fact that you've completely settled for something average when you could have reached for something spectacular." He opened the door. "Madelyn's address and phone number are on that paper. You can go after her and beg for her forgiveness...or refuse to see reason, but at the very least, make sure Felicia doesn't harm her."

Brody remained silent as Gregg walked through the door and closed it softly behind him.

MADELYN

"Rhodes, you've checked my room for your 'security breaches' about half a dozen times now. I think it's safe for me to go to bed," Midge said as she sank onto her mattress and began pulling the covers over her body, allowing herself to snuggle into the softness of her pillow.

"Your window doesn't latch properly," he grumbled. He shifted his bulky weight and sat on the bed next to her.

"We're two stories up. I don't think Felicia has any secret ninja skills we need to worry about."

"I wouldn't put it past that woman to be capable of flying due to some strange mutation she developed as a fetus."

"Are you calling Felicia Davenport a mutant?"

"If the shoe fits!"

Midge allowed herself a rare smile and reached for Rhodes' hand.

"Thank you for taking care of me."

"I'd like to take care of you on a more permanent basis," he said as he leaned down to kiss her forehead.

Midge blocked him with a hand to the chest and eased him back.

"You know I love you Rhodes, but it's always been a friendly kind of love. A sisterly kind of love."

Rhodes sighed and stretched back to his full height. "I know, Midge, but you can't blame a guy for seeing something wonderful and wanting it for his own."

Midge nearly shed a few tears, wondering why Brody hadn't felt the same way.

"Do you know who else is absolutely wonderful and just happens to live in this apartment?"

"Who?"

"Stacey."

"Stacey? I thought she was dating someone."

Midge burst out laughing.

"I'm not sure what gave you that impression, but she's definitely interested in dating *you*. Maybe give that a try?"

Rhodes gave her an affectionate grin. "Sure. I'll think about it." He reached down for a hug this time, and then stood up, heading for the door.

"I'll be staking out the apartment for the night. If for some reason you hear or see anything out of order you just give me a call."

Midge glanced at her cell phone on the stand and nodded.

"I'll not fail to sound the alarm in case of an emergency."

Once Rhodes left, Midge sank back into the bed and prepared herself for another sleepless night filled with thoughts of Brody and why he'd suddenly turned on her.

BRODY

Brody sat in his car just outside Madelyn's apartment, wondering for the millionth time why he had decided to take an interest in the safety of a woman who didn't give a darn about him.

The answer, of course, was simple. He loved Madelyn, even if she was a heartless man eater who had wreaked havoc on his emotions, his future, and his own sanity.

A light flicked on in a second-story window. He nearly jumped out of his seat at the sight of Madelyn. He grabbed his binoculars, something he considered a necessity when staking out an ex-girlfriend's abode, and brought them to his face. Her sweet expression came into focus as well as the cute bunny pajamas she had on. He couldn't believe she managed to pull off a sexy look with bunny pajamas that covered the entirety of her figure.

He nearly allowed himself a smile—until another person he wasn't expecting came into view.

Rhodes!

Several expletives rang throughout the stillness of his car as he vented his anger and frustration to absolutely no one in particular. Hadn't he known that Rhodes had his eye on Madelyn? Hadn't he wondered if there was anything going on between them? Feeling like the idiot, he lowered his binoculars down and considered leaving Madelyn to her fate. If Rhodes was by her side then she had enough security to ensure that nothing happened to her.

Then again, maybe that was the only reason he was there, though that failed to explain his presence in her bedroom. Brody raised his binoculars again. It also failed to explain why Rhodes was on the bed embracing her. The fury that ignited his temper nearly took over as he grabbed the door handle and prepared himself to scale the wall and rip Madelyn from Rhodes' greasy embrace.

He restrained himself once he realized that Rhodes was leaving the room instead of spending the night. The relief he felt at this turn of events gave him cause to thank his lucky stars that he was sitting rather than standing since the shakiness in his legs wouldn't have supported him at the moment.

He hunched down in his seat when Rhodes left the building and circled to a car parked right under Madelyn's window.

Was the pervert expecting a peep show?

Fortunately, Madelyn's light flipped off and all was dark and silent, forcing

Brody to take in huge gulps of cool air as he tried again to cool his mounting temper.

Then he waited, and so did Rhodes, confirming his assumption of Rhodes' real reason for being there, though he still wasn't pleased that the man had been in Madelyn's room...hugging her. Silence stretched as he and the security guard waited for a threat that most likely didn't exist.

Brody cursed himself again for the decision to come here. All he'd managed to do tonight was prove to himself that he was still in love with Madelyn. How was he supposed to marry Charlene when he couldn't get through a single moment without thoughts of Madelyn disrupting his emotional stability? He couldn't break it off with the girl. Not now. Charlene certainly didn't deserve such callous treatment when she had been nothing but kind and loving. It would break her heart, and he didn't have it in him to do something like that to her.

No. Madelyn had been the dream, but it was time to grow up and finally get married to someone who actually wanted and needed him. Someone who was charming, pretty, kind, and accomplished. Charlene would make the perfect wife of a CEO. What else was there to consider?

Nothing.

So why was his mind in constant turmoil over a certain redhead?

Brody had almost convinced himself that it was time to turn in and head home for the night when a slight movement just ahead of Rhodes' vehicle caught his attention. A figure dressed in black darted toward the space two stories below Midge's window and threw something against the wall of the building. The object exploded, erupting into flames.

Rhodes jumped from his car and began chasing after the figure. Brody grabbed the door handle, ready to head into the lobby of the building to find a fire extinguisher when he noticed another figure climbing the fire escape—a fire escape that passed right next to Madelyn's window. Without hesitating, Brody dashed across the street and into the building, making his way to the second floor.

CHAPTER 35

Midge

Midge heard what sounded like an explosion outside but couldn't be sure due to the noise of her neighbors in the apartment directly above. She would never understand the appeal of violent video games. The sound of bullets ricocheting against steel cars on the gamers' TV caused her to pull her pillow over her head to cover her ears, which was why she failed to hear her window squeak open. The pressure on her pillow suddenly increased.

Someone else was in her room!

Midge tried to pull the material from her face, but the pillow was brutally shoved down much harder this time. She immediately kicked the covers off and caught her assailant in the leg. The pressure on her face released. She threw the pillow from her head and jumped from the bed. Felicia Davenport stood before her, wearing a dark jumpsuit and holding something thin and shiny in her hand.

"Felicia, what in the world do you think you're doing?"

She gave Midge a creepy smile and inched herself forward.

"I'm not sure how you connected those murders to me, but I *am* sure that you were the one to give that information to the police. They mentioned they have a witness prepared to testify to the skeletons in my closet. I'm sure you understand why I can't have you living long enough to confirm everything you've discovered."

Midge couldn't contain her hysterical laughter.

"As much as I would love to take credit for bringing you down, I simply can't claim that honor. You have a lot of enemies Felicia. You'll have to look elsewhere for your witness, and no doubt do some more killing in the process."

"Don't lie to me. You knew about my past. Who else would benefit from my incarceration?"

"Anyone who's ever met you would benefit from your incarceration, Felicia. You're not exactly a pleasant person to be around."

"Oh, I am so going to enjoy this."

Felicia brought her arm up and swung it down, attempting to plunge something into Midge's chest. Midge dodged to the right, and then brought her knee up into Felicia's stomach, knocking the wind out of her. She regrouped on the other side of the room, screaming for Stacey and Lisa.

Why hadn't they heard the commotion in her room? She didn't have time to worry about it further as Felicia turned and swung at her again. This time the knife's blade gleamed wickedly against the firelight from outside.

Wait! Fire?

Midge's focus broke as she stared in horror at the flames licking the outside of her window. Felicia took advantage of that moment and delivered a swift kick, knocking her feet out from under her and sitting herself on top of Midge's stomach.

"You set fire to my building? You are absolutely crazy, Felicia. You should have been institutionalized years ago."

"The fire was a distraction, you idiot. Do you think anyone is going to hear your pitiful cries for help when their apartment is going up in flames?"

Midge bucked and kicked to dislodge the crazy senator's daughter, but Felicia was much stronger than she looked.

"I know that a dagger to the heart is a little dramatic, and even though you were rejected so spectacularly on live television, I still feel like your heart deserves one more jab just to seal the deal."

Felicia raised her arm above her head and brought the dagger down just as Midge bucked again and shifted to the left. The blade came down hard and plunged into the woolly carpet with a dull thud. Another thud sounded to her right, and then a loud crack rippled through the room as the door busted open and someone barreled through, knocking Felicia to the floor. Vision blurry, Midge heard a loud smack and then another thud. Felicia landed next to her completely unconscious.

"I'm not an advocate for hitting women, but that particular woman has had it coming for quite some time."

Midge's heart sped at the hushed, familiar tones of the man's voice.

"Brody?" she whispered.

Strong hands secured her by her shoulders and pulled her to her feet.

"We need to get you out of here. The building is on fire, and the fire department is on its way."

Midge nodded, unable to form any of the questions that begged to be answered. Instead, she allowed herself to lean into him for support, swallowing her pride in the process. It wasn't exactly easy to accept help from the man who had so thoroughly ripped her heart from her chest.

"Thank you for coming to save me," she whispered.

There was a pause as they made it out of the apartment, and then, in a very quiet voice he said, "You're welcome, Madelyn."

Midge continued leaning against Brody's car while the police finished taking his statement. Apparently, upon hearing news of Felicia's release, he immediately assumed Felicia would be headed Midge's way, and he came over to stake the place out.

She couldn't fathom why. The chaos of ambulances and firemen taking care of apartment residents and those who were injured mirrored the chaotic thoughts moving around like floating topography within her mind.

Why in the world would he have troubled himself with her safety when he couldn't be bothered to trouble himself with her very tender feelings? Public humiliation one moment and then savior the next? His behavior within the last month had become so contradictory she wasn't sure how to feel or react to this unexpected moment of chivalry.

Of course, he'd also turned around and headed back into the apartment for Felicia once he'd brought Midge outside. He'd saved Felicia even though he hated that woman. She was glad he'd saved her. As despicable as Felicia was, she was also a human being who didn't deserve to burn to death in an apartment building.

Brody finished answering the officer's questions and made his way over to his car. She couldn't help but admire his quick and confident steps and then cringe when his steps slowed and became hesitant after spotting her standing by his car.

So? Did he not expect some gratitude on her part or was she supposed to behave as if the last thirty minutes hadn't happened? Midge began to look for her father's camera crew just in case this entire fiasco had been nothing more than another staged attempt at adding more excitement to the show. Brody Prescott: all American good guy and national hero.

She supposed it had a nice ring to it.

He eased himself up to the car and leaned on it, leaving several inches of space between them. The distance may as well have encompassed the whole of the United States. The Brody she knew and loved never would have allowed that kind of distance to exist between them.

After a moment, Midge cleared her throat, deciding she would take the high road and say something nice even though she wanted to attack him for his hurtful betrayal.

"Thank you for keeping an eye on me. I owe you my life, and I'm very grateful to you."

She cringed at the formality lacing her tone. She didn't know how to behave in his presence anymore. Offering his love one moment and then denying he'd ever felt a thing for her the next made her feel like she was tiptoeing around land mines.

"You already thanked me. You didn't have to hover by my car simply to state it again." His gruff voice felt as abrasive as sand paper might against her fair skin.

"Well...I guess I feel like a thank you just isn't enough to repay you for what you did."

"Who says I'm not going to expect payment? You can certainly afford my exorbitant fee now that you have your trust fund back."

Midge's temper came to a boil. All thoughts of civility were wiped clean as her pent up anger and frustration came bubbling to the surface.

She turned to face him, hands on her hips as she flung off the stupid blanket the paramedics had provided for her.

"What is your problem, Brody? Why did you even bother to stake out my apartment and save me when it's so obvious that you absolutely cannot stand me?"

Brody's look of surprise immediately morphed as his jaw clenched and a small vein in his neck began to pulse.

"*I* can't stand *you*? That's incredibly ironic coming from someone who faked an interest in me and then quickly tossed me aside at the first threat against her trust fund and her manuscript. You proved you didn't have one ounce of feeling for me long before I dumped you on national television."

Midge's jaw nearly came unhinged. "What are you talking about? You knew why I came on the show in the first place. I was very transparent about that, and I have no idea what my manuscript has to do with this."

"Don't you?" Brody moved closer and roughly grabbed her shoulders. "I heard your little conversation with Felicia. I know she tried to blackmail you into lying about your feelings for me, though it turns out it wouldn't have been much of a lie for you since you feel nothing. You told her you would dump me after the show and that was that. Do you really think that after watching that video I would wait around for you to completely destroy me?"

Midge's shock and confusion rendered her speechless. Her reaction appeared to confirm Brody's dark assumptions.

"Get away from my car. Charlene and I are having dinner together and I'm already late."

Midge grabbed his arm. "Wait. You watched a video? I don't understand—"

"Felicia filmed the whole thing and made a copy. Charlene found it and brought it to me, and can I tell how awful it was for her to be put in such an uncomfortable position?"

Midge shook her head, trying to make sense of his explanation. "Charlene? What? Why did she even have access to it? Brody, whatever you saw or heard was taken out of context. Please believe me."

Brody ripped his arm from hers. The fury in his eyes had her backing up a pace. He was too angry to hear her and too angry to accept a different alternative to what he believed.

"Not possible, Madelyn. It won't do you any good to backpedal now." He got in his car and slammed the door. "Besides," he yelled through the open window, "what good does denying it do? You have what you came on the show for. I hope that money makes you as miserable as you deserve."

Midge stepped forward, trying one more time to plead her case and explain why she had said those things in the first place, but Brody gunned the engine as a warning, forcing her to back up. He pulled away from the side of the road and left her standing there unable to fix this misunderstanding.

"I knew this was some huge mistake," Stacey said, bouncing excitedly in her chair and nearly toppling off it.

The three roommates had to relocate to another living space since their apartment was technically a crime scene. Unfortunately, the only person in the group who actually had family living close by was Midge. After failing to convince the girls to let her pay for a comfy hotel, she reluctantly called her father to let him know what had happened and to ask to be put up for the night. He'd sounded upset when she related the news of her near-death experience and personally came to pick the girls up after the police had finished taking their statements.

Despite the rift in their relationship, her father had always taken care of her even if most of that care had been dictated by his hectic work schedule.

Now they were in his kitchen, sitting at a round table and snacking on cold cuts, cheddar cheese, and grapes. Midge found near-death experiences made one hungry. The familiarity of the white cupboards, aged tile flooring, and marble counter tops gave her a sense of peace and tranquility, a sense of finally coming home.

"Well, now I feel kind of sorry for punching him in the face," her father said, bringing her out of her reverie.

Midge gaped at him in horror. "You punched Brody?"

He lifted his chin and folded his arms defensively. "I warned him right from the beginning that I would make his life a living hell if he hurt you."

"When did this conversation take place?"

"When he told me he'd joined the show to get close to you."

Feeling a little bowled over by that news she said, "You knew why he was really there? The whole Cinderella story wasn't just an angle for your show?"

"Of course it was an angle for the show, but it also benefited you in the process, so I figured there wasn't any harm in taking full advantage of the situation."

Lisa let out an amused chuckle. "Your dad's an opportunist. Can't say I wouldn't have done the same thing."

"That's because you're cut from the same cloth. I've decided that TV producers are every bit as criminal as computer hackers," Midge said.

Knightly's eyes gleamed with interest as he really took Lisa in for the first time. "You're a professional hacker?"

Lisa shrugged. "I can neither confirm nor deny such accusations at this time, especially in front of someone who makes a living filming people."

"Well, these skills you may or may not possess might be helpful in getting to the bottom of what Brody was given," he said.

Lisa slapped her forehead and turned to Midge. "Of course! I should have considered it much sooner. Let me grab my laptop from my bag and we'll take a look at Brody's computer."

"Do you really think you can find that information?" Stacey asked, bouncing again in her excitement. Midge was beginning to wonder if her three cups of coffee had been a mistake. Her energy rivaled that of Charlene's at the moment

"If Brody downloaded the video on his computer or if he even watched it, then I should be able to access the information."

The group waited anxiously for Lisa to grab her laptop, fire it up, and begin the process of hacking into Brody's computer. After a few minutes, Midge had to stand up and pace since her nervous energy made sitting an impossibility.

"I'm in," Lisa shouted.

"This is so exciting. I'm participating in criminal activities," Stacey giggled as she reached for the coffee pot in the middle of the table. Midge quickly stayed her hand and shook her head.

"I'm cuttin' you off, Stacey. You're so wired right now your hair follicles are twitching."

Stacey gave a morose glance toward the coffee pot but must have noticed her shaking hand because she nodded in agreement and reached for a couple of grapes instead. They never managed to make it into her mouth. It was like watching a basketball player with Parkinson's Disease.

"Found it. Brody emailed it to his assistant—Gregg, I think—and had him verify that the video hadn't been edited to misrepresent what you were saying."

Lisa pushed play and the very beginning of Midge's awful conversation with Felicia played back at the group.

"I tell Brody I don't love him and I never did, and in return you give me back my manuscript?"

"I'll mail it to your home address the day you leave the mansion," Felicia said.

"But I don't love him, Felicia. I'll admit that he's extremely likable, but for you to think that I'm still here due to any interest in Brody Prescott is simply ludicrous. I can't leave the show until Brody eliminates me; otherwise, no trust fund."

As the video progressed, Midge's heart sank even further. No wonder

Brody felt so hurt and betrayed. He didn't realize that she had been bluffing in an attempt to outmaneuver Felicia. The video stopped right after her emphatic denial of her love for Brody and her interest in his money.

"Harsh, Midge," Lisa said after the video finished.

"I was bluffing. I didn't mean any of that. There was far more to that conversation than what Brody was allowed access to."

"And you say Brody mentioned Charlene's involvement in this? How would she have had access to that video, and why would she sabotage you? I thought you two were friends?"

"There's no such thing as a friend in show business, especially when an eligible billionaire is on the line," Knightly said, adding his own jaded yet accurate assessment of the situation.

"If Charlene had access to that video footage it stands to reason she was a lot closer with Felicia than she let on. Which leads me to the sad conclusion that Charlene might have been Felicia's accomplice," Lisa said.

Midge shook her head at the treachery. "She seemed so kind. I find it hard to believe she didn't just stumble upon the edited copy and then try to warn Brody of the heartbreak she thought he was headed for."

Lisa and Stacey exchanged skeptical glances while Midge's father let out a short huff of laughter.

"Well, we can settle this right now by snooping around the contents of her computer. Like I wasn't going to do that anyway." Lisa got back to work while Stacey suddenly decided she needed to jog around the outside pool for a bit. Knightly hovered over Lisa's shoulder to observe her work.

After a few moments he asked, "You wouldn't be interested in coming to work for me, would you?"

"Pay me in cash, off the books, and I set my own hours."

"Done."

Midge gave her father a stern glare. "What on earth do you need a hacker for?"

"I work in Hollywood. When would I *not* need a hacker? Having access to secrets in this business is like having your own brand of currency."

She lifted her hand to prevent him from explaining further.

"The less I know about that the better."

"I'm inclined to agree."

"This Charlene chick is definitely not who she says she is. Charlene isn't even her real name." Lisa said.

"What?" Midge asked. She circled around the table to hover over Lisa's other shoulder.

"Your friend's real name is Elizabeth Jude Ramsey. Does that last name ring any bells?"

Midge stared in shock at Lisa's screen.

"Didn't Elizabeth Ramsey die in that fire along with her brother and her father?"

"That's what we all assumed, but what if she hadn't been there at all and the police simply believed she had?"

"Why didn't she come forward? Why didn't she point the finger at Felicia?"

"Maybe she didn't have the proof she needed and felt it best to remain dead for the time being," Knightly said. "Maybe she was the one who leaked that information to the press."

"That doesn't make sense. Why be her accomplice in any of this if she hated Felicia?" Midge wondered.

"Keep your enemies close, Midge girl. She must have pretended to be someone else to get close to Felicia in order to take her down."

"That's an elaborate agenda. There was no way for her to know if she would be a contestant on the show."

"You know, I can't even remember how she became a contestant on the show." Knightly looked truly puzzled. "I actually don't remember approving her."

"She probably approved herself," Lisa said. "She knows her way around a computer. A lot of these files are encrypted. It might take me some time to find the footage we're looking for...no, wait." Lisa turned to Midge and smiled. "She didn't even bother to hide the footage. She couldn't have made it any easier to find than if she'd embedded a flashing red arrow above it."

Lisa played the footage which went well beyond the version she had given Brody.

"She cut it off before Brody could see that you were bluffing. It definitely sent him the wrong message."

"That doesn't excuse his failure to communicate with my daughter," Knightly said, still attempting to justify the damage he must have done to Brody's face.

"He should have come to me and asked me about the video, but in all fairness, I also received the wrong impression about his intentions and failed to communicate or give him the benefit of the doubt. I can hardly condemn him for his actions afterward when I spent quite a bit of time refusing to place any of my faith or trust in him."

"Have we figured out if the wench is a witch?" Stacey asked, suddenly bursting into the kitchen looking severely wind-blown and disheveled.

"I thought you were going for a run. Did you have a fight with a tree?" Lisa asked, pointing to some leaves and a few twigs sticking haphazardly out of Stacey's long mane of hair.

"Of course not. I just felt like climbing one."

"At two-thirty in the morning?"

Her swift nod implied she didn't understand what was so wrong with that.

"Yeah. No more coffee for you, Stacey," Midge said as she motioned for her to sit down.

"Can you make a copy of this, Lisa?" Knightly asked.

"What are you thinking, Dad?"

Her father gave her a mischievous grin. "I'm thinking the 'Tell All' episode is going to get extremely interesting."

"You want to clear things up with Brody by televising this huge misunderstanding and the hurt his rejection caused me?"

"She could just take this copy to Brody in private and show him what really passed between her and Felicia," Stacey suggested.

Knightly and Lisa gave Stacey a withering glare which Stacey failed to notice due to the fact that she was once again jumping up and running out the back door, most likely headed for another round of tree climbing.

"You have to do it on TV, Midge!" Lisa said. "So many viewers were upset and confused when you left the show. It would be the perfect ending to this fairy tale that your dad so expertly wove for the series."

"I couldn't have said it better myself, Lisa. I've decided to include health benefits in your employee package."

"Could you possibly add in a gym membership and one spa day a month?"

"Done."

"I am so working for you." Lisa turned to Midge with a smile and jerked a thumb toward Knightly. "Why is this the first time I've ever met your father?"

"Come on, Midge girl. I know you hate the idea of your private life being aired on TV, but your story with Brody isn't finished, and everyone who was rooting for a fairy tale ending is still reeling from the shock of Brody choosing Charlene over you. We have to make this right and finish the story. Surely from a director's point of view you can see why this would make for great television."

Midge shook her head, getting ready to turn her back on the idea of collaborating with her father just as she had six years ago, but the pleading look and hopeful smile stopped her long enough to consider how much she missed working with him on anything.

Though Corbin Knightly had kept his distance over the last six years, he had done an admirable job of working on their relationship over the past two weeks. He even let his assistants film the rest of the season so he could be there for her after what he dubbed an "emotionally and morally debilitating debacle" courtesy of Brody Prescott. For him to hand the reins over to someone else in the middle of a project was huge, and he'd done it just for her. She knew it was her turn to make a gesture here.

In this instance, her gesture would help not only her father but Brody as well. If she put herself out there on television to let the whole world know how she truly felt about him then maybe he would actually believe she genuinely loved him. He went on the show just for her. She could handle the spotlight and allow herself some vulnerability on TV for his sake.

"Okay," she finally agreed, meeting her father's eyes and giving him a warm smile. "Let's do it your way."

Knightly rubbed his hands together in anticipation. It made him look like a diabolical scientist ready for some sick lab experiments. Lisa stood up and did a funky little happy dance.

"This is gonna be epic. I've already got the whole thing mapped out in my head," he said.

Midge didn't doubt that for a second.

CHAPTER 36

Midge

Midge's stomach twisted as she battled her anxiety, wishing she could simply run away from this entire ordeal. Each contestant sat in their very own limo, waiting in line to be dropped off at the entrance of the live filming of the "Tell All" episode. It was the proverbial red carpet event where she'd have to face down photographers and reporters. Midge likened it to a pathway filled with burning coals where she'd have to paste a smile on her face and pretend the burning sensation was completely manageable.

Who doesn't like smoldering footwear?

She reminded herself that she was facing down her own fears and insecurities for Brody. He hadn't rejected her due to any indifference on his part. He'd simply protected himself from being rejected. She hoped he would still care for her once she had the chance to explain her side of the story.

She studied her gown of burnished gold. The color reminded her of Bell's ball gown from Disney's *Beauty and The Beast,* though her skirt wasn't quite as full as Belle's had been.

Her wild mane of red hair had been straightened and tamed into an elegant forties styled wave, brushing just below her shoulders. She looked ready to hit the red carpet. Inwardly, she squashed down her trepidation as her limo pulled up to the curb and an attendant opened the door for her. She lifted her hand and allowed herself to be assisted from the limo. The moment she stepped onto the carpet a wall of noise accosted her. It took her a few disorienting moments to realize that the people along the sidelines were cheering for her at a deafening level.

Her forced grin soon morphed into a genuine smile as she saw a few teenagers pushing past reporters and photographers to get a good look at her. Midge began what she hoped was an elegant glide down the carpet but couldn't resist stopping to take one of the teen's outstretched hands, allowing herself to be pulled into a hug by the young girl.

"We don't understand what happened. We wanted you to be Brody's future wife. You guys are so perfect together!" one of the girls said in her ear.

Midge pulled back to give her an encouraging smile.

"It's not over yet, ladies," she said.

The girls squealed in delight, their youthful enthusiasm becoming too much for Midge to resist. She continued down the carpet, buoyed by their words and attitude, smiling and posing for photographers just like her mother had taught her all those years ago.

It was a relief to make it into the building, but her inordinately good mood was shattered when she was ushered backstage and ran smack dab into Charlene and Brody.

The surprise on Brody's face was swiftly wiped away by an angry scowl. Charlene gave Midge an enthusiastic hug. It was all Midge could do to not rip the she-devil's eyes out after discovering the part she'd played in this debacle.

"So good to see you again, Charlene," Midge said.

"Oh, isn't this little reunion just wonderful," Charlene gushed. "I just can't wait for everyone to rehash the good, the bad, and the ugly."

"Oh, it's definitely going to get ugly."

"What was that?"

"I'd rather not relive the bugs again." Midge assembled a serene look to cover her near blunder, and then her eyes swiveled to Brody. "You look really wonderful, Brody. It's nice to see you."

Brody swallowed with some difficulty, appearing to use that time to muster some kind of comment void of emotion.

"You always look nice, Midge. See you on set." He grabbed Charlene's hand and swiftly stole away from her.

Midge frowned in dismay.

He's so eager to get away from me he may as well be running.

Not an auspicious start to the evening. Midge briefly wondered if he would still reject her once she got a chance to level the playing field. She shook such traitorous thoughts from her mind. Losing her nerve was pointless. The events ready to unfold couldn't be reversed. Her father wouldn't allow it.

She had no more time to worry about Brody's reaction to her plan because more make-up and hair personnel began primping and adding finishing touches here and there. Cambria sidled up next to her in the midst of this, giving her a friendly smile.

"I'm glad to see you, Midge," she said. "I'm kind of relieved you actually came. After the way things ended with you and Brody, I wasn't sure you would even want to attend the taping."

"Well, I guess I figured Brody and I have some unfinished business we need to deal with."

"Oh, I'm so happy to hear you say that. I've been wondering along with everyone else what the heck happened between you two." She looked nervous for a second and then continued, "I mean, don't get me wrong, Charlene is nice and all, but you and Brody had this chemistry that sizzled whenever you were together. He isn't the same with Charlene. Seems a bit forced."

"Well, I guess we'll see what happens. Maybe I can make him change his mind."

Cambria's eyes widened in hungry anticipation. "Sounds like some fun entertainment to me. I'll be sure to sit next to you when the party starts."

Midge squeezed her shoulder. "Great idea."

Soon Midge and the other contestants were ushered to their seats. They faced the audience and a comfortable looking couch in the middle of the stage where Les Lassiter sat in his own interview chair like a king awaiting the arrival of his court. Midge couldn't help but grin at the way he soaked in the audience's applause when he announced the show would start in one minute.

As the countdown began, Midge's grin slipped away. The nervous tension in her neck reminded her of how much was on the line tonight.

"We're here tonight to talk to America's favorite sweethearts and get the gritty details of Brody's journey to finding true love," Les began, pausing for more applause before continuing on. "Let's start by introducing you to the man of the hour, Mr. Brody Prescott."

Midge sucked in some much needed oxygen as Brody entered from stage right, waving to the audience and flashing that killer smile of his. Oxygen eluded her, refusing to enter her lugs, flitting away as she gripped the arms of her chair.

One breath after another allowed her more mental clarity and focus.

"Brody, we have several women wanting to have their say at the moment."

For the next grueling hour, Midge had to sit through the agonizing vista of beautiful contestants sitting next to Brody on the couch, hashing out misunderstandings, resolving conflicts and issues, and wishing him all the best while squeezing his arm and initiating far too much physical contact. Another twenty minutes was spent discussing Felicia Davenport's participation on the show and her attack on Midge.

"Many people had a difficult time with your controversial decision to eliminate Madelyn Knightly from the show, especially after the many heartfelt moments you two shared together. Just what went wrong? What made you decide that Ms. Knightly wasn't the right girl for you?"

Brody's smile looked a bit forced to Midge. The strain in the lines around his mouth and the corners of his eyes couldn't been hidden by any of the cosmetics used to enhance his features.

"Les, there are points in every relationship where you discover aspects of a person's personality or character that simply don't mesh well with yours. It was better for us to part ways, but I wish Madelyn the very best, and I hope she finds the love she is searching for."

The audience seemed a bit disappointed with Brody's response. Midge couldn't tell if it was because they still didn't agree with the decision or because his response was superficial and vague.

Midge swallowed hard, appreciating his sentiment, but feeling more grateful that he chose not to air out the real reasons behind his decision to eliminate her. Most men might have tried to drag her reputation through the mud by discussing the contents of the video, however misleading they had been.

"Well, I think Madelyn had a few things she wanted to say to you before we bring Charlene on stage and talk about your future wedding plans. Madelyn?" Les motioned to the empty space next to Brody.

Midge did her best to close out the applause and sympathetic crying that a few more zealous fans of the show had unleashed as she approached the center of the room and took a seat on the couch. She kept a healthy bit of distance between she and Brody.

He could hardly look at her. She noticed the gargantuan effort it took for him to stand and give her a quick embrace before retreating to his side of the couch.

Once the room quieted down, Les dug right in to the hard questions.

"Madelyn, I think it's safe to say from your reaction to Brody's decision during your last diamond ceremony that you hadn't expected him to let you go."

Midge cleared her throat as the uncomfortable sensation of everyone's rapt attention on her threatened to choke off her vocal chords. She gritted her teeth, willing some kind of response to come, but she hadn't expected her stage fright to hit her with such force after all her mental preparation. She felt so alone even though Brody was within reaching distance. Les must have mistaken her inability to speak as a show of extreme emotion.

"It's okay, Madelyn. I understand this must be painful for you to talk about."

A warm hand slipped into hers. She glanced at Brody's strong fingers wrapped around her own and had a difficult time processing this show of support even though he was convinced she had betrayed him. Then her eyes did fill with tears. She gave him a grateful smile as the tears spilled down her cheeks. A momentary glimmer of surprise flashed across his expression before disappearing into that restrained façade he'd mastered so well.

"It is painful to talk about, Les, but I think what pains me more is that the relationship ended because of my inability to open up and trust the love that Brody so willingly offered. I never came right out and told him I loved him."

A hushed gasp from the audience prevented her from speaking for a moment. She felt Brody squeeze her hand, but she knew if she looked at him and found pity rather than acceptance she would never get through the rest of her speech.

"Brody made it very clear how he felt about me, but I've always struggled to believe that there is anything about me worth pursuing. So many people in my life were interested in me because of what my connections to Hollywood could offer them. I've always been Corbin Knightly's daughter rather than Madelyn Knightly. I refused to believe that Brody was sincere in his pursuit of me, and when I did finally decide to give him the benefit of the doubt and take that leap it was too late. At that point, something very damaging was given to him, something that convinced him I didn't care for him. I didn't give him a reason to trust in what I felt for him, and as a result, he let me go."

The murmuring of the audience became more audible, and Les had to wait until they quieted down.

"Madelyn, are you saying that Brody was given something that discredited you in his eyes?"

She felt the full force of Brody's gaze on her. No doubt he was surprised that she would shed light on something so damaging for her when he had been gallant enough to sidestep that information.

"He was given a video that misrepresented how I felt about him. In truth, he was only given half the video, but I'd like to show the entire video right now so that everyone, including Brody, will know exactly how I feel about him."

The lights dimmed as the large projector screen to the right lowered. Soon a video of Midge starring front and center was airing for all the world to see. In the background she could hear Felicia's voice as she began blackmailing Midge.

Brody, whether consciously or unconsciously, tightened his hand around Midge's. She didn't know if it was another show of support or if watching her claim she didn't love him again was too much for him. The shadows dancing around his eyes certainly made it look as if he was grimacing at the display. The audience wasn't happy with her response to Felicia's blackmail.

Les paused the video and turned to look at Midge.

"This is the part Brody saw?"

"Yes. This next part was cut from his version of the video footage."

Les nodded and allowed the video to continue. Midge tried to track Brody's reaction from the corner of her eye as the conversation between her and Felicia progressed.

She felt the same shame when she heard herself say her career was more important than her relationship with Brody, but she hoped her next words would redeem her in his eyes. His muscles remained tense and his jaw kept that hard edge that hinted at pain and suppressed anger.

Finally, that moment of redemption arrived.

"I can always write another book, but I can never replace someone as amazing and wonderful as Brody Prescott. So if you plan on publishing that book under your name or destroying the only copy in existence, I suppose that's up to you. I love him. It's taken me far too long to get to the point where I can actually admit that out loud, and I can't give it up now. I can't give him up ever. Brody means far more to me than my success as an author, and if you had any concept of what true love feels like you might have found your own happiness by now rather than lying and murdering others in an attempt to grab it."

The video ended once Felicia stormed out of the room. As the lights came up and the projector went white, the audience, the contestants, and even Les stood up applauding. She turned her head to take in the vast expanse of the audience to her right and the contestants on her left offering her their support and their applause. She met Cambria's eyes and Cambria nodded as if to say, "Well done."

Once the applause subsided, Midge allowed herself to look at Brody full on. His varied expressions flashed across his face so quickly they nearly canceled each other out. He hadn't let go of her hand, its vise-like grip only tightening further.

"Charlene was working with Felicia to discredit me. She wanted you all to herself, and to be honest I don't blame her. I share the sentiment."

Brody shook his head. "I'm sorry, Madelyn, I should have allowed you to explain—"

"You have nothing to apologize for. I simply wanted to set the record straight. You need to know that I love you. I've always cared for you, but I never trusted in myself enough to allow it to grow like it needed to. I'm sorry I waited so long, and I have no idea if this changes anything now, but I couldn't let you leave this show without knowing how I really feel about you."

Midge leaned over and planted a soft kiss on his cheek, and then she pulled from her purse a small branch with a Lehua flower attached to it. She set it on the couch between them and said, "Lehua and Ohia, never to be parted."

Then she stood, and instead of heading back to her chair like she was expected to, her feet guided her toward the audience, through the walkway separating the fans from the stage, and out the exit.

She'd overcome her fears, left her heart wide open, and told him everything, but she'd be darned if she was going to sit in that chair while she watched Charlene, or Liz, or whatever that she-devil's name was, put her hands all over the man she loved. This was all she could do. It was all she could handle.

As she stepped outside and onto the red carpet, she was surprised to see so many reporters, photographers, and fans of the show still out there offering their enthusiastic support.

She did her best to paste on that same smile she'd managed for so long, but this time it wouldn't take. The tears came anyway. She held her head high and continued walking down the longest red carpet of her life, heading for what looked like a very accommodating limo.

BRODY

If Madelyn's revelation and declaration of love hadn't been so unexpected, he might not have sat there like an idiot for so long while the girl he loved left the stage and exited the building.

"Is she leaving?" Les asked. His panic managed to break Brody from his frozen state.

Leaving? She couldn't leave. It didn't matter that he knew how to find her now. She couldn't walk away from him thinking for even one moment that he wasn't going to chase after her like he always had. He grabbed the flower Midge left behind and stood.

"Excuse me, Les. My future wife is, once again, trying to get away from me."

The audience laughed and cheered while Les looked around at the camera crew and asked, "He's leaving, too? Can they do that?"

Brody rushed off the stage down the aisle and toward the exit, bursting through the doors into the outer lobby and then moving into a full on sprint as he headed for the front doors of the building.

He broke through them and paused on the red carpet, slightly disoriented from the remaining crowd still in attendance. Spotting Madelyn a few yards ahead of him was like emerging from a black curtain of fog that had refused to dissipate.

He ran down the red carpet as she opened the door of her limo and prepared herself to get in. He reached her before she could escape him again, placing his hands at her hips and swiftly turning her to face him.

The sweet tears flowing freely over her soft cheeks tore at his heart. He brushed them away with a finger and tilted her chin so that their lips were mere centimeters away.

Her shy smile caused adrenaline to shoot through his veins.

"This is the last time I'm chasing after you, Madelyn."

"Why is that?" she asked.

"Because I want you to consider yourself good and caught."

He melded his lips to hers and reveled in her uninhibited response, enjoying the mutual give and take of affection with no reservations or lingering doubts. She was his. Wholly and completely his.

He broke the kiss long enough to get down on his knee, holding up the Lehua blossom he said, "Madelyn Knightly, I think it's about time you agreed to marry me. Will you do me the honor?"

Her smile, showered with tears, was the most beautiful sight he had ever seen.

She extended her hand and accepted the flower, then she knelt before him and threw herself into his arms.

"Yes," she whispered, placing another long, lingering kiss on his lips.

The chaos around them couldn't override the enormous sense of love and fulfillment they found in each others arms as fans cheered and photographers captured one of the most important moments of their lives.

MIDGE

Midge breathed in the sweet smells of Giacomo's croissants as she leaned back, enjoying the warm strength of Brody's arm draped across her chair.

"Oh, my word. These things are to die for," Blanche cooed as she took another bite of her warm croissant. "I can't believe I've never been to this place."

"Café Canapé is the best kept secret in the area," Midge said in a conspiratorial whisper.

"I think between Blanche and my daughter, we're going to have to fight for any chance at keeping one for ourselves, Brody," Knightly stated. He reached for the last croissant on the table, but Lisa sneaked up right behind him and swiped it from his grasp. With a cheeky grin she took a large bite and strutted victoriously around the table.

"Scratch that," Knightly muttered. "Keeping these women fed is going to break your bank, Brody. Good thing you have some money to spare."

"Speaking of money," Lisa managed around another mouthful, "I just found out that Elizabeth Ramsey is not only testifying against Felicia at her trial next month, but she's suing that psycho wench for pain and suffering due to the loss of her family and her home. When are you scheduled to testify, Midge?"

"Right around the same time as Elizabeth."

"I'm still amazed at how cordial you've been with her ever since we discovered her involvement with Felicia. She nearly succeeded in ruining everything, for Heaven's sake!"

"Once we sat down and actually talked it out, it was easy to see that she was simply trying to survive. I'm not condoning her actions, and we'll certainly never be close, but getting a feel for what she went through gave me some perspective. She will have her own legal issues to deal with for threatening my life, but I can hold hatred in my heart for her."

"There's pretty much no end to all of Madelyn's amazing qualities, forgiveness being one of them," Brody said.

"Yes, you were certainly on the receiving end of her forgiveness while down on one knee a few months ago. I'm just glad things worked out the way they did," Blanche said. "I was not pleased when I had to watch my son eliminate you, Midge. That whole situation was so wrong, I was about ready to throttle him through the television."

Brody chuckled. "Yes, you weren't exactly too friendly to the other women I brought home to meet you."

"And who could blame me? I'd already picked out my daughter-in-law. You were suffering from severe brain damage by the end of the season." Blanche reached across the table and patted Midge's hand. "Lucky for us, this young lady never gave up on you."

"I'm certainly happy things worked out the way they did. The press is already hounding me for exclusives during your wedding two weeks from now," Knightly said. He rubbed his hands together in excitement.

"No," Midge and Brody emphatically stated.

Knightly held up a placating hand. "Just hear me out for a moment. I'm thinking I'll be the one to film the entire thing. We'll add touching interviews, behind the scenes footage of the day before preparations—where we'll have exclusive access to any bridezilla behavior on Midge's part—and then we can broadcast the ceremony live."

Brody stood and shook his head while offering Midge his hand.

"If you even think about making our wedding a public spectacle, we'll elope to the nearest church and forget to invite you," Midge teased.

There were other reasons Brody and Midge had opted for a quiet gathering away from the public eye. Her mother was coming to the wedding. Celeste had immediately taken to Brody when Midge had brought him to Garden Cove Sanitarium to meet her. Even though her mother's mental clarity remained mostly unchanged, a small spark of recognition lit her features when Midge greeted her, and Celeste had cried when Midge told her about the wedding. It was a huge step toward rebuilding a relationship with her mother.

Brody went to pay for their sweets and then motioned Midge out the door while Blanche, Lisa, and Knightly discussed the pros and cons of a reality TV series about psychotic brides and their elaborate weddings.

"Are you ready to become Mrs. Brody Prescott?" he asked. He placed an arm around her shoulder and snuggled her close to him as they strolled along the sidewalk.

"Absolutely. It better happen sooner rather than later. I'm never going to fit into my gown with all of the croissants you've been feeding me."

He laughed as they slowly meandered their way towards the beach.

"You've got the metabolism of a sixteen-year-old boy. You have nothing to worry about."

"Be that as it may, I'm thinking a healthy game of beach tag is in order. I have to hold onto this girlish figure!" She turned to face him and began a slow backwards run so she could taunt him a little. "Think you've got what it takes to catch me?"

Brody's dazzling smile nearly stopped her in her tracks.

"I'm not worried," he said in a low voice. "I've caught you before, and I'll catch you again."

"Prove it, Brody Prescott!" She tapped him lightly on the shoulder and sprinted away. "Tag, you're it.

Brody sprang into action and easily caught up with her. He wrapped his arms around her and spun her in circles.

"I suppose I should consider myself good and caught," she murmured after their laughter died down.

He turned her to face him and dove his fingers into the soft curls at the nape of her neck.

"It's about time," he said.

Then he took her lips with his and sealed their happily ever after with kiss after kiss after kiss.

Thank you so much for reading this fun romcom.
If you enjoyed Brody and Madelyn's love story,
then you'll love *Rescuing the Billionaire*,
Book 2 in *The Reluctant Bride Series*

Afterword

The idea for this book can be blamed on our foreign exchange student from Switzerland, Alyssia Keller, who came to live with us during the school year of 2014-2015. She'd been a fan of *The Bachelor* for quite some time, while I had done an admirable job of avoiding that show like I would a sugar-free diet. I couldn't think of anything more ridiculous than watching desperate women fighting over a knuckle head who probably joined the show just so he could get laid. What were these women thinking? Why in the world put yourself through all of that drama? No guy could be worth such heartache.

Right?

I knew you'd understand.

These were all of the arguments—valid arguments—I posed to Alyssia when she insisted I sit down and start the new season of *The Bachelor* with her. The bachelor in question? Chris Soules.

Because I'm a good sport...and also because she promised me an endless supply of Swiss chocolate, I agreed and sat down to watch the show.

Holy crap! I was hooked within the first ten minutes.

Dang it.

It was like watching a train wreck and waiting for the inevitable carnage to follow. You know you should probably shield your eyes, but you simply can't tear yourself away.

So entertaining.

As I watched Chris begin his first round of make-out sessions, I thought about how no one in the world could have paid me nearly enough money to put myself in that situation.

Then I wondered what might happen if someone didn't want to be on the show but was forced into it. What would motivate a woman to agree to something like that? What if the bachelor in question decided she was the one for him and refused to let her leave?

How delicious!

So I got to work on it right away. Of course, I had to continue watching the show. Purely for the sake of research, mind you, lest you think I couldn't pull myself away from the TV to go make dinner...or do laundry...or wash the dishes. And then it was absolutely imperative that I continue my research by watching *The Bachelorette*.

Right?

I knew you'd understand.

For the record, I still think the idea of a dating reality TV series is ridonculous, but that's what makes it so entertaining. Plus, I became super attached to the contestants and their relationships with the bachelor...which is exactly what those devious TV producers want you to do.

Stinkers.

Needless to say, my foreign exchange student and I spent many evenings planted in front of the TV with an unhealthy amount of popcorn and chocolate in front of us, arguing the finer points of life married to Whitney versus life married to Becca or even Kaitlyn. And who can dispute Kaitlyn's extreme likability? And how awesome was it to witness every single emotional melt down, including the fake panic attack from Kelsey and her tactless claim that the death of her husband was the best backstory on the entire show?

Classic.

I do so love research.